COLLECTED STO

The author of eight novels, Peter Ca
Australia. In 2001 he became the se
Booker Prize twice. He lives in New York.

PETER CAREY

Collected
Stories

faber and faber

First published in Great Britain in 1995
by Faber and Faber Limited
3 Queen Square London WC1N 3AU
This UK paperback edition first published in 1996

Printed and bound in Great Britain by
Mackays of Chatham PLC, Chatham, Kent

A CIP record for this book is
available from the British Library

ISBN 0–571–17586–4

4 6 8 10 9 7 5

Contents

ACKNOWLEDGEMENTS

Four of these stories have not been previously collected: 'Joe' (first printed in *Australian New Writing*), 'Concerning the Greek Tyrant' (*The Tabloid Story Pocket Book*, Wild & Woolley), 'A Million Dollars' Worth of Amphetamines' (*Nation Review*) and 'A Letter to Our Son' (*Granta*). The remaining stories were first published in *The Fat Man in History* (University of Queensland Press, Australia, 1974) and *War Crimes* (University of Queensland Press, Australia, 1979). A number of stories from both these collections were included in the British edition of *The Fat Man in History* (Faber and Faber, 1980).

"Do You Love Me?"

1. *The Role of the Cartographers*

Perhaps a few words about the role of the Cartographers in our present society are warranted.

To begin with one must understand the nature of the yearly census, a manifestation of our desire to know, always, exactly where we stand. The census, originally a count of the population, has gradually extended until it has become a total inventory of the contents of the nation, a mammoth task which is continuing all the time — no sooner has one census been announced than work on another begins.

The results of the census play an important part in our national life and have, for many years, been the pivot point for the yearly "Festival of the Corn" (an ancient festival, related to the wealth of the earth).

We have a passion for lists. And nowhere is this more clearly illustrated than in the Festival of the Corn which takes place in midsummer, the weather always being fine and warm. On the night of the festival, the householders move their goods and possessions, all furniture, electrical goods, clothing, rugs, kitchen utensils, bathrobes, slippers, cushions, lawn mowers, curtains, doorstops, heirlooms, cameras, and anything else that can be moved into the street so that the census officials may the more easily check the inventory of each household.

The Festival of the Corn is, however, much more than a clerical affair. And, the day over and the night come, the householders invite each other to view their possessions which they refer to, on this night, as gifts. It is like nothing more than a wedding feast — there is much cooking, all sorts of traditional dishes, fine wines, strong liquors, music is played loudly in quiet neighbourhoods, strangers copulate with strangers, men dance together, and maidens in yellow robes distribute small barley-sugar corncobs to young and old alike.

And in all this the role of the Cartographers is perhaps the most important, for our people crave, more than anything else, to know the extent of the nation, to know, exactly, the shape of the coastline, to hear what land may have been lost to the sea, to know what has been reclaimed and what is still in doubt. If the Cartographers' report is good the Festival of the Corn will be a good festival. If the report is bad, one can always sense, for all the dancing and drinking, a feeling of nervousness and apprehension in the revellers, a certain desperation. In the year of a bad Cartographers' report there will always be fights and, occasionally, some property will be stolen as citizens attempt to compensate themselves for their sense of loss.

Because of the importance of their job the Cartographers have become an elite — well paid, admired, envied, and having no small opinion of themselves. It is said by some that they are overproud, immoral, vain and footloose, and it is perhaps the last charge (by necessity true) that brings about the others. For the Cartographers spend their years travelling up and down the coast, along the great rivers, traversing great mountains and vast deserts. They travel in small parties of three, four, sometimes five, making their own time, working as they please, because eventually it is their own responsibility to see that their team's task is completed in time.

My father, a Cartographer himself, often told me stories about himself or his colleagues and the adventures they had in the wilderness.

There were other stories, however, that always remained in my mind and, as a child, caused me considerable anxiety. These were the stories of the nether regions and I doubt if they were known outside a very small circle of Cartographers and government officials. As a child in a house frequented by Cartographers, I often heard these tales which invariably made me cling closely to my mother's skirts.

It appears that for some time certain regions of the country had become less and less real and these regions were regarded fearfully even by the Cartographers, who prided themselves on their courage. The regions in question were invariably uninhabited, unused for agriculture or industry. There were certain sections of the Halverson Ranges, vast stretches of the Greater Desert, and long pieces of coastline which had begun to slowly disappear like the image on an improperly fixed photograph.

It was because of these nebulous areas that the Fischerscope was introduced. The Fischerscope is not unlike radar in its principle and is able to detect the presence of any object, no matter how demateri- alized or insubstantial. In this way the Cartographers were still able to map the questionable pairs of the nether regions. To have returned with blanks on the maps would have created such public anxiety that no one dared think what it might do to the stability of our society. I now have reason to believe that certain areas of the country disap- peared so completely that even the Fischerscope could not detect them and the Cartographers, acting under political pressure, used old maps to fake in the missing sections. If my theory is grounded in fact, and I am sure it is, it would explain my father's cynicism about the Festival of the Corn.

2. *The Archetypal Cartographer*

My father was in his fifties but he had kept himself in good shape. His skin was brown and his muscles still firm. He was a tall man with a thick head of grey hair, a slightly less grey moustache and a long aquiline nose. Sitting on a horse he looked as proud and cruel as Genghis Khan. Lying on the beach clad only in bathers and sun- glasses he still managed to retain his authoritative air.

Beside him I always felt as if I had betrayed him. I was slightly built, more like my mother.

It was the day before the festival and we lay on the beach, my father, my mother, my girlfriend and I. As was usual in these circum- stances my father addressed all his remarks to Karen. He never considered the members of his own family worth talking to. I always had the uncomfortable feeling that he was flirting with my girl- friends and I never knew what to do about it.

People were lying in groups up and down the beach. Near us a family of five were playing with a large beach ball.

"Look at those fools," my father said to Karen.

"Why are they fools?" Karen asked.

"They're fools," said my father. "They were born fools and they'll die fools. Tomorrow they'll dance in the streets and drink too much."

"So," said Karen triumphantly, in the manner of one who has become privy to secret information. "It will be a good Cartographers' report?"

My father roared with laughter.

Karen looked hurt and pouted. "Am I a fool?"

"No," my father said, "you're really quite splendid."

3. *The Most Famous Festival*

The festival, as it turned out, was the greatest disaster in living memory.

The Cartographers' report was excellent, the weather was fine, but somewhere something had gone wrong.

The news was confusing. The television said that, in spite of the good report, various items had been stolen very early in the night. Later there was a news flash to say that a large house had completely disappeared in Howie Street.

Later still we looked out the window to see a huge band of people carrying lighted torches. There was a lot of shouting. The same image, exactly, was on the television and a reporter was explaining that bands of vigilantes were out looking for thieves.

My father stood at the window, a martini in his hand, and watched the vigilantes set alight a house opposite.

My mother wanted to know what we should do.

"Come and watch the fools," my father said, "they're incredible."

4. *The I.C.I. Incident*

The next day the I.C.I. building disappeared in front of a crowd of two thousand people. It took two hours. The crowd stood silently as the great steel and glass structure slowly faded before them.

The staff who were evacuated looked pale and shaken. The caretaker who was amongst the last to leave looked almost translucent. In the days that followed he made some name for himself as a mystic, claiming that he had been able to see other worlds, layer upon layer, through the fabric of the here and now.

5. *Behaviour when Confronted with Dematerialization*

The anger of our people when confronted with acts of theft has always been legendary and was certainly highlighted by the incidents which occurred on the night of the festival.

But the fury exhibited on this famous night could not compare with the intensity of emotion displayed by those who witnessed the earliest scenes of dematerialization.

The silent crowd who watched the I.C.I. building erupted into hysteria when they realized that it had finally gone and wasn't likely to come back.

It was like some monstrous theft for which punishment must be meted out.

They stormed into the Shell building next door and smashed desks and ripped down office partitions. Reporters who attended the scene were rarely impartial observers, but one of the cooler-headed members of the press remarked on the great number of weeping men and women who hurled typewriters from windows and scattered files through crowds of frightened office workers.

Five days later they displayed similar anger when the Shell building itself disappeared.

6. *Behaviour of Those Dematerializing*

The first reports of dematerializing people were not generally believed and were suppressed by the media. But these things were soon common knowledge and few families were untouched by them. Such incidents were obviously not all the same but in many victims there was a tendency to exhibit extreme aggression towards those around them. Murders and assaults committed by these unfortunates were not uncommon and in most cases they exhibited an almost unbelievable rage, as if they were the victims of a shocking betrayal.

My friend James Bray was once stopped in the street by a very beautiful woman who clawed and scratched at his face and said: "You did this to me, you bastard, you did this to me."

He had never seen her before but he confessed that, in some irrational way, he felt responsible and didn't defend himself. Fortunately she disappeared before she could do him much damage.

7. *Some Theories that Arose at the Time*

1. The world is merely a dream dreamt by god who is waking after a long sleep. When he is properly awake the world will disappear completely. When the world disappears we will disappear with it and be happy.

2. The world has become sensitive to light. In the same way that prolonged use of, say, penicillin can suddenly result in a dangerous allergy, prolonged exposure of the world to the sun has made it sensitive to light.

The advocates of this theory could be seen bustling through the city crowds in their long, hooded black robes.

3.   The fact that the world is disappearing has been caused by the sloppy work of the Cartographers and census takers. Those who filled out their census forms incorrectly would lose those items they had neglected to describe. People overlooked in the census by impatient officials would also disappear. A strong pressure group demanded that a new census be taken quickly before matters got worse.

8. *My Father's Theory*

The world, according to my father, was exactly like the human body and had its own defence mechanisms with which it defended itself against anything that either threatened it or was unnecessary to it. The I.C.I. building and the I.C.I. company had obviously constituted some threat to the world or had simply been irrelevant. That's why it had disappeared and not because some damn fool god was waking up and rubbing his eyes.

"I don't believe in god," my father said. "Humanity is god. Humanity is the only god I know. If humanity doesn't need something it will disappear. People who are not loved will disappear. Everything that is not loved will disappear from the face of the earth. We only exist through the love of others and that's what it's all about."

9. *A Contradiction*

"Look at those fools," my father said, "they wouldn't know if they were up themselves."

10. *An Unpleasant Scene*

The world at this time was full of unpleasant and disturbing scenes. One that I recall vividly took place in the middle of the city on a hot, sultry Tuesday afternoon. It was about one-thirty and I was waiting for Karen by the post office when a man of forty or so ran past me. He was dematerializing rapidly. Everybody seemed to be deliberately looking the other way, which seemed to me to make him dematerialize faster. I stared at him hard, hoping that I could do something to keep him there until help arrived. I tried to love him, because I believed in my father's theory. I thought, I must love that man. But his face irritated me. It is not so easy to love a stranger and I'm ashamed to say that he had the small mouth and close-together eyes that I have always disliked in a person. I tried to love him but I'm afraid I failed.

While I watched he tried to hail taxi after taxi. But the taxi drivers were only too well aware of what was happening and had no wish to spend their time driving a passenger who, at any moment, might cease to exist. They looked the other way or put up their NOT FOR HIRE signs.

Finally he managed to waylay a taxi at some traffic lights. By this time he was so insubstantial that I could see right through him. He was beginning to shout. A terrible thin noise, but penetrating nonetheless. He tried to open the cab door, but the driver had already locked it. I could hear the man's voice, high and piercing: "I want to go home." He repeated it over and over again. "I want to go home to my wife."

The taxi drove off when the lights changed. There was a lull in the traffic. People had fled the corner and left it deserted and it was I alone who saw the man finally disappear.

I felt sick.

Karen arrived five minutes later and found me pale and shaken. "Are you all right?" she said.

"Do you love me?" I said.

11. *The Nether Regions*

My father had an irritating way of explaining things to me I already understood, refusing to stop no matter how much I said "I know" or "You told me before".

Thus he expounded on the significance of the nether regions, adopting the tone of a lecturer speaking to a class of particularly backward children.

"As you know," he said, "the nether regions were amongst the first to disappear and this in itself is significant. These regions, I'm sure you know, are seldom visited by men and only then by people like me whose sole job is to make sure that they're still there. We had no use for these areas, these deserts, swamps, and coastlines which is why, of course, they disappeared. They were merely possessions of ours and if they had any use at all it was as symbols for our poets, writers and film makers. They were used as symbols of alienation, lovelessness, loneliness, uselessness and so on. Do you get what I mean?"

Yes," I said, "I get what you mean."

"But do you?" my father insisted. "But do you really, I wonder."
He examined me seriously, musing on the possibilities of my understanding him. "How old are you?"

"Twenty," I said.

"I knew, of course," he said. "Do you understand the significance
of the nether regions?"

I sighed, a little too loudly, and my father narrowed his eyes.
Quickly I said: "They are like everything else. They're like the cities.
The cities are deserts where people are alone and lonely. They don't
love one another."

"Don't love one another," intoned my father, also sighing. "We no
longer love one another. When we realize that we need one another
we will stop disappearing. This is a lesson to us. A hard lesson, but,
I hope, an effective one."

My father continued to speak, but I watched him without listening. After a few minutes he stopped abruptly: "Are you listening to
me?" he said. I was surprised to detect real concern in his voice. He
looked at me questioningly. "I've always looked after you," he said,
"ever since you were little."

12. *The Cartographers' Fall*

I don't know when it was that I noticed that my father had become
depressed. It probably happened quite gradually without either my
mother or me noticing it.

Even when I did become aware of it I attributed it to a woman.
My father had a number of lovers and his moods usually reflected
the success or failure of these relationships.

But I know now that he had heard already of Hurst and Jamov,
the first two Cartographers to disappear. The news was suppressed
for several weeks and then, somehow or other, leaked to the press.
Certainly the Cartographers had enemies amongst the civil servants
who regarded them as overproud and overpaid, and it was probably
from one of these civil servants that the press heard the news.

When the news finally broke I understood my father's depression
and felt sorry for him.

I didn't know how to help him. I wanted, badly, to make him
happy. I had never ever been able to give him anything or do

anything for him that he couldn't do better himself. Now I wanted to help him, to show him I understood.

I found him sitting in front of the television one night when I returned from my office and I sat quietly beside him. He seemed more kindly now and he placed his hand on my knee and patted it.

I sat there for a while, overcome with the new warmth of this relationship, and then, unable to contain my emotion any more, I blurted out: "You could change your job."

My father stiffened and sat bolt upright. The pressure of his hand on my knee increased until I yelped with pain, and still he held on, hurting me terribly.

"You are a fool," he said, "you wouldn't know if you were up yourself."

Through the pain in my leg, I felt the intensity of my father's fear.

13. *Why the World Needs Cartographers*

My father woke me at 3.00 a.m. to tell me why the world needed Cartographers. He smelled of whisky and seemed, once again, to be very gentle.

"The world needs Cartographers," he said softly, "because if they didn't have Cartographers the fools wouldn't know where they were. They wouldn't know if they were up themselves if they didn't have a Cartographer to tell them what's happening. The world needs Cartographers," my father said, "it fucking well needs Cartographers."

14. *One Final Scene*

Let me describe a final scene to you: I am sitting on the sofa my father brought home when I was five years old. I am watching television. My father is sitting in a leather armchair that once belonged to his father and which has always been exclusively his. My mother is sitting in the dining alcove with her cards spread across the table, playing one more interminable game of patience.

I glance casually across at my father to see if he is doing anything more than stare into space, and notice, with a terrible shock, that he is showing the first signs of dematerializing.

"What are you staring at?" My father, in fact, has been staring at me.

"Nothing."

, don't."

nervously I return my eyes to the inanity of the television. I don't
know what to do. Should I tell my father that he is dematerializing?
If I don't tell him will he notice? I feel I should do something but I
can feel, already, the anger in his voice. His anger is nothing new. But
this is possibly the beginning of a tide of uncontrollable rage. If he
knows he is dematerializing, he will think I don't love him. He will
blame me. He will attack me. Old as he is, he is still considerably
stronger than I am and he could hurt me badly. I stare determinedly
at the television and feel my father's eyes on me.

I try to feel love for my father, I try very, very hard.

I attempt to remember how I felt about him when I was little, in
the days when he was still occasionally tender towards me.

But it's no good.

Because I can only remember how he has hit me, hurt me, humiliated me and flirted with my girlfriends. I realize, with a flush of panic
and guilt, that I don't love him. In spite of which I say: "I love you."

My mother looks up sharply from her cards and lets out a surprised cry.

I turn to my father. He has almost disappeared. I can see the
leather of the chair through his stomach.

I don't know whether it is my unconvincing declaration of love
or my mother's exclamation that makes my father laugh. For whatever reason, he begins to laugh uncontrollably: "You bloody fools,"
he gasps, "I wish you could see the looks on your bloody silly faces."

And then he is gone.

My mother looks across at me nervously, a card still in her hand.
"Do you love me?" she asks.

The Last Days of a Famous Mime

1.

The Mime arrived on Alitalia with very little luggage: a brown paper parcel and what looked like a woman's handbag.

Asked the contents of the brown paper parcel he said, "String." .

Asked what the string was for he replied: "Tying up bigger parcels."

It had not been intended as a joke, but the Mime was pleased when the reporters laughed. Inducing laughter was not his forte. He was famous for terror.

Although his state of despair was famous throughout Europe, few guessed at his hope for the future. "The string," he explained, "is a prayer that I am always praying."

Reluctantly he untied his parcel and showed them the string. It was blue and when extended measured exactly fifty-three metres.

The Mime and the string appeared on the front pages of the evening papers.

2.

The first audiences panicked easily. They had not been prepared for his ability to mime terror. They fled their seats continually. Only to return again.

Like snorkel divers they appeared at the doors outside the concert hall with red faces and were puzzled to find the world as they had left it.

3.

Books had been written about him. He was the subject of an award-winning film. But in his first morning in a provincial town he was distressed to find that his performance had not been liked by the one newspaper's one critic.

"I cannot see," the critic wrote, "the use of invoking terror in an audience."

The Mime sat on his bed, pondering ways to make his performance more light-hearted.

4.

As usual he attracted women who wished to still the raging storms of his heart.

They attended his bed like highly paid surgeons operating on a difficult case. They were both passionate and intelligent. They did not suffer defeat lightly.

5.

Wrongly accused of merely miming love in his private life he was somewhat surprised to be confronted with hatred.

"Surely," he said, "if you now hate me, it was you who were imitating love, not I."

"You always were a slimy bastard," she said. "What's in that parcel?"

"I told you before," he said helplessly, "string."

"You're a liar," she said.

But later when he untied the parcel he found that she had opened it to check on his story. Her understanding of the string had been perfect. She had cut it into small pieces like spaghetti in a lousy restaurant.

6.

Against the advice of the tour organizers he devoted two concerts entirely to love and laughter. They were disasters. It was felt that love and laughter were not, in his case, as instructive as terror.

The next performance was quickly announced.

TWO HOURS OF REGRET.

Tickets sold quickly. He began with a brief interpretation of love, using it merely as a prelude to regret, which he elaborated on in a complex and moving performance which left the audience pale and shaken. In a final flourish he passed from regret to loneliness to terror. The audience devoured the terror like brave tourists eating the hottest curry in an Indian restaurant.

7.

"What you are doing," she said, "is capitalizing on your neuroses.

Personally I find it disgusting, like someone exhibiting their club foot, or Turkish beggars with strange deformities."

He said nothing. He was mildly annoyed at her presumption: that he had not thought this many, many times before.

With perfect misunderstanding she interpreted his passivity as disdain.

Wishing to hurt him, she slapped his face.

Wishing to hurt her, he smiled brilliantly.

8.

The story of the blue string touched the public imagination. Small brown paper packages were sold at the doors of his concerts.

Standing on the stage he could hear the packages being noisily unwrapped. He thought of American matrons buying Muslim prayer rugs.

9.

Exhausted and weakened by the heavy schedule he fell prey to the doubts that had pricked at him insistently for years. He lost all sense of direction and spent many listless hours by himself, sitting in a motel room listening to the air-conditioner.

He had lost confidence in the social uses of controlled terror. He no longer understood the audience's need to experience the very things he so desperately wished to escape from.

He emptied the ashtrays fastidiously.

He opened his brown paper parcel and threw the small pieces of string down the cistern. When the torrent of white water subsided they remained floating there like flotsam from a disaster at sea.

10.

The Mime called a press conference to announce that there would be no more concerts. He seemed small and foreign and smelt of garlic. The press regarded him without enthusiasm. He watched their hovering pens anxiously, unsuccessfully willing them to write down his words.

Briefly he announced that he wished to throw his talent open to broader influences. His skills would be at the disposal of the people, who would be free to request his services for any purpose at any time.

His skin seemed sallow but his eyes seemed as bright as those on a nodding fur mascot on the back window ledge of an American car.

11.

Asked to describe death he busied himself taking Polaroid photographs of his questioners.

12.

Asked to describe marriage he handed out small cheap mirrors with MADE IN TUNISIA written on the back.

13.

His popularity declined. It was felt that he had become obscure and beyond the understanding of ordinary people. In response he requested easier questions. He held back nothing of himself in his effort to please his audience.

14.

Asked to describe an aeroplane he flew three times around the city, only injuring himself slightly on landing.

15.

Asked to describe a river, he drowned himself.

16.

It is unfortunate that this, his last and least typical performance, is the only one which has been recorded on film.

There is a small crowd by the river bank, no more than thirty people. A small, neat man dressed in a grey suit picks his way through some children who seem more interested in the large plastic toy dog they are playing with.

He steps into the river, which, at the bank, is already quite deep. His head is only visible above the water for a second or two. And then he is gone.

A policeman looks expectantly over the edge, as if waiting for him to reappear. Then the film stops.

Watching this last performance it is difficult to imagine how this man stirred such emotions in the hearts of those who saw him.

Kristu-Du

The man who brings water shall be blessed.
He carrieth fat to the cattle,
ears to the corn.
The sound of such water can be likened
to the laughter of children.

(Traditional Deffala Song)

1.

While the architect's wife carefully folded a pair of white slacks, five men were hanged. As she hunted through the drawer for her cosmetics and packed them neatly, one by one, in a small leather carrying case, an old man died of dehydration and starvation beside a dusty road. As she slipped the case shut and fiddled inexpertly with its lock, teams of imported builders laboured on the great domed building in the middle of the cruel rock-filled valley.

The architect sat on the edge of the neatly made bed and watched his wife. He was a slim tall man in his late forties. He had fine blue eyes, unusually large eyelids, and a high forehead made even higher by the receding crop of curling grey hair. His mouth was perhaps his best feature, containing as it did the continual promise of a smile. But now the promise was not honoured. His eyes were red-rimmed and tired. His long-fingered hands were clasped on his lap and he watched his wife make her final preparations for her departure. She was leaving him and returning to Europe.

Now she was packed she sat on the bed beside him. They had entered those white corridors where there is neither shadow nor feeling.

He wished to say many things to her but he had said them all already. He said them badly and she had not listened in any case.

He wished to say: the building I have designed will last a thousand years and will endure beyond the tyrant who rules this place.

He would have added: you are only leaving because you saw a soldier shoot a dog, not because of anything else.

But all these things had been covered time and time again and she was returning to the civilization of Europe and he was to remain to build his masterpiece, the great dome of the desert, Kristu-Du, the meeting house of the tribes.

He picked up her two cases from the bed and took them out to the Land Rover. When he returned she was standing in the living room looking at an old book of his work. As he walked in she put it down on the coffee table.

Neither of them said anything.

On their way out she placed her front door key on top of the refrigerator. Then, hesitating, she opened her handbag and took out a small bottle of pills. These she placed beside the keys.

They were sleeping pills, difficult to come by.

The noise of the Land Rover always made conversation difficult, but now it made the lack of it somehow more bearable. Gravel rattled against the aluminium floor, the engine and the transmission were loud and unrelenting, rock samples in the back jumped and crashed on the tray with every bump. He saw now, as he had seen when he first arrived three years ago, the terrible bleakness of the town, a bleakness that did not even have the redeeming virtue of being exotic. The buildings constructed by the now departed Russians all looked like grey hospitals. They stood at the grand height of four storeys, towering over a collection of ugly shops and houses of white concrete blocks. In the unpaved streets stunted palm trees died from lack of water. He saw the terrible poverty of the people as they squatted on the footpath or walked aimlessly in groups along the broken streets. Tall Itos, Berehvas with pierced ears, Deffalas with the yellow eyes of desert people. It was nobody's home, everyone's exile. A city planned where no one had ever wished to live.

Only the soldiers seemed well fed. They lounged everywhere, these tall warriors of the president's own tribe, clustering in doorways or patrolling in groups of two or three, machine-guns slung over their shoulders.

He saw the big white colonial building which he now recognized as a place to be feared, the detention centre, and behind it in the high-walled garden of the palace, a tasteless mock-Spanish edifice built on the president's instruction to a photograph torn from a badly printed American newspaper.

From here the president ruled with a skilful and unique blend of violence and magic. The magic, of course, was not magic at all, but rather an array of technological tricks which were impressive to a primitive and unlettered people. Oongala was a giant of a man, half-educated, barely literate, but he understood his people all too well. Those who were too educated or enraged to be impressed by magic could be handled with simple violence, torture and murder. With the rest he reinforced his claim to be the Great Magician of tribal myth by utilizing a continual array of new tricks.

The great canal which would have brought water to the drought-stricken land had been abandoned when he came to power. The railway which would have joined its disparate peoples lay unfinished with two stations built and the rails lying on the parched soil like pick-up sticks abandoned by a bored child. This was not the technology Oongala preferred.

The man who has known throughout the world as a comic-strip dictator, a clown, a buffoon and a mass murderer, chose to travel across his land in a hovercraft, to drop out of the sky in a white helicopter, or simply to star in one more badly made motion picture which he wrote, directed, produced and starred in. These films were the staple diet of his starving populace. They cheered him as he jumped thirty feet from ground to roof top to battle and destroy armed villains. They watched open-mouthed as he defeated bands of machine-gunning renegades. Bullets could not harm him, gravity hold him, or the engines of war overpower him.

And now they were treated to the works of the man whom Gerrard had privately named Mr Meat, the ex-arms dealer Wallis, who was now making a fortune from constructing holograms in the bigger villages. The work had barely begun but if the reaction to the one in the capital was any indication, it was a popular piece of magic. Inside a concrete building that had all the charm of a public urinal the faithful could see a three-dimensional image of their dictator levitating above the desk in his big office.

Now, as the Land Rover left the town and rattled down the track towards the airport, Gerrard looked across at his wife. She caught his eye for a moment and then looked hurriedly away, she who had once encouraged him with his plans, bolstered him in the face of failure and criticism, who had stood by him fiercely when his controversial works had been disbanded by one municipal authority because of cost, another because of a provincial sense of what was

beautiful. And now, here, when a great building was near comple-
tion, she was leaving him, washing her hands of him, joining the
ranks of the old associates who had publicly criticized his role in
working for the glorification of a mass murderer.

The hypocrites, he thought now, they sit in their exquisite offices
while their own governments torture and kill, and because there isn't
a scandalized headline in the newspapers they pretend these things
don't go on. They are so clean, so pure, and I am so terrible. They
want me to say: no, I shall abandon this project, the greatest domed
structure in the world. I should walk away from it and leave it
unfinished or to be ruined by incompetent fools. Would they? Would
his fine pure friends have walked away from such a triumph simply
because a government had changed? A building seven times as big
as St Peter's in Rome? He smiled thinly.

The airport was almost empty. He checked in his wife's baggage
whilst she looked in the duty-free shop. When he came back he saw
that she had bought perfume. He said nothing and gave her the
ticket.

"There is no point in you waiting," she said.

He looked at her: eyes that had once looked at him with love, now
dull and lustreless, lips that had covered his body in soft passionate
kisses, now thin and full of tension.

"I wanted to say ..." he began.

"What?" she interrupted nervously, on the defensive, worried
that he would ask anything of her, make any claim.

He had wanted to say that he would miss her dreadfully, that he
would think of her continually, that he would endure his loneliness
in the hope that the separation would not be permanent.

But instead, he merely smiled a wry smile and said, "I just wanted
to say goodbye."

"Goodbye," she said. She kept her hands clutched around her
perfume and handbag. She did not lean towards him. "Goodbye,"
she said again.

"Goodbye," he said, then turned on his heel.

She watched him walk away, casually throwing his keys up and
down in his hand. It was the walk of a person who might have
been on his way to an expensive lunch. She never forgave him for
it.

2.

There were many who would have described Gerrard Haflinger as a solitary man. It is true that conversation did not come easily to him and he had a peculiar mixture of shyness and arrogance in his character that normally made him appear more than a little aloof. His dealings with governments, municipal authorities and the Medicis of modern business had always been made more difficult by his inability to unbend, to be anything other than the bristling defendant of the purity of his vision. But solitary he was not.

In an interview in a popular European magazine he had once been asked what was most precious to him in life and he had answered, without hesitation, that it was to be with true friends. And what was a true friend? A true friend, he had answered, was someone you could stand naked before, who would never judge you, whom you could share your darkest secrets with, and so on.

By this definition Gerrard Haflinger had no more friends. He had been judged and found guilty not only by the three men he respected and loved most, but also by his wife.

Gerrard Haflinger no longer remembered the interview but if he had he would have reflected that he had not answered truthfully: his work was the most precious thing in his life. For this, this one project, he had been prepared to give up everything else. Possibly if his other work had proceeded properly, if the theatre complex had not been bungled, if the state library had ever gone ahead, he might have abandoned the Kristu-Du on the day Oongala took power and parliamentary democracy was abolished, or, if not then, at least in the following months when it became clear to everyone what sort of a leader Oongala would be.

But he was forty-six years old and the Kristu-Du was all that stood between him and the terrifying abyss of the total and complete failure of his life's ambition. To abandon the domed building would be to throw away everything he had ever worked for and join the faceless ranks of those clever men and women who had seen their dreams crash and splinter through lack of drive, charm, talent, or, as Gerrard saw this issue, courage.

His refusal to abandon his project had brought him to sit in this white sparse living room by himself. He felt like a man who comes to stand on the edge of a desert which stretches as far as the eye can see. He felt the cold wind already stinging him and was sorry that

he had come to stand here. Yet he felt also, in the midst of the jumbled
emotions of fear, loneliness, and self-pity, a certain tingling of excitement that he did not know what to do with.

He walked to the bedroom and stared at the neatly made bed. The
sight gave him a sharp and sudden pain and he turned quickly. In
the kitchen he opened the refrigerator door and stood for some time
staring into it. He was shutting its door when his eye lighted on the
key and the bottle of sleeping tablets. He put the key in his pocket
and walked to the sink, carefully reading the instructions on the label
of the pills. He poured a glass of boiled water and returned to the
living room where he made himself comfortable on the big black
Italian couch. He took the two pills and waited for them to work.

It was seven o'clock at night.

3.

It was just after eight o'clock in the morning and the air was still crisp
and cold when he arrived at the small pass which opened onto
Hi-Dahlian (the Valley of the Spirits). As he drove to the rise he
waited impatiently, as he always did, for the moment when the poor
dusty drought-stricken landscape would suddenly cease and there
before him would lie the harsh boulder-strewn valley filled with
dazzlingly white round rocks, a great basin of egg-smooth boulders
that stretched to the mountains on every side. And there, in the
middle, would stand his Kristu-Du, its soaring walls as smooth and
white as the rocks themselves, its copper dome gleaming golden in
the morning sun.

The Land Rover lumbered onto the pass, and there it was. He
stopped, as he always stopped, and looked at it with pride and
satisfaction. For now there was no doubting the greatness of the
work, its perfect scale, its harmonious integration into the spectacular landscape. It was a glistening rock in a sea of shining pebbles, of
them and yet apart from them. Only as one came very close did one
appreciate the immense size of the building: 1,000 feet high, 850 feet
in diameter, seven times the size of St Peter's. In its glowing eggshell
interior there was room for 100,000 tribesmen.

It had been designed to the brief of Oongala's first victim, the late
president, as a unifying symbol for the eight tribes, sited in the
holiest place, a neutral ground where a new democracy would start
to spread its fragile wings. Gerrard, in the early days when the plan

had been selected, had spoken of its function with a fierce obsessive poetry, likening it to a vast machine which would take an active role in the birth of a new democracy. It was not a symbol, he said. It was not a building. It was one of those rare pieces of architecture which would act on the future as well as exist in the present.

In those innocent days the plans provided for an extensive water system, with supplies for the watering of horses, mules and camels. There was to have been a small lake around which shade trees were to be planted, pleasant camping for those who had journeyed so far. But there was, of course, no water now. Oongala had stopped work on the great canal and the drought, the terrible drought, continued to kill the people and their livestock and to raise the very earth itself so that on some days the sun was blotted out by an endless ocean of flying dust.

As he drove down into the valley Gerrard looked at what he saw with a selective eye. He did not see the section of roof that was still missing. He eliminated the giant blue and red cranes, the bird's-nest ugliness of scaffolding, the twisted piles of abandoned reinforcing mesh, the glistening corrugated-iron offices and the workers' amenity blocks. He saw trees which would one day be planted and fountains that would burst spectacularly from fissured rock. But most of all he adjusted his vision to ignore the grey and white clusterings of figures that gathered around the west entrance of the building like swarms of virulent organisms which would destroy their host. Yet in this he was not wholly successful, so that as he entered the plain itself, winding along the carefully planned road between the giant rocks, lines of tension formed across his face and two small vertical lines appeared on his forehead, just to the left of his nose.

The road was planned to be a continuous series of surprises, of opened vistas and closed canyons, of startling glimpses of the building, and veiled promises of what was to come. Now, at the last moment, he came round the rock he had named "Old Man Rock" and he was at the edge of the site itself and the great building towered above him in all its breathtaking beauty. And now he could eliminate things no more and the lines on his forehead deepened as the white and grey clusterings of figures revealed themselves to be a meeting of one hundred and fifty skilled European workers.

A strike.

He drove past them slowly, aware of the turned eyes but unable to acknowledge them in any natural way. He parked outside his office and went in to wait.

He sat on his swivel chair and played with some paperclips, his apprehension showing in the way he took them, one by one, and twisted them and bent them until they grew hot and snapped with fatigue. It was here that he was bad, here that he ruined things. It was here that his associates succeeded and he failed. For they were charming and persuasive men who could sway hard-headed businessmen in their own language, and overcome the problems of site disputes with their negotiators' skills and hard-headed bargaining.

He no longer talked to the men who were building his dream. Even his assistants found him distant and cold. And he had so badly offended the engineers that they would barely speak to him. It was not as he wished it. He would have dearly loved to have taken them to town, to have bought them beers, to have gone whoring with them, to have shared the easy relaxed talk he had overheard between them. But there was something stiff in him, something that would not bend.

So he waited in his office for the deputation, breaking paperclips and throwing them into the rubbish bin.

4.

He disapproved of bribes and so gave this one badly. Rather than speeding his interview with the minister it produced the opposite effect. The minister's secretary, a uniformed sergeant from the 101, was now punishing him for such a tasteless and inelegant performance.

He had now waited an hour, his agitation becoming more and more pronounced. He crossed his long legs and then uncrossed them. He stared at a yellowed five-year-old copy of *Punch* and could find nothing funny in it. He stared at the bleak anteroom with a practised eye, observing a thousand defects in workmanship and finish, noting a wall that was not quite vertical, automatically relocating a window so that it was lower, wider, and placed on a wall where it might have collected some of the chilly winter sunshine.

He stood and examined the tasteless paintings on the walls.

He sat and looked at his fingernails, wondering if it was true that the long curved shells indicated a propensity to lung disease as he had once been told.

As to how he would persuade the minister to make extra funds available to meet the men's demands, he had no idea. If he had been Mr Meat he would not have bothered with the minister, he would have gone straight to Oongala, played polo with him and spent a night at the billiard table. He would have laughed at the dictator's jokes and told even cruder ones of his own. But he was not Mr Meat and his grey formal reserve made the dictator uneasy, as if he were being secretly laughed at. Oongala would no longer see him.

What the men wanted was fair and reasonable. It was quite correct. But the correctness did not help. Everything in him wanted to say: "Give the money, find it, do anything, but let the work proceed." But that, of course, was not an argument.

Finally the secretary had had enough of the agitated movements of his prisoner. He phoned through to the minister and told Gerrard he could go in.

Gerrard smiled at the secretary, thanking him.

The secretary stared at him, the merest flicker of a smile crossing his stony face.

5.

The minister sat behind his large desk doing the *Times* crossword. He was, for this country, an unusually short man. He had a sensitive face and particularly nervous hands, which seemed to flutter through a conversation like lost butterflies. On occasions they had discussed Proust and the minister had talked dreamily of days at Oxford and invited the Haflingers to visit socially, an invitation that Gerrard, had he been a trifle more calculating, would have realized was an important one to accept. Yet he managed to neither accept nor decline and had left the minister with the feeling, correct as it happened, that Gerrard found his company unstimulating. The minister was a man of sensitive feelings and weak character, a failing that had kept him alive while stronger men had long since disappeared into jail.

"Good morning, Gerrard. What would you make of this — Ah! A cross pug leaps across funereal stone? It is eleven letters," he smiled apologetically, "beginning with S."

"I don't know."

"Neither do I." He folded the delicate rice-paper pages of the airmail edition and plugged in a small electric jug which sat on the low filing cabinet beside him. "Coffee?"

"That would be pleasant, thank you," Gerrard was trying to be pleasant, to unbend, to relax, to be patient enough to discuss all ten volumes of *Recherche du Temps Perdu* if it was necessary. He sat in the low visitor's chair and they both waited for the jug to boil.

"How is Mrs Haflinger?"

"Gone, I'm afraid."

The eyebrows raised and the tongue clucking sympathetically. "Our country is not to everybody's taste," he picked up *The Times*, weighed it, and let it fall to the desk, "as I read every day."

"Unfortunately it isn't." Gerrard attempted to match the sad ironical smile on the other's face.

"Black with two?"

"Thank you." Gerrard watched as the minister fussed over the coffee and thought how much he hated the metallic taste of Nescafé.

"Excuse me," said the minister, "I seem to have spilled some into the saucer. Now what is the problem? I take it the visit isn't social." And he allowed the merest glint of malice to enter his voice.

"I have a strike."

"And the particular matter of the dispute? Ah," he smiled, "if only our industrial relations laws were in a more advanced stage. But," the smile again, "I'm sure you understand that as well as I."

"There is no particular matter. It is a question of conditions generally. The shortage of water, the absence of power in their quarters, the quarters themselves." Gerrard thought of the old army barracks where his men were quartered: squalid rows of huts with no partitions and a complete lack of privacy for even the most basic matters.

The minister nodded sympathetically: "Oh, I know, I know. The latrines, I imagine, are also a problem. One cannot blame them. I would be upset myself."

"There is a list." Gerrard was beginning to hope. Against his best sense he hoped that this man might actually have the guts to do something. He gave the minister the list of the men's complaints. It contained ten points.

"What do they ask?"

"Either that matters be upgraded or they be paid at a special penalty rate."

"And," the minister blew into the steaming coffee, "if that is not possible, and I mean 'if'?"

"They will leave, en masse."

"Oh dear."

"Yes."

"And you think they will carry out the threat?"

In his blind anxiety it had never occurred to Gerrard that they wouldn't, but he said simply: "They will carry it out."

"Oh dear."

"Quite," said Gerrard. "What shall we do, what can we do?"

"For me," the minister held his pale palms upwards, "my hands are tied. I myself can do nothing." The hands came together in an attitude of prayer and the index fingers plucked nervously at the pendulous lower lip. "My department's funds are already over-committed. It would take the president himself to approve a special allowance."

"And the president," Gerrard smiled thinly, "is not likely to be sympathetic."

"As you know," the minister clasped his hands across his breast and leant back dolefully in his big squeaking chair, "as you know, the president is of the view that they are being paid far too much as it is. It was only after my most earnest plea ..."

"For which I am most grateful." The minister was lying. Gerrard lied in return. He had never spoken in these terms to the minister before. He was finding it repulsive. He felt vaguely ill. "But if there were anything ..."

The minister snapped forward in his chair and leant across the table. "I will speak to him," he said with the air of a man who has made a reckless decision. "I will go to him this morning. The president is most anxious that the project be finished quickly. He feels that in the absence of rain," and here he allowed the merest trace of treasonable sarcasm to enter his voice, "the people are in need of a boost in morale. He is relying on the Kristu-Du. He will be most eager to end the dispute."

"Which means?"

"It means," the minister winked slyly, "that I will speak on your behalf and that finally you need not worry. Your building will go ahead without serious delay. You have my word for it. You will not be unhappy with the result." And the wink came again. Gerrard, who wondered if he had seen the first wink, had no doubts about the second.

"And the men?" he asked.

"The men," said the minister, "will not leave, I promise you."

Gerrard stood, unsure of what he had done. He looked at the minister's face and wondered if it was capable of winking. "You will be in touch?" he said.

"Most definitely. And perhaps, when this little crisis is over, you might like to join my family for a luncheon. Next Sunday perhaps — the eleventh."

"Thank you. That would be delightful."

The minister held out his small hand. It clung to Gerrard's hand, spreading a damp film of secret fear around it.

6.

When the Land Rover entered the site on the following morning he understood immediately the agreement he had made with the minister. As he turned off the engine he finally admitted that he had known all along. He had understood exactly and precisely what would happen but he had not allowed himself to look at it. The minister's wink had produced a tightening in his stomach. The sweat he had felt in the handshake had been as much his as the minister's. Their fears had met and smudged together between their two hands.

As he walked between the big khaki trucks of Oongala's army he felt shame and triumph, elation and despair. They mixed themselves together in the terrible porridge his emotions had become.

All around him the work continued, watched by the keen arrogant eyes of Oongala's elite force: the notorious 101s.

The English doctor had seen the Land Rover approach and now he watched angrily as the tall man in the grey safari suit walked towards him. His walk did not belong here, amongst these harsh rocks and calloused hands. It was a city walk, the walk of a man who strolls boulevards and sips vermouth in side-walk cafés. The doctor detested the walk. "Like an evil little spider," he thought, "who will soon proclaim his innocence."

Now the tall man stopped. Now he ran. He sprinted towards the doctor, jumping across a pile of piping. The doctor grimaced and transferred his attention to the young Danish worker who lay on the ground before him. The injection had at last eased the pain. Soon he'd be able to shift him to town. He heard rather than saw Gerrard squat beside him. He said nothing and busied himself repacking the syringe with exaggerated care. He picked up the two ampoules from the dusty ground, tossed them in his hand, and with a sudden expression of rage threw them against the wall of the building.

"What's up?"

The architect smelt of expensive shampoo. The doctor couldn't bear to look at him. He took the young man's pulse and was surprised to find his own hand shaking. "I would have thought it was obvious."

"What may be obvious to you is not obvious to me. Kindly tell me what has happened." There was a tremor in the architect's voice, and the doctor, looking up, was astonished to see despair in the other's eyes. "Kindly tell me what has happened."

"He was shot by your friends here. He told them he was a free man and didn't have to work. He made quite a speech. It is a shame you missed it," he smiled nastily, "all about freedom and democracy."

Gerrard looked down at the young man on the ground. He was no more than twenty. Someone had placed a shirt under his naked back. His left calf was heavily bandaged, but his clear blue eyes showed no trace of pain. It was a romantic face, Gerrard reflected, with its sparse blond beard, its tousled hair and those luminous eyes. As Gerrard watched he saw, on the young man's face, the beginning of a smile. He knelt, bending hungrily towards the smile, hoping to kill his own pain with it. He saw the lips move. He bent further, reaching towards words. So he was only six inches from the young face when the lips parted and a hot stream of spittle issued from them with hateful speed, hitting Gerrard on the left cheek. He stood, as if stung, and turned on his heel towards the office. Then, changing his mind, he returned to his Land Rover.

As he left the site in a cloud of dust the Kristu-Du continued its inexorable progress as inch by inch, pound by pound it moved towards its majestic finale.

7.

For two days Gerrard Haflinger remained in his house without going out. Each hour he stayed away from the site made it harder for him to return to it. The thought of a return was hateful to him. The thought of not returning was impossible to contemplate.

Dirty clothes lay on the living room floor beside the sleeves of twenty recordings, not one of which had given any solace. The empty bottle of sleeping pills lay in the kitchen, its white plastic cap on the dining table.

It was night and the black windows reflected his unshaven face as he stared out into the empty street.

He sat down at the desk in the living room and began to type a letter, but he stopped every few characters, cocking his head and listening. He had become nervous, fearful of intruders, although he could not have explained who these intruders might be or why they would wish to enter his house.

He loosened the tension of the typewriter roller so that the paper could be removed silently from it, flattened the sheet, and began to write by hand.

As he wrote the letter to his son the only noises he heard were the loud scratching of the pen and the regular click of a digital clock.

The difficulty with both of us is that we were raised to believe that we were somehow special. In my case this has resulted in my coming to this: to build a grand building for a murderer because it is the only path left to me to realize my sense of "specialness" (an ugly inelegant word but it is late at night and I can think of no other). You, for your part, could find nothing in the world that corresponded with your sense of who you were, or rather who we had taught you you were. I now understand as I never did before how very painful and disappointing this must have been for you.

Yet tonight, sitting in an empty room and thinking about you in America and your mother in Paris, I envy you the good luck or misfortune in avoiding the trap we laid so lovingly for you.

For now I recognize this sense of specialness as the curse and conceit that it is and I would rather be without it.

Yesterday I was responsible for a man being wounded. The same man spat in my face when I bent to speak to him. And it is this thing, a small thing when compared with the great charges that have been laid against me, that has brought me to toy (flirt is a better word) with the idea of abandoning the project totally. My mind is not made up either way, but I have come to the position of recognizing the possibility. The final straw for your mother was the sight of a dog being machine-gunned by a drunk soldier. I thought that ridiculous, a piece of dishonest sentimentality. But now I understand that too. It is not the wounding of the man that brings me to my present state, but the fact that he spat in my face.

It is too late for me to be forgiven by my self-righteous colleagues (architects are surely the most hypocritical group on earth) but possibly not too late for me to forgive myself.

When we last heard from you you were just starting the vegetable shop. Please write and tell me if the venture has proven successful.

What is your life like?

Love, Father

When he had finished the letter he folded it hastily, placed it inside an envelope, and, having consulted a small notebook, addressed it. Then he sat with his head in his hands while the digital clock clicked through four minutes. His thoughts were slippery, elusive, tangled strands of wet white spaghetti which he could neither grasp nor leave alone.

He stood up then and went to the bathroom where he looked for pills in the little cabinet above the basin. There were none, but he found instead a small bottle of nail polish which he considered with interest.

He shut the door.

First he washed his arm with soapy water. Then he methodically worked up some shaving cream into a thick, creamy lather. Sitting on the small stool in front of the mirror, he brushed the lather into the dense black hair along his left arm. When he was done, he took a safety razor and, very carefully, shaved the arm until it was perfectly smooth.

He washed his arm and examined it in the mirror: a slender tanned arm with long delicate fingers.

Seeing hair on the knuckles he also lathered these and, being careful not to knick himself, shaved them.

Now he picked up the nail polish and applied it carefully. It took him three attempts to get it right.

When the nail polish had dried he undressed completely, folding his white trousers carefully and placing them on the carpeted floor in the passage outside.

He shut the door again and sat on the basin and watched in the mirror as the red fingernailed hand of a beautiful woman crept across his stomach and took his penis, stroking it slowly.

"I've missed you," said the voice, a quiet, shy, tentative voice that seemed afraid of derision or rejection, and then, gathering confidence: "I love you, my darling."

In the street outside a man laughed.

At the detention centre a young shopkeeper was being given the merest touch of an electric cattle prod.

At the Merlin Hotel, Wallis, alias Mr Meat, the man who sold holograms, picked up his telephone and dialled Gerrard's number.

When the number finally rang Gerrard Haflinger grabbed a bathrobe and ran to answer it. He stood in the living room accepting a dinner invitation, semen dripping down his stomach like spittle.

8.

In a minute or two Mr Meat would change Gerrard's mind entirely about the whole question of his involvement with the building. He would do it quite unintentionally. In a minute or two he would give Gerrard his scenario. In fact it was one of four such scenarios that he considered to be possible, but he would insist on the veracity of this one because it was the most likely, in his calculation, to frighten Gerrard, to undo a little of his arrogance and moral superiority.

Mr Meat thought Gerrard was a pompous pain in the arse, but he was bored and lonely and wished to fill in one last night before he escaped this dung hole of a country and went back to more predictable and respectable work selling armaments.

So he was not aware that the ascetic man who sat opposite him in the deserted dining room of the Merlin Hotel was more than a little unhinged with guilt and despair, that he was on the point of renouncing his life's work, and entering the cold empty landscape he had always feared.

But first they had to sit through this circus that was going on at the bar, all because Haflinger had ordered a Campari and the waiters didn't know what in the hell a Campari was, even though it was sitting on the shelf in the bar, practically biting their silly snub noses.

"You're going to have to help them," Wallis said, "or we'll never get a bloody drink."

The architect turned in his seat to look at the embarrassed conference of white-coated waiters. "Oh," he said, "they'll work it out."

Wallis sighed. "You're about to get a Drambuie."

Gerrard began to get up but sat down again as the Drambuie was returned to the shelf.

"Oh Christ, I can't stand it." Mr Meat pushed his chair back and Gerrard watched him as he strode across to the bar, this big beefy-faced man with the arrogant aggressive walk of a military policeman. He saw the waiters' mortified faces. He saw the big impatient hand haul the Campari from the shelf, snatch a glass, and pour an unmeasured quantity into it. He couldn't bear to watch any more and looked instead at the bleak empty tables of the dining room, too depressed to be amused by the fake Doric columns.

Wallis brought back Campari, soda and a beer for himself. "Now you know why I stick to beer," he said, "they can't fuck it up." He raised his glass, holding it with peculiar daintiness with thumb and middle finger. "Here's to the drought."

"You've made them embarrassed."

"So they should be. Christ, it's their job to know a Campari from a Drambuie. They bloody should be embarrassed."

"Still ..."

Wallis leant his bulk into the table, the beakish nose thrusting from the great florid face, his big index finger poking in the direction of the Campari. "Listen, old son, you're too sensitive. People in our line of work can't afford to be so sensitive. Skol." He drank again.

"Our occupations are hardly similar."

"Oh come on, tell me what the difference is." Wallis smiled. He was starting to enjoy himself.

"I think there's a difference." Gerrard attempted a smile. It didn't work out very well. "There is a difference between an important work of architecture and what you yourself describe as magic." None of this exactly reflected Gerrard's viewpoint but he had no intention of discussing anything so serious with Wallis.

"It's all magic here, old son, so don't look so superior. As a matter of fact I'll lay you a thousand U.S. dollars that it'll be your magic that brings Oongala undone. There is a limit to magic when people are starving. The holograms might be a big hit here, but they're not very popular in the villages. In fact I'd say they were very counter-productive. I would say that Oongala is not a popular man with the tribes at the moment. I'd give him three months at the most. When will your great work" — he pronounced "Great Work" slowly and sarcastically — "be completed?"

"Four, five months."

"Then it'll be four or five months before Oongala gets kicked out and things get very nasty for you. Look, I can tell you exactly what'll happen. And listen to me, because this is something I bloody well know about. I am an expert, old boy, in knowing when to leave a country. You can't survive in my business without knowing that."

Gerrard looked at the great red face with fascination. "Go on."

But they were interrupted by the approach of a waiter and Wallis fell suddenly silent. They ordered the Merlin's safest and most predictable dishes: pea soup followed by vegetable omelette. Wallis, in spite of his avowed dedication to beer, ordered Veuve Clicquot.

The food arrived too quickly and the champagne too slowly.

As he alternated sips of pea soup with Veuve Clicquot, Wallis continued: "Let me give you the exact scenario, as a little present, eh? Oongala will not know how unpopular he is. There is not a man left who is brave enough to tell him. However, he will know that things are not exactly rosy. People are dying. They are upset because there is no water and by now they all know about the canal and they know Oongala stopped it to spend money on your building. They're angry about that, but Oongala can't know how angry otherwise he'd drop your building like a hot cake and get stuck into the canal. However, he does know he needs a very powerful piece of magic and your building is about the only trick he has left up his sleeve. But," Wallis smiled, delighting in the drama of his scenario, "but to impress everyone with the dear old Kristu-Du he'll have to bring them to see it, eh? He will bloody well be forced to have the famous gathering of the tribes." He laughed a strange dry cackle. "How about that, eh, isn't that neat?"

"It was exactly what Daihusia asked me to design it for."

"Sure." Wallis brushed that aside like the misunderstanding of a rather dull pupil. "But Daihusia was smart enough to have never built it."

Gerrard laughed indulgently. "You're very cynical."

Wallis's black eyebrows shot up and his small eyes narrowed and became dark and challenging. "You don't believe me? You're living in a dream world. It was a stunt. You, of all people, should have known that. It was a symbol. It was useful to Daihusia as an idea, but he was clever enough to know that the canal was more useful to him as a fact, and he couldn't afford to have both. If he'd given them water he would have ruled until he was a hundred, a fact our present fellow doesn't seem to have cottoned on to."

"You really think so?"

"I know so. Dear fellow, you wouldn't be building your great masterpiece if Daihusia was in power. Or, if you were, you'd still be buggering around with the foundations and not having money for anything else."

"Go on with your scenario."

Wallis looked at him sharply, aware of a new interest in the architect: the contempt had gone from his eyes and been replaced by a deep, quiet interest. "My scenario," he said, "is that in order to control the tribes, Oongala is going to do what Daihusia would never have done: he is going to have to bring them here to see the Kristu-Du. And when he does that, when god knows how many thousands arrive to see this spectacle, they will be coming as very angry people. They will be angry enough to forget their differences. They may be superstitious and primitive, but they are not stupid."

"The army, surely ..."

Wallis waved his hand disdainfully, tidying up minor objections before he came to deliver his *coup de grâce*. "Apart from his beloved 101s, the rest of them are all tribally mixed. They're not going to shoot their own people. The army, old son, will not be worth a pinch of shit." And he brought thumb and index finger together as if offering Gerrard a pinch of it there and then. As he did so he noted the strange excited light in the architect's eyes. He interpreted it, incorrectly, as fear. "When the day comes," he said softly, "they will not love you." And he drew his index finger across his throat.

He leant back and waited for this to sink in.

"Oh," Gerrard smiled, "I'm staying if that's what you mean."

The smile irritated Wallis beyond belief. "Look." He put his champagne glass down on the table and riveted Gerrard with his dark eyes. "Look, Mr Architect, you better listen to me. I know what I'm talking about. I've seen this sort of thing before. I have had conversations, almost identical conversations, with people like you before. You will be no different from the bastards who run the detention centre. No one who has helped Oongala will be safe. They won't indulge in fine discussion about the history of architecture. If you stay, you're as good as dead."

"How do I know that what you say is true?"

Quietly, smugly, Wallis took out his wallet. From it he removed an airline ticket. He threw it across to Gerrard, who opened it and read it.

"Tomorrow," Wallis said.

"But you haven't finished."

"I've finished everything I'm going to do."

"Then you really think it's true?"

"I know it." He retrieved the ticket and returned it to the wallet.

Gerrard returned to his cold half-eaten omelette with a new enthusiasm. His mind was kindled again with the fierce hard poetry of his obsession: a structure whose very existence would create the society for which it was designed.

Wallis saw him smiling to himself and felt an almost uncontrollable desire to punch him in the face.

9.

Three months later the letter to his son lay forgotten in the top drawer of his desk, documentation of a temporary aberration, a momentary loss of faith.

In the spare white-walled house not an item was out of place, not a match, a piece of fluff, a suggestion of lint, an unwashed plate or a carelessly dropped magazine disturbed its pristine tidiness. The records were stacked neatly, the edge of each sleeve flush with the shelf, arranged in faultless alphabetical order.

The dirty clothes in the laundry basket were folded as fastidiously as the dresses in a bride's suitcase.

Gerrard, sitting at the desk, continued work on the fourth draft of an ever lengthening article which he planned for world release. It had many titles. The current one was "A Machine Built for Freedom". The title, of course, referred to the Kristu-Du. The treatise itself was gradually becoming less coherent and more obscure, as it attributed almost mystical power to the great domed building. What had begun as a simple analogy with a machine had long since ceased to be that. The building was a machine, an immense benevolent force capable of overthrowing tyrannies and welding tribes into nations.

Now he was speeding through a long and difficult section on the architecture of termites in relationship to their social structure. The handwriting became faster and faster as the pen jabbed at the paper and stretched small words into almost straight lines. There was little time, a week at most, and the more he wrote the more he thought of that he should include. For now, today, it seemed that his faith had been well placed: the scenario was going through its first movement. As the site had at last been tidied, as most of the workers had left, the rumours had begun about a gathering of the tribes, and now today it had been publicly proclaimed. Gerrard read the morning newspaper with the tense elation of a man who is three good shots away from winning a golf tournament. He knew he was not there yet. Not yet. Not yet.

But the gamble would pay off, it must pay off. It had not been an easy time and his faith in the scenario had been by no means constant, but a cautious inquiry here, a journey there, a piece of gossip from the minister, little odds and ends had confirmed the probability of the events the departed Wallis had predicted.

If three months ago he had been despised at the site, he had become openly hated. If he had once been distant, he had since become rude. If once he had been insensitive, he had become ruth-less. He was anaesthetized, a man running over hot coals towards salvation. The second shooting barely touched him, the reported beatings had become technical difficulties to overcome. A list had been compiled by the staff and the workers containing serious allegations about him. Even as he wrote his treatise this list was being released to the world press. Had he known, he would have considered it part of the gamble. As he introduced Pericles into the termite society, he was afire with faith.

This time next week the Kristu-Du would have produced a new society. He prayed feverishly that it wouldn't rain.

10.

It was happening.

It was said that Oongala skulked in his palace afraid. It was said openly in the streets.

Already the tribes had been gathered for four days. They camped around the Kristu-Du in their hundred thousands and inside it as well. Oongala's army brought them water in trucks, and delivered food daily. Goats were slaughtered and fires lit.

The minister was no longer to be found in his office and Gerrard found only a chicken clicking down the tiled corridors of the state offices.

Tanks were in evidence in the town and helicopters hovered anxiously.

Gerrard remained in his house, waiting for the call that would tell him Oongala was on his way to the site. One visit to the site had convinced the architect that he had nothing to fear about the accuracy of Wallis's scenario. The mood amongst the tribes was distinctly hostile. Soldiers of the army were spat on and dared not retaliate. Gerrard himself, an unknown white man, was bustled and shouted at. The hatred thrilled him. Each curse brought him closer to the realization of his dream. He saw Itos talking to Berehvas, Joflas to Lebuya, and in the midst of such violent concorde he felt an excitement of almost sexual dimensions.

Finally, on the fifth day, Oongala emerged from the palace, an uncertain parody of a triumphant smile on his huge cruel face. Gerrard, receiving his long-awaited phone call, followed the entourage in his Land Rover.

It was not a sensible thing to do, to associate himself publicly with the ruling party, but he followed it like a child following a circus parade.

The tribes waited sullenly, united beside and beneath the awesome dome.

In the four days Gerrard had been away from the site many words had been spoken. As tribe spoke with tribe, brother with brother, as they fired each other with their common anger, their breath rose high inside the great copper dome. So many people, each one breathing, speaking, some shouting, singing, and from each the breath rose and was held and contained by the copper cupola.

By the third day the roof of the dome was no longer visible to those who sat 1,000 feet below on the tiered steps. A fine mist, like a fog, hung there, a curious contradiction to the cold cloudless day outside.

By the fourth day the mist had turned to a definite cloud. And Gerrard, had he seen this, would have immediately understood the enormity of the mistake he had made. For the copper dome was acting as an enormous condenser and the breath of the people swirled in strange clouds inside the dome, regarded with fear and apprehension by the tribes.

Oongala entered the valley at precisely four o'clock on the fifth day, just as the weak sun disappeared behind the mountains and a sharp chill descended on the valley.

He drove through the crowd to the door, waving and smiling. Their mood was uncertain, and if there was a little cheering there was also much silence. Oongala entered the Kristu-Du in full military uniform, one large man going to meet death with more courage than many would have thought him capable of.

Gerrard Haflinger strode jauntily towards the building in a crisp white suit, not yet aware that he had built a machine that would keep these primitive people in Oongala's murderous grip for another forty-three years.

For at this instant the great clouds inside the cupola could hold the water no more and rain fell inside the Kristu-Du, drenching the drought-stricken people in a heavy continuous drizzle.

Gerrard Haflinger had designed a prison, but he did not know this yet and for the eighty seconds that it took him to force his way through the hysterical crowd he still remained, more or less, sane.

Crabs

Crabs is very neat in everything he does. His movements are almost fussy, but he has so much fight in his delicate frame that they're not fussy at all. Lately he has been eating. When Frank eats one steak, Crabs eats two. When Frank has a pint of milk, Crabs drinks two. He spends a lot of time lying on his bed, groaning, because of the food. But he's building up. At night he runs five miles to Clayton. He always means to run back, but he always ends up on the train, hot and sweating and sticking to the seat. His aim is to increase his weight and get a job driving for Allied Panel and Towing. Already he has his licence but he's too small, not tough enough to beat off the competition at a crash scene.

Frank drives night shift. He tells Crabs to get into something else, not the tow truck game, but Crabs has his heart set on the tow trucks. In his mind he sees himself driving at 80 m.p.h. with the light flashing, arriving at the scene first, getting the job, being interviewed by the guy from 3UZ's Night Watch.

At the moment Crabs weighs eight stone and four pounds, but he's increasing his weight all the time.

He is known as Crabs because of the time last year when he claimed to have the Crabs and everyone knew he was bullshitting. And then Frank told Trev that Crabs was still a virgin and so they called him Crabs. He doesn't mind it so much now. He's not a virgin now and he's more comfortable with the name. It gives him a small distinction, character is how he looks at it.

Crabs appears to be very small behind the wheel of this 1956 Dodge. He sits on two cushions so he can see properly. Carmen sits close beside him, a little shorter, because of the cushions, and around them is the vast empty space of the car — leopard skin stretching everywhere, taut and beautiful.

The night is sweet, filled with the red tail lights of other cars, sweeping headlights, flickering neon signs. Crabs drives fast, keeping the needle on the 70 mark, sweating with fear and excitement as he chops in and out of the traffic. He keeps his small dark eyes on the rear-vision mirror, half hoping for the flashing blue lights that will announce the arrival of the cops. Maybe he'll accelerate, maybe he'll pull over. He doesn't know, but he dreams of that sweet moment when he will plant his foot and all the power of this hotted-up Dodge will roar to life and he will leave the cops behind. The papers will say: "An early model American car drew away from police at 100 m.p.h."

Beside him Carmen is quiet. She keeps using the cigarette lighter because she likes to use it. She thinks he doesn't see her, the way she throws away her cigarettes after a few drags, so she can use the cigarette lighter again. The cigarette lighter and the leopard skin upholstery make her feel great.

The leopard skin upholstery is why they're going to a drive-in tonight. Because Carmen whispered in his ear that she'd like to do it on the leopard skin upholstery. She was shy. It pleased him, those small hot words blowing on his ear. She blushed when he looked at her. He liked that.

He didn't tell Frank about the leopard skin. He didn't think it was good for Frank to know how Carmen felt about it. Anyway Frank hates the leopard skin. He normally keeps it covered with a couple of old grey blankets. He didn't tell Frank about the drive-in either because of the Karboys.

The Karboys have come about slowly and become more famous as the times have got worse. With every strike they seem to grow in strength. And now that imports are restricted and most of the car factories are closed down they've got worse. A year ago you only had to worry if your car broke down on the highway or in a tough suburb. They'd come and strip down your car and leave you with nothing but the picked bones. Now it's different. If you buy a used car part (and you try and get a *new* carbie, say, for a 1956 Dodge) it's sure to come from some Karboy gang or other and who's to say they didn't kill the poor bastard who owned the Dodge it came off. Every time Frank buys a part he crosses himself. It's a big joke with Frank, crossing himself. Crabs too. They both have this big thing going about crossing themselves. It's a joke they have. Carmen doesn't get it, but she never was a Catholic anyway.

The official word is not to resist the Karboys, to give them all your car if you have to, but you don't see a man giving his car away that easily. So a lot of drivers are carrying guns, mostly sawn-off .22s. And if you've got any sense you keep your doors locked and windows up and you keep your car in good nick, so you don't get stranded anywhere. The insurance companies have altered the wars and civil disturbances clauses to cover themselves, so you take good care of your car because you'll never get another one if you lose it.

And you don't go to drive-ins. Drive-ins are bad news. You get the odd killing. The cops are there but they don't help much. Last week a cop shot another cop who was knocking off a bumper bar. He thought the cop was a Karboy but he was only supplementing his income.

So Crabs hasn't told Frank what he's doing tonight. And he's got some of Frank's defensive gear out of the truck. This is a sharpened bike chain and a heavy-duty spanner. He's got them under the front seat and he's half hoping for a little trouble. He's scared, but he's hoping. Carmen hasn't said anything about the Karboys and Crabs wonders if she even knows about them. There's so much she doesn't know about. She spends all day reading papers but she never takes anything in. He wonders what she thinks about when she reads.

There are more cars at the drive-in than he expected and he drives around until he finds the cop car. He plans on parking nearby, just to be on the safe side. But Carmen is very edgy about the police, because she is only just sixteen and her mother is still looking for her, and she makes Crabs park somewhere else. In the harsh lights her small face seems very pale and frightened. So Crabs finds a lonely spot up in the back corner and combs his thick black hair with a tortoiseshell comb while he waits for the lights to go out. Carmen arranges the blankets over the windows. Frank has got this all worked out, from the times when he went to drive-ins. There are little hooks around the tops of all the windows so they can be curtained with towels or blankets. Frank is ingenious. In the old days he used to remove all the inside door handles too, just in case his girl friends wanted to run away.

They put down the lay-back seats and Carmen unpins her long red hair. She only pinned it up because Crabs said how he liked her unpinning it. He sits like a small Italian buddha in the back seat and watches her, watches her hair fall.

She says, you're neat, you know that, very neat.

When she says that he doesn't know how to take it. She means that he is almost dainty. She says, you're sort of ... She is going to say "graceful" but she doesn't.

Crabs says, shut up, and begins to struggle with the buckle of his motor-cycle boots. Crabs never had a motor bike, but he bought the boots off Frank, who was driving one night when there was a bike in a prang. He got them from the ambulance driver for a packet of fags. Crabs bought them for three packets of Marlboro. There was a bit of blood, but he covered it up with raven oil.

Crabs really likes heavy things. Also he dislikes laces. All his shoes have zips, buckles, or slip on. When he was at the tech they used to tie him to the chain-wire fence by his shoelaces, every lunchtime. They tied him to the fence right in front of the Principal's window and the only way he could ever get out was to break the laces, because he couldn't bend down — if he bent down they kicked him in the arse. Crabs's father was always coming up to see the Principal and complaining about the shoelaces but it never did any good. Once Crabs came to school with zip-up boots and they stole them from him so he had to wear the laces, for his own protection.

The first film is crackling through the loud speaker and Carmen sits up near the front window with only her black pants on, her hair down, covered with a heavy sweet perfume she always wears. Crabs shyly eyes her breasts which are small and tight. He would like her to have big boobs, like the girls in *Playboy*. That is the only way he would like to improve her, for her to have big boobs, but he never says anything about this, even to himself. He says, help me with my boot. He is embarrassed to ask her. He knew this would happen and it was worrying him. He says, just pull. Normally Frank pulls off his boots for him. The boots are one size too small but they don't hurt too much.

Crabs lies back with his shirt off, his black jeans down, and one sock off while Carmen pulls at the second boot. Crabs is coming on fuzzy as he watches Carmen stretched back, her face screwed up with concentration and effort. He watches the small soft muscle on the inside of her thigh and the small soft hollow it has, just where it disappears into her pants.

She says, hey, careful. The boot is still half on the foot.

He is on top of her and she, giggling and groaning, manoeuvres sweetly below him, reciting nursery rhymes with her arse. He thinks, for the hundredth time, of the change that comes over her when she screws. Until now she is nothing much, talking dumb or sleeping or listening to the serials on the radio. It is only now she wakes up. And you could never guess, no matter how much you knew, that this girl would turn on like this. She sits around all day eating peanut butter and honey sandwiches or reading the *Women's Weekly* or reading the Tatts results or the grocery advertisements. Crabs feels he is drowning in a sea of honey. He says, "humpty-dumpty". Carmen, swerving, swaying, singing beneath him says, "Wha?"

Crabs says, bang, bang-bang-bang.

Carmen, her mascara-smudged eyes blinking beneath his mascara-smudged lips, giggles, groans, arches like a cat.

Crabs says, bang, bang, bang-bang.

Carmen arches. Crabs thinks she will break in half. Him too. She falls. He rolls and keeps rolling down to the left hand side of the car. He says shit, oh *shit!*

The car is on one side, listing sharply. Carmen lies on her back, smiling at the ceiling. She says, mmm.

Crabs says, Jesus Christ, someone's knocked off the wheels, Jesus CHRIST.

Carmen turns on her side and says, the Karboys. So she knew about them all the time. She sounds pleased.

Crabs says, you'll stain the upholstery. He searches for the other boot and the bike chain.

He runs through the cars. He doesn't know what he is looking for, just those two wheels, one will do because he has the spare. His white jacket is weighed down by the chain. He runs through the cars. Sometimes he stops. He knocks on windows but no one will answer. Everyone's too scared.

He rounds the back of a late model Chevvy and comes face to face with the cop car. One of the cops is putting something in the boot. Crabs is convinced that it's the wheels. He keeps going past the car, walks round the perimeter of the drive-in and returns to the Dodge. Carmen has taken the blankets down and is watching the film. He tells her his theory about the cops and she says, shh, watch.

The manager fills out the two forms and gives them meal tickets. He is a slow fat man with a worn grey cardigan. He explains the meal ticket system — the government will supply them with ten dollars' worth of tickets each week, these tickets can be spent at the Ezy-Eatin right here on the drive-in. If they run out of tickets, that's too bad, because it's all they'll get. If they want blankets they have to sign for them now. Carmen asks about banana fritters. The manager looks at her feet and slowly raises his half-shut eyes until they meet hers. He says that banana fritters are only made at night, but she can purchase anything sold in the cafeteria.

The manager then asks if there's anyone they want to notify. Crabs begins to give him Frank's name and then stops. The manager waits and licks the stubby pencil he is using. Crabs says, it doesn't matter. The manager says, that's your decision. Crabs says, no it doesn't matter, forget it. He can see Frank when he gets the notification, when he learns that his Dodge has lost two wheels, when he learns Crabs took it to a drive-in. He'd come out and kill them both.

Carmen says, we'll walk home next Saturday.

The manager sighs loudly and scratches his balls. Crabs wonders if he should hit him. He's got the chain in his jacket. The manager is saying, "Now this time listen to what I tell you. First, you ain't got no public transport ..."

Carmen says, I didn't *mean* public transport. I ...

"... you don't have a bus or a train because buses and trains don't come to the Star Drive-in. They've got no reason to, do they? Secondly, you can't walk down that highway, young lady, because it's an 'S' road. And if you know the laws of the land you ain't permitted to walk on or near an 'S' road."

He looks across at Crabs and says, "And dogs aren't allowed on 'S' roads, or bicycles or learner drivers. So we're not allowed to let you out of that gate until this bloody government finds a bus that they can spare to get you all home. There are now seventy-three people in your situation. I don't like it either. I don't make a profit from you so don't think I want you around. So we'll all have to wait until something is done. And we all pray to God that something's done soon." He crosses himself absently and Carmen laughs.

The manager stares at her blankly. Crabs would like to lay that chain across his fat face. The man says, "You want me to notify your mother?" and Carmen becomes very quiet and smoothes her skirt with great concentration. She says "no" very quietly.

The manager is standing up. He shakes them both by the hand. He advises them to sign for blankets but they say no, they have some. He has become very fatherly. At the door he shakes their hands again and says he hopes they can make themselves comfortable.

It is bright sunlight outside. Carmen says, he seemed nice.

Crabs says, he's a bastard. I'll get him.

Carmen says, for what?

Crabs says, for being a bastard.

Carmen takes his hand and they walk to the Ezy-Eatin, dodging in and out of the temporary clothes lines that have sprung up since last night. There are about thirty cars scattered throughout the drive-in. Some kids are playing on the swings beneath the screen. In front of the Ezy-Eatin a blonde woman of about forty is hanging out her washing and wearing a grey blanket like a cape. She smiles at them. Crabs scowls. When they pass she calls out, "Honeymooners", and a man laughs. Crabs takes his hand out of Carmen's but she grabs it back.

The woman at the Ezy-Eatin explains to Carmen about the banana fritters, that they only have them at night, so she has an ice cream sundae instead. Crabs has a chocolate malted with double malt. The woman takes the coupons. Carmen says, isn't it lovely, like a picnic.

It takes him a week to collect the bricks for the back wheel. When he has enough he chocks them under the rear axle and then puts the spare on the front. Carmen reads comics and listens to the music they play through the speakers. Crabs goes looking for another Dodge to get a wheel from. There aren't any.

At night he wanders round the drive-in tapping on car windows. He plans to get a lift out, get a wheel somehow, and return. But no one will open their windows.

He begins to collect petrol caps and hub caps, just to keep himself occupied. When he has enough he'll find a Karboy to swap his lot for a wheel. He feels heavy and dull and spends a lot of time sleeping. Carmen seems happy. She eats banana fritters at night and watches the movie. Crabs strips down the engine and puts it together again. A lot of the day he spends balancing the flow through the twin carbies, until, one afternoon at about four o'clock, he runs out of petrol.

There is no way out. Carmen tells him this every day. Each day she comes back from the Ladies' with new reasons why there is no way out. At the Ladies' they know everything. They stand and squat for hours on end, their arms folded, holding up their breasts. At the Men's it is the same. But Crabs shits in silence with his ears disconnected. He has no wish to know why there is no way out.

He is waiting for the arrival of a 1956 Dodge. He eats little, saving his coupons to exchange for a wheel and hubcap he will need. There are dozens of other wheels he could use, but he wants to return Frank's Dodge in perfect condition. So he waits, lying on the leopard skin upholstery he has come to hate. He tries not to think of Frank but he has nothing else to think of. He is not used to this, doing nothing. He has always been busy before, getting fit, or going to the pictures or out in the truck with Frank. And all day he has worked, delivering engravers' proofs in the Mini Minor. He hated that Mini. He misses that hate. He misses driving it, knocking shit out of its piddling little engine, revving it hard enough to burst, waiting for the day when he would work at Allied Panel and Towing.

But his mind keeps coming back to Frank and every day the pain is worse. He tries to think of reasons why Frank will forgive him. He can't think of any. He tries to make Frank's big spud face smile at him and say, forget it, mate, it happens to the best of us. But the face contorts, the big knobbly jaw juts and he sees Frank take out his teeth, ready for a fight. Or he sees Frank's hand holding the shifting wrench.

Frank said, you get a nice car, people respect you when you got a nice car. You go somewhere, a motel, and you got a nice car, they look after you. Frank looked after Crabs. Frank said, you build up your body, then you can stand up for yourself anywhere. You build up your body and you can walk in anywhere and know how to look after yourself. He gave him the chest expanders and an old photo he had of Charles Atlas. Frank said, that man is a genius.

Crabs hid in the Dodge and tried to keep his mind free of all these things. He tried to keep his mind free by keeping busy with Carmen but she didn't like doing it in the daylight.

Carmen lies on the roof, sunbaking, while Crabs hides in the Dodge. He makes plans for getting out and he tells them to Carmen. But the wire is now electrified. But the drive-in is closed to visitors. But the security cars circle the perimeter all night.

Crabs walks through the drive-in each morning after breakfast, looking for the Dodge he is sure will arrive, somehow, one night. He picks his way through the clothes lines, around the temporary toilet facilities, skirts round the rubbish disposal holes, edges by the card games and temporary cricket pitches. It is like the beach when he was a kid. Everybody is doing something. He would like to blow them all up.

He looks at Carmen's face and tries to see exactly what has happened to it. It is older. Her sweater is covered with small "pills" of wool. Her hair is pulled back and done in a plait but doesn't hold in her ears which seem to stick out. She has got fatter. Her mouth is full of hamburger while she tells him. He knows. He has seen it. He watched it all. She knows he saw it. She wipes her mouth clean of hamburger grease with the arm of her sweater, and tells him about what happened last night.

He says, I know, I saw.

But she tells him, because she feels he sees nothing. She has told everyone at the Ladies' about him and they've come to gaze at him, individually and in groups. He puts up the blankets to keep out their stares, but Carmen invites them in. Their husbands come and invite him to cricket or two-up. He thinks of Frank and the Dodge that will come.

He says, I saw.

He saw, last night, the convoy of trucks come in through the main gate of the drive-in. Everybody went to look. Crabs went afterwards and stood on the edge of the crowd. For some reason they cheered, they cheered the trucks and the drivers as if they were liberating troops. But the trucks only held more cars, cars without wheels, cars without engines, crippled cars, cars unable to move. Crabs watched silently, wondering what it meant.

He watched while the huge mobile crane shifted the cars from the trucks to the ground. He watched the new cars being arranged in lines, in vacant spaces. And when everyone else had lost interest he still watched. He saw the prefabricated Nissen huts come on a huge Mercedes low-loader. He watched the Nissen huts unloaded under the harsh glare of searchlights that had been mounted on top of the old projection room, on top of the Ezy-Eatin.

And he was still there at dawn, when the low-loaders, the cranes, and the other trucks had gone, he was there when the buses began to arrive.

He was there, removing two wheels from a 1956 Dodge.

* * *

Everybody goes to stare at the arrivals. Carmen is frantic, she begs him to come. He has never seen her so happy, so angry. Her eyes are sharp and clear. He would like to screw her but he is busy. He would love to hold her, to calm her, warm her, cool her. But he has two wheels from a 1956 Dodge and he is busy. In the corner of his eyes he sees exotic things: cloaks, robes, dark skin, swarthy complexions. He hears voices he doesn't understand, he thinks of the tower of Babel and then he thinks of the Sunday School where he heard about the tower of Babel and then he thinks about peppercorn trees and then he thinks of the two wheels and he tells Carmen, soon, I'll come soon.

The jack is in good shape. He has kept it in good shape. He jacks up the back of the car and removes the bricks. Then he puts on the new wheel. The tyre is a little flat. He guesses at about fifteen pounds per square inch, but it is good enough. Then he removes the front wheel, and puts it back in the spare compartment, and then he puts on the new front wheel.

He will need petrol. Maybe oil too.

He feels as if he is alive again. He will bring the car back to Frank. He will tell a story to him, a fantastic story. He was driving in the country. He was forced off the road by a Mercedes low-loader, and cut off by a jeep. They lifted the Dodge onto the low-loader with Crabs and Carmen inside, and drove off to a country rendezvous. There was a gang. Crabs joined the gang. At night they drove off with the low-loaders. Crabs drove one of them, a Leyland. They stole cars from off the highway. Made the drivers walk home. Crabs became their leader after a fight. He regained the Dodge. Rebuilt it. Then he escaped and brought it back here, to you, Frank.

He is happy. There is tumult around him. He will need to check the oil and petrol. He lifts the bonnet and has the dip stick half out when he notices the carbies are missing. He stops, frozen. Then, slowly he begins the check. The generator is gone. The distributor also. The fan and fan belt. The battery together with the leads. Both radiator hoses and the air cleaner.

Something inside him goes very taut. Some invisible string is taken in one more notch.

He walks, very slowly, back to the newly arrived Dodge. There are people in it. He ignores them. He opens the door and tugs the bonnet release catch. Someone pulls at his clothing. He knocks them off. He opens the bonnet and looks in, looking for the parts he will salvage. There is nothing there. No engine. A dirty piece of plywood has been placed inside to give the engine compartment a floor. Some small chickens, very young, are drinking water from a bowl in the middle.

He lies back on the leopard skin and gazes at the sights outside. Carmen is beside him. She is snuggled up against him. She is saying a lot. Slowly Crabs begins to see what his eyes see.

A large group of Indians, dressed in saris, are gathered around a battered blue Ford Falcon. One of them, an old man, squats on the roof. The Ford Falcon was delivered last night. A group of men, possibly Italians, lean against the front of Frank's Dodge. They are laughing. They seem to be playing a game, taking turns to throw a small stone so that it lands near the front wheel of a bright yellow Holden Monaro. Small children, black, with swollen bellies run past shouting, chased by a small English child with spectacles.

Carmen is crying. She is saying, they are everywhere. They stare at me. They want to rape me.

Crabs has been thinking. He has been thinking very deeply. Things have been occurring to him and he has reached a conclusion. He has formed the conclusion into a sentence and he tells Carmen the sentence.

Crabs says, to be free, you must be a motor car or vehicle in good health.

Carmen is crying. She says, you are mad, mad. They all said you were going mad.

Crabs says, no, not mad, think about the words — to be free, you …

She puts her hand over his mouth. She says, it stinks. It stinks. The whole place stinks of filthy wogs. They're dirty, filthy, everything is horrible.

Crabs sees a car moving along the lane that separates this line of cars from the next. It is a 1954 Austin Sheerline. Inside is the manager, he sits behind the wheel stiffly, looking neither left nor right. It is moving. Crabs is excited for a moment, wondering if he can buy the car with his meal tickets. The car narrowly misses the Indian family and, as it passes in front of him, he sees that the Austin is being pushed by an English family, a man, a woman, and three young boys.

Crabs says, a motor car or vehicle in good health.

* * *

Flags, some of them ragged and dirty, flutter in the evening breeze. With every step Crabs smells a different smell, a different dish, a different excretion. He walks slowly along the dusty lanes filled with bustling people. Carmen is in the Dodge. He left her with the bicycle chain and the doors locked.

The situation has become such that no progress is possible. Crabs is now formulating a different direction. Movement is essential, it is the only thing he has ever believed. Only a motor car can save him and he is now manufacturing one. Crabs has decided to become a motor vehicle in good health.

As yet, as he walks, he is unsure of what he will be. Not a Mini Minor. He would like something larger, stronger. He begins to manufacture the tyres, they are large and fat with heavy treads. He can feel them, he feels the way they roll along the dusty lanes. He feels them roll over an empty can and squash into the dust. Then the bumper bars, huge thick pieces of roughly welded steel to protect him in case of collision. Mud guards, large and curving. They feel cool and smooth in the evening breeze. There is something that feels like a tray, a tray at the back. He can feel, with his nerve ends, an apparatus, but as yet he doesn't know what the apparatus is. The engine is a V8, a Ford, he feels the rhythm of its engine, the warm, strong vibratings. A six-speed gearbox and another lever to operate the towing rig. That is what the apparatus is, a towing rig.

He feels whole. For the first time in his life Crabs feels complete. He shifts into low gear and cruises slowly between the lanes of wrecked cars, between the crowds, the families preparing their evening meals.

And he knows he can leave.

He has forgotten Carmen. He is complete. He changes into second and turns on the lights, turning from one lane into the next, driving carefully through the maze of cars and Nissen huts, looking for the gate. The drive-in seems to have been extended because he drives for several miles in the direction of the south fence. He turns, giving up, and shifting into third looks for the west fence where the gate was.

It is late when he finds it. His headlights pick up the entry office. No one seems to be on guard. As he comes closer he sees that the gates are open. He changes down to second, accelerates, and leaves the drive-in behind in a cloud of dust.

On the highway he accelerates. He feels the light on top of him flashing and, for the pure joy of it, he turns on the siren. The truck has no governor and he sits it on 92 m.p.h., belting down the dark highway with the air blasting into the radiator, the cool radiator water cooling his hot engine.

He has gone for an hour when he realizes that the road is empty. He is the only motor vehicle around. He drives through empty suburbs. There are no neon signs. No lights in the houses. A strong headwind is blowing. He begins to take sideroads. To turn at every turn he sees. He feels sharp pains as his tyres grate, squeal, and battle for grip on the cold hard roads. He has no sense of direction.

He has been travelling for perhaps three hours. His speed is down now, hovering around 30. He turns a corner and enters a large highway. In the distance he can see lights.

He feels better, warmer already. The highway takes him towards the lights, the only lights in the world. They are closer. They are here. He turns off the highway and finds himself separated from the lights by a high wire fence. Inside he sees people moving around, laughing, talking. Some are dancing. He drives around the perimeter of the wire, driving over rough unmade roads, through paddocks until, at last, he comes to a large gate. The gate is locked and reinforced with heavy-duty steel.

Above the gate is a faded sign with peeling paint. It says, "Star Drive-in Theatre. Please turn off your lights."

Life & Death in the South Side Pavilion

I was employed, originally, as a Shepherd 3rd Class. That was in the days of the sheep and even now that the sheep have been replaced by horses I believe that my position is still Shepherd 3rd Class although I have had no confirmation of this from The Company. My work place is, to the best of my knowledge, known officially as THE SOUTH SIDE PAVILION but it is many years since I saw this written on a delivery docket and I have never seen it anywhere since.

Yesterday I wrote to The Company asking to be relieved of my post and I used the following description: "I am employed as a Shepherd 3rd Class in the South Side Pavilion." I hope it makes sense to them. I had considered a more detailed description, something that would locate the place more exactly.

For instance: "The pavilion is bathed in a pale yellow light which enters from the long dusty windows in its sawtooth roof. In the centre, its corners pinned by four of the twenty-four pillars which support the roof, is a large sunken tank which resembles a swimming pool. The horses require the greater part of this area. I, the Shepherd in charge, have a small corner to myself. In this corner I have, thanks to the generosity of The Company, a bed, a gas cooker, a refrigerator, and a television set. The animals give me no trouble. However they are, as you must be aware, in danger from the pool ..."

I didn't send that part of the letter, for fear of appearing foolish to them. The people at The Company must know my pavilion only too well. Probably they have photographs of it, even the original architect's plans. The pool in the centre must be known to them, also the dangers associated with the pool. I have already made many written requests for a supply of barbed wire to fence off the pool but the experts have obviously considered it unnecessary. Or perhaps they have worked out the economics of it and, taking the laws of chance into account, must have decided that it is cheaper to lose the odd horse than to buy barbed wire which, for all I know, might be expensive these days.

I have placed empty beer cartons around the perimeter of the pool, in the foolish hope that they will prove to be some kind of deterrent. Unfortunately they seem to have had quite the opposite effect. The horses stand in groups perilously close to the edge of the pool and stare stupidly at the cardboard boxes.

2.

The television is showing nothing but snow. The pavilion is bathed in its blue electric blanket. Another horse has fallen into the pool. Its pale bloated body floats in the melancholy likeness of a whale.

3.

Marie arrived early and discovered me weeping amongst the horses.

"Why are you weeping?"

"Because of the horses."

"Even horses must die, sooner or later."

"I am weeping because of the swimming pool."

"The swimming pool is there to help them die."

When Marie tells me that the swimming pool is there to help the horses die, I believe her. She has an answer for everything. But when she leaves her answers leave with her and the only comfort in the pavilion is distilled into a couple of small sad marks on the sheets of my bed.

4.

I AM HERE TO STOP THE HORSES FALLING INTO THE SWIMMING POOL.

5.

Marie, who helped me get into the pavilion, now wants to help me out. Personally I would like to leave. I have sent my resignation to The Company and am, at present, awaiting the replacement. Marie said, "Fuck The Company." She arrived today with colour brochures and an ultimatum: either I leave the horses or she will leave me.

"Do you love the horses?"

"No, I love you."

"Then come with me."

"I can't leave them alone."

"They fall into the pool anyway. You can't stop them."

"I know."

"Then you might as well come."

"I can't come until they've all fallen into the pool."

"But you are trying to stop them falling into the pool."

"Yes."

"You can't love the horses if you're just waiting for them to fall in and drown."

"No, I love you."

"Ah, but I know you love the horses."

And so it continues.

6.

Marie sleeps beside me, enveloped in the sweet heavy smell of sleep and sperm.

There is some movement in the pavilion. I lick my fingers and wipe my eyes with spittle. For the moment the tiny shock of the wetness is enough to keep me awake. I stare into the dark, among the grey garden of gloomy horses, trying to distinguish movement from stillness.

There is a large splash. A high whinnying. I block my ears. Once they are in the pool there is nothing they can grip on to get them out.

7.

The men came with a truck fitted with winches. They dragged the horse from the pool and put it on a trailer. They had to break its back legs to fit it in properly.

I imagined that they looked at me reproachfully. Probably it is simply that this is a part of their job that they dislike, and, having paid me five visits to remove dead horses, they are not kindly disposed towards me.

I asked them if any of the dead horses would be replaced. They seemed too busy to answer me, but I have always assumed the answer is no.

Today I explained that I wished to be relieved of the job. When they could offer no helpful suggestions I asked about the barbed wire. They looked shocked and expressed the opinion that barbed wire was cruel.

8.

Marie didn't come tonight. She is giving me a free sample of her absence, letting me know in advance what it will taste like. She needn't have bothered. It's just as bad as I thought it would be.

I leaf through the brochures she has left for me, staring at beaches I can never imagine visiting. I have never seen so many beaches. On the beaches there are beautiful girls, girls more beautiful than Marie. Perhaps she thinks that the beautiful girls in the brochures will provide the extra incentive. What she will never understand is that I want to go with her to these beaches more desperately than anything else in the world. She accuses me of having a misplaced loyalty to The Company but I care nothing for The Company which has never deigned to answer my letters. If I could leave the pavilion I would go to The Company's offices and settle everything once and for all. If need be I would kidnap a member of The Company's staff and bring him back here as a replacement.

The strange thing is that once I have left the pavilion I know I will detest the horses. I can feel this new attitude waiting in the wings of my mind, waiting to take over. I have tried to explain this to Marie but she thinks I am being dishonest with myself, that I simply wish an excuse not to go with her.

But now I am responsible for the horses. Each death is my responsibility and I have no wish to be responsible for so many deaths.

And now that I am unable to make love she thinks it is because I have an unnatural attraction to the horses and that I find her unattractive in comparison. But I am unable to make love because every time I make love a horse falls into the pool.

EVERY TIME I FUCK MARIE I KILL A HORSE.

Perhaps the noise of fucking upsets them and they panic and lose their bearings. I told Marie about my feelings, that the lovemaking was unsatisfactory because of the danger to the horses.

She said, "You attribute great power to your cock."

"While it is limp it will do no harm."

"No harm," said Marie, "and no good either."

9.

Another night without Marie.

Her absence has cured my limp cock more quickly and effectively than either of us could have guessed. I toss and turn in my tangled bed dreaming of involved and passionate love on the distant beaches of her brochures.

At this moment I am prepared to fuck until the pool is full of horses.

10.

The horses are standing in a circle around the pool, their tails swishing through the grey air. It is not difficult to imagine that they have gathered around the pool to look into the black water and dream about death. The blackness of death must seem attractive to them after the grey nights and yellow days of the pavilion. Or perhaps they are simply aware of my decision and are now standing in readiness.

The whip has always been there, thoughtfully provided by the same company that refused to supply me with barbed wire.

I have no wish to remember the manner in which I drove the horses into the pool. It was sickeningly easy. They fell into the water like overripe fruit from a tree, often before the whip had touched them. In five minutes the pavilion was empty and the pool was boiling with horses. I retired to my bed and pulled the pillow over my head.

In less than an hour there were twelve horses floating in the pool. They bumped softly into one another like bad dreams in a basin.

11.

They have brought replacements. They unload the twelve new horses from the truck with the flashing yellow light on its roof. Then they proceed to winch the drowned horses from the pool.

I plead with the men not to leave the live horses in my care, to transfer them to another pavilion. I offer them everything I have: my television set, my refrigerator, my bed, the brochures Marie left with me.

The driver flicks through the brochures sullenly: "The TV is company property." He adds that he intends to confiscate the brochures.

Room No. 5 (Escribo)

I scratch my armpit and listen to the sound, like breakfast cereal. The hotel room has a title, *Escribo*. It was an office. Occasionally there is a rumbling upstairs, a vibration, and water cascades through the ceiling and splashes into the bidet beneath.

Trucks rumble through the town. They are filled with soldiers. It is likely that Timoshenko is finally dying, in which case there may be a coup, or possibly none, possibly a dusty road stretching across the plain and a wrapper from one of those bright green confections lost somewhere among the grasses.

The restaurant smells of piss and is humid. Condensation covers the tiled floor which is streaked with a fine grime. A large footprint with a rubberized pattern repeats itself. Jorge was here yesterday. Jorge may not be important to anything. He is a captain in Timoshenko's army but his ability to affect things is probably small.

Jorge's customs post is six kilometres along the road over the bridge. It will probably rain. If Timoshenko dies things may alter. The wind may blow from a different direction. It may continue hot. The sound of gunfire could be mistaken for thunder, or vice versa. In the urinal humidity of the restaurant possibilities smear into one another. Some young boys drink Coca-Cola and lean against the coffee machine. Outside there are more, revving Zundapps.

You lie on the bed and smile at the ceiling. I wonder what you think. Your smile is permanent and I have given up asking you about it. I have decided that you are smiling about a day five years ago. I have not yet decided what happened on that day. And, as you won't tell me, it is I who must decide, but later. I can think of nothing that might make you smile.

I asked you if you were frightened to die, now. You smiled and said nothing.

I asked the question to stop you smiling.

I don't know who you are. You have not stopped smiling since I found you at Villa Franca. You have not stopped smiling except to make love, and then you frown, as if you had forgotten what you

were going to say. Your smile is full and gentle. It is a smile of softness
and of complete understanding but you refuse to explain it and I do
not know what you understand and you continue to refuse me this.

You wish for more yoghurt. Again, for the eighth time today, we
leave this room and go to the café opposite the Restaurant Centrale.
You eat yoghurt. I watch. The soldiers who sit at the other tables
watch loudly. They watch us both. You frown, as if making love,
eating yoghurt. I cannot bear the sight of it, the yoghurt, the texture
of it is repulsive to me, like junket, liver, kidney, brains, Farax, and
Heinz baby foods.

Your yoghurt finished, you look at me and smile. Your eyes crease
around the edges. The strange thing about your smile is that it has
never once become less real or less intense. It is a smile caught from
a moment in a still photograph, now extended into an indefinitely
long moving film. You look around the café. I tell you not to. The
soldiers are not schooled in the strange ways of your smile and may
misinterpret it. They have already misinterpreted it and sit at tables
surrounding us.

If Timoshenko dies they will rape you and shoot me. That is one
possibility, have you considered it?

I watch the spider as it crawls up your arm and say nothing. You
know about it as you know about many things. You insisted on going
through the border post ten minutes after me. Is it for that reason,
because of your inexplicable behaviour, that they held you there so
long. I saw, through the window of the verandah, the officials going
through your baggage. They held up your underwear to the light
but did not smile. Things are not happening as you might expect.

I wish you to frown at me. What would happen if I asked you,
gruffly, to frown at me here, in public? You would smile, suspecting
a joke.

When the soldiers see us walking towards the café they call to us.
I ask you to translate but you say it is nothing, just a cry. They wait
for us to come and eat yoghurt. It is a diversion. While they remain
at the café there cannot be a general alert. For that reason it is good
to see them. They, for their part, are happy to see us. They call out
"Yoguee" as we walk up the hill towards them. When we arrive at
the table there are two bowls of yoghurt waiting. For the third time
I send one bowl back. The waiter refuses to understand and jokes

with the soldiers. You say that his dialect is difficult to catch. It is a diversion.

The heat hangs over the town like a swarm of flies. Trucks rumble over the old stone bridge. It stinks beneath the bridge. If you couldn't smell the stink by the bridge the scene would be picturesque. I have taken photographs there, eliminating the stink. Also a number of candid shots of you. I wish you to appear pensive but you seem unable to portray yourself.

There are some good dirty jokes concerning the Mona Lisa's smile and the reasons behind it. Your smile is not so enigmatic. It is supremely obvious. It is merely its duration that is puzzling.

I do not know you. Your accent is strange and contains Manchester and Knightsbridge, but also something of Texas. You have been to many places but are vague as to why. You have no more money but expect some to arrive at the Banco Nationale any day. We wait for your money, for Timoshenko, for night, for morning, for the ceiling to rumble and the water to pour down. I have put newspaper in the bidet to stop the water from the ceiling splashing. I have begun a letter to my employers in London explaining my absence and there is nothing to stop my finishing it. I have hinted at a crisis but am unable to be more explicit. They, for their part, will interpret it as shyness, discretion, or the result of censorship.

At this moment the letter lies conveniently at the top of my suitcase. If the suitcase is searched the letter will be found easily. It is possibly incriminating, although it is constructed so as to reveal nothing. Knowing nothing, it is possible to reveal everything. That is the danger.

Night

It is night. You lie in the dark with your face hidden in the pillow. You lie naked on top of the blanket; you like the texture of the blanket. It is hot and the blanket is grey and I lie beside you on the sheet, peering at the light entering the room through closed shutters. I have considered it advisable to keep the shutters pulled tight — the room is at street level and has a small balcony that juts out a foot or two above the cobbled roadway.

I touch your thigh with my toe and you make a noise. The noise is muffled by the pillow and I do not understand it.

I sleep.

When I wake you are no longer there. My body is electrified by short pulses of panic. The shutters arc open and a truck drives by, beside the balcony and above it. I hear the driver cough. Men in the back of the truck are singing sadly and softly. I listen to them hit the bump at the beginning of the bridge and hear the hard thump and clatter. The sad singing continues uninterrupted, as if suspended smoothly above the road.

You are no longer there. I dare not look for your bag, but you have left a handkerchief behind. I could rely on you for that, to leave small pieces of things behind you.

It is not the money. I am not concerned with the money. The Banco Nationale has not impressed me with its efficiency and I have no faith in its promises and assurances. They cashed your last traveller's cheque and gave a hundred U.S. dollars instead of ten. You laughed and took the money back, but not from a sense of caution.

In the bank there was an old woman in black who had her money in a partially unravelled sock. You stood behind her and smiled at her when she turned to stare at your dress. If the money were to arrive in an old sock I would have more confidence, but you say it is coming from Zurich and I have little hope. No, it is not the money, which we both undeniably need. The panic is not caused by the thought of you disappearing with or without the money, nor is it caused by the thought of the secret police, although I am not unconcerned by them.

But the panic is there. I fight it consciously. In my mind I rearrange the filing system in my London office. There are some red tabs I have been anxious to order. I busy myself writing classifications on these red tabs. I write the names of my districts: Manchester, Stockport, Hazel Grove. At Hazel Grove I lose my place. I lie on the sheet covered by small pinpricks of energy and hear a man shout something that sounds like *"Escribo"* . I am sure he could not know the sign on the door of our room. Unless you have told them, and they have shouted it deliberately, to frighten me. For you say nothing of the police or the political situation when I attempt to discuss it. As for the newspapers, you say they are boring, not worth translating, and that, in any case, they are unlikely to report Timoshenko's death immediately. You say you have no idea why they would not let us back across the border last Sunday and claim that you accept their story as reasonable and correct. You have also suggested that it was because "the border closes on Sunday" but that was not a very good joke. And, by now, it is essential that we wait "until my cheque comes from Zurich". You seem bemused, as patient as a sunbather.

Is it because you want to see the ending, how the story works out? Because I remember the way you were in Riano when we went to the cinema to see that American film, something about the F.B.I. You laughed continually and the audience made small hissing noises at you. But you waited, because you wanted to see the end. Then we went to a café for a drink and you sipped your sweet vermouth and said, "Wasn't it awful?"

There is a scratching at the door. You enter quietly, wearing my shirt over your dress. I can hear that your feet are bare. And I can smell you, the smell of your pulse. It is as if you opened a window on the inner regions of your soul. The smell is of rain on the wheat plains. Water and sand, seeds, cow dung, spit, wild flowers, and dry summer grass.

You enter the room softly on your bare feet and I lie on the cool sheet watching you watching me.

I say, where were you?

You say, I went for a walk ... by the river.

I say, it stinks by the river.

You say, I know.

You have nothing but your skirt and my shirt on. You shed them limply and come to my bed, frowning gently.

Day

The shutters are still open and a small boy watches us. He has climbed up from the roadway onto our small raised balcony. I place a sheet over you and stand up, gesturing to the child that he must go. He refuses to budge, staring fixedly at my cock. He has a large square head and small stupid eyes. Go, I say. But I do not move out onto the balcony where I could be viewed from the street. I could possibly be misinterpreted and that would be unfortunate.

Instead, I close the shutters and wait for him to go. I wait five minutes by the watch on your sleep-limp wrist. He is still there. I make myself comfortable and wait.

He is probably from the police. That amuses me, but not sufficiently, because it is not totally impossible. Things are becoming less and less impossible.

I do not care about the police but would like to know why they refused to let us back across the border last Sunday.

Jorge is a captain in Timoshenko's army at the border post. I am informed of his name because he has been called that, Jorge, by people in the restaurant. Jorge has told you that there is a war across the border. Either that or that the people across the border are anxious to attack this country when Timoshenko dies. Or possibly both things. You say there was a difficulty with the grammar, a doubt about the meaning of a certain verb and one or two words that are phonetically confusing. But you have accepted all three possibilities as being true and reasonable. He bought you a drink and insisted that you sit at his table to drink it. I was more confused than hurt, more anxious than angry. It seemed possible that he was teasing, that he had fabricated or arranged a war to have you sit at his table.

That is why we now eat at the Restaurant Centrale. But sooner or later he will come to buy you a second drink and to announce that the war is continuing indefinitely. I have no plan for dealing with him. He appears to be well covered and practically invulnerable.

In all likelihood I shall watch you both from my table.

Jorge's small spy is still there on the balcony and is peering through the shutters. I turn my back on him and go back to the filing system which is now devoted to the streets of London. I begin to arrange them in alphabetical order but can get no closer to A than Albermarle Street.

Outside the boys are revving up their Zundapps. Trucks continue to pass over the bridge but there seem to be more of them. It is as if they have been brought out by the heat. Today will be most unpleasant. It is hotter now than it was at noon yesterday.

The ceiling rumbles and the water begins to pour through, slowly at first and then in a torrent. I place fresh newspaper inside the bidet and watch Timoshenko's face absorb the water, becoming soggy and grey.

Afternoon

I watch you eat your yoghurt. You appraise each spoonful carefully, watching the white sop slide and drip from your spoon. There are beads of perspiration on your lip and you ask me to ask for the water. I have forgotten the word and remember it incorrectly. The waiter appears to understand but brings coffee and you say that coffee will do. Later, when I pay, I notice that he does not include the price of the coffee. Has he forgotten it? Or is it an elaborate joke, to bring coffee, pretending all the time that it is water. After eight days in this town it is not impossible.

We leave the café and walk up towards the museum. You shade your eyes and say, perhaps it will open today, although you know it will be closed.

After the museum we walk through the same cobbled streets we have walked for eight days, attempting to find new ones. There are no new streets, they are the same. They contain the same grey houses faced with the same ornate ceramic tiles. I photograph the same tiles I photographed yesterday. You take my arm as we enter the square for the last time and say, the money has come, I can feel it.

We walk slowly to the Banco Nationale. It is still early. After we have checked there we will return to our room, there is nothing else.

The money has arrived. You discuss it with the teller. You appear uncertain, moving from one foot to the other as you lean against the counter watching him calculating the exchange on the back of a cigarette packet. The two of you consult frequently. You look at me uncertainly and produce some dark glasses from your handbag. Among your numerous small possessions these are a surprise to me. I thought I could number your possessions and had, one night, compiled a mental list of them. It is called Kim's game, I believe, although I have no idea why.

It is cool and quiet in the bank. You whisper to the teller in his language. The rest of the bank staff sit in shirtsleeves at their desks and watch. Occasionally they say something. A thin-faced clerk addresses a question to me. I shrug and point to you. Everybody laughs and I light a cigarette.

I have no confidence in the money or its ability to get us back across the border. There is a bus later this afternoon.

I ask you to ask the teller about the war across the border. You lean towards him, kicking up your legs behind the counter as you lean. He replies earnestly, removing his heavy glasses and wiping perspiration from his badly shaven face. I notice that he has a small tic in his cheek. He has the appearance of an academic discussing a perplexing problem. When he has finished he replaces his glasses and resumes his calculations.

You say nothing.

I ask you. The anxiety is returning — I cannot connect your behaviour to anything. I am not anxious for the course of the war itself, nor for the sake of the money. I touch your flesh where it is very soft, above the elbow, and you jump slightly. I ask you what he has said.

You say, he says everything is OK . . . he heard on the radio that it is OK.

And Timoshenko? I ask you. The clerk looks up when he hears the words but resumes his work immediately. My finger plays with the fabric of your blouse where it clings to your arm. And Timoshenko?

You say, Timoshenko is OK ... the operation was a success . . .

Did he say?

No, I read it this morning ... in the newspaper ... I meant to say. You look at your dusty sandalled foot and scratch the bare calf of your leg. I notice now how you scratch the bare calf of your leg like that. I wonder how such a habit starts. There are many small red scratch marks on your leg. You say, Timoshenko is OK.

I go to stand at the window and look across to our hotel. A number of small boys are fighting on the balcony of our room.

I return to the counter and lean against it as if it were a bar and I were in a western. I lean backwards with my elbows on the bar and watch you sideways. I say, ask him about the border, will they let us across?

He wouldn't know.

I know, I say, it doesn't matter.

Before

In Villa Franca you were in the Banco Nationale when I met you. You wore the same blouse and asked if I would mind you travelling with me. I said, I would be happy for you to. Your eyes were soft and grey, seeming wise and gentle. You had, so it seemed, lived less than a block from me in London. It was difficult to work out the chronology, you appeared to shift around so often.

You said, you don't look as if you work in insurance. And I wasn't sure what you meant.

Border

I prepare for Jorge as the bus groans around the mountain road towards the border. It is full of old women and stops constantly to let them off. There are also a few men who wear squat hats, heavy farmers' boots, and black umbrellas. The heat is intense. You gaze out the window and say nothing. We have not discussed the border or any of its implications. I do not believe in the war or Timoshenko.

The border post is at a break in the mountains. There is a small wooden bridge and two buildings that look like filling stations. Soldiers stand around the bridge with machine-guns hung casually from their limp shoulders. One kicks a stone. There is a woman and a child sitting in the dust by the customs house steps. The woman waves flies away from her face with a newspaper. The child sits stock still and stares at the bus with dull interest.

There are now only six of us in the bus. Three men with squat hats and black umbrellas and an old woman who carries two chickens by the legs, one in each hand. The chickens appear to be asleep.

We have been here before. Last Sunday. We wait for Jorge and the continuation of his little joke. You sit beside me in the bus and huddle into the window, alone with your reflection in the dusty fly-marked glass. I say, it is OK. You say, yes it is OK. Your eyes hide behind dark glasses and I see only my own face staring at me questioningly.

In the customs shed we form a line. There is an argument about the chickens and one is confiscated. A soldier tethers its feet to the bottom of an old hat stand from which a machine-gun hangs heavily.

Jorge stands at the head of the line looking along it like a sergeant major. He waves to us and waddles down, a riding crop tucked under his fat folded arm. The riding crop betrays his heroes but looks ludicrous and somehow obscene. He has two broken teeth which appear to be in an advanced state of decay.

You talk to him and he continues to look across at me. Finally you turn to me and say, he says it is OK ... the war was nothing ... an incident ... they often have them.

You do not appear happy. Your forehead is wrinkled with a frown that I yearn to smooth with my palm.

I shake Jorge's hand. I am immediately sorry. The chicken is in danger of upsetting the hat stand. The soldier removes the machine-gun and places it on the counter.

After

The bus travels through the flat grey granite as dusk settles. Large rocks pierce the gloomy surface of the earth. There are no trees but a few sheep who prefer the road to the country on either side, possibly because it is softer. It is cooler here on the other side of the border, on this side of the mountains.

Rain begins to fall lightly on the windows, making soft patterns in the dust. I open the window to smell the rain. You are frowning again. I hold my hand out the window until it is wet and then place my palm on your forehead.

I say, why do you frown?

You say, because I love you.

I say, why do you smile?

Because I love you.

Postscript

In Candalido I ask you about the first time we crossed the border and why you crossed separately.

You say, it is because of the underwear, because they always do that ... at the small border posts ... take out the underwear.

I say, why should I mind?

You say, it was dirty.

Happy Story

1.

Marie was critical of his ideas about flying. "You're really in a bad way about this."

"I don't think it's a bad way," he said.

"It's an obsession," she said, "all this talk about flying and birds. I think you're simply unhappy and want to escape."

He lay on his back on the beach and watched a seagull ride the wind, dropping, sliding, turning. "I think it'd be good," he said, "look at that seagull."

Marie closed her eyes. "I've seen them," she said. "They're white and have orange beaks." She was silent a moment. "And orange legs," she added. Later she broke the silence to say, "If you could fly you'd want to do something else, like swim."

"Seagulls can swim," he said.

"Not under water."

"They can dive under water," he said, "but they can't stay under for long."

"That's what I mean," she said, "they can't stay under for long. They can't swim under water, not like a fish."

"No," he said, "that's true, they're not like fish."

"Doesn't that make you unhappy?"

"No," he said, "I'm more interested in the flying."

She turned on the sand. "You're exasperating," she said. "I know you'll never be happy."

"I'd be happy if I could fly."

"That doesn't seem very likely."

"It isn't impossible either."

"No," she sighed, "I guess it's not impossible."

2.

"You're crying," she said.

"No, not really."

"I know why you're crying. You're crying because of your wife."

"No, I don't think that's true."

"I'm sure it's true."

"It's not, really."

"Then it's because you can't fly."

"No."

"Then what is it?"

"It's nothing," he said. "I wasn't crying."

3.

After making love she was still restless. "What is it?" she asked him.

"What's what?"

"You know."

"No, really, I don't. I feel good. Do you feel good?"

"Yes, I feel good, but what about you? What is it?"

"I'm fine."

"You're staring at the ceiling in a funny way."

"I'm lying on my back. I'm staring at the ceiling because I'm lying on my back."

"You're thinking about flying," she said accusingly.

"I'm not."

"You are. I can tell you are. I always know when you're thinking about flying. Will you stop, please."

"OK," he said.

Later she said, "You were thinking about it, weren't you? Tell me honestly."

"No," he said, "I don't think I was."

"You frighten me when you think about flying. Promise me you won't."

"I promise," he said.

4.

"What's this?" she asked, looking over his shoulder.

"It's a water pump," he said.

"It has wings."

"No, they're not wings. They're the blades of the wheel. They lift the water. It's a water pump."

"I think it's about flying," she said. "You promised me you wouldn't."

"It's a water pump," he said, "really."

"Well," she said, "in any case, there are little eggs all over the cabbages. I came in to tell you."

5.

No one had said anything about flying for a long time. They were drying the dishes one night when Marie broached the subject: "If you built something for flying in," she said, "just say you did ..."

"Yes," he said.

"Well, if you did, how many people would it carry?"

"The two of us."

"It could fly with the two of us?"

"Of course."

She looked happy and kissed him suddenly. Her hands left lumps of soap suds in his hair. Then she became thoughtful. "If you built it," she said, "would there be room for the dog?"

"Yes," he said, "that could be done. I hadn't thought of it, but that could be done."

"It wouldn't be difficult?"

"No. It'd be easy."

"That sounds like a good idea," she said.

6.

"Well," he said, "where do you want to go?"

Marie buckled up her helmet and picked up the dog. "I don't know," she said. "Where do you want to go?"

"Wherever you want to go," he said.

"Well," she said, "I wouldn't mind going to ..." She stopped. "I'm being selfish. Where do you want to go?"

"Wherever you want to go."

"Well," she said, "I've always wanted to go to Florence."

"All right," he said.

He looked up at the sky. It was a good night for flying.

A Million Dollars' Worth of Amphetamines

1.

When Carlos was arrested the rock'n'roll band fled immediately. In the confusion of the moment they left many valuable things behind them that would later be confiscated by due legal process, by Carlos's lawyers: cars, paintings, houses — most, in fact, of the vast material wealth they had accumulated.

The connection between Carlos and the band was not well known, although later, of course, it was public knowledge that he had not only managed their business affairs to his own advantage, but thoughtfully supplied them with heroin and cocaine, thus assuring himself of a huge potential income in blackmail if the need should ever arise.

Julie, Carlos's twenty-two-year-old lover, escaped at the same time, slipped across the border and then flew as far south as her savings would permit. She arrived almost destitute.

Unlike the band, she had no skills to sustain her. Her only talent was her life, her addiction to fear and danger.

The town she arrived in suggested no avenues of opportunity for the one piece of business her financial security might have depended on.

She knew where there was half a million dollars' worth of amphetamines.

Apart from Carlos, who was in prison, she was the only person in the world who knew.

The town contained nothing she understood. The streets were wide and straight and without surprise. It boasted thirty-three buildings higher than five storeys, a single strip club, three expensive restaurants serving bad food, one discotheque full of thirteen-year-olds, and an ugly shrine to fallen soldiers which stood on a slight hill at the intersection of the two main boulevards.

The only opportunities the town presented were paid employment. Her only qualification was a typing course she had begun when she had planned to run away from Carlos the year before.

She took a room in a boarding house and began walking the wide, wet streets in search of a job.

It was the worst part of winter.

In an architect's office she found Claude hunching over a single-bar radiator while he interviewed her with curious shyness. He was forty-one years old and not particularly successful. He didn't give her a job, instead he asked her out for dinner.

2.

This is what Claude found out about her.

She had hair the colour of a field of corn. She had a strutting walk she conducted with pointed fingers. She had been born with a cancer and still had the scar. She had lived with a gangster. She was full of fears and nightmares and had left her clothes in another city, running down back stairs to stolen cars with cocaine in her handbag and one shoe missing.

She smiled crookedly. She had a lisp. Her voice was as soft as velvet. She had the start of a double chin. She had the face of someone who had come out of a sad movie at three o'clock in the afternoon. She could change from a Renaissance Bacchus to a gargoyle in less than a second. She had an extraordinarily beautiful smile.

She believed that heroin was the best cure for the common cold. When she frowned it was like a pond shivering. She had a nightmare she couldn't talk about. She had a sob that wet his sleep. She had a chin that went wobbly when she was having an orgasm. She knew Mick Jagger. She could define a band's music by the drugs they used. She was in love with South America and had never been there. She was possibly wanted by the police in connection with the man-slaughter Carlos was charged with, a crime involving the sale of a speedball that had gone wrong.

Her handbag contained a huge bottle of Mandrax and a small one of Valium.

She knew where there was half a million dollars' worth of amphetamines.

She drank with enthusiasm and kept a bottle of wine by the bed.

It was their second night together.

3.

She came to him as a visitor from Mars, a dazzling carpet of arcane information which he read with doubt and wonder in the perpetual Sunday evenings of his life.

She moved into his house on the slow muddy river and left her clothes scattered on the floor beside his.

She lost two jobs in three days and said: "I could always become a whore." As usual she was asking difficult questions by making confident assertions.

In the cold nights they lit fires and interrogated each other about their lives, smoked grass, fucked and complained, each in their own way, of the life in the town.

They were two particles, vibrating uncertainly in puzzled attraction.

She could not understand the eccentricities of his bourgeois life, his two marriages, the gossip of a town that ostracized him, his dissatisfaction with his life but his depressed acceptance of it.

She had begun by believing she was fucking for her dinner and had been surprised to find him warm, gentle, full of whimsies as beautiful as a fairy-tale. She recognized in him a romanticism similar to her own. While he slept she watched the warm lines beside his eyes, the softness of his mouth, the tousled lion's mane of dark hair, and all the marks of hope and disappointment that forty years had etched into his olive face. She watched him tenderly, without understanding.

After the third job, it was accepted that she would stay in the house while he went to his office where he worked on the detailing of the town's thirty-fifth tall office block, overflow work from a larger, more successful practice than his own.

The days were difficult for her. The quietness was depressing, the future uncertain. She read the foreign newspaper for information about Carlos, fearing a successful appeal by his lawyers. She dwelt continually on the night Carlos had given Jean the speedball, uncertain as to whether he had meant to kill him or if it had been a mistake. The panic in Jean's eyes haunted her and made her heart palpitate and her scalp itchy. She knocked herself out with Valium and wine. She woke yellow-tongued and dry-mouthed and wandered around the huge adobe house that Claude had built for himself after his first marriage. It resembled nothing she had ever known, either her parents' Tudor mansion or the shifting motel rooms of her gangster adventures. The walls needed painting and the air smelt damp. A fine clay dust settled on tables and chairs and spread across the slate floor like talcum powder so that each evening her footsteps stood as a diary of her restless day.

She had battle fatigue but couldn't slow down. The days with Carlos had been full of fast movements, dangers she only half understood. She had been swept along in a swift current of meetings conducted in Spanish and Italian, electric cocaine concerts with the rock'n'roll band, border crossings with damp hands holding one of Carlos's five passports, a heavy pistol in a motel drawer, and the continual wonder of living a B-grade movie when your father was a director of a multinational corporation famous for its detergents and insecticides.

To come from that, to this.

Days of wine and Valium and yellow rivulets running under willow trees to the wide muddy river at the bottom of Claude's neglected garden which reminded her of some melancholy story she had been read as a child.

She had reached the safety she had ached for and now she was prey to the boredom that safety brought with it.

"Let's go and dance somewhere," she said, but there was nowhere to dance but the discotheque for thirteen-year-olds and the expensive restaurants for dirty old men.

On a Wednesday afternoon she wrote eleven letters to Evelyn, the back-up vocalist with the rock'n'roll band. She posted the eleven letters to five friends and six poste restantes, hoping that one of them would reach her. In the letters she promised safety, a refuge in this provincial city. She recognized the stupidity of the letters, the possibility of one of them reaching Carlos's friends. She said nothing of Claude in the letters. There was no way she could explain Claude to Evelyn, or anyone else.

And she thought about the half a million dollars' worth of amphetamines safely stored in an underground passage in a small northern town. And she thought about them timidly, for now she had time to consider the matter, she admitted she had none of the business skills needed to dispose of them.

More seriously, she doubted that she had the courage to double-cross Carlos on anything so important.

All I am, she thought, is a fucking groupie.

She took ten milligrams of Valium and stood in the rain, pretending she was a cow.

4.

She waited for him each evening with an anxiety she denied even to herself. She resisted temptations to cook him meals, yet thought she should be doing something. She wondered who was exploiting who. She didn't understand the rules of the relationship. She didn't understand why he let her stay, but she only thought about that when he wasn't there. And then she felt she had nothing to offer him, if to do something as simple as cook a meal might be interpreted as an attempt to lay a claim on him. So together they opened tins of tuna and beans. They rarely ate out. He seemed to have no social life, although he discussed friends and recent dinner parties. She wondered if he was socially ashamed of her.

She didn't understand that she was a storybook for him, an encyclopedia of adventure, a Persian carpet of his imagination that he stared at with wonder, never hoping to understand all the mysteries of it.

He interrogated her gently, never sure of whether she was exaggerating or lying. He lay gentle traps for her, smiled to catch her out on inconsistencies, enjoying the slow unravelling of her story.

He was fascinated by the rock'n'roll band (samurais, magicians, keepers of Rosicrucian secrets), by Carlos, and by all the drugs he knew by name but not from experience.

Lying in bed he might ask her about Carlos, feeling the wonder of a child asking a parent about worlds he didn't understand.

"He was really amazing," she said. "Carlos was the most amazing person. He had a terrible temper. He wasn't really bright. He killed a man, Claude, while I waited in the car."

"Did you love him?"

"He was really amazing."

And then there was the morning Carlos was taken away by two other gangsters.

"Were they mafiosi?"

"I think he double-crossed them."

"But were they mafiosi?"

"He was in his dressing gown. It was the only time I saw him scared. He was scared shitless. They took him away."

"What did they do to him?"

She shrugged. "He didn't come back for two weeks."

"What did you do?"

"I went and hid. I knew a lot of things he knew. Do you want a million dollars' worth of amphetamines?"

"You said half a million before."

"What the fuck does that matter. It's a lot of money, baby." And her face which had been clouded with frowns burst into a smile of pure sensual excitement as she waved straight-fingered hands and clicked her tongue.

"Where?"

"Come with me and I'll tell you."

"Where?"

"Carlos can't go near it, even if he gets out of jail."

He smiled at her, wondering. "Why not?"

"You don't understand Carlos. He wouldn't tell anyone. He'll wait."

He kissed her then, very gently. "I think you're bullshitting."

"You think I'm bullshitting because you've never known anyone like Carlos."

"You keep changing your story."

"Don't be boring, honey. You're a boring old man." And then she would kiss him, as gently as he had kissed her, looking into his eyes to ask him puzzled questions she couldn't begin to form. "Do you want me to go away?"

"No, not unless you want to go away."

His skin was younger than his eyes. He lay there languidly, without apparent need.

"I found a photograph of your wife. She looks very beautiful," she said, asking another question.

"What else did you find?"

"A mouldy sandwich under the bed."

"Anything else?"

"Let's go to a club."

"There aren't any clubs."

"Well, let's go to a bar."

"I hate bars."

"You're a boring old man, Claude."

"Yes," he said. "I know."

And she began then to kiss him, first his neck, then his chest, and then his limp cock until it was stiff and hard inside her mouth. She moved her mouth and tongue slowly, sweetly, and listened with pleasure while he groaned softly.

Outside the frogs croaked beside the river.

They held hands tightly, fucking slowly, feeling curiously happy in their puzzlement with each other.

5.

And then, in the last week of winter, the letters began and each night, it seemed, she had some word of the odyssey of the rock'n'roll band who were now wanted for questioning due to information that Carlos had passed on to the police.

"He's trying to do a deal," she said.

"How?" he asked.

"He's a cunning little bastard," she said.

Claude read the letters with wonder and fear, wonder at the adventure he was watching, and (to his own surprise) fear that the band would arrive at his house and take Julie from his dull world to their exciting one.

As he detailed the plumbing of the six-storey office block and watched the melancholy streets of the town with their predictable goings and comings, he thought only of the rock'n'roll band and the million dollars' (half a million dollars'?) worth of amphetamines.

Ho-Chin, the legendary drummer, was coming down from the north and sneaking through borders for an unstated rendezvous with Eric, the lead guitarist. Evelyn, having laid low in Hong Kong, had slipped out to a cattle boat and was heading this way laden with cocaine and a plan to slip in through Daru in New Guinea and Thursday Island.

And each of them, it seemed to Claude, drawing his dreadful plumbing and considering the placement of mirrors for successful typists to lipstick in front of, was a king amongst kings and their coming together would be more thrilling and threatening than the meeting of rivers from the mountains.

And then there were setbacks, delays.

Paul had been arrested in Bangkok for busking. (Claude sent

money.) Evelyn was having an affair with a Muslim in Surabaya and walked amongst pilgrims for Mecca with her infidel's secrets, blue Muslim cocks on pale mornings, white sheets and slowly turning fans above the vagueness of mosquito nets. She who had once worked the London tube with her twelve-string guitar (click-click-cocaine-click), with her beautiful Eurasian face and blue-black straight hair, as thin and nervous as a million dollars' worth of amphetamines.

Eric wrote letters about music, drugs and police that Claude didn't understand.

He came to hate the letters. He also became obsessed by them. And as he concentrated on the method of attaching fire-escape banisters to walls, his mind wandered through impossible concerts in the municipal auditorium. Eric, in fur boots, eyes closed, singing electrical magic with his guitar until audiences were transformed into rivers and white water dispersed down streets where it flooded the houses and left them full of fish.

And as he worked on the relationship between the lift doors and the placement of the call buttons, he saw the second concert where the people would come and be transformed into large white birds who would circle in slow loops before going to live beside rocky seas, catching fish and making eggs which they would guard against predators.

Stoned on hope and anxiety he saw a concert where the applause became locusts and the audience became fields of grass and were devoured by the locusts and left barren and desolate. Wind came through the municipal auditorium blowing gritty sand into the faces of the rock'n'roll band as they travelled out into the desert, cruel bandits looking for new audiences, coming at last to a city in the north surrounded by orange groves and date palms where they would be taken in and adopted by the people and taught crafts such as cabinet making and net weaving and some would learn how to pick an orange, at what time, by what method, for the people in that place had no music in their lives and didn't understand the purpose of the band, seeing them simply as vagabonds to be befriended and taught a purpose in life.

Such were Claude's dreams of the rock'n'roll band, against whom he was already building defences.

6.

She made up her eyes with charcoal in the manner of Indian men, so they suggested secrets and sorcery.

She pored over newspapers, reading between the lines of local news.

The mayor, she suggested, was a Cocairo.

How was she so sure?

"Look at his cheekbones. Cocairos are like that. That's how you tell them. The skin stretches tight over their cheekbones. They got a crazy look in their eyes."

A local murder was obviously centred around heroin.

"How? Why?"

"It's very weird, you know, the guy wasn't from here at all and the girl was. I think she lured him into the bush where the other guy killed the first guy. He probably double-crossed him. It was a heroin deal, I bet."

"How?"

"It's just very weird, that's all." And she couldn't say any more, retreating simply into her own certainty, unable or unwilling to explain why it was a heroin killing or possibly not believing it anyway, but simply wanting to transmit the incredible life she had lived with Carlos.

"This town is a fucking bore."

"You don't have to stay here."

"I can't afford to go anywhere else … unless …" she flashed wide sparkling Indian eyes and snapped her fingers, click, click, click, "unless you want to come and get some amphetamines with me, honey."

He thought of Bonnie and Clyde Barrow taking photographs of themselves in hotel rooms, posing as gangsters in a movie, cigarettes dangling from their mouths, guns pointed on camera.

"You're a French gangster movie," he told her.

"You don't make any sense," she said. "There's half a million dollars' worth of amphetamines. We can get them."

She was chubby. She cried in her sleep. Her palms sweated continually. He saw her cowering in a corner while Carlos beat her up.

"Where are they?"

"I'll tell you when we're on our way."

"I can't leave anyway," he said. "I've got a building to finish."

"You're a boring old man, Claude, come and get drunk."

"We got drunk last night."

"We could try and score some coke."

"You said you didn't want any more coke."

And there she was again, in her underwear, the grey hat tipped forward on her curly blonde head, the revolver dangling in her small damp hand. "Just a sniff, honey. Cocaine is a really amazing drug. It's a really *nice* drug."

"We could always go and see the mayor," he said.

"Oh, that mayor. Claude, you don't know anything about what goes on in this town."

7.

"Are you really serious about these amphetamines?" he asked her.

"It's a very heavy scene."

"Do you really know where they are?"

"Do you think everything I tell you is a lie?"

"No, but you do exaggerate."

She smiled.

"Are they really worth a million dollars?"

"That's retail," she grinned.

"How would you sell them?"

"You'd never come with me, would you? We could go to South America together. It's a really amazing place."

"No," he said. "I'm an architect with responsibilities to my clients. And I won't come with you because I'm a coward." They were curled up on the couch in front of the fire listening to Mozart. "Why don't you go and get them yourself? I'll wait for you here."

"People there know me. I was there with Carlos. They know the stuff is hidden somewhere but they don't know where. It's very heavy. They kill people for money like that."

"But not respectable middle-class architects," he said thoughtfully.

For one fleeting, terrible moment she thought his interest might be serious. The thought chilled her. "Oh baby, don't you ever get mixed up with these people. They don't care about anyone." She cradled his head in her lap. "Let's get stoned and watch TV."

8.

One day he returned home and found that she had swept the house.
A stew was cooking on the stove. There was a bottle of wine open
on the table.

"Why did you do that?" he asked her. He was astonished. It
seemed out of character.

"I cut the grass, too, some of it."

"What with?"

"The scythe," she said simply, "only the postman came and saw
my boobs because I got hot and took my shirt off. Do you mind?"

"No, I don't mind. Did he mind?"

"He's a really nice man," she said, "he came in for a drink."

"He came in for a fuck," Claude said more sharply than he had
expected to.

"You really don't understand twenty-two-year-old ladies, do
you?" she said, frowning at him. "All you understand is cheating on
wives and getting divorced."

As usual in matters of sexual morality, he felt she was right. "Was
there any mail?"

"Evelyn's left Surabaya," she said. "How's your shitty building?"

"Shitty. Did you fuck the postman?"

"No, baby. I didn't fuck the postman."

The house smelt clean and good and the stew made a slow
comforting noise. He filled a glass of wine and looked at Evelyn's
letter without reading it.

Julie stood over the stove, thoughtfully stirring the stew with a
wooden spoon.

He was going to ask, what happens when the band arrives?

But he didn't. Instead he said, "Do you want a joint?"

9.

Julie with her T-shirt off cutting grass with a scythe.

Julie planting five small trees and watering them with a plastic
bucket.

Claude buying records by the rock'n'roll band and staring at
photographs.

"Is that like Evelyn?"

"Is that a good photograph of Eric?"

"Does Evelyn screw Paul? It looks like it from the photo."

Julie reading *Social Banditry* by the river.

Julie in blinding sun on the roof of the house, removing leaves from guttering.

Julie trying to draw pictures of parrots and Claude and hiding them afterwards.

Claude buying detailed maps of a northern city where a million dollars' worth of amphetamines are hidden.

Julie with sunburn.

Claude with maps.

In the late spring many things were changing and Julie went into town and bought a long white cheesecloth dress with small blue flowers embroidered on it.

"Feel my hands," she said.

"Yes," he wondered.

"Dry."

They lay on clean sheets nowadays but Claude didn't sleep well, his dreams were twisted in the tangled roads of his threat and his salvation: the rock'n'roll band and a million dollars' worth of amphetamines.

10.

She saw him as soft and slow and sleepy as a lizard. She would have dressed him in pale mohair sweaters and soft leather slip-ons. She saw him playing svelte snooker at 3.00 a.m., his dark eyes smiling in concentration. She saw him by firelight. By deep dusk light on warm evenings. She was wrapped in blankets with him and by him. She would have done nothing to unwrap the cocoon they had built. He had asked nothing of her, ever, and she would have given him anything.

Yet he seemed somehow restless and untouchable. His movements, normally so fluid, had become less certain.

They played the amphetamine game now only because he wanted to.

She talked to him about the amphetamines because she had come to love him. She considered, by brown rivers on hot days, saying I love you in the evening but never did. She came to fear that he wanted her to leave, that his restlessness was an indication of this.

"Do you want me to go away, honey?" she asked him.

"Do you want to go away?"

"No."

"Aren't you bored?"

"No," she smiled, "I'm not bored."

"You keep saying I'm a boring old man."

"Ah," she said, "I only say that to flatter you."

"I have often thought," he said, not unkindly, "that you perhaps say it to flatter yourself."

"How do you mean?"

"That it makes you feel dangerous."

She reacted by making pistols of her fingers and with wrinkled nose, swivelling hips, shooting him with imaginary Magnums. "Zap. Zap."

"Do you want to rob banks?" he said.

"Only if I can do it with you," she said. "Come and look at the trees. I think they might need watering."

11.

She had begun to guess about the rock'n'roll band and its effect on him. She had tried to tell him that it affected nothing, would affect nothing. But because he hadn't really declared his fears there was no way she could successfully allay them.

He thought she was a Bedouin princess who would return to her own people.

She was an orphan with damp hands and bad dreams that she had postponed with wine and Valium and electric fears.

Sometimes she felt she had been invented by Leonard Cohen, whom she hated.

She regretted her letters to Evelyn.

She regretted the answers. She took the letters as they arrived and hid them where he wouldn't find them.

But he found them and misinterpreted her reasons for hiding them.

She began to fear losing him.

She had made him hate his job. She had made him ashamed of his life. She had never told him that she loved him, that her eyes filled with tears watching him sleep, without her knowing why.

And she knew that he was plotting something. His dark face was as secretive as shuttered windows on winter mornings. When she kissed him he returned her kisses distractedly. When he got stoned he looked miserable. And when he asked her about the amphetamines she knew it was because he thought she was a liar so she told him plainly, in detail, exactly where they were and she drew a plan that could not have been invented and explained that in the city in question there was an old quarter in which all the houses had disused interconnecting passages, a protection against seventeenth-century winters.

"Now do you believe me?" she said when she had finished.

"Yes, I believe you," he said, without apparent conviction.

And although she should have guessed what was on his mind she didn't, because he wasn't interested in money, because drugs had no fascination for him, because he was unlike Carlos and had no need to prove himself in acts of machismo and because it was unthinkable that a gentle-faced amateur should attempt anything so patently foolish.

He said he was going to an architects' convention in another city.

She knew he was lying and didn't ask to come.

She knew he was going to fuck some lady who was more beautiful and more interesting than she was.

She bought him a mohair sweater in a very pale blue.

12.

He had become more than slightly mad. His actions were dictated by a logic so strict that it allowed no variation. He was a sleepwalker strolling on the ledges of sixty-storey buildings. He was a beach-comber removing seashells from a minefield. He flew into a northern city, took a taxi to an address he had copied down, asked the taxi to wait and emerged in five minutes with a large crate.

In his hotel room he packed the contents of the crate into sixty small cardboard boxes and posted them to himself, to his home, to his office and to seven different suburban post offices in the town where he lived.

Not one of them was intercepted by customs. It had never occurred to him that they might be.

13.

He had always wanted to take Polaroid photographs of her face to show her its incredible variety, most beautiful in laughter, most childlike when solemn, ugly in tears, as mischievous as a gargoyle, as decadent as Bacchus.

But when finally, two weeks after he returned, he presented her with a million dollars' worth of amphetamines, he was in no way prepared for the undiluted horror that widened her eyes and dropped her jaw and made her literally gasp for breath.

For she knew, as she looked at the peculiarly beautiful capsules with their pink and yellow stripes, that her haven had been ripped apart and laid waste.

She stared at him, shaking her head, not even trying to wonder how he had succeeded in doing what he had done.

She shivered in anger and despair.

He had understood nothing.

He had thought it was a game.

He had finally believed her story but he had never believed how serious it was.

He was standing in front of her now, smiling proudly, like a dog with a hand grenade in its mouth, wagging its tail.

Carlos had an ugly mouth. Carlos had treated her like shit. Carlos was stupid and vindictive and in jail. But he was also a businessman who had just been relieved of the biggest deal he had ever conceived. Carlos would kill a hundred men to get those little pills. He would do it tomorrow, or the next day, or next year, but he would do it.

There was nothing she could say to him. There was no advice she could offer him for his own safety. She could think only of her own survival. She felt ill. She could not even kiss him goodbye.

14.

Clay dust falls from adobe walls and settles on slate floors, chairs, tables and filters through the cracks of a crate containing a million dollars' worth of amphetamines which have never been discovered.

He tried one once, but it made him feel unpleasant.

In nights of Valium and wine he remembers times when he held her in his arms and pressed his body full of dreams.

Peeling

She moves around the house on soft slow feet, her footsteps padding softly above me as I lie, on my unmade bed of unwashed sheets, listening. She knows, as she always knows, that I am listening to her and it is early morning. The fog has not risen. The traffic crawls outside. There is a red bus, I can see the top of it, outside the window. If I cared to look more closely I could see the faces of the people in the bus, and, with luck, my own reflection, or at least the reflection of my white hair, my one distinction. The mail has not yet arrived. There will be nothing for me, but I wait for it. Life is nothing without expectation. I am always first to pick up the letters when they drop through the door. The milk bottles, two days old, are in the kitchen unwashed and she knows this too, because she has not yet come.

Our relationship is beyond analysis. It was Bernard, although I prefer to name no names, who suggested that the relationship had a Boy Scout flavour about it. So much he knows. Bernard, who travels halfway across London to find the one priest who will forgive his incessant masturbation, cannot be regarded as an authority in this matter.

Outside the fog is thick, the way it is always meant to be in London, but seldom is, unless you live by the river, which I don't. Today will not disappoint the American tourists.

And she walks above my head, probably arranging the little white dolls which she will not explain and which I never ask about, knowing she will not explain, and not for the moment wishing an explanation. She buys the dolls from the Portobello Road, the north end, on Friday morning, and at another market on Thursdays, she has not revealed where, but leaves early, at about 5 a.m. I know it is a market she goes to, but I don't know which one. The dolls arrive in all conditions, crammed into a large cardboard suitcase which she takes out on her expeditions. Those which still have hair she plucks bald, and those with eyes lose them, and those with teeth have them removed and she paints them, slowly, white. She uses a flat plastic paint. I have seen the tins.

She arranges the dolls in unexpected places. So that, walking up the stairs a little drunk, one might be confronted with a collection of bald white dolls huddled together in a swarm. Her room, which was once my room, she has painted white; the babies merge into its walls and melt into the bedspread which is also white. White, which has become a fashionable colour of late, has no appeal to her, it is simply that it says nothing, being less melodramatic than black.

I must admit that I loathe white. I would prefer a nice blue, a pretty blue, like a blue sky. A powder blue, I think it is called. Or an eggshell blue. Something a little more feminine. Something with — what do you call it? — more character about it. When I finally take her to bed (and I am in no hurry, no hurry at all) I will get some better idea of her true colour, get under her skin as it were.

Did you get the pun?

I have found her, on numerous occasions, playing Monopoly in the middle of her room, drinking Guinness, surrounded by white dolls.

Several times a week she comes to wash my dishes and to be persuaded to share a meal with me. The consumption of food is, for the moment, our most rewarding mutual occupation. We discuss, sometimes, the experience of the flavours. We talk about the fish fingers or the steak and kidney pies from Marks & Sparks. She is still shy, and needs to be coaxed. She has revealed to me a love for oysters which I find exciting. Each week I put a little of my pension aside. When I have enough I will buy oysters and we will discuss them in detail. I often think of this meal.

At an earlier stage I did not understand myself so well, and achieved, on one or two occasions, a quiet drunken kiss. But I have not pursued the matter, being content, for the moment, with the meals and the company on these quiet nights now that the television has been taken away and now that I, unemployed, have so little money to spend with the ladies in Bayswater, the cinema, or even a pint of best bitter in the Bricklayers Arms which, to tell the truth, I always found dull.

I am in no hurry. There is no urgency in the matter. Sooner or later we shall discuss the oysters. Then it will be time to move on to other more intimate things, moving layer after layer, until I discover her true colours, her flavours, her smells. The prospect of so slow an exploration excites me and I am in no hurry, no hurry at all. May it last for ever.

Let me describe my darling. Shall I call her that? An adventure I had planned to keep, but now it is said. Let me describe her to you. My darling has a long pale face with long golden hair, slightly frizzy, the kind with odd waving pieces that catch the light and look pretty. Her nose is long, downwards, not outwards, making her appear more sorrowful than she might be. Her breasts, I would guess, are large and heavy, but she wears so many sweaters (for want of a better term) that it is hard to tell; likewise the subtleties of her figure. But she moves, my darling, with the grace of a cat, pacing about her room surrounded by her white dolls and her Monopoly money.

She seems to have no job and I have never asked her about her occupation. That is still to come, many episodes later. I shall record it if and when it is revealed. For the moment: she keeps no regular hours, none that I can equate with anything. But I, for that matter, keep no regular hours either and, never having owned a clock, have been timeless since the battery in the transistor radio gave out. Normally it seems to be late afternoon.

She is making up her mind. I can hear her at the top of the stairs. Twice, in the last few minutes, she has come out onto the landing and then retreated back into her room. She has walked around her room. She has stood by the window. Now she moves towards the landing once more. She is there. There is a silence. Perhaps she is arranging dolls on the landing.

No. She is, I think, I am almost positive, descending the stairs, on tiptoe. She plans to surprise me.

A tap at the door. My stomach rumbles.

I move quickly to the door and open it. She says hello, and smiles in a tired way.

She says, phew. (She is referring to the smell of the bad milk in the unwashed bottles.)

I apologize, smooth down my bed, pull up the cover, and offer her a place to sit. She accepts, throwing my pyjama pants under the bed for the sake of tidiness.

She says, how is your situation?

I relate the state of the employment market. But she, I notice, is a little fidgety. She plays with the corner of the sheet. She is distracted, appears to be impatient. I continue with my report but know she is not fully listening.

She leaves the bed and begins to wash up, heating the water on the small gas heater. I ask her of her situation but she remains silent.

The water is not yet hot enough but she pours it into the tub and begins to wash up, moving slowly and quickly at the same time. I dry. I ask her of her situation.

She discusses George, who I am unsure of. He was possibly her husband. It appears there was a child. The child she visits every third Sunday. For the hundredth time I remark on how unreasonable this is. The conversation tells neither of us anything, but then that is not its purpose. The dishes she dispenses with quickly, an untidy washer, I could do better myself — she leaves large portions of food behind on plates, bottles, and cutlery, but I do not complain — I keep the dishes to attract her, like honey.

I relate a slightly risqué joke, a joke so old it is new to her. She laughs beautifully, her head thrown back, her long white throat like the throat of a white doll, but soft, like the inside of a thigh. Her throat is remarkable, her voice coming softly from it, timorously, pianissimo.

She is, how to call it, artistic. She wears the clothes of an ordinary person, of a great number of quite different ordinary persons, but she arranges them in the manner of those who are called artistic. Small pieces of things are tacked together with a confidence that contradicts her manner and amazes me. Pieces of tiny artificial flowers, a part of a butcher's apron, old Portuguese boots, a silver pendant, medal ribbons, a hand-painted stole, and a hundred milk bottle tops made unrecognizable. She is like a magpie with a movable nest.

Her name, which I had earlier decided not to reveal, is Nile. It is too private a name to reveal. But it is so much a part of her that I feel loath to change it for fear I will leave something important out. Not to mention it would be like forgetting to mention the white dolls.

The washing-up is finished and it is too early yet to prepare a meal. It is a pleasant time, a time of expectation. It needs, like all things, the greatest control. But I am an expert in these matters, a man who can make a lump of barley sugar last all day.

We sit side by side on the bed and read the papers. I take the employment section and she, as usual, the deaths, births, and marriages. As usual she reads them all, her pale nail-bitten finger moving slowly over the columns of type, her lips moving silently as she reads the names.

She says, half to herself, they never put them in.

I am at once eager and reluctant to pick up this thread. I am not sure if it is a loose thread or one that might, so to speak, unravel the whole sweater. I wait, no longer seeing the words I am looking at. My eardrums are so finely stretched that I fear they may burst.

She says, don't you think they should put them in?

My stomach.rumbles loudly. I say, what? And find my voice, normally so light, husky and cracked.

She says, babies ... abortion babies ... they're unlisted.

As I feared, it is not a loose thread, but the other kind. Before she says more I can sense that she is about to reveal more than she should at this stage. I am disappointed in her. I thought she knew the rules.

I would like, for the sake of politeness, to answer her, but I am anxious and unable to say any more. I do not, definitely not, wish to know, at this stage, why she should have this interest in abortion babies. I find her behaviour promiscuous.

She says, do you think they have souls?

I turn to look at her, surprised by the unusual pleading tone in her voice, a voice which is normally so inexpressive. Looking at her eyes I feel I am being drowned in milk.

She pins back a stray wisp of hair with a metal pin. I say, I have never thought of the matter.

She says, don't be huffy.

I say, I am not huffy.

But that is not entirely correct. Let us say, I am put out. If I had any barley sugar left I would give her a piece, then I would instruct her in the art of sucking barley sugar, the patience that is needed to make it last, the discipline that is required to forget the teeth, to use only the tongue. But I have no barley sugar.

I say, I am old, but it will be a little while before I die.

She says (surprisingly), you are so morbid.

We sit for a little while quite silently, both looking at our pieces of newspaper. I am not reading mine, because I know that she is not reading hers. She is going to bring up the subject again.

Instead she says, I have never told you what I do.

Another thread, but this one seems a little less drastic. It suits me nicely. I would prefer to know these things, the outside layers, before we come to the centre of things.

I say, no, what do you do?

She says, I help do abortions.

She may as well have kicked me in the stomach, I would have preferred it. She has come back to the abortions again. I did not wish to discuss anything so ... deep?

I say, we all have our jobs to do, should we be so lucky as to have a job, which as you know ...

She says, the abortionist is not a doctor, there are a number of rooms around London, sometimes at Shepherd's Bush, Notting Hill, there is one at Wimbledon, a large house.

I have not heard of this sort of thing before. I examine her hands. They are small and pale with closely bitten nails and one or two faintly pink patches around the knuckles. I ask her if she wears rubber gloves. She says, yes.

I am quite happy to discuss the mechanics of the job, for the moment.

She says, I have always thought that they must have souls. When she ... the woman I work for ... when she does it there is a noise like cutting a pear ... but a lot louder. I have helped kill more people than live in this street ... I counted the houses in the street one night ... I worked it out.

I say, it is not such a large street ... a court, not very large.

She says, twice as many as in this street.

I say, but still it is not so many, and we have a problem with population. It is like contraception, if you'll excuse the term, applied a little later.

My voice, I hope, is very calm. It has a certain "professional" touch to it. But my voice gives no indication of what is happening to me. Every single organ in my body is quivering. It is bad. I had wished to take things slowly. There is a slow pleasure to be had from superficial things, then there are more personal things like jobs, the people she likes, where she was born. Only later, much later, should be discussed her fears about the souls of aborted babies. But it is all coming too fast, all becoming too much. I long to touch her clothing. To remove now, so early, an item of clothing, perhaps the shawl, perhaps it would do me no harm to simply remove the shawl.

I stretch my hand, move it along the bed until it is behind her. Just by moving it … a fraction … just a fraction … I can grasp the shawl and pull it slowly away. It falls to the bed, covering my hand.

That was a mistake. A terrible mistake. My hand, already, is searching for the small catch at the back of her pendant. It is difficult. My other hand joins in. The two hands work on the pendant, independent of my will. I am doing what I had planned not to do: rush.

I say, I am old. Soon I will die. It would be nice to make things last.

She says, you are morbid.

She says this as if it were a compliment.

My hands have removed the pendant. I place it on the bed. Now she raises her hands, her two hands, to my face. She says, smell …

I sniff. I smell nothing in particular, but then my sense of smell has never been good. While I sniff like some cagey old dog, my hands are busy with the campaign ribbons and plastic flowers which I remove one by one, dropping them to the floor.

She says, what do you smell?

I say, washing-up.

She says, it is an antiseptic. I feel I have become soaked in antiseptic, to the marrow of my bones. It has come to upset me.

I say, it would be better if we ceased this discussion for a while, and had some food. We could talk about the food, I have fish fingers again.

She says, I have never told you this but the fish fingers always taste of antiseptic. Everything …

I say, you could have told me later, as we progressed. It is not important. It is good that you didn't say, you should not have said, even now, you should have kept it for later.

She says, I'm not hungry, I would rather tell you the truth.

I say, I would rather you didn't.

She says, you know George?

I say, you have mentioned him.

My hands are all of an itch. They have moved to her outermost garment, a peculiar coat, like the coat of a man's suit. I help her out of it and fold it gently.

She says, George and my son … you remember.

I say, yes, I remember vaguely, only vaguely … if you could refresh my memory.

She says, you are teasing me.

I deny it.

I have started with the next upper garment, a sweater of some description which has a large number 7 on the back. She holds her arms up to make it easier to remove. She says (her voice muffled by the sweater which is now over her head), I made up George, and the son.

I pretend not to hear.

She says, did you hear what I said?

I say, I am not sure.

She says, I made up George and my son ... they were daydreams.

I say, you could have kept that for next year. You could have told me at Christmas, it would have been something to look forward to.

She says, how can you look forward to something you don't know is coming?

I say, I know, I knew, that everything was coming, sooner or later, in its own time. I was in no hurry. I have perhaps five years left, it would have filled up the years.

She says, you are talking strangely today.

I say, it has been forced on me.

There is another garment, a blue cardigan, slightly grubby, but still a very pretty blue.

I say, what a beautiful blue.

She says, it is a powder blue.

I say, it is very beautiful, it suits you.

She says, oh, it is not really for me, it belonged to my sister ... my younger sister.

I say, you never mentioned your younger sister.

She says, you never asked me.

I say, it was intentional.

Now I have all but lost control. The conversation goes on above or below me, somewhere else. I have removed the powder blue cardigan and the red, white, and blue embroidered sweater beneath it. Likewise a blouse which I unfortunately ripped in my haste. I apologized but she only bowed her head meekly.

She says, you have never told me anything about yourself ... where you work ...

I am busy with the second blouse, a white silk garment that looks almost new. I say, distractedly, it is as I said, I am unemployed.

She says, but before ...

I say, I worked for the government for a number of years, a clerk ...

She says, and before that?

I say, I was at school. It has not been very interesting. There have been few interesting things. Very boring, in fact. What I have had I have eked out, I have made it last, if you understand me, made my few pleasures last. On one occasion I made love to a lady of my acquaintance for thirty-two hours, she was often asleep.

She smiles at me. She says, that sounds ...

I say, the pity was it was only thirty-two hours, because after that I had to go home, and I had nothing left to do. There was nothing for years after that. It should be possible to do better than thirty-two hours.

She smiles again. I feel I may drown in a million gallons of milk. She says, we can do better than that.

I say, I know, but I had wished it for later. I had wished to save it up for several Christmases from now.

She says, it seems silly ... to wait.

As I guessed, her breasts are large and heavy. I remove the last blouse to reveal them, large and soft with small taut nipples. I transfer my attentions to her skirt, then to a second skirt, and thence to a rather tattered petticoat. Her stockings, I see, are attached to a girdle. I begin to unroll the stocking, unrolling it slowly down the length of her leg. Then the second stocking. And the girdle.

Now she sits, warm and naked, beside me, smiling.

There is only one thing left, an earring on the left ear.

I extend my hand to take it, but she grasps my hand.

She says, leave it.

I say, no.

She says, yes.

I am compelled to use force. I grasp the earring and pull it away. It is not, it would appear, an earring at all, but a zip or catch of some sort. As I pull, her face, then her breasts, peel away. Horrified, I continue to pull, unable to stop until I have stripped her of this unexpected layer.

Standing before me is a male of some twenty odd years. His face is the same as her face, his hair the same. But the breasts have gone, and the hips; they lie in a soft spongy heap on the floor beside the discarded pendant.

She (for I must, from habit, continue to refer to her as "she") seems as surprised as I am. She takes her penis in her hand, curious, kneading it, watching it grow. I watch fascinated. Then I see, on the right ear, a second earring.

I say, excuse me.

She is too preoccupied with the penis to see me reach for the second earring and give it a sharp pull. She sheds another skin, losing, this time, the new-found penis and revealing, once more, breasts, but smaller and tighter. She is, generally, slimmer, although she was never fat before.

I notice here that she is wearing a suspender belt and stockings. I unroll the first stocking and find the leg is disappearing as I unroll. I have no longer any control over myself. The right leg has disappeared. I begin to unroll the left stocking. The leg, perhaps sensitive to the light, disappears with the rolling.

She sits, legless, on the bed, apparently bemused by the two coats of skin on the floor.

I touch her hair, testing it. A wig. Underneath a bald head.

I take her hand, wishing to reassure her. It removes itself from her body. I am talking to her. Touching her, wishing that she should answer me. But with each touch she is dismembered, slowly, limb by limb. Until, headless, armless, legless, I carelessly lose my grip and she falls to the floor. There is a sharp noise, rather like breaking glass.

Bending down I discover among the fragments a small doll, hairless, eyeless, and white from head to toe.

A Windmill in the West

The soldier has been on the line for two weeks. No one has come. The electrified fence stretches across the desert, north to south, south to north, going as far as the eye can see without bending or altering course. In the heat its distant sections shimmer and float. Only at dusk do they return to their true positions. With the exception of the break at the soldier's post the ten-foot-high electrified fence is uninterrupted. Although, further up the line, perhaps twenty miles along, there may be another post similar or identical to this one. Perhaps there is not. Perhaps the break at this post is the only entry point, the only exit point — no one has told him. No one has told him anything except that he must not ask questions. The officer who briefed him told the soldier only what was considered necessary: that the area to the west could be considered the United States, although, in fact, it was not; that the area to the east of the line could be considered to be Australia, which it was; that no one, with the exception of U.S. military personnel carrying a special pass from Southern Command, should be permitted to cross the line at this point. They gave him a photostat copy of an old pass, dated two years before, and drove him out to the line in a Ford truck. That was all.

No one in the United States had briefed him about the line — its existence was never mentioned. No one anywhere has told him if the line is part of a large circle, or whether it is straight; no one has taken the trouble to mention the actual length of the line. The line may go straight across Australia, for all the soldier knows, from north to south, cutting the country in half. And, even if this were the case, he would not know where, would not be able to point out the line's location on a map. He was flown from the United States, together with two cooks, five jeeps, and various other supplies, directly to the base at Yallamby. After they landed there was no orientation brief, no maps — he waited fifteen hours before someone came to claim him.

So, for all he knows, this line could be anywhere in Australia. It is even possible that there are two parallel lines, or perhaps several hundred, each at thirty-mile intervals. It is even possible that some lines are better than others, that not all of them stretch through this desert with its whining silence and singing in the line.

The road crosses the line, roughly, at a right angle. The fact that it is not exactly a right angle has caused him considerable irritation for two weeks. For the first week he was unable to locate the thing that was irritating him, it was something small and hard, like a stone in his boot.

The bitumen road crosses the line at the slightest angle away from a right angle. He has calculated it to be, approximately, eighty-seven degrees. In another month those missing three degrees could become worse.

The soldier, who is standing on double white lines that run the length of the road, kicks a small red rock back into the desert.

The soldier sits inside the door of the caravan, his eyes focused on the dusty screen of his dark glasses, his long body cradled in his armchair. He was informed, three weeks ago, that he would be permitted to bring a crate of specified size containing personal effects. From this he gathered some ill-defined idea of what was ahead of him. He is not a young soldier, and remembering other times in other countries he located an armchair that would fit within the specified dimensions. The remaining space he packed with magazines, thrillers, and a copy of the Bible. The Bible was an afterthought. It puzzled him at the time, but he hasn't thought of it or looked at it since.

He had expected, while he put the crate together, that he would have a fight on his hands, sooner or later, because of that armchair. Because he had envisaged a camp. But there was no camp, merely this caravan on the line.

The soldier polishes and cleans his dark glasses, which were made to prescription in Dallas, Texas, and stands up inside the caravan. As usual he bumps his head. His natural stoop has become more exaggerated, more protective, because of this caravan. He has hit his head so often that he now has a permanent patch that is red and raw, just at the top, just where the crew cut is thin and worn like an old sandy carpet.

But this is not a caravan, not a real caravan. It resembles an aluminium coffin, an aluminium coffin with a peculiar swivelling base constructed like the base of a heavy gun. The soldier has no idea why anyone should design it that way, but he has taken advantage of it, changing the direction of the caravan so that the front door faces away from the wind. Changing the view is what he calls it, changing the view.

No matter which way you point that door the view doesn't alter. All that changes is the amount of fence you see. Because there is nothing else — no mountains, no grass, nothing but a windmill on the western side of the line. The corporal who drove him out in the Ford said that things grew in the desert if it rained. The corporal said that it rained two years ago. He said small flowers grew all over the desert, flowers and grass.

Once or twice the soldier has set out to walk to the windmill, for no good reason. He is not curious about its purpose — it is like the road, an irritation.

He took plenty of ammunition, two grenades, and his carbine, and while he walked across the hot rocky desert he kept an eye on the caravan and the break in the wire where the road came through. He was overcome with tiredness before he reached the windmill, possibly because it was further away than it appeared to be, possibly because he knew what it would look like when he got there.

The day before yesterday he came close enough to hear it clanking, a peculiar metallic noise that travelled from the windmill to him, across the desert. No one else in the world could hear that clanking. He spat on the ground and watched his spittle disappear. Then he fired several rounds in the direction of the windmill, just on semi-automatic. Then he turned around and walked slowly back, his neck prickling.

The thermometer recorded 120 degrees inside the caravan when he got back.

The walls are well insulated — about one foot and three inches in thickness. But he has the need to have the door open and the air-conditioner became strange and, eventually, stopped. He hasn't reported the breakdown because it is, after all, of his own making. And, even if they came out from Yallamby and fixed it, he would leave the door open again and it would break down again. And there would be arguments about the door.

He needs the air. It is something he has had since he was small, the need for air coming from outside. Without good air he has headaches, and the air-conditioner does not give good air. Perhaps the other soldiers at the other posts along the line sit inside and peer at the desert through their thick glass windows, if there are any other soldiers. But it is not possible for him to do that. He likes to have the air.

He has had the need since he was a child and the need has not diminished, so that now, in his forty-third year, the fights he has fought to keep windows open have brought him a small degree of fame. He is tall and thin and not born to be a fighter, but his need for air forced him to learn. He is not a straight fighter, and would be called dirty in many places, but he has the ability to win, and that is all he has ever needed.

Soon he will go out and get himself another bucket of scorpions. The method is simple in the extreme. There are holes every two or three inches apart, all the way across the desert. If you pour water down these holes the scorpions come up. It amuses him to think that they come up to drink. He laughs quietly to himself and talks to the scorpions as they emerge. When they come up he scoops them into a coffee mug and tips them into the blue bucket. Later on he pours boiling water from the artesian bore over the lot of them. That is how he fills a bucket with scorpions.

To the north of the road he marked out a rough grid. Each square of this grid (its interstices marked with empty bottles and beer cans) can be calculated to contain approximately one bucket of scorpions. His plan, a new plan, developed only yesterday, is to rid the desert of a bucket full for each day he is here. As of this moment one square can be reckoned to be clear of scorpions.

The soldier, who has been sitting in his armchair, pulls on his heavy boots and goes in search of yesterday's bucket. The glare outside the caravan is considerable, and, in spite of the sunglasses, he needs to shade his eyes. Most of the glare comes from the aluminium caravan. Everything looks like one of those colour photographs he took in Washington, overexposed and bleached out.

The blue bucket is where he put it last night, beside the generator. Not having to support the air-conditioning, the generator has become quiet, almost silent.

He takes the blue bucket which once held strawberry jam and

empties a soft black mass of scorpions onto the road, right in the middle, across those double white lines. In another two weeks he will have fifteen neat piles right along the centre of the road. If you could manage two bucketfuls a day there would be thirty. Perhaps, if he became really interested in it and worked hard at it, he could have several hundred buckets of scorpions lined up along those double lines. But sooner or later he will be relieved from duty or be visited by the supply truck, and then he will have to remove the scorpions before the truck reaches the spot.

He walks slowly, his boots scuffing the road, the blue bucket banging softly against his long leg, and enters the caravan where he begins to search for a coffee mug. Soon he will go out and get himself another bucket of scorpions.

The sun is low now and everything is becoming quieter, or perhaps it is only that the wind, the new wind, suggests quietness while being, in fact, louder. The sand which lies on the hard rocky base of the desert is swept in sudden gusts and flurries. Occasionally one of these small storms engulfs him, stinging his face and arms. But for all the noises of sand and wind it appears to him that there is no sound at all.

He stands in the middle of the road, his shoulders drooping, a copy of *Playboy* in his hand, and gazes along the road, as far as he can see. Somewhere up towards the western horizon he can make out an animal of some type crossing the road. It is not a kangaroo. It is something else but he doesn't know exactly what.

He gazes to the west, over past the windmill, watching the slowly darkening sky. Without turning his legs he twists his trunk and head around to watch the sun sinking slowly in the eastern sky.

He squats a little, bending just enough to place the copy of *Playboy* gently on the road. Walking slowly towards the caravan he looks once more at the windmill which is slowly disappearing in the dark western sky.

The carbine is lying on his bunk. He clips a fresh magazine into it, and returns to his place on the road, his long legs moving slowly over the sand, unhurriedly. The noise of his boots on the roadway reminds him of countless parades. He flicks the carbine to automatic and, having raised it gently to his shoulder, pours the whole magazine into the sun which continues to set in the east.

* * *

He lies on the bunk in the hot darkness wearing only his shorts and
a pair of soft white socks. He has always kept a supply of these socks,
a special type purchased from Fish & Degenhardt in Dallas, thick
white socks with heavy towelling along the sole to soak up the sweat.
He bought a dozen pairs from Fish & Degenhardt three weeks ago.
They cost $4.20 a pair.

He lies on the bunk and listens to the wind in the fence.

There are some things he must settle in his mind but he would
prefer, for the moment, to forget about them. He would like not to
think about east or west. What is east and what is west could be
settled quickly and easily. There is an army-issue compass on the
shelf above his head. He could go outside now, take a flashlight with
him, and settle it.

But now he is unsure as to what he has misunderstood. Perhaps
the area to the geographical east is to be considered as part of the
United States, and the area to the west as Australian. Or perhaps it
is as he remembered: the west is the United States and the east
Australian; perhaps it is this and he has simply misunderstood
which was east and which west. He was sure that the windmill was
in the United States. He seems to remember the corporal making
some joke about it, but it is possible that he misunderstood the joke.

There is also another possibility concerning the sun setting in the
east. It creeps into his mind from time to time and he attempts to
prevent it by blocking his ears.

He had been instructed to keep intruders on the outside but he is
no longer clear as to what "outside" could mean. If they had taken
the trouble to inform him of what lay "inside" he would be able to
evaluate the seriousness of his position. He considers telephoning
the base to ask, and dismisses it quickly, his neck and ears reddening
at the thought of it.

It is hot, very hot. He tries to see the *Playboy* nude in the dark,
craning his head up from the pillow. He runs his dry fingers over the
shiny paper and thinks about the line. If only they had told him if it
was part of a circle, or a square, or whatever shape it was. Somehow
that could help. It would not be so bad if he knew the shape.

Now, in the darkness, it is merely a line, stretching across the
desert as far as his mind can see. He pulls his knees up to his

stomach, clutching his soft socks in his big dry hands, and rolls over on his side.

Outside the wind seems to have stopped. Sometimes he thinks he can hear the windmill clanking.

The alarm goes at 4.30 a.m. and, although he wakes instantly, his head is still filled with unravelled dreams. He does not like to remember those dreams. A long line of silk thread spun out of his navel, and he, the spinner, could not halt the spinning. He can still taste the emptiness in his stomach. It is not the emptiness of hunger but something more, as if the silk has taken something precious from him.

He bumps around the caravan in the dark. He does not like to use the light. He did not use it last night either. He is happier in the dark. He spills a bottle of insect repellent but finds the coffee next to it. With his cigarette lighter he lights the primus.

He could go outside, if he wanted, and take boiling water straight from the artesian bore, but he is happier to boil it. It makes a small happy noise inside the caravan which is normally so dense and quiet, like a room in an expensive hotel.

It will become light soon. The sun will rise but he doesn't think about this, about the sun, about the line, about what the line divides, encircles, or contains, about anything but the sound of boiling water.

The blue flame of the primus casts a flickering light over the pits and hollows of his face. He can see his face in the shaving mirror, like the surface of a planet, a photograph of the surface of the moon in *Life* magazine. It is strange and unknown to him. He rubs his hands over it, more to cover the reflected image than to feel its texture.

The coffee is ready now and he dresses while it cools off. For some reason he puts on his dress uniform. Just for a change, is what he tells himself. The uniform is clean and pressed, lying in the bottom of his duffle bag. It was pressed in Dallas, Texas, and still smells of American starch and the clean steam of those big hot laundries with their automatic presses.

In the middle of the desert the smell is like an old snapshot. He smiles in soft surprise as he puts it on.

He stands in the middle of the road. It is still cold and he stamps up and down looking at the place where the horizon is. He can make nothing out, nothing but stars, stars he is unfamiliar with. He could never memorize them anyway, never remember which was the Bear or the Bull, and it had caused him no inconvenience, this lack of knowledge.

He stands in the middle of the road and turns his head slowly around, scanning the soft horizon. Sooner or later there will be a patch, lighter than any other, as if a small city has appeared just over the edge, a city with its lights on. Then it will get bigger and then it will get hot, and before that he will have settled one of the questions concerning east and west.

He turns towards the east. He looks down the road in the direction he has known as "east" for two weeks, for two weeks until he was crazy enough to watch the sun set. He watches now for a long time. He stands still with his hands behind his back, as if bound, and feels a prickling along the back of his neck.

He stands on the road with his feet astride the double white line, in the at-ease position. He remains standing there until an undeniable shadow is cast in front of him. It is his own shadow, long and lean, stretching along the road, cast by the sun which is rising in the "west". He slowly turns to watch the windmill which is silhouetted against the clear morning sky.

It is sometime later, perhaps five minutes, perhaps thirty, when he notices the small aeroplane. It is travelling down from the "north", directly above the wire and very low. It occurs to him that the plane is too low to be picked up by radar, but he is not alarmed. In all likelihood it is an inspection tour, a routine check, or even a supply visit. The plane has been to the other posts up "north", a little further along the line.

Only when the plane is very close does he realize that it is civilian. Then it is over him, over the caravan, and he can see its civilian registration. As it circles and comes in to land on the road he is running hard for the caravan and his carbine. He stuffs his pockets full of clips and emerges as the plane comes to rest some ten yards from the caravan.

What now follows, he experiences distantly. As if he himself were observing his actions. He was once in a car accident in California where his tyre blew on the highway. He still remembers watching himself battle to control the car, he watched quite calmly, without fear.

Now he motions the pilot out of the plane and indicates that he should stand by the wing with his hands above his head. Accustomed to service in foreign countries he has no need of the English language. He grunts in a certain manner, waving and poking with the carbine to add meaning to the sounds. The pilot speaks but the soldier has no need to listen.

The pilot is a middle-aged man with a fat stomach. He is dressed in white: shorts, shirt, and socks. He has the brown shoes and white skin of a city man. He appears concerned. The soldier cannot be worried by this. He asks the pilot what he wants, using simple English, easy words to understand.

The man replies hurriedly, explaining that he was lost and nearly out of petrol. He is on his way to a mission station, at a place that the soldier does not even bother to hear — it would mean nothing.

The soldier then indicates that the pilot may sit in the shade beneath the wing of the aircraft. The pilot appears doubtful, perhaps thinking of his white clothing, but having looked at the soldier he moves awkwardly under the wing, huddling strangely.

The soldier then explains that he will telephone. He also explains that, should the man try to move or escape, he will be shot.

He dials the number he has never dialled before. At the moment of dialling he realizes that he is unsure of what the telephone is connected to: Yallamby base which is on the "outside", or whatever is on the "inside".

The phone is answered. It is an officer, a major he has never heard of. He explains the situation to the major, who asks him details about the type of fuel required. The soldier steps outside and obtains the information, then returns to the major on the phone.

Before hanging up the major asks, what side of the wire was he on?

The soldier replies, on the outside.

It takes two hours before the truck comes. It is driven by a captain. That is strange, but it does not surprise the soldier. However, it disappoints him, for he had hoped to settle a few questions regarding the "outside" and "inside". It will be impossible to settle them now.

There are few words. The captain and the soldier unload several drums and a handpump. The captain reprimands the soldier for his lack of courtesy to the pilot. The soldier salutes.

The captain and the pilot exchange a few words while the soldier fixes the tailboard of the truck — the pilot appears to be asking questions but it is impossible to hear what he asks or how he is answered.

The captain turns the truck around, driving off the road and over the scorpion grid, and returns slowly to wherever he came from.

The pilot waves from his open cockpit. The soldier returns his greeting, waving slowly from his position beside the road. The pilot guns the motor and taxis along the road, then turns, ready for take-off.

At this point it occurs to the soldier that the man may be about to fly across the "inside", across what is the United States. It is his job to prevent this. He tries to wave the man down but he seems to be occupied with other things, or misunderstands the waving. The plane is now accelerating and coming towards the soldier. He runs toward it, waving.

It is impossible to know which is the "inside". It would have been impossible to ask a captain. They could have court-martialled him for that.

He stands beside the road as the small plane comes towards him, already off the road. It is perhaps six feet off the road when he levels his carbine and shoots. The wings tip slightly to the left and then to the right. In the area known as the "west" the small aeroplane tips onto its left wing, rolls, and explodes in a sudden blast of flame and smoke.

The soldier, who is now standing in the middle of the road, watches it burn.

He has a mattock, pick, and shovel. He flattens what he can and breaks those members that can be broken. Then he begins to dig a hole in which to bury the remains of the aeroplane. The ground is hard, composed mostly of rock. He will need a big hole. His uniform, his dress uniform, has become blackened and dirty. He digs continually, his fingers and hands bleeding and blistered. There are many scorpions. He cannot be bothered with them, there is no time. He tells them, there is no time now.

It is hot, very hot.

He digs, weeping slowly with fatigue.

Sometimes, while he digs, he thinks he can hear the windmill clanking. He weeps slowly, wondering if the windmill could possibly hear him.

Concerning the Greek Tyrant

1.

Homer has a fever.

His bedclothes have fallen. His face is contorted. His whispering mouth is like a small rose in a sea of soft chamois leather. His blind eyes look like the eyes of old statues that have lost their paint. His ageing naked body is soft and white with baby-creases where the arms and legs meet the body. The floor beside his bed is a mess of tangled clothes, as if the turbulent sea had spilled out of his raging mind and been left to run wild and crash around the room.

His dreams rage against the white walls and he curses them petulantly, telling them to go away.

But Echion won't go away.

He can see Echion and Diomedes quite clearly. They are lying on a beach in a foreign land. It is unlike any land he has ever seen: a hot, humid tropical place left over from an old legend. Homer's mind is a mass of old legends. They wind around each other like the bedclothes on his floor and in his confusion he tries to untangle them but succeeds only in winding them closer together. For a week this battle has continued and it shows no signs of abating.

Now there's this damn Echion again. Echion on an unpleasantly beautiful tropical beach. The landscape is full of gaping white holes that Homer is desperate to fill in. Through the white holes are the fragments of landscape he cannot immediately imagine and now, from habit, he begins to work at them like a cunning old stone mason, patiently filling them in tree by tree, cloud by cloud, grain of sand by grain of sand. The work gives him no pleasure or satisfaction. It is merely one more problem to be solved.

The beach is lined with great tall trees that resemble palm trees but they are not palm trees at all. They bear large orange fruit the size of a man's head. When the orange fruit fall they split open to reveal purple seeds and bright red flesh. These seeds now litter the beach like beads from a broken necklace and Echion lies talking to a native girl who doesn't understand his words.

Echion is stocky and squat and his body comprises a wild landscape of bumps and bulges that runs from his huge knotted calves to his wide powerful shoulders. His nose has been broken, a portion of his left ear is missing, and his black curling hair is beginning to bald, right in the centre of his great head. These marks are the result neither of battles nor of age, but of small spiteful injuries inflicted on him by Homer — repayments for imagined slights against a master Echion doesn't even know exists. For Echion is a worrier. He worries at the reasons for his dreams, questions the logic of his terrible battles. He has nagged at Odysseus, asking him continual questions about the blind oracle he is known to consult.

The time has not yet come to kill Echion for the last time. When the time comes his death will be used to achieve a certain effect. Echion is an annoying small coin, but he will not be spent lightly. He is also a dangerous coin to keep. Sooner or later his infuriating questions will contaminate Diomedes and then the other men. Echion is the seed of the mutiny which Homer dreads.

But Echion is wearing down. His black eyebrows almost meet across his perpetually furrowed brow and his eyes look like windows onto a windswept sky, one instant the most brilliant blue and the next grey with heavy clouds. He looks like a man who has fought too many battles and wants nothing more than to lie down and die amongst his friends.

Homer looks along the beach, walking his mind past the twenty-eight other men who are also there. Some sleep under the tall strange trees. Others recline under large wooden structures that have been built for them by friendly natives. In the shade of these shadow factories they retell old legends and bawdy stories. Others, like Echion, lie with women who are puzzled and afraid of these hairy light-skinned strangers.

The laughter on the beach is loud and coarse. There is a grim determination in it, as if the men were committed to being happy at any cost. They are soldiers on leave. They wish to behave like soldiers on leave but at the same time they cast silent glances at the palm trees and their giant orange fruit and examine the seeds carefully while they caress their girl or tell their story or pretend to gaze out at the misty sea. The girls accept the caresses silently and offer their strange companions rich drinks from goblets shaped like pigs' heads and the soldiers laugh and play at being happy.

For the thousand things they talk and joke about, they say nothing about their most recent experiences. They say nothing of the lands they have visited, driven on the seas of Homer's fever, a great yellow storm which has washed them onto impossible shores where they have met threat and horror and deprivation.

They are suffering from the shock which is the necessary protection for those who are the victims of dreams. Their memories of their roles in Homer's dreams seem simply to be recollections of nightmares too horrible to mention.

Thus they remember but dismiss the time that Odysseus was set alight and ran amongst them in panic, setting each of them alight in turn. Likewise Diomedes' castration and decapitation. Likewise a thousand other horrible things.

Only Echion ponders on these matters. His brows knot continually as he tries to put down his memories.

Odysseus, of course, is excepted from all this. It is necessary that he collaborate. He alone is not protected and will clearly remember the pain and the hardships and soon he will come in search of Homer and accuse him once more of neglect and mismanagement.

Homer turns wearily in his bed, attempting to turn his back on the beach. If only he could remember where he was sending these men he could put everything to rights. But he's lost. His memory has broken its anchor and is drifting loose and he's stuck with this contingent of soldiers who lie on a foreign beach and drown the noises from their dreams with false laughter.

The seas shimmer.

A large white fluffy cloud in the sky threatens to solidify, to become granite. Homer, moaning, tastes the rock between his teeth.

Diomedes leans on his elbow. His flesh is smooth and unmarked. His wounds have been healed by Homer. Diomedes is a good soldier, tough and strong, delighting in discipline and comforting himself in the superiority of his leaders. Homer's spite has not been visited on him. He is a strange contrast to the battle-scarred veteran who lies by his side.

"Are you awake?" he asks the veteran.

"Yes," says Echion, "I'm awake." He is staring at the granite cloud.

"Do you like your girl?" Diomedes' voice is uneasy. He wishes to be continually assured that everything is excellent. He is young and Echion is old.

Echion smiles. He finds his friend's concern for the quality of the girl amusing. "Yes, I like my girl. Do you like yours?"

Diomedes doesn't look at his girl. It seems as if he wasn't asking about the girl at all, that he wanted to know something more important. "Yes," he says, "I like my girl."

He picks up one of the purple seeds and examines it minutely. For a moment it seems that he is about to ask another question, the real question.

"Tell me," Echion says gently, "tell me what's on your mind."

"Nothing," says Diomedes, "I was just thinking how good it is that we both like our girls."

2.

Later, while Diomedes was asleep, Echion dug sullenly in the sand and puzzled at his problem. His problem nagged at him continually. It was something so stupid it made him angry to think about it. But he couldn't leave it alone.

Echion's problem was that he had forgotten the purpose of their mission. It was stupid of him. It was so stupid he couldn't even ask any of the others. He had once made the mistake of broaching this subject with Diomedes and Diomedes, his closest friend, had flared into a wild temper and called him a traitor and a weakling and many other things which, his eyes brimming with tears, he came later to apologize for. He had, he said, been having bad dreams. They had upset him. He was sorry. Echion had forgiven him instantly but they had not discussed the matter since.

As for the matters of the dreams, Echion had considered talking about that but he thought better of it. He had also been afflicted by these dreams. He had mentioned them to Odysseus, who had taken such a keen interest in them that he had become suspicious.

Echion now abandoned his sand-digging so that the girl could scratch his back more easily. He gazed out at the small flotilla of canoes from which brown bodies fell into the water. Probably, he thought, probably they are collecting food for a feast. The voices of the divers wandered across the water like memories from a hundred years ago and Echion was suddenly homesick and yearned for the voice of a wife he could hardly remember and the arms of a child whose name he had forgotten.

"Where did he go?" It was Diomedes again.

"Who?"

"Odysseus."

"I thought you were asleep."

"I was thinking about Odysseus. I wondered where he was."

"I suppose," said Echion, "that he's talking to the blind man."

Diomedes sighed. "Do you like your girl?" he asked.

"Yes," said Echion, "I like my girl. Do you like yours?"

"Yes, yes I do. Do you want to swap?"

"I don't care. Do you want to?"

The sky was full of clouds like a melted jigsaw puzzle, "I don't know," said Diomedes, "I was just thinking about Odysseus."

3.

Reality returns to Homer's fever only to take his sight and go away again. Light falls on his blind eyes like coloured rain on a tiled roof.

He is walking down a street in the country of his fever. Odysseus is pursuing him. The street is uneven and littered with small stones. He stumbles continually. He worries about his dignity. The street is full of unseen foreigners. Hands touch him. It is difficult to understand the intention of the numerous small pinches and sharp tugs he is assailed by.

He fears that Odysseus has passed the limit of his endurance and gone mad, that he carries the knife that will kill them all, Homer and the battle-weary population of his mind.

He is assailed by strange smells, rotten fish mixed with acrid smoke. Someone is burning something foul and the strangeness of the smells and the impudent touches of these unknown hands cause him to panic.

He turns, first left, then right, and then sits, quite suddenly, in the middle of this foreign street.

The hands are trying to drag him up. He is angry and afraid and also irritated that these ignorant people should dare to touch him, Homer. The voices in his ears are uncultured and angry. They shriek curses at him. He cannot understand the language but knows what they are saying. They know of his mistreatment of Odysseus and the men. They have a list. His crimes are all numbered. They plan to kill him.

He curls up on the ground, as helpless as a child, and waits for the first rock to strike him.

And then he hears the sound of Odysseus's voice speaking in the language of the country of his fever. That Odysseus should have learned this language without his knowledge seems a vicious betrayal. Odysseus is shouting. Slowly Homer realizes that he is ordering the people to leave him alone.

Odysseus is going to rescue him.

"I am blind," says Homer suddenly. "I am blind. I can't see." He pretends that Odysseus is not there. The prospect of being rescued by Odysseus is humiliating. Homer pretends to rescue himself. "Get away from me," he says, "I'm blind."

"They can't understand you."

Homer composes himself and attempts to look as if he is totally in charge of the situation, sitting in the middle of this filthy street in his good clothes.

"Who's that?"

"You know who it is."

"Oh, Odysseus, is it? Sit down, Odysseus, I've been expecting you."

"You're stopping a funeral procession," says Odysseus. "Come over to the side and let them get through."

Homer doesn't like the sound of his voice. It's made from steel, like a dagger.

When they're sitting by the side of the street, Odysseus says, "You've been running away."

"Don't talk nonsense. I've been waiting for you for hours. Have you brought everything?"

He hears a rustle of cloth as Odysseus squats beside him. "Are you still ill?"

Homer can feel the face peering closely at his. He puts a hand out and pushes the face away. For an instant he is in a room in Greece and the smell of hot broth is under his nose.

"I'm better now," he says. "Fever is not a very pleasant thing for a man."

"It's possibly worse," says Odysseus, "for the creatures of his imagination."

"It's been a hard time for all of us," the poet says, "for me, for you, for the men. Is Echion still causing trouble?"

"He was never causing trouble," Odysseus speaks patiently. "I've explained it to you before. I don't know why you want to misunderstand me."

"I can't have men who spread rumours."

"He remembered his dreams, that's all. He wanted to talk about his dreams."

Homer thumps his staff on the street. "I won't have men talking about their dreams. I can't afford the risk. You can't either. Once they know, they don't want to do what they're told," he sighs. "Sometimes I'm sorry I told you."

"I'm sorry you told me," says Odysseus, "always."

"I've been watching this Echion," Homer insists. "He's a good soldier?"

"Yes, yes he is."

"I have a plan for him. Did you bring the writing materials?"

"I said so, yes. Are you still lost?"

"Homer is never lost," says Homer. "We have made a few minor explorations and now it's time to get back to the main story. I've been thinking, Odysseus, that if Echion wants to know the meaning of his dreams, we might as well tell him."

And then the blind man begins to speak in a curiously soft voice which rises and falls in a steady rhythmical pattern. Odysseus writes down his words, sitting at the blind poet's feet like a servant in front of his master.

4.

"Your girl has a wart on her hand," said Diomedes.

"Has she?" said Echion. "I hadn't noticed."

"She's got a wart on her left hand, just near her little finger. Why don't you look?"

Echion looked instead at Diomedes and smiled, in spite of himself, at the earnestness of his friend's face. He wondered what was really bothering him. "Do you have funny dreams?" he asked.

Diomedes looked embarrassed. "I wasn't criticizing her," he said. "Do you think she has a lover? She's very beautiful." The girl smiled at Diomedes and he began to play with her long black hair.

"Do you have funny dreams?" said Echion. "I have funny dreams."

"I have beautiful dreams," Diomedes smiled at the girl, "about love."

"You don't have strange dreams about battles?"

"No."

Echion caught his friend's gaze and held it hard. "Is that the truth?"

"Yes," Diomedes averted his eyes, "of course it's the truth."

"I had a dream," Echion began very slowly, as if remembering with great difficulty, "that we had all been captured and we were assembled in a great courtyard. The walls of the courtyard were like giant staircases and our captors were women. For some reason they chose me. They selected me and took me to the centre of the courtyard and pulled my arm, this arm, off. All the time I was there I was watching you. You were weeping. And ..." Echion stopped, his voice breaking. "Did you have that dream, Diomedes?"

"I don't know." Diomedes had turned on his stomach and hidden his face in his folded arms.

"I know you did." Echion now spoke very calmly. "I know you had that dream, Diomedes. I know we all had that dream. And all the other dreams. I don't think they were dreams. I think these terrible things have really happened and Odysseus has used magic to make us forget."

Diomedes looked at his friend's serious face and suddenly burst out laughing. "Who put your arm back?" he said.

"I don't know," said Echion, "I don't know. Do you want to swap?"

"All right."

Echion suddenly felt very tired. "You don't mind about the wart?"

"There isn't a wart," said Diomedes. "I only said it to make you look at her. You haven't looked at her since we came here. I think she's offended."

Diomedes leant across and took the girl's hand and Echion looked at her for the first time. Yes, she was a beautiful girl. So was Diomedes' girl. They were both beautiful. They seemed to Echion to be almost identical with their long blue-black hair and high foreheads and small noses. Only the colour of their simple garments which they tucked so shyly around their breasts separated them from each other in his mind.

His girl had been blue.

He held out his hand towards the red girl and she came, reluctantly, he thought, to his side. She touched his ear, the ear with the piece missing from it. She touched the cut edge with her finger. It tickled. She said something questioningly in her own language and Echion answered in his: "It's all right," he said, "it was long ago, a long time ago."

Diomedes stood up with the blue girl and walked slowly towards the mountains.

Left alone with this young girl, Echion felt very old and very lonely. "Are you happy," he asked her hoarsely, "do you have a lover?"

The girl raised her thick black eyebrows.

"Lover," he said, "do ... you ... have a ... lover?"

The girl stood and pulled him up slowly, a great bulky parcel of bad dreams with a piece missing from his ear. "Are you happy?" he said as he followed her reluctantly towards the mountains.

Up and down the beach, men were gathered in groups, some sleeping, some talking, some with girls. Somewhere Odysseus was talking to a blind man.

As they left the sand and began to walk along the path to the village, Echion caught a glimpse of their craft: a wooden horse with its head poking out above the strange trees. It looked sad and lonely, like some creature lost in a dream.

5.

It is dark in Homer's room and the inside of the wooden horse is like a huge barn in midsummer. The heat is stifling. The horse was not designed for the tropics and the air is heavy with the smell of the men who left it this morning: it seems to ooze from the wood as it exhales in the daytime what it has inhaled in the night.

But now Echion is here. He is puzzled and guilty to find himself doing this, but he is reading Odysseus's papers. The papers he had always assumed to be navigation charts and calculations now reveal themselves to be merely pages of verse. Why should Odysseus spend so many hours reading these verses as if they were maps or instructions? Perhaps Echion has found the wrong thing. Perhaps he is mistaken.

His dark eyes scan the pages hurriedly, and then a little more slowly, and then very slowly indeed.

Because Echion has just stepped inside the blueprints for his own bad dreams.

Each page of verse has a thick line drawn through it diagonally, as if it were some kind of mistake, but the words on these pages describe, in more detail than Echion had remembered, the details of his bad dreams. The verse records the incident with the female warriors, tells how Odysseus was set afire by mechanical monsters, how Diomedes was castrated and then decapitated. The verse contains more battles than a man could fight if he lived for a hundred years and Echion is in every one. As he reads them he feels a great weariness, the weariness he has been trying to deny, sweep over him. His dark eyes fill with huge tears as he reads of the pain and death of his dearest friends. The pages seem cruel and hard to him, the work of merciless gods who have been playing with his life. The handwriting sweeps on and on, seemingly never ending. He begins to skip through the thousands of pages until he comes, at last, to those at the end. These have not been crossed out.

These later pages appear more normal. There are no monsters. Instead they talk about a city called Troy and a wooden horse and a battle in which thirty men will fight against the Trojans, assisted by others who will come in ships. There is a roughness about the verse, as if it were not quite finalized. Small alterations have already been made. Words have been crossed out and not replaced. Echion reads this with relief and then his eye catches his own name near the bottom of a page.

He reads quickly and then, suddenly, lets out a great bellow of rage.

The verse tells how Echion is so eager for battle that he is the first to emerge from the horse at Troy. He is so keen that he falls and breaks his neck. Echion doesn't know what he has stumbled into. He knows only that he feels a greater rage than he has ever felt in his life. Someone is playing tricks with him. His whole life has been controlled by some evil practical joker who has manipulated him, tortured him, and killed him a thousand times. And now it seems that they wish to kill him one more time.

"The bastards." He shouts the word. He doesn't know who he shouts it at. Perhaps at Odysseus. He doesn't know who it is.

The wooden horse now seems to him to be a terrible jail, a torture chamber from which he must escape before this next death can take place. He has no possessions. There is nothing to delay him. He will disappear for ever into the depths of this land. He would rather spend his life amongst strangers than be subjected to one more death.

He turns from the pages of verse with his jaw set hard and finds himself face to face with a frail old blind man with a pampered face. He has never seen him before. He dislikes him instantly.

"Excuse me," says the blind man, "I'm blind. I can't see."

Echion remains still and doesn't make a sound. He watches the blind man like a cat watching a snake.

"Put my hand on your shoulder."

The old man looks so frail that Echion takes the hand and lays it on his shoulder. The hand is small and soft and his shoulder is hard and heavy. With his heart beating hard Echion begins to walk towards the trapdoor.

"Perhaps," says the blind man, "it might be better to stay."

"I'm going."

"You are going ... to Troy," the blind man smiles. His hand is like a vice on Echion's shoulder. Echion feels as if the marrow has been sucked from his bones. He is like a blown-out candle. He stands helplessly and looks at the rose petal mouth of this man. Finally he manages to speak. He says, "I read what Odysseus wrote."

"My name is Homer," says the blind man, "and you read what I told Odysseus to write and you read it because I permitted you to. This will be the last time for you. The other times were mistakes. But this business in Troy is what I needed you for, I need you to fall from the horse," the poet says, "for the irony."

Homer leads Echion to a place by the door where he ties his hands with leather thongs and binds them to a post. Echion doesn't protest. He feels like an ox in a slaughter yard. The blind man ties on a gag to stop him bellowing.

6.

When the night came his companions returned to the horse to sleep. They had been told some story about Echion and no one, not even

Diomedes, looked his way. It was as if he were invisible, already dead and buried in the pages of Homer's verse.

When they had all drunk their wine Odysseus explained the nature of the battle to be fought the next day. He said nothing of how the wooden horse was to be moved to Troy. He mentioned "allies" and once talked of a "powerful friend". The men's minds, accustomed to living on the waves of Homer's fevers, accepted all this without question and retired to bed early to be ready for tomorrow's battle.

Echion lay in the dark and waited for Diomedes, but when he didn't come to release him he began to work quietly on his leather bindings, gnawing on them with his broken teeth until his gums bled and his mouth was full of the sticky juices of his veins.

Around him the horse groaned and creaked like a ship weathering a heavy sea. Outside he fancied he could hear voices and hammering and the crash of masonry. His jaws ached and his arms twitched and it wasn't until early morning that his bindings were finally undone.

He crept stiffly to the door and lowered the great trapdoor. The rope ladder flopped down in the dark. His arms were stiff and his hands so cramped that he could barely clench them. His head was strange from lack of sleep and as he lowered himself onto the first rung he was overcome with giddiness.

His foot slipped on the second rung, and he fell.

In the grey hours before dawn a giant wooden horse could be seen enclosed by the walls of Troy. The first Greeks who descended the rope ladder found Echion already there. He was lying on the dusty ground with his neck broken.

7.

Echion hadn't died immediately. He had written some words in the fine clay dust with a bleeding finger. The words were as follows:

"KILL THE PIG TYRANT HOMER WHO OPPRESSES US ALL."

But the words were erased by the blind feet of his companions as the whole incident concerning Echion was later erased by Homer, who no longer found the incident interesting enough to tell.

Withdrawal

1.

The front room of Eddie Rayner's shop is like many other shops in
High Street. It's busy on Saturdays and quiet for the rest of the week.
The shops around him sell the same things he sells: stripped pine
furniture, bentwood chairs, old advertising signs, blue and white
china, and odds and ends like butter churns and stained-glass
windows. The prices are high and the work isn't too hard. On
weekdays the second-hand dealers stand in the street, chatting about
prices and the pieces they've picked up at the auctions.

Eddie is no longer welcome to these little conferences. It's because
of the back room. There are many stories about Eddie's back room.
They are all guesses, because Eddie has never invited any of the other
dealers to inspect it. However, a recent exhibition in the front room
has given rise to a new spate of stories more shocking than anything before. Sixteen photographs of the bodies of murder victims
lying on lino, on carpet, on cobblestone, surrounded by such every-
day things as children's toys, policemen's shoes, and old cigarette
packets. There is an ordinariness about the photographs which
makes them all the more shocking. This new revelation of Eddie's
has brought his neighbours back into his shop. They haven't liked
what they've seen.

Even before this recent event he has been something of a scandal
amongst them. They gossip about his women, they guess about his
men friends, they shake their heads about the state of his Porsche
which is now so battered and rusted that it is almost unrecognizable.
And they wonder about the clients, some of them very well known
and very wealthy, who come to visit Eddie's back room and emerge
carrying unidentified articles hidden in beer cartons or wrapped in
newspaper.

Second-hand dealers are naturally jealous and bitchy about each
other but Eddie Rayner somehow acted as a common bond to those
in High Street. They said he paid too much at the auctions, that his

prices were too high or too low, that his taste was dated, that he had
no taste, that he knew nothing about business, that he received stolen
goods, that he was a homosexual, that he was involved in witchcraft.
All symbols by which they tried, somehow, to make the contents of
the back room more concrete.

When Eddie hung the exhibition of murder victims they held a
meeting and decided to send a deputation to ask him to remove the
photographs at once. Eddie received the deputation with his cool,
stoned, beautiful smile and left the photographs exactly where they
were.

Incensed, they wrote him a very formal letter wherein they
repeated their request in more forceful language. Eddie had the letter
framed and hung it in the window.

It was, as Eddie said every day, a very interesting summer.

It was a terrible summer. Fires ringed the city itself, burning
fiercely around the outer suburbs. At night the horizon glowed
bright red as if the city were being fried on some incredible hot plate.
The north wind pushed the fire into suburban streets where the
sounds of its flames were picked up by excited men from radio
stations and the same north wind brought ashes and still-burning
leaves to float down High Street past Eddie's shop, down Caroline
Street, past his flat.

It was Eddie's summer. Not the summer of white beaches and
bronzed bodies, but the summer of burnt houses and blackened
bodies, a summer you could believe was the beginning of the end
of the world. At night Eddie sat on the balcony with Daphne smoking
grass, watching the red glow in the sky and feeling an intensity of
emotion that he had rarely experienced when confronted with
nature.

2.

Eddie is waiting in Casualty at the Alfred Hospital. He is waiting for
an intern called Dean Da Silva. He moves awkwardly from one
foot to the other, tall and thin and lonely as a lighthouse.

He is unsure of whether he should have come. It is possibly
dangerous, it is certainly indiscreet. Now, with the inquisitive rabbit
eyes of the admissions clerk asking him silent questions, he feels that
it has certainly been a bad move.

He sits, once more, on the vinyl bench, next to the weeping

woman who continues to drop fat tears onto an old copy of *Time*. He can see the rabbit-eyed clerk saying something to a nurse about him. The nurse has a big arse and a small nose. She wrinkles her nose and Eddie sends her his most sinister sexual look. He is a master of this particular look and the nurse averts her eyes and whispers some cowardly message to the clerk, who waits a few seconds before looking up again.

Eddie Rayner has a face like Captain Hook in the Walt Disney version of *Peter Pan & Wendy*. His lower lip protrudes slightly, not enough to make him look stupid, but just enough to make him look vaguely debauched. He decorates this remarkable face with the marks of his caste: wire-flamed spectacles, thin drooping moustache that runs in parallel lines down his long chin, and shoulder-length hair of an undecided colour.

His body, however, is his real face. Legs so long and thin and tightly skinned in slinky velvet that he takes on something of the nature of a spider. It is an effect he is not unaware of. Now he stands and moves, once more, from leg to leg, dancing to some silent sensual music while he waits uncertainly for Dean Da Silva, who he has never met before. Dean Da Silva has a severed hand to sell him, or, more correctly, has hinted to a mutual friend that a severed hand might become available.

Dean Da Silva is somewhere in the unmapped area that lies behind the wall behind the counter where the admissions clerk is trying to locate a teddy-bear biscuit. Eddie hears him ask the nurse if she has seen a teddy-bear biscuit.

"Mr Rayner."

Eddie jumps. He sees a plump, smooth, neatly suited, white-coated, shiny-shoed Dr Dean Da Silva standing in front of him. Dr Dean Da Silva has a smooth, bland, olive-skinned face. He asks Eddie, "What's the trouble?"

"I'm Eddie Rayner."

"That I know."

"Yeah, well I believe my name has been mentioned ..."

Eddie always finds these first contacts awkward. He looks at the clerk, who is peering at him over the top of a half-eaten teddy bear. He leads the way to a corner and Da Silva follows, frowning impatiently. Eddie hesitates. Then, with a shrug, he limply sheds his clothing: "It's about the hand ... a hand ... you're selling."

"I see." Da Silva's face registers nothing. In it Eddie reads greed, fear, caution, superciliousness. He takes all his own anxieties and plants them in the empty bed of Da Silva's face.

"That's true, I take it, that you are?"

"More or less."

Eddie smiles. He tries to plant a smile on Da Silva's face. He encourages it with the serenity of his own smile but Da Silva only nods and waits. So he asks, "It's OK for you to talk here, about this?"

"It is a little premature. What do you want it for, this... item?"

"I have a ... you know ... client."

"A client?" Da Silva picks up the word and examines it critically with stainless-steel tweezers.

"Yes, a client."

Dean Da Silva is doing his first year as an intern. Already he has found that fine balancing point between reserve and disdain. "It is not a very ethical request."

"It is not a very ethical offer." Eddie understands this language. The talk of ethics is really all about money. The less ethical it is the more expensive it will be.

"The offer has not been made. In any case," Da Silva looks at his watch, a complicated piece of machinery which is probably a graduation present, "in any case, I believe I can contact you through our mutual friend."

"The thing is a delivery date."

"I'll contact you when it becomes available. If," he consults his graduation present again, "if it does become available."

Eddie leaves the hospital wishing he hadn't come. He has fallen victim, once more, to his own fierce impatience. Da Silva would have come to him sooner or later. There was no one else he could have gone to. Then Eddie could have controlled the deal and bought, if not cheaply, at a reasonable price. Now it was all going to be a hassle.

He guns the Porsche down Punt Road towards Caroline Street and then, on second thought, does a U-turn and heads back towards High Street so he can drive past the shop. As he comes up High Street he can see them: Jim Kenny and Alex Christopolous and someone he doesn't know. They're peering into his shop reading the letter that they themselves have signed. As he cruises past the shop he toots the horn, hoping they'll jump. Instead they peer mildly in his direction and he watches them in the rear-vision mirror as they retreat slowly to Jim Kenny's shop across the road.

He drops back into second and does a screaming wheelie that brings him to the front of Kenny's shop, then another wheelie that brings him to his own front door. Now he has no idea what he should do next.

He could go back to the flat and see if Daphne is there. But if she isn't there it'll be worse. Better imagine she is there and go and check out the stocks in the back room.

He opens the door to the back room. There is nothing really to check out. He knows the extent of his wealth but enjoys, once more, looking at it with the assumed eyes of a stranger, saying to himself: you have never been here before, you wander down a street and browse in a shop, by mistake you open this door and find yourself in this room, this room that the world has always denied you. And there: the gold filling from Belsen. The phial of blood said to have once pulsed through Marilyn Monroe's veins. The large file of genuine obscene letters and suicide notes obtained through his contact in the police department. Likewise the police photographs, recording details of crimes large and small, dead bodies and empty ashtrays set together in silver bromide. Many, many other items. A stained shirt with a foul smell which was certainly worn by Guevara in Bolivia, sold by a traitor to a policeman to a tourist to a woman collecting examples of folk weaving, and finally to Eddie. Less seriously there are a variety of trusses in glass cases with metal plaques attributing their ownership to important historical figures. These last are amusing fakes and are not expensive.

It is cool and dark here in the back room with its black walls and careful spotlights. Sharing the imaginary stranger's delight Eddie wishes, once more, that the back room was not a back room. The exhibition of murder victims in the front room is a flirtation with his fantasy of declaring the back room open for general viewing. It is a calculated experiment.

The pine furniture and bentwood chairs bore him to death. But the things in this back room thrill him beyond measure, some strange mixture of fear and disgust and something else sends his nerve ends tingling. He is not an analytical man and has never wondered deeply about his love for these items. When challenged he has defended himself as a liberator, a man who has opened a door and let fresh air into a room musty with guilt. It is not a brilliant defence.

It was here, in this room where he is most sure of himself, that he first met Daphne. At that time she was the mistress of a cabinet minister who had a public reputation for Protestant austerity. The cabinet minister was an old customer of Eddie's, a collector of strange photographs. Doubtless he could have obtained the same photographs through the police department but it would have been a risky business and he valued Eddie's reputation for discretion. His particular interest was sadistic rape and these photographs, for some reason even Eddie wasn't sure of, were the most difficult to obtain.

And it was here that Daphne saw Eddie, standing in his kingdom like the devil himself, talking in measured professional tones to the minister who, in his excitement and embarrassment, was stammering like a schoolboy.

On that day Eddie, with great subtlety and spiderlike certainty, humiliated the minister simply by asking him very specific questions about the photographs he wished to see. He was very, very polite, but his persona had changed, and he talked to the minister with the voice of the world outside. Normally he would have let him leaf through the files, but this was not to be a normal occasion. It was to be something of a duel. It was to be one of those strange occasions when neither the attacker nor the victim could really believe what was happening and thus smiled at each other throughout, each attempting to persuade the other of the supreme ordinariness of the occasion.

But the minister, like a man whose throat has been slashed by a very sharp razor, didn't discover the damage till he had left the premises, and then only because it was reflected so painfully in the eyes of his mistress.

Daphne was not a beautiful girl, although she had a striking body with very long legs and big tits which she displayed to their most incredible advantage. Her face, however, had a flabbiness, a laxness about it that was not attractive. She had a large, loose mouth and a birdlike nose which lay beneath layers of make-up she applied so skilfully. There was, however, something about her, a combination of recklessness, sensuality, and strength. She had a novelist's fascination for people, and an intuitive understanding of them. Her life was devoted to the study of people. She gossiped about them, fought

with them, and fucked them and had, in a very few years, collected
an incredible array of lovers including a professional gangster, an
English footballer, a visiting Shakespearian actor, and a well-
known second-hand car dealer.

And during this summer she moved in with Eddie and Eddie was
frightened, flattered, and almost in love with her. He felt like a man
who's bought a racing car he's too frightened to drive fast. A sense
of inadequacy overwhelmed him every time he thought about
Daphne because Daphne had certain very set ideas about who Eddie
was and Eddie wasn't entirely sure that he could live up to them.

Daphne put great store by her honesty. They had played on that
first incredible night, a long, exciting game of emotional strip-tease
where they dared each other to be honest about their feelings. It had
ended with Eddie declaring his total infatuation with Daphne and
Daphne hinting that the feeling might be mutual. Somewhere along
the line Eddie felt that he had lost the game, but he continued to play
it and was disconcerted to discover that his most honest admissions
were not received well. Honest admissions of previous dishonesty
did not go down well with Daphne, whose reservations about him
began when she sensed weaknesses and secrets she had not suspected. She regarded him curiously, unsure of his authenticity.

Eddie was wondering whether he might now go and see if
Daphne was home when he heard the front door of the shop open.
He came out to find the smack freaks tilting back dangerously on his
bentwood chairs.

Jo-Jo, before the beauties of heroin had led him along more private
paths, had once been a friend. But Pete had never been. Pete had mad
eyes and a psychotic, derisive smile that struck a chill in Eddie's
heart. He had once seen Pete at work with a broken beer bottle. In
the end nothing had happened. Pete had laughed in his victim's pale
face and smashed the bottle at his feet. But it had been a nasty scene
and Eddie didn't like to remember it. Pete had since done time for
possession. He looked like someone who had done time, his hair still
cut short by Pentridge barbers.

Eddie began to talk about the fires. Pete and Jo-Jo knew nothing
about the fires and weren't interested in them. Jo-Jo told him how
they had been driven from their haven in Williamstown by other
natural forces. They couldn't stand it any more — the dead woman
sitting in the room with the pen in her hand, forever about to write

something which they would never know about. Jo-Jo hated the
blank paper almost as much as he hated the corpse of their landlady,
an old woman of seventy or more who refused to decompose in spite
of the heat, or because of it. Eddie thought he could see the fear
showing through the unshaven whiskers of Jo-Jo's baby face, but it
was probably only malnutrition.

While the landlady sat at the table refusing to decompose, the
house she had died in proved to be made of weaker stuff. Huge
hunks of plaster, two inches thick and exceptionally dangerous, had
begun to fall with frightening regularity. One such fall had ripped
down a heavy bookshelf in the living room, another had knocked
the bathroom cabinet from its wall and filled the bath with rubble.
The dunny was blocked and they couldn't shit in it.

Pete and Jo-Jo had lived in a small flat adjoining the main house.
What had once been a quiet suburban refuge had now come to
disturb them so much that they preferred to enter the inner city
where they were both known to the cops.

When he heard about the body something inside Eddie went very
tight and began to reverberate very fast. A thought so outrageous
that it terrified him to consider it. An impossible thought, but the
more he was frightened of it the more he knew he had to do it. Not
for the money, although the money would be incredible. But ...
because ...

But for now he was relieved that Jo-Jo had brought a subject for
conversation along with him. Jo-Jo's silences were somehow like
threats. Now while he talked to them about the old lady he managed
not to feel so fucking straight. Smack freaks always made him
nervous. They were so private, so exclusive, living in their own
dangerous world which he would never have the courage or foolishness to enter.

Even now he felt their curious ambivalence towards him, their
envy of his success, and also their contempt for it. Pete didn't say
much. He went off to the windowless dunny where he shot up
and splattered blood over the door. He came back rubbing his arm
and smiling secretively to Jo-Jo.

Eddie said, "She hasn't rotted or anything?" He'd never seen a
dead body. He wondered about it.

No, she hadn't even ... started ... to decompose. She was like (grimace) perfect. Nothing was happening. That's what was freaking them.

Eddie wanted to be sure they hadn't told anyone.

Pete curled his lips. Who in the fuck're we going to tell? The cops?

Jo-Jo nodded. They were waiting for some ... stuff ... and they were going to take the truck up to Queensland maybe tomorrow. They were waiting for a ... delivery. They were going to Queensland to stay with ... relatives.

The "relatives" were somehow a big joke. Eddie grinned with them and then felt stupid when he saw how they looked at him. They'd caught him out. They rubbed his nose in his own fraud. They knew he didn't know the joke about relatives. Fucking smack freaks, always talking in code.

He told them he wanted to see the old lady and Jo-Jo told him the address although Pete told him not to. Pete was mumbling. Eddie wished they'd get out of his shop but when they asked if they could stay at his place for a night he couldn't bring himself to say no.

3.

They moved in that night and began to fuck up his record collection as soon as they arrived. Eddie followed after them, putting records back in their plastic sleeves and placing ashtrays in strategic positions while Daphne, bright-eyed, talked to them about Queensland. Eddie didn't know she'd been to Queensland. But she had. She'd lived there for nearly a year.

"You know Cairns?" she asked Pete.

"Yeah."

"Cairns is a groove."

"Holloway Beach."

"Oh Christ yeah, Holloway Beach." Pete exchanged some look with Jo-Jo that could have meant anything.

Eddie nearly asked, what's Holloway Beach, but he stopped himself. He'd never seen Pete hold a human conversation with anyone. He would rather that it wasn't happening here.

"You ever go to Martin's caravan?"

"Oh yes," Daphne smiled, a very large warm smile.

"He got busted."

"Yeah I know." Daphne smiled like she knew a lot about Martin and his caravan. It was a quite explicit smile which made her look a little soft and sentimental round the eyes.

Pete nodded, "You knew Martin." He laughed.

Eddie sat on the floor and grinned good-naturedly. He remembered Daphne telling him once how she'd lived in a caravan.

"Martin was a good guy," said Jo-Jo. "When he got busted his mum flew up from Lismore and bailed him out. You ever meet his mum?"

"Yeah," Daphne giggled. "He took me down to Lismore once to see his mum."

"The Golden Wattle Café ..." grinned Pete.

"Yeah, The Golden Wattle Café, and she looked me up and down and everything. It wasn't very cool. I had to sleep in a room out the back. That's when I pissed off from Martin. His mum came in one morning and said, Daphne what do you think of Martin? I don't know what she wanted me to say. But I said, well Mrs Clements he's certainly a good fuck."

"What'd she do?"

"*She* didn't do anything. She just pretended she hadn't heard. I got a bus."

Eddie waited for them to start talking about drugs. Sooner or later it'd come up. He hadn't told her they were smack freaks. Now, sometime, the hypodermic would come out and no one needed to go and hide in the dunny to do the job. And then. And then, Daphne would want to try it. Anything once, she'd say, anything once. And leave Eddie standing like a shag on a rock.

They made him feel so fucking straight. He would have loved to have kicked them out but that would have made him feel even more straight. And when they began to shit in his red plastic rubbish bin he didn't complain.

4.

Eddie went down to the shop the next morning to make a few private phone calls and found Detective Sergeant Mulligan from the vice squad waiting for him. Eddie knew Detective Sergeant Mulligan from the days when he'd managed the Brown Paper Book Shop in the Metropole Arcade. When he saw Mulligan he knew what had happened: his High Street friends had lodged an official complaint.

Eddie parked the Porsche behind Mulligan's unmarked Holden

and waved to the dapper man in the suit and suede waistcoat who stood waiting patiently outside the shop. Mulligan looked more like a used-car salesman than a cop. He had a seedy handsome face and favoured big cufflinks and interesting tie-pins.

He was going to be busted. He didn't mind. Finally it'd be good for business.

"You're a dirty bastard," said Mulligan. "This is Constable Fisher."

Fisher looked like a farmer. He gazed solemnly at Eddie like a child looking at a dangerous snake in the zoo.

Eddie opened the shop for them and they wandered around getting a better look at the photographs. "You know who this is?" Mulligan tapped a man lying on what seemed to be a kitchen floor.

"No."

"Name's Hogan. His wife's in Fairlea now, the silly bitch. You mind telling me where you got these?"

"From the North Melbourne tip."

"*You* found them at the North Melbourne tip. Just wandering through were you?"

"A friend."

"You're a bit sick in the head, Eddie."

"Do you think?" Eddie smiled. He found it ironic that he was being busted for possessing the art of the police force.

Constable Fisher watched one, then the other, like a man watching a game of tennis.

"Corrupt and deprave."

"I'm what?"

"These," Mulligan indicated the photographs, "are likely to corrupt and deprave." He grinned. "So I'll have to give you a receipt."

Eddie thumped his forehead with his fist. "They've got their clothes on."

"How many photographs?"

Fisher counted them twice. "Sixteen."

"Listen," said Eddie, "there's no pricks, no genitals, they've got their clothes on."

"Sixteen … photo … graphs," wrote Mulligan, "size?"

Fisher guessed: "Ten by eight?"

"They've got their clothes on. They're just dead people with their clothes on."

But the truth of the matter is that Mulligan had a better idea of what Eddie was up to than Eddie did himself. He recognized him for what he was: a pornographer of death. He gave Eddie the receipt and went off with the photographs under his arm.

5.

Eddie spent the rest of the day trying to find a lawyer, an embalmer, and a man who made crates.

He phoned the lawyer and made an appointment. Then he contacted the crate maker and gave him the dimensions of the crate he wanted made. He allowed the dimensions on the generous side because Jo-Jo and Pete couldn't seem to agree on whether their landlady had been large or small.

The embalmer was a little more difficult. He arranged one meeting at the Clare Castle Hotel in Carlton. It was not a satisfactory meeting. Eddie said he had to have a piss and crept out the back door and didn't go back.

He'd have to solve that problem later. He contacted friends at St Vincent's hospital but nobody knew anybody.

This job was going to have its difficulties.

Preoccupied with processes and techniques, he didn't have much time to think about the old lady herself but her presence dominated his day and made him not unpleasantly tense. His nerve ends tingled and he clenched and unclenched his long fingers in an ecstasy of anticipation.

He planned to take Daphne with him. He had a very clear idea of the power politics of their personal relationship and he knew that the visit to the house would swing the balance once more his way, bring it back to where it had been on the first afternoon when he had humiliated the cabinet minister.

But when the morning finally came Pete and Jo-Jo presented him with the red plastic rubbish bin they'd been shitting in.

"What's this?"

Pete stared at him incredulously. "It's for the pig."

"The cops?"

"Not the cops, the fucking pig. We got a pig out at Williamstown. You give it to the pig to eat."

Eddie nodded slowly. They were doing to him what he had done to the cabinet minister. He put the plastic bin of shit in the passenger seat of the Porsche and was forced to leave Daphne behind with the freaks.

6.

When Eddie left the city he was still busy planning the complicated details of what would surely be his masterpiece. The embalmer had fucked things up a bit. Still, that could be fixed. Somehow it'd all work. And then, Jesus Christ, what an auction he'd have.

What he had in mind was a tableau. The tableau would consist of the whole house. In one room of this house there'd be a real old lady sitting at a table about to write a letter. That would be the centre of the work. The other rooms would be needed too, if only to establish the authenticity of the central room.

It was ambitious. It was dangerous. It involved skill and organization and a lot of luck. If one thing fucked up it wouldn't work. If she had relatives who wanted to live in the house he wouldn't be able to buy it. If the neighbours had found the body before he got there the whole thing would be ruined. If she'd started to decay, the embalmer (another problem) mightn't be able to do a good job. He'd have to sneak her out of the house and crate her and store her for however long might be necessary.

But, with all these little difficulties taken care of, Eddie would have the most incredible auction sale of all time. Selected invitations to twelve of his richest customers. They would bid against each other to take possession of this most outrageous of all Eddie's little curios.

But now as he drove out to Williamstown with the bucket of shit beside him on the seat he began to get a little nervous. His nervousness was nothing to do with the embalmer or the cops or difficulties with relatives. No, what was beginning, only now, to make him just a little bit nervous was the thought of the dead body.

He'd never seen a dead body.

He wished Daphne was with him. Daphne would have been freaked by it all. Her fear would have made him strong and confident. The thought of the body wouldn't have worried him then. But now, by himself ...

He tucked the Porsche behind a petrol tanker, deciding not to pass it. There was no hurry. Eddie cruised into Williamstown at 25 m.p.h.

7.

The house was perfect, right down to the cypress pines that lined the rickety wooden fence at the front. From this exquisite beginning it never faltered. The drive was made from bricks which had sunken so that the surface resembled the surface of the sea in a slight swell. Beside the drive were lines of dead irises and beyond the iris beds were seas of tall brown grass amongst which Eddie could see neglected garden tools and the handle of an old-fashioned lawn mower.

It was perfect. It was also a little terrifying. He wished, once more, that Daphne had been there. It would have been easy. He wouldn't have stayed sitting in his car as he was now. He could see the house through the wire gate. There was a dead woman sitting inside that house. Blistering weatherboard. Brown holland blinds drawn. Walls marked with the water from a leaking spout. It was nothing like the house in *Psycho*. It was also exactly like the house in *Psycho*.

If it hadn't been for the bucket of shit which was now slowly boiling in the sun it is possible that Eddie would never have left the car. But finally the foul smell became worse than his fear and he lifted the plastic garbage can from the car and carried it obediently up the drive.

It was then, halfway up the drive, that he heard the noise. An incredible screaming, high-pitched and terrible. Its effect on Eddie was shattering. His tall, thin frame jerked. He dropped the bin. And stood absolutely still.

There was a horrible prickling feeling down the back of his neck. He would have turned, right then, and run. But he was too frightened to run. He stood on that brick drive riveted to the spot while the squealing continued.

And then, very slowly, it dawned on him.

It was the fucking pig.

Hot and embarrassed he picked up the bin and continued up the drive. At the back of the house he found the pig writhing in the dust of its yard like a possessed thing. Not a smooth-shaven pig like he'd seen in the butcher shops, but a black hairy hog with a long evil snout and wild red eyes. He stood at the rails of the pig's yard and watched it writhe like a man watching his own nightmares.

And then he realized. He thought of something he had read about:

WITHDRAWAL

The word flashed in the sky of his mind in red neon letters. And he understood the rubbish bin.

He took the bin of shit and tossed it into the pig yard. The pig gobbled the lot in two seconds, still whimpering.

Later, when he was inside the house, the pig became quiet. So, he thought, the pig is a junkie too, addicted from eating the shit of junkies.

8.

The episode with the pig had somehow cauterized his fear. Now he entered the house from the back verandah, tiptoeing selfconsciously across the creaking boards, the eyes of a thousand imaginary neighbours and vice-squad men boring into his black velvet back. He opened the door slowly, like a man defusing a dangerous bomb. His professional mind observed small details with fascination: the worn linoleum floor, the strange old lady's hat on the hat stand, the plastic raincoat on the floor, the large white cat huddled in a ball in a far corner, the stained glass on the front door, far away. The first room, a bedroom, obviously unused. Several dead ferns in pots on the floor, a gardener's glove, an airmail letter from Malaysia. He touched nothing, silently celebrating the perfect neglect, the authentic symbols of death. He approached, once more, that perfect no man's land where fear is thrilling and almost pleasant.

To the left, another door. And he knew, as his hands touched the large black door knob, that this was the room. He held his breath, preparing himself for a smell he had read about. He waited for the air, heavy with the perfume of death, to overwhelm him.

But there was no smell, except perhaps a sweet woody smell like the inside of a walnut.

She sat, sedately, at the table, wearing a moth-eaten fur coat over a pair of men's pyjamas that were a size too big. A slight old lady with thin grey hair pulled back into a bun on a very round head. Rimless glasses on a small pert nose. Tiny white hands, one resting on a table, one holding a fountain pen which rested on a blank piece of white writing paper. The table she sat at was large. On the other side of the table lay the remains of some plaster ceiling which had crushed a vase of flowers. Eddie noted the pieces of art noveau vase with satisfaction. Somehow they were almost better than the old lady herself, a more frightening natural symbol of the old lady who he now ignored, feeling a little embarrassed in her presence.

The blinds were drawn and the lights were on. This also was perfect: low-wattage lights, yellow and weak.

In search of other equally perfect symbols he wandered from room to room. He found photograph albums, old postcards, more letters than he could have hoped for, a wardrobe full of clothes, some of them expensive period pieces in their own right, a grand piano with a broken leg, paintings of irises and, in the kitchen, best of all, a ham sandwich slowly growing a green beard of mould.

And then, as he re-entered the living room where the old lady sat so quietly at the table, quite suddenly, without warning, it all went very flat. Well, perhaps not flat, but let us say that Eddie lost that tingling, that feeling of too much blood in the veins, that sensation that the curious fingers might themselves burst open under pressure, that curious irritating feeling at the back of the neck, all the delicious sensations that had always accompanied one of his finds.

Accustomed to standing on the edge of giddy chasms of disgust and terror, he was surprised to find himself standing on a wide, flat plain.

It was all so ... ordinary.

He had dealt, all his professional life, with pieces of death, the cunts and pricks and tits of death, bottled, embalmed, and photographed close up. But here he had crossed that vague, disputed territory that separates the pornographic from the erotic. Accustomed to peering through keyholes, he was surprised to discover that he had walked through a door and it was all quite different from what his tingling hysterical nerves had told him it would be. He felt no suspicion of fear, no disgust, no exhilaration. Merely a kind of curious calm like a good stone.

The house was not, in spite of the body, in spite of the symbols, a house of death. The pornographer of death had been confronted with, of all things, a life.

9.

Like a child who, after weeks of ringing doorbells and running away, is caught and made welcome in the house whose doorbells he has been so excitedly ringing, Eddie shyly availed himself of the feast that was now offered him.

He travelled humbly through the rooms and passageways of the old lady's life. He read letters from her mother which had been written fifty years ago. He leapt ten years forward to discover a love affair and back twelve years to read a school report, then forward to a concert where the old lady had sung with some distinction, then forward again, far forward, to the letter of an American who wrote to ask about a new hybrid iris which had been named after her and was difficult or impossible to obtain in Connecticut; there was a letter from a niece who worried that she might be lonely, the dignified letter of a rejected lover, then, quite recently, strange letters from a man who had once been a lodger who might well have been a con man but who inquired, just the same, about the health of a dog called Monty and who promised to return soon from Bundaberg, where he was engaged in the cane harvest.

He wandered through the pages of photograph albums and was able to put faces to many of the people who wrote the letters. He saw in the unchanging eyes of the old lady a peculiar mixture of vulnerability and bravado, the look was still there, gazing at him from across the table. He met her father, her mother, her brother the architect, her other brother who had been killed in a motor accident on his twenty-first birthday, the man who had written the first love letters but not the man who had written the more recent ones.

He read the letters sitting across the table from the old lady, who seemed as if she might, at any moment, begin to reply to any one of this vast horde of correspondents.

He stayed until dusk but he knew long before then that it would be wrong to make the tableau. It would be wrong because it would be wrong, and it would be wrong because it wasn't shrill, or disgusting, or even vaguely spooky. He knew also that there was a lot of money to be made from selling the individual parts. The body, once removed from its environment, would be sufficiently scandalous to bring ten thousand dollars, possibly much more. Even in his new humbled state he recognized that this was a considerable amount of money. Likewise the letters, the postcards, the clothes would bring a lot. The letter telling her of her brother's death could bring fifty dollars, nicely mounted in a clinical aluminium frame.

Still, he managed to evade the issue of what he would actually do with all this.

He left the house as he found it, succumbing only at the last moment to the letter announcing her brother's death. This he folded lightly and put in his pocket.

Leaving by the back door he remembered the pig which was now sleeping contentedly in the corner of its yard. Some strange combination of his new-found feelings and some more practical, cautious, bet-hedging consideration made him decide to take the pig back with him to the smack freaks, who were, after all, responsible for its condition. Left alone it would suffer. Left alone it would also attract attention to the house and perhaps remove the old lady from his grasp at a time when he was unsure of what he might or might not do with her.

I will not record here the difficulties, some of them amusing, that confronted Eddie when he decided to truss the pig, nor those that beset him when he tried to get it into the car. Suffice it to say that he was badly bitten and that he finally succeeded in arriving back at Caroline Street with one pig which was already starting to worry about where its next fix was coming from.

10.

"You what?" said Jo-Jo.

"I brought the pig back. It's downstairs in the car."

The three of them looked up at him derisively. They sat together on the couch, Pete, Daphne, and Jo-Jo, and Eddie didn't like to see them like that, all together, all aligned against him. There wasn't much room on the couch. He could see how the thighs pressed into other thighs. Here, in his fucking flat, all pressed together and sitting in judgment on him, in his own flat.

"It was screaming." His eyes sent desperate signals to Daphne, but Daphne wasn't receiving.

"Did you give it the shit?"

"Yeah, of course I gave it the fucking shit, but I'm not going to make a shit run out there every day just to keep it quiet."

Pete stared at him with dreadful anaesthetized eyes and Daphne smiled at him. It wasn't much of a smile. It could have meant a number of unpleasant things. It occurred to him that she'd been shooting up, but he didn't ask.

"If I let it keep screaming someone's going to call the cops and I stand to lose several thousand bucks."

That did it. Not so cool now, his smack freak friends. They wanted to know what was out there that they'd missed. Diamonds? They'd looked through the house for valuables but the only thing they found was a wrist watch on the corpse itself.

Eddie felt better. He rolled himself a joint and didn't pass it round. He pulled out the letter and let them read it.

The freaks didn't know where they were but he could see that Daphne knew the value of the letter. Still, even she hadn't guessed. She wanted to know what else was out there. Gold fillings?

Eddie very nearly didn't tell them. He had decided on the way back from the house that he wasn't going to sell the old lady. He felt strong and together. He was going to call a doctor or the cops or whoever you call about an old lady, and that would be it. And if it hadn't been for this problem with people sitting on his couch, it would have been it.

Now, however, he found himself saying, "That little old lady you left behind is worth ten grand, just the body alone."

Pete shifted in his seat and looked at Eddie with his head on one side: "Who'd buy an old lady?"

"Lots of people would buy an old lady. Daphne knows at least four people who'd buy an old lady. I know maybe a dozen."

Pete shook his head. "Shit, you're weird, man, you're really weird."

Eddie smiled his stoned, cool, people-loving smile and went to sit on a tall stool. He felt better and worse all at once. In spite of his triumph a great sadness had begun to fall around him. He began to feel that the victory hadn't been worth it. However, he continued: "I'm going to sell that little old lady. I'm going to buy the whole fucking house, man. THE DEAD LANDLADY IN HER HOUSE. Price on application."

"Man, you're on a weird trip."

"Sure. Now if you guys help me upstairs with the pig, I'll go out there tonight and bring her back."

"You going to bring her *here*?"

"Sure. She can sit at the table there. Now you guys give me a hand with the pig and if it starts to yell you give it some stuff. I'll pay for it, but you give it a fix if it needs it. I don't want those pricks next door calling the cops because they hear a pig screaming."

"OK, Eddie," said the freaks.

11.

He drove the old lady back to Caroline Street with the hood down. She didn't seem to mind. In fact, Eddie felt that the wind had put a smile on her face. Even now he was unsure of whether he would really sell her or not. With every mile he changed his mind and changed it back again.

In a confused state of mind he stopped off at High Street and the old lady waited patiently in the car while he went into the back room. The back room didn't help. It all looked a little foolish to him, but maybe it was just because of the old lady waiting so meekly in the car outside.

12.

Exhausted by the events of the day, Eddie slept well that night. The freaks had given the pig a hit and it also slept soundly in the bath. The old lady sat at the table, the pen once more in her hand, gazing thoughtfully at Janis Joplin on the cover of *Rolling Stone*.

When Eddie woke in the morning Daphne was already up. He went out to inspect the old lady and found she wasn't there. No one else was there, either.

Instead, he found a note from Daphne which said that they'd taken the old lady to Sydney to sell and they were going on up to Queensland to stay with relatives. The note said there was some stuff in the bathroom cupboard, enough for a couple of hits, and she'd marked the pig with lipstick to show where to put the needle in. There were other instructions, all quite helpful and explicit.

She also left the name of a man who could sell Eddie more smack and said where to contact him and how much to pay. "In my opinion," she wrote, "the best thing might be just to give it an O.D., love, Daphne."

Report on the Shadow Industry

1.

My friend S. went to live in America ten years ago and I still have
the letter he wrote me when he first arrived, wherein he describes
the shadow factories that were springing up on the west coast and
the effects they were having on that society. "You see people in dark
glasses wandering around the supermarkets at 2 a.m. There are great
boxes all along the aisles, some as expensive as fifty dollars but most
of them only five. There's always Muzak. It gives me the shits more
than the shadows. The people don't look at one another. They come
to browse through the boxes of shadows although the packets give
no indication of what's inside. It really depresses me to think of
people going out at two in the morning because they need to try their
luck with a shadow. Last week I was in a supermarket near Topanga
and I saw an old negro tear the end off a shadow box. He was arrested
almost immediately."

A strange letter ten years ago but it accurately describes scenes
that have since become common in this country. Yesterday I drove
in from the airport past shadow factory after shadow factory, large
faceless buildings gleaming in the sun, their secrets guarded by
ex-policemen with Alsatian dogs.

The shadow factories have huge chimneys that reach far into the
sky, chimneys which billow forth smoke of different, brilliant colours. It is said by some of my more cynical friends that the smoke
has nothing to do with any manufacturing process and is merely a
trick, fake evidence that technological miracles are being performed
within the factories. The popular belief is that the smoke sometimes
contains the most powerful shadows of all, those that are too large
and powerful to be packaged. It is a common sight to see old women
standing for hours outside the factories, staring into the smoke.

There are a few who say the smoke is dangerous because of
carcinogenic chemicals used in the manufacture of shadows. Others
argue that the shadow is a natural product and by its very nature

chemically pure. They point to the advantages of the smoke: the beautifully coloured patterns in the clouds which serve as a reminder of the happiness to be obtained from a fully realized shadow. There may be some merit in this last argument, for on cloudy days the skies above our city are a wondrous sight, full of blues and vermilions and brilliant greens which pick out strange patterns and shapes in the clouds.

Others say that the clouds now contain the dreadful beauty of the apocalypse.

2.

The shadows are packaged in large, lavish boxes which are printed with abstract designs in many colours. The Bureau of Statistics reveals that the average householder spends 25 per cent of his income on these expensive goods and that this percentage increases as the income decreases.

There are those who say that the shadows are bad for people, promising an impossible happiness that can never be realized and thus detracting from the very real beauties of nature and life. But there are others who argue that the shadows have always been with us in one form or another and that the packaged shadow is necessary for mental health in an advanced technological society. There is, however, research to indicate that the high suicide rate in advanced countries is connected with the popularity of shadows and that there is a direct statistical correlation between shadow sales and suicide rates. This has been explained by those who hold that the shadows are merely mirrors to the soul and that the man who stares into a shadow box sees only himself, and what beauty he finds there is his own beauty and what despair he experiences is born of the poverty of his spirit.

3.

I visited my mother at Christmas. She lives alone with her dogs in a poor part of town. Knowing her weakness for shadows I brought her several of the more expensive varieties which she retired to examine in the privacy of the shadow room.

She stayed in the room for such a long time that I became worried and knocked on the door. She came out almost immediately. When I saw her face I knew the shadows had not been good ones.

"I'm sorry," I said, but she kissed me quickly and began to tell me about a neighbour who had won the lottery.

I myself know, only too well, the disappointments of shadow boxes for I also have a weakness in that direction. For me it is something of a guilty secret, something that would not be approved of by my clever friends.

I saw J. in the street. She teaches at the university.

"Ah-hah," she said knowingly, tapping the bulky parcel I had hidden under my coat. I know she will make capital of this discovery, a little piece of gossip to use at the dinner parties she is so fond of. Yet I suspect that she too has a weakness for shadows. She confessed as much to me some years ago during that strange misunderstanding she still likes to call "Our Affair". It was she who hinted at the feeling of emptiness, that awful despair that comes when one has failed to grasp the shadow.

4.

My own father left home because of something he had seen in a box of shadows. It wasn't an expensive box, either, quite the opposite — a little surprise my mother had bought with the money left over from her housekeeping. He opened it after dinner one Friday night and he was gone before I came down to breakfast on the Saturday. He left a note which my mother only showed me very recently. My father was not good with words and had trouble communicating what he had seen: "Words Cannot Express It What I feel Because of The Things I Saw In The Box Of Shadows You Bought Me."

5.

My own feelings about the shadows are ambivalent, to say the least. For here I have manufactured one more: elusive, unsatisfactory, hinting at greater beauties and more profound mysteries that exist somewhere before the beginning and somewhere after the end.

Joe

We are quite content. The meal is finished and we have all washed up the dishes together. It is typical of us that we should all wash up the dishes together, even though it is less convenient than two of us doing it, one washing and one drying. The kitchen is small and we all crowd in, eager that we should do our share. That is so like us, you have no idea. We stick together through thick and thin. After all, that's what families are for.

We sit around in the lounge room now and don't say much. Doreen has put on the *Perry Como Show* but the sound is low and no one is paying much attention to it. All that comes from the TV is a faint electrical hum.

We are all quite well known to each other by our various characteristics, some of which are common to the whole family, others of which are held and treasured by individual members. Jack, for instance, is good at getting information from books. He is often reminded of this. To give one example, he learned about playing golf from a book Doreen gave him. This gave him a head start when he played for the first time.

In small ways like this we know of each other's talents. It is a great comfort to us.

In all likelihood we are not so different from other families. We like to joke about family jokes and we have a great respect for the police. I mention the police at this stage because they have a difficult job to do and don't get much thanks for it. The police strike of the thirties brought this fact home to many people for the first time. If any of us were to enter the police force he would lose no respect in our eyes.

Joe doesn't seem to have any characteristics. I don't know if we've ever actually said that out loud. But when it comes to the time of night when we discuss such things, Joe doesn't seem to come up. Also, there are no little stories concerning him. Perhaps it is because he is too young at the moment to have characteristics. I would be forced to admit that he does not look too much like us. We all have characteristic long noses; both Mother and Father have them, Roman noses we call them, and also pointed ears, which is why we have all been called Pixie at school or in our work from time to time. Joe has the ears, but not the nose. That is perhaps his one characteristic. Mother often says, Joe doesn't have the family nose. Joe himself will point this out when various things are discussed.

Actually the reason we all washed up tonight is because Joe raped Harry Bush's youngest last night during interval at the pictures. Last night was Thursday night. I must admit I was surprised.

Most nights Joe sits at home and picks the scabs on his knees — he's still at that stage where he has scabs on his knees from falling over all the time. In addition, he was never circumcised but I have never heard Mother or Father discuss this characteristic or the reason for it. I wouldn't be surprised if this lack of circumcision was the psychological reason for Joe doing over Shirley during the interval. It was out the back, by the rainwater tank. Harry Bush brought her panties round before tea and shoved them in my father's face. Later on, my father said they were none too clean anyway and it was hard to tell. In happier days, with a different subject, this observation of Father's would have had all the makings of a famous family joke. He has some good ones which he remembers; we all remember them.

As I mentioned before, Joe doesn't have the family nose. He was sixteen yesterday and went off to the pictures by himself after the early birthday tea. We always have an early tea on birthday nights. It is one of the things we do. Afterwards we sing songs.

However, Joe excused himself after his birthday tea and went to the bathroom where he shaved the fuzz off his lip with my razor and then he changed into a clean shirt and Jack's tartan tie. Then he borrowed my white sports coat and wore his own trousers and brown desert boots. The sports coat was too big for him across the shoulders.

Then he went out. It was his birthday tea and no one was too upset, although of course we were.

Joe doesn't have the family nose, is what my father said. Then we all sang songs and my mother played the accordion and we were still at it when Joe came home. He sang a number or two with us and then went off to bed. I remember that he didn't clean his teeth. That is one of the things we are particular about, cleaning teeth, because once you've lost them they're gone for good. It is the same with crossing the road and taking precautions during the bush-fire season. People always think it's too much bother and go on as if it's a big joke. But you don't see anyone laughing when they get knocked down on the road or when there's a fire burning up their place. If you've ever seen anything like that you won't easily forget it, believe me. Father saw Reg McLeod's little girl get run over by a semi-trailer and he's never forgotten it.

Anyway, Joe went straight to bed. None of us said anything. After all, it was his birthday. We finished up the cake just the same. Mother said it would have gone stale if we'd left it.

Harry Bush claims our Joe raped his Shirley during the interval. The picture theatre is just out the back of our place; its back fence is next to ours. I mean, we share a back fence. So he probably heard us singing songs for his birthday, while he did her.

We are all in the lounge. Joe is sitting on the floor with his back against the wall. It is where he usually sits. You can see the mark where his head touches the wall. He is reading *Modern Motor*. Everybody else is doing things. Doreen looks a bit fidgety and is knitting booties for Alice Craig's baby which is due any day now. Mother has her knitting too. She is knitting a birthday jumper for Joe and is casting off the last arm. It is one of those bulky sweaters. Joe hasn't said anything about it. Father hums a little tune as he fills his pipe. It is one of his characteristics that he sings when he is edgy or angry or at all upset, which he naturally is.

No one has said anything to Joe yet. We are all looking at him. He has rolled up the leg of his jeans and started to pick a scab. Naturally, we study him picking his scab — nothing else is moving in the room, except for Perry Como, and no one seems to have much interest in that. So we all look at Joe picking the scab and he looks up at me and says, it's a wart.

Dad says, do you know Shirley Bush?

Joe looks at his scab very hard and tries to lift its lid. He says, yes. Then he scratches his brown skinny arms and leaves white scratch marks behind.

Dad says, I hear she was abused.

Joe says, I never abused her. I don't think Dad made himself too clear. Joe has bare feet. He starts hunting for things between his toes.

Doreen says, don't do that, Joe.

Joe looks a bit startled and says, what?

Jack says, don't pick at your tinea.

Joe says, I haven't got tinea.

I say, none of us have got tinea, Jack. No one in the family has got tinea. If one of us had it we'd all have it.

Joe says, you get it from not drying between your toes.

Doreen says, it's a fungus, it grows in the bathmats.

Exactly, I say, that was exactly my point.

Dad lights his pipe again and we all be quiet and watch him to see what he will say to Joe.

Dad says, were you familiar with Shirley Bush?

When?

Answer the question.

Joe looks around at all of us and sees we all know. I feel a bit sorry for him.

Joe looks at Mother and Father and Doreen and Jack and me and then he grins from ear to ear like he'd just won Tatts.

He says, yes, last night during the interval.

He looks happy. Obviously, he has not understood the meaning of the question or, alternatively, of his answer.

Dad says, do you know what rape is?

Joe grins and says, yes.

Dad says, did you rape Shirley Bush?

Joe laughs and Doreen gets up to walk out. She drops the knitting for Alice Craig's baby and bends down to pick it up. When she bends down I can see she doesn't have any pants on. Doreen walks out with her feet scuffling on the floor and her legs rubbing together; I can hear them.

Dad says, did you?

Joe is going a bit red at last and he tries to put his skinny brown arms somewhere comfortable. He unbuttons his shirt and hugs his chest. He says, I don't think it was.

Dad says, how do you mean?

Joe looks sort of embarrassed. He begins to pick at the scab again. He bends his head to look at it closer, so all we can see is the top of his head. He says something we can't hear.

Dad says, what?

Joe says, is it rape … if you do it standing up?

Jack says, only if she didn't want to.

Dad says, did she want to Joe? You can tell us.

Joe says, no.

No one says anything for a bit. Dad looks at Joe as if he was seeing him for the first time. Joe looks up and grins.

Dad says, well?

Joe rolls over and lies on the floor on his stomach. He looks at some pages in *Modern Motor*. Then he says, she wanted to do it lying down … but …

Mother has been counting a row of stitches for some time. She appears to have been losing count. She says, yes … go on …

Her voice sounds high and tense, like it does when she wants to go to the lav and someone is already there.

Joe says, she wanted to do it lying down, but I said there wasn't time during the interval.

Then he cries, looking around at all of us. His grinning mouth melts like a wax doll in an oven. His face slowly caves and he cries without noise.

No one moves for a while. We sit and watch Joe crying.

Then Jack turns the TV off and Dad goes over to the phone to get in touch with Phil Cooper, the solicitor.

The Puzzling Nature of Blue

PART 1

Vincent is crying again. Bloody Vincent. Here I am, a woman of thirty-five, and I still can't handle a fool like Vincent. He's like a yellow dog, one of those curs who hangs around your back door for scraps and you feed him once, you show him a little affection, and he stays there. He's yours. You're his. Bloody Vincent, crying by the fire, and spilling his drink again.

It began as stupidly as you'd expect a thing like that to begin. There was no way in which it could have begun intelligently. Vincent put an ad in the *Review*: Home and companionship wanted for ex-drunken Irish poet shortly to be released from Long Bay. Apply V. Day Box 57320.

I did it. I answered it. And now Vincent is crying by the fire and spilling his drink and all I can say is, "Get the Wettex."

He nods his head determinedly through his tears, struggles to get up, and falls over. He knocks his head on the table. I find it impossible to believe that he hasn't choreographed the whole sequence but I'm the one who gets up and fetches the Wettex. I use it to wipe up the blood on his head. God save me.

Yesterday I kicked him out. So he began to tear down the brick wall he'd started to build for me. Then he gave up and started crying. The crying nauseated me. But I couldn't kick him out. It was the fifth time I couldn't kick him out.

I'm beginning to wonder if I'm not emotionally dependent on the drama he provides me. What other reason is there for keeping him here? Perhaps it's as simple as pity. I know how bad he is. Anyone who knew him well wouldn't let him in the door. I have fantasies about Vincent sleeping with the winos in the park. I refuse to have that on my head.

"How many people answered your ad?" I asked.

"Only you."

Thus he makes even his successes sound pitiful.

Tonight I have made a resolution, to exploit Vincent to the same extent that he has exploited me. He has a story or two to tell. He is not a poet. He was never in Long Bay. But he has a story or two. One of those interests me. I intend to wring this story from Vincent as I wring this Wettex, marked with his poor weak blood, amongst the dirty dishes in the kitchen sink.

Before I go any further though, in my own defence, I intend to make a list of Vincent's crimes against me, for my revenge will not be inconsiderable and I have the resources to inflict serious injuries upon him.

Vincent's first crime was to lie to me about having been in Long Bay, to ask for sympathy on false grounds, to say he was a poet when he wasn't, to say he was a reformed alcoholic when he was a soak.

Vincent's second crime was to inflict his love on me when I had no wish for it. He used his dole money to send me flowers and stole my own money to buy himself drink. He stole my books and (I suppose) sold them. He gave my records to a man in the pub, so he says, and if that's what he says then the real thing is worse.

Vincent's third crime was to tell Paul that I loved him (Vincent) and that I was trying to mother him, and because I was mothering him he couldn't write any more.

Vincent's fourth crime was to perform small acts that would make me indebted to him in some way. Each time I was touched and charmed by these acts. Each time he demanded some extraordinary payment for his troubles. The wall he is propped against now is an example. He built this wall because he thought I couldn't. I was pleased. It seemed a selfless act and perhaps I saw it as some sort of repayment for my care of him. But building the wall somehow, in Vincent's mind, was related to him sleeping with me. When I said "no" he began to tear down the wall and call me a cockteaser. The connection between the wall and my bed may seem extreme but it was perfectly logical to Vincent, who has always known that there is a price for everything.

Vincent's fifth crime was his remorse for all his other crimes. His remorse was more cloying, more clinging, more suffocating, more pitiful than any of his other actions and it was, he knew, the final imprisoning act. He knows that no matter how hardened I might become to everything else, the display of remorse always works. He knows that I suspect it is false remorse, but he also knows that I am not really sure and that I'll always give him the benefit of the doubt.

Vincent is crying again. I'd chuck him out but he's got nowhere else to go and I've got nothing else to trouble me.

I can't guarantee the minor details of what follows. I've put it together from what he's told others. Often he's contradicted himself. Often he's got the dates wrong. Sometimes he tells me that it was he who suggested Upward Island, sometimes he tells me that the chairman mumbled something about it and no one else heard it.

So what happens here, in this reconstruction, is based on what I know of the terrible Vincent, not what I know of the first board meeting he ever went to, a brand-new director who was, even then, involved with the anti-war movement.

The first boarding meeting Vincent ever went to took place when the Upward Island Republic was still plain Upward Island, a little dot on the map to the north of Australia. I guess Vincent was much the same as he is now, not as pitiful, not as far gone, less of a professional Irishman, but still as burdened with the guilt that he carries around so proudly to this day. It occurs to me that he was, even then, looking for things to be guilty about.

Allow for my cynicism about him. Vincent was never, no matter what I say, a fool. I have heard him spoken of as a first-rate economist. He had worked in senior positions for two banks and as a policy adviser to the Labor Party. In addition, if he's to be believed, he was a full board member of Farrow (Australasia) at thirty-five. It is difficult to imagine an American company giving a position to someone like Vincent, no matter how clever. But Farrow were English and it is remotely possible that they didn't know about his association with the anti-war movement, his tendency to drink too much, and his unstable home life.

In those days he had no beard. He wore tailored suits from Eugenio Medecini and ate each day at a special table at the Florentino. He may have seemed a little too smooth, a trifle insincere, but that is probably to underestimate his not inconsiderable talent for charm.

Which brings us back at last to the time of the first board meeting.

Vincent was nervous. He had been flattered and thrilled to be appointed to the board. He was also in the habit of saying that he had compromised his principles by accepting it. In the month that elapsed between his appointment and the first meeting his alternate waves of elation and guilt gave way to more general anxiety.

He was worried, as usual, that he wasn't good enough, that he would make a fool of himself by saying the wrong thing, that he wouldn't say anything, that he would be expected to perform little rituals the nature of which he would be unfamiliar with.

The night before he went out on a terrible drunk with his ex-wife and her new lover, during which he became first grandiose and then pathetic. They took him home and put him to bed. The next morning he woke with the painful clarity he experienced in those days from a hangover, a clarity he claimed helped him write better.

He shaved without cutting himself and dressed in the fawn gaberdine suit which he has often described to me in loving detail. I know little about the finer details of the construction of men's suits, so I can't replay the suit to you stitch for stitch the way Vincent, slumped on the floor in his stained old yellow T-shirt and filthy jeans, has done for me. I sometimes think that the loss of that suit has been one of the great tragedies of Vincent's life, greater than the loss of his fictitious manuscripts which he claims he left on a Pioneer bus between Coffs Harbour and Lismore.

But on the day of his first board meeting the suit was still his and he dressed meticulously, tying a big knot in the Pierre Cardin tie that Jenny and Frank had given him to celebrate his appointment. His head was calm and clear and he ignored the Enthal asthma inhaler which lay on his dresser and caught a cab to the office.

Whenever Vincent talks about the meeting his attitude to the events is ambivalent and he alternates between pride and self-hatred as he relates it. He has pride in his mental techniques and hatred for the results of those techniques.

"As a businessman," he is fond of saying, "I was a poet, but as a poet, I was a fucking whore." He explains the creative process to me in insulting detail, with the puzzled pride of someone explaining colour to the blind. He is eager that business be seen as a creative act. He quotes Koestler (who I know he has never read) on the creative process and talks about the joining of unlikely parts together to create a previously unknown whole.

There were a number of minor matters on the early part of the agenda, the last of which was a letter from the manager of the works at Upward Island. Upward was a vestige of an earlier empire when the company had been heavily involved in sugar, pearling, and other colonial enterprises. Now it was more an embarrassment than a source of profit and no one knew what to do with it. No one in the company was directly responsible for affairs there which is why such a trivial matter was now being referred to the full board for a decision.

The letter from the manager complained about pilferage from the company stores. He apologized profusely for the trouble he was causing but stressed at the same time the importance of his complaint. The natives had less and less respect for the company and were now stealing not only rum (which was traditional and accepted) but many other things for which they could have no conceivable use. For instance a whole case of 25-amp fuses had disappeared and their absence had put the company Land Rover out of action. The manager was now forced to travel around the island by mule, a sight which caused him much embarrassment and the natives much amusement.

Vincent, cool and professional in his new suit, searched his mind for some dramatically simple answer to this problem, but he came up with nothing. When the chairman asked him his opinion, he felt embarrassed to say that he could think of nothing.

As usual with matters concerning Upward Island, the matter was delegated to the chairman's secretary, who would, it was expected, send the manager a beautifully typed and completely useless letter.

With the matter of Upward Island thus disposed of, the next item on the agenda was considered. This was a problem which caused the board some serious anxiety and was to do with two million dollars' worth of Eupholon which was at this moment on the seas and heading for Australia.

You may or may not be aware of the nature of Eupholon. There was some coverage in the international press when the American Food and Drug Administration committee ordered its withdrawal from the U.S. market and most western governments followed suit. During the late sixties Eupholon had been prescribed as a central nervous system stimulant not unrelated to amphetamines. However, prolonged use of the drug produced a number of nasty side effects, the most dramatic of these being a violent blue colour in the extremities of the body. Normally the fingers and hands were first affected, but cases of feet, noses and ears were also mentioned in the reports.

Farrow International was thus left with an inventory of millions of dollars' worth of Eupholon which it had little hope of selling but which it also refused to destroy. The Birmingham head office lived in the fond hope that the Food and Drug Administration's earlier decision would be reversed. However, the drug was still legally available in Australia, and the U.K. office, in an attempt to minimize its losses, had planned a big push on the Australian market. The two-million-dollar shipment at present on the water was to be sold in the first six months.

Unfortunately the Australian government had banned the drug soon after the ship entered the Pacific. And now the Australian board was meeting to decide what to do with such a large quantity of such an undesirable drug.

The international directive was to warehouse it and wait. But warehouse space in Melbourne and Sydney was at a premium and the cost of hiring space for what might be an indefinite period gave the board members worried faces and expensive frowns.

It was then that Vincent asked his question about Upward Island which, at first, seemed so irrelevant that nobody bothered to answer him. His question had been about harbour facilities.

The chairman reminded him that the Upward Island matter had been settled but Vincent insisted on an answer and was told that Upward Island had an excellent harbour.

He then asked about the company store.

He was told that the company store was very large indeed.

Could it accommodate the Eupholon?

Yes, it could.

Could the ship be diverted to Upward?

Yes, it could.

Vincent must have smirked. He would have felt it childish to smile, and his repressed smiles look like nasty little smirks. So I can see the board members looking with wonder at his face, not knowing whether to be pleased with his suggestion or irritated by the smirk.

Vincent had solved the problem but he was not content to leave it at that and, in a demonstration of his creative genius, went on to spell out the ramifications of this plan.

The problem of pilferage on Upward Island would be simply

cured. When the Eupholon arrived it would certainly be subject to pilferage. This in itself didn't matter and would hardly occasion huge losses, but perhaps this pilfering could be used to stop other pilfering.

Assuming the islanders maintained their habits (the manager, in a crude attempt at humour, had euphemistically detailed the effects on several men who had stolen a carton of laxatives), then whoever stole the Eupholon would quickly become visible. Their hands would turn blue. They would not only become visible to the authorites but would provide a living demonstration of the powers of the company to mark those who transgressed its laws.

Thus, Vincent explained, the two problems could be solved at once. Pilferage on Upward Island would be prevented effectively and the Eupholon could be warehoused at no extra cost to the company.

It seems likely that no one gave a damn about the pilferage problem, but Vincent was so obviously thrilled with the neatness of his solution and they were so grateful for a place to put the Eupholon that they were in no mood to nit-pick or to criticize the more far-fetched aspects of the scheme.

As soon as his plan was formally adopted and a cable sent to Birmingham with a request to re-route the ship, Vincent was immediately stricken with terrible remorse. He had fallen, once more, victim to his own terrible brilliance. He had helped a colonial power (Farrow) wreak havoc and injury on an innocent people (the Upward Islanders) and he had been proud to do it.

The thought of those islanders walking around with blue hands suddenly seemed obscene and terrible to him and he immediately sent a memo to the managing director wherein he requested that an armed guard be placed on the warehouse at all times and that the man be given instructions to shoot anyone attempting to enter the warehouse without proper reason. He was confident that one wounding (unfortunate though that might be) would act as an effective deterrent and prevent the realization of the nightmare he had created. He investigated the award rates for armed guards and included in his memo a breakdown of all costs involved in the scheme. The amounts were so minor that the matter was approved without comment, although it seems likely that Vincent was pushing the Upward Island idea to the point where it would become a private joke amongst his fellow directors.

Satisfied with all this Vincent went off to a meeting of the Vietnam Moratorium Committee where, dressed in faded jeans and a blue workshirt, he was among those who supported a call for physical confrontation with the police. Excepting the few who suspected he was an agent provocateur, those who saw him speak were impressed by the emotion of his appeal and the fact that there were tears in his eyes when he spoke about the Vietnamese people.

It would be wrong to think that the tears were false or his appeal cynical. Vincent was continually in a state of conflict between his heartfelt principles and his need to be well thought of by people.

I don't think that there's any need to say any more about Vincent's life at this time. The shipment duly arrived at Upward Island and was stored as expected. Considerable quantities of Eupholon were stolen. Several islanders were shot dead by overzealous guards, many were wounded.

It is thought that the Gilbert and Sullivan revolution which took place on Upward Island last week may well have been directly attributable to these shootings. Vincent himself chooses to believe this, which is no reason for believing that it isn't true. Certainly it was a painless revolution and the small island, against the advice but not the wishes of the Australian government, was granted its independence. The company was expelled and its stocks of Eupholon confiscated. This caused Farrow International no pains at all as by this time it had become obvious, even to Birmingham, that Eupholon would never be acceptable to the market again.

Reports of the revolution have noted the blue hands of certain members of the revolution, but these have been generally described in the press as "war-paint".

It is on account of those blue hands that Vincent is sitting in my room and weeping.

In the year that has elapsed since the first board meeting he has slowly and gracelessly slid downhill. He became more and more outspoken in his anti-war activities until such time as these activities became an embarrassment to the company and he was fired on the direct instruction of Birmingham. It is perhaps unfortunate that at the same time the members of the Moratorium Committee discovered that he was actually a director of Farrow (whose French subsidiary was actively involved in the production of chemical warfare agents) and expelled him for his moral duplicity.

With these two emotional props removed Vincent went to pieces. He departed for Queensland to write but only got as far as Lismore where he was looked after briefly by communards.

His memory of events after this time is either unclear or so embarrassing to him that he is not prepared to reveal any significant details. He still insists that it all came to a climax two months ago with him being interned in Long Bay for assaulting a policeman at a demonstration, but I know this is untrue. It is possible he would have liked the idea of going to Long Bay, but he never has.

Now I can let you into a secret.

This is something I've been hoping might happen as I've worked. Had it not happened, this little account of Vincent's involvement with Upward Island would still have been of some real interest. However, recent events mean that I may be able to pursue the matter in a more purposeful way.

Vincent assaulted me last night. He came home with some people I'd never seen before, demanded I feed them, abused me when I refused, and punched me in the mouth when they left.

I'm afraid that I am now angry with him. I can no longer be dispassionate. The tiny part of me that observed Vincent with god-like pity has gone. I talked of revenge before. I was speaking of some minor bitching revenge of exploiting his story for my own gain. Now, however, I have a broken tooth which will have to be capped. It'll cost me two hundred dollars. My warfare with Vincent has come into the open.

I have told him to go and I will not change my mind. He knows it. At this moment his bags are packed but he is staying to finish dismantling the brick wall, a job he does with sullen thoroughness. He watches me typing over the top of it, a self-satisfied smirk on his face. I'd love to know what he thought he was doing with that brick wall. I'm sure it represents all kinds of incredible things for him. There is mortar dust over the dishes in the kitchen and all the furniture. There is mortar dust over the typewriter and between my teeth.

Well, Vincent my friend, the paper I work for is committed to sending me to Upward Island to look at this quaint little revolution. And now I've got a little background information from you, I'll use it and broaden it in the best way I can. I shall publicize you, Vincent, both here and on Upward Island. I'm sure the leaders of Upward Island will be most interested to know who is responsible for their blue hands. I'm not sure if you're legally responsible but I'm sure you should be.

PART 2

I have led you on with promises of a spectacular revenge, and now I will tell you that there shall be no revenge. Instead, I hope, a more substantial meal awaits you.

In four days on Upward Island I have seen three months' planning come undone. Am I so shallow, so easily swayed? Am I like an adolescent girl, jumping from love to hatred with every change in the weather?

Whatever my mental balance, there is more than a little explaining to do. Vincent is sitting on my bed in the Rainbow Motel, Upward Island. The fan turns overhead. The cockroaches stroll casually across the concrete floor. In the corner, above the basin, a little lizard lies, occasionally making small bird noises.

Vincent informs me that he is a chee-chuk.

He leans back against the pillow and I observe for the twentieth time what I never saw until this week: what lovely legs he has: long, slim straight legs as deeply tanned as rich students on long holidays. He looks so clean, so healthy. His beard is gone and there is no longer anything to veil his fine sensitive chiselled features with those beautiful sad grey eyes. Vincent, did I tell you that even when I was most angry with you I loved your eyes? They are less of an enigma to me now.

We have not arrived easily at this still, calm moment in this little room. We have travelled via suspicion and rage. I have watched him, on other days, as he earnestly helped me prepare my article, providing me with facts I hadn't known about his past, and easing my way into knowledge of his present. He has acted as my guide and denied me nothing and I watched carefully for his sleight of hand as he prepared the scaffolding for his own execution.

But there have been no tricks. Neither has there been remorse, tears, demands, or violence.

Instead I have come to envy him his calm, his contentment, his ability to sit still and keep his silence.

Vincent left for Upward Island on the day I threw him out. He had been planning it from the time he met me. He paid for the fare with money from my stolen books and records and a number of even less savoury transactions. I can imagine him arriving: bedraggled, dirty, full of guilt and speed in equal proportions, going from one bar to the next in search of someone who would forgive him the sin he hadn't the courage to confess. He had no money, no plan, and existed in drunken agony at the bottom of the big black pit he had dug for himself. He had come, classically, with remorse, but the remorse would not go away and with each day he fell further and further into the grips of despair. He couldn't leave. It was impossible to stay.

It was finally Solly Ling, the new president himself, who picked him up off the floor and took him home. Taking him for a derelict (which he was) Solly set about drying him out. He found him clothes and gave him food and then, sternly, put him to work.

Vincent had never done sustained physical labour in his life. But now he was forced to work on the building of the Upward Island school. There was no alternative. He dug stump holes until his hands were raw and bleeding. He carried bricks until his arms only existed as a nagging pain in his brain. He poured concrete.

He spoke little and never complained. There was a logic in it. It was a penance. He accepted it.

Solly had cleared out an old shed in his backyard and there Vincent, wide-eyed and sleepless, listened with terror to toads and rats and flying foxes and other nocturnal mysteries slither and flap and eat and dig around the hut.

Vincent and Solly ate together, mostly in silence, for Vincent was terrified of revealing anything of his past. But Solly was a patient man and a curious one. He sensed Vincent's education and with one question one day and another the next he finally learned that Vincent was a lawyer and an economist, that he had worked for big companies including several banks. At that time the island council was making heavy weather of the constitution and one night Solly broached the subject with Vincent and he watched with pleasure as Vincent took the thing apart and put it together in a neat, simple and logical way. The next day Vincent met the council. He was patient and self-effacing. Solly watched him and saw a sensitive diplomat, a man who listened to every speaker and was able to see the value of a sensible objection, but who could also politely point out the disadvantages of a less sensible one.

It was a touchy business. The council could have rejected him, found him patronizing, or too clever by half. But none of these things happened. Vincent's guilt had made his nerve ends as raw as his blistered hands and he felt their feelings with a peculiar intensity. He acted as a servant, never once imposing his own will.

His service to the council, however, was but a drop of water on the fires of his guilt. He sat in the old Waterside Workers Union shed where the council meetings were held and all he could see were the blue hands of the councillors. Surrounded by the evidence of his crime there was no room for escape.

He drafted three new prawning contracts and volunteered for the unpleasant job of cleaning the mortar off the old bricks for the school. He painted Solly's house for him and went on to start the vegetable garden.

These acts were in no way intended to curry favour or gain friendship (in fact they were some sort of substitute for wrath) but they succeeded in spite of that. The islanders took to him: not only was he educated but he was also prepared to work at the nastiest jobs side by side with them, he could tell funny stories, he didn't flirt with their wives, and he'd negotiated the best damn prawn contracts they'd ever had.

It is doubtful if Vincent noticed this. He was not accustomed to being liked and would have never expected it on Upward Island.

Given his skills, it's natural enough that he should have been co-opted as an assistant to the council. But that he should be elected formally to the council after only two months is an indication of the popularity he had begun to enjoy. Again, it is doubtful if he saw it.

On the night after his election to the council he sat on the verandah with Solly and looked out at the approaching night, a night that was still foreign to him and full of things he neither liked nor understood.

Solly was a big man. The stomach that bulged beneath his white singlet betrayed his love of beer, just as the muscular forearms attested to his years as a waterside worker. The great muscled calves that protruded from his rolled-up trousers were the legs of a young man, but the creased black face and the curly greying hair betrayed his age. It was a face that could show, almost simultaneously, the dignity of a judge and the bright-eyed recklessness of a born larrikin.

He sat on the verandah of his high-stilted house, one big blue hand around a beer bottle, the other around a glass which he filled and passed to Vincent. The hand which took the glass was now calloused and tough. The arm, never thick, was now wiry and hard, tattooed with nicks and scratches and dusty with mortar. A flea made its way through the hairs and dust on the arm. Vincent saw it and knocked it off. It wasn't worth killing them. There were too many.

As the darkness finally shrouded the garden a great clamour began in the hen house.

"Bloody python," said Solly.

"I'll go." Vincent stood up. He didn't want to go. He hadn't gone yet, but it was about time he went.

"I'll go," Solly picked up a shotgun and walked off into the dark. Vincent sipped his beer and knew that next time he'd have to go.

There was a shot and Solly came back holding the remains of a python in one hand and a dead chicken in the other.

"Too late," he grinned, "snake got him first."

He sat down, leaving the dead bird on the floor, and the snake draped across the railing.

"Now you're on the council," he said, "we're going to have to do something to get your hands in shape."

"Ah, they're all right. The blisters have all gone." Vincent wondered what blisters had to do with the council.

"I wasn't talking about blisters, Mr Economics. I was discussing the matter of your hands." Solly chuckled. His white teeth flashed in the light from the kitchen window. "You're going to have to take some medicine."

Vincent was used to being teased. He had faced poisonous grasshoppers, threatened cyclones and dozens of other tricks they liked to play on him. He didn't know what this was about, but he'd find out soon enough.

"What medicine is that, Sol?"

"Why," laughed Solly, "little pills, of course. You need a few little pills now you're on the council. We can't have you sitting on the council with the wrong-coloured hands."

Vincent couldn't believe what he was hearing. They'd never discussed the blue hands. His mind had been full of it. Not a day had gone by when the blue hands hadn't caused him pain. But he had avoided mentioning them for fear of touching so nasty a wound.

"Eupholon?" He said it. The word.

"For a smart boy, you're very slow. Sure, that's what they call it."

Vincent's scalp prickled. He had said the name. How did he know the name? They knew about him. It was a trap. Now it would be the time for justice to be done. They would force him to take the poison he'd given them.

There was a silence.

"Solly, you know where I worked before?"

"Sure, you was the great Economics man."

"I mean what company."

"Sure, you worked for Mr Farrow." Solly's voice was calm, but Vincent's ears were ringing in the silence between the words.

"How you know that, Solly?"

"Oh, you got a lady friend who reckons you're a bad fella. She wrote us a letter. Three pages. Boy, what you do to her, eh?" He laughed again. "She's a very angry lady, that one."

"Anita."

"I forget her name," he waved an arm, dismissing it. "Some name like that."

In the corner of his eye, Vincent saw the headless python twitch.

"That why you want me to take the pills?"

"Christ no." Solly roared with laughter, a great whooping laugh that slid from a wheezing treble to deepest bass. "Christ no, you crazy bastard." He stood up and came and sat by Vincent on the step, hugging him. "You crazy Economics bastard, no." He wiped his eyes with a large blue hand. "Oh shit. You are what they call a one-off model. You know what that means?"

"What?" Vincent was numb, almost beyond speech.

"It means you are fucking unique. I love you."

Vincent was very confused. He slapped at a few mosquitoes and tried to puzzle it out. Every shred of fact that his life was based on seemed as insubstantial as fairy floss. "You don't care I sent the pills here?"

"Care!" the laughter came again. "To put it properly to you, we are fucking delighted you sent the pills here. Everything is fine. Why should we be mad with you?"

"The blue hands ..."

"You are not only crazy," said Solly affectionately. "You are also nine-tenths blind. Don't you notice anything about the blue hands?"

"What do you mean?"

"I mean you're bloody blind. All the best men got blue hands. All the bravest men. We're bloody proud of these hands. You got blue hands on Upward, Vincent, you got respect. How come you can live here so long and not notice that? We had to beat that damn guard to get these hands, Vincent. When the time came to kick out Farrow, everyone knows who's got the guts to do it, because we're the only ones that's got the hands."

"So I've got to have blue hands, to be on the council?"

"You got it. You got perfect understanding."

"OK," Vincent grinned. He felt as light as air. He poured himself another beer. He wanted to get drunk and sing songs. He didn't dwell on the idea of the blue hands. That was nothing. All he said was, "Where do I get the pills?"

Solly scratched his head. "Well, I suppose there must be some up at the warehouse. You better go up and take a look."

Vincent started laughing then, laughing with pure joy and relief. The more he thought about it, the funnier it was and the more he laughed. And Solly, sitting beside him, laughed too.

I imagine the pair of them hooting and cackling into the dark tropical night, a dead chicken at their feet, a headless python twitching on the railing. Not surprisingly, they were laughing about different things.

Late the next morning Vincent set off to walk to the warehouse. He felt marvellous. In the kitchen he cut himself some sandwiches and on the dusty road he found a long stick. He walked the three-mile track with a light heart, delighting in the long seas of golden grass, finding beauty in the muddy mangrove shoreline and its heat-hazed horizon.

Vincent in white shorts with his cut lunch and walking stick like a tourist off to visit Greek ruins.

The warehouse shone silver in the harsh midday sun. There was something written on the side. As he came up the last steep slope he finally made it out: someone had painted a blue hand on the longest side of the building and added, for good measure: WARNING — DEATH. He wondered vaguely if this had been the manager's work.

How gloriously ineffective it had been. What total misunderstanding had been displayed.

He was still a hundred yards from the warehouse when he saw a man, dressed in white shorts like himself, standing at the front of the building.

The man called.

Vincent waved casually and continued on, wondering who it was. The man was white. He had seen no white people until now.

As he walked up the hill, being careful not to slip on the shale which made up the embankment, the man disappeared for a second and then came back with what looked like a rifle. Vincent's first thought was: a snake, he's seen a snake. He grasped his stick firmly and walked ahead, his eyes on the ground in front.

So he didn't see the man lift the rifle to his shoulder and fire.

The bullet hit the ground a yard ahead of him and ricocheted dangerously off the rocks.

Vincent stopped and yelled. The man was a lunatic. The bloody thing had nearly got him. Even as he shouted he saw him raise the rifle again.

This time he felt the wind of the bullet next to his cheek.

He didn't stay to argue any longer, he turned to run, fell, dropped the sandwiches and stick and slithered belly down over shale for a good twenty feet. When he stood up it was to run.

From the next hill he saw the man with the gun walk down the hill, pick up the sandwiches and slowly saunter back to the warehouse.

Imagine Vincent, cut, bruised, covered in sweat, his eyes wide with outrage and anger as he strode into the Royal Hotel and found Solly at the bar.

"Solly, there's some crazy bastard at the warehouse. He shot at me. With a fucking rifle."

"No," said Solly, his eyes wide.

"Yes," said Vincent. "The bugger could have killed me."

They bought drinks for Vincent that night and he finally learned that the guards he had once employed for Farrow were now employed by the council to continue their valuable work. Those with blue hands did not want them devalued.

And Vincent, nursing his bruises at the bar, tried to smile at the joke. It was not going to be as easy to get his blue hands as he'd thought.

Faced with the terrifying prospect of death or wounding, he began to consider the possibility of blue hands more carefully. Whilst they would give him some prestige on Upward Island, they would make him grotesque anywhere else, of interest only to doctors and laughing schoolchildren on buses. He saw himself in big cities on summer days, wearing white gloves like Mickey Mouse. He saw the embarrassed eyes of people he knew and, he says, my own triumphant face as I revelled in the irony of it: Dr Strangelove with radiation poisoning.

If there had been anywhere left to run to, he would have gone. If there was a job he could have taken, he would have taken it. Even without this, he would have gone, if he'd had the money.

But he had no money. No chance of a job. And he was forced to consider what he would do.

And as he thought about it, lying on his bed, drinking with Solly, nailing down the roof on the schoolhouse, he came to realize that not only couldn't he leave, he didn't want to. He came to see that he was liked, respected, even loved. For the first time in his life he considered the possibility of happiness. It was a strange thing for him to look at, and he examined it with wonder.

What was so wrong with Upward Island?

He couldn't think of anything.

Did he miss the city? Not particularly. Did he miss friends? He didn't have any. Did he miss success? He had failed. Strangely, he had become somebody: he was Vince, he worked down at the school, he cleaned bricks, he did the prawn contracts.

On the morning of the second day after the shooting he came to the realization that he had no option but to stay. And if he was to stay he had no option but to get his hands the right colour. He looked the prospect of the warehouse in the eye and was filled with terror at what he saw.

Vincent was frightened of snakes, lizards, bats, spiders, scorpions, large ants, and noises in the night he didn't understand. He used what daylight he could and crept to the point in the track where the warehouse was just visible, then he sat on a rock and waited for darkness.

His face and hands were blackened. His shirt sleeves were long. In his pocket he carried the torch Solly had given him. As the sun set a crow flew across the sky, uttering a cry so forlorn that it struck a chill in Vincent's heart.

The sky turned from melodramatic red, to grey, and slowly to darkness. He edged painfully up the path convinced he would put his hand on a snake. A rustle in the grass kept him immobile for two minutes. He stared into the darkness with his hair bristling. A toad jumped across his boot and he slipped backwards in fright. He pressed on, crawling. His hand grasped a nettle. A sharp rock pierced his trousers and tore his skin. Tiny pieces of gravel inflicted a hundred minor tortures on his naked hands. A flying fox, its wings as loud as death itself, flew over him on its way to a wild guava bush.

Yet there were few noises loud enough to distract him from his beating heart. It felt as if his head was full of beating blood.

Slowly, very slowly, he edged his way to the warehouse. Once it had been nothing more than a word in a memo, but now it gleamed horribly under a bright moon, the colourless words on its side clearly visible and exactly calculated in their effect.

The guards were well paid and took three shifts. They were established in very good houses, were given three months' holiday a year and were encouraged to bring their families to Upward. They were stable, serious men, and if they mixed little in the society, they were certainly vital to it.

Tonight it was Van Dogen. They had teased Vincent about this, saying Van Dogen was the best shot of them all.

He could hear Van Dogen above him, walking up and down on the gravel. Once his face flared white from the darkness as he lit a cigarette. Vincent watched the tiny red speck of cigarette as it swung around the building like a deadly firefly.

Now, he made his way slowly to where there was no red dot, to the back of the warehouse where the water tank stood. For here, he knew, was the way to the roof. Onto the wooden stand, then to the tank, a slow dangerous arm lift to the roof. Now he moved on borrowed sandshoes across the vast expanse of metal roof, a loud footstep disguised by the noises caused by the contraction of the metal in the cool night air.

The third skylight from the end awaited him as promised. He climbed through slowly and his dangling feet found the rafter.

Slowly, quietly, he closed the skylight and giddily, fearfully, lowered himself from the rafter.

He let go, hoping the superphosphate sacks were still below. It was further than he thought. He fell onto the hard bags with a frightened grunt.

In an instant there was a key in the door and the guard stood flashing a strong torch. Vincent rolled quietly from the bags. As he lay on top of two metal U-bolts he wanted to cry. He wanted to stand up and say: "Here I am."

Van Dogen couldn't shoot him. Not in cold blood. The whole thing was impossible. It was he, Vincent, who had constructed Van Dogen's original salary. He had invented Van Dogen. He had arranged aeroplanes to fly him through the sky. He had arranged for a gun. He had told Van Dogen to shoot.

Van Dogen walked the aisles of the vast warehouse. It took everything in Vincent to stop himself standing up. "Here I am. I'm a friend." He was like a man who jumps from a tall building because he is frightened of falling from it.

Van Dogen was faceless. A lethal shadow behind a bright light, the formless creature of the very brain that was now sending panic signals to every part of a prickling body.

But Van Dogen noticed nothing. It was simply part of his nightly routine and he left after a couple of minutes.

Vincent lay still for a long time, caught in the sticky webs of his nightmare. When he moved it was because a mouse ran across his shoulder and down his back. He shuddered and jumped back onto the superphosphate. Then although he felt himself already condemned, he moved to the crates of Eupholon. He blinked the torch on for half a second, then off. Another lightning flash. He found them. He took the hateful bottles and filled his shirt pockets and his trouser pockets with them. He didn't know how much to take. He took everything he could fit in.

And now he faced the side door. It was one of four doors. One was the right choice. Two were dangerous. One was deadly. He stood behind the side door and waited. He could hear nothing. No footstep, no breathing, nothing. Slowly, silently, he slid back the latch and waited. Still nothing.

He opened the door and ran. He had been told not to run. He ran straight into Van Dogen who had been standing in front of it.

Vincent shrieked with fear. The shriek came from him without warning, high and piercing, as horrible as a banshee wail. Van Dogen fell. Vincent fell. The track lay ahead. Vincent was berserk. He kicked Van Dogen's head and threw his rifle against the wall where it went off with a thunderclap.

Half falling, half running, Vincent was on the track down the hill. He tripped, fell, stood and ran. As he tripped the third time he heard a shot and felt a shock in his leg. But he could still run. He felt no pain. In his pockets the broken Eupholon bottles gently sliced his unfeeling skin.

When he woke he was in bed. There was a bandage on his leg and another on his chest. But the first thing he noticed were the three Eupholon bottles standing beside his bed. Beside them, the contents of the five other broken bottles were piled in a little saucer.

The little yellow capsules seemed as precious and beautiful as gold itself. He lay on his bed, laughing.

He balanced the little saucer on his stomach and smiled at the capsules. He took one, not bothering with water. He looked through the open door of the shed to where Solly was digging in the vegetable garden. He took another, impatient for the moment when he would have hands as beautiful as those that now grasped the garden spade.

My revenge lies about me in tatters. Shredded sheets of confusion drift through the air. My story written, but not a story I intended or one my editor will accept.

But I know, if I know anything, that he changed, and I now like him as much as I once despised him.

If I said I was a child, an adolescent, do not take me too literally. Whatever questions you ask of me I have asked myself. We might start with the simplest: has he conned me by helping me prepare my case against him?

It is a possibility. I can't reject it.

Am I reacting to the esteem in which he is held here? When I despised him he was a public joke. Now he is liked. Is this why I like him?

A possibility. I grasp it. It does not sting unduly.

Do I like him because he no longer demands my affection? Do I wish to conquer him now that he has less need of me?

Possibly. But so what?

Do I lack any solid system of values? Is this why I now find blue hands beautiful where once I called them grotesque?

Certainly I have changed. But there must be a functional basis for aesthetics. Blue hands on Upward Island are not blue hands anywhere else.

But then, what of this function? What of the regard blue hands are held in? Should prestige be granted only to the brave? Does physical bravery not suggest a certain lack of imagination? Is it a good qualification for those who will rule?

I don't know.

Is bravery seen to be a masculine virtue? Where are the women with blue hands?

There are none, as yet.

Then am I like a crippled female applauding male acts of bravado? No, I am not.

I know only that he walks slowly and talks calmly, is funny without being attention-seeking, accepts praise modestly and is now lying on my bed smiling at me.

I don't move. There is no hurry. But in a moment, sooner or later, I will go over to him and then I will, slowly, carefully, unzip his shorts and there I will see his beautiful blue penis thrusting its aquamarine head upwards towards me. It will be silky, the most curious silkiness imaginable.

I will kneel and take it in my mouth.

If I moan, you will not hear me. What I say, you will never know.

Questions, your questions, will rise like bubbles from deeper water, but I will disregard them, pass them, sinking lower to where there are no questions, nothing but a shimmering searing electric blue.

Conversations with Unicorns

1.

The unicorns do not understand.

We have had long conversations but it is difficult for them. They insist that I have come to collect the body of one of their number, but at the same time they point out that there is no body, that it was collected by another man before I arrived. They continue to insist on these points, laughing that I have come for something that is not there.

I have asked them why they think that I could only have come for one reason, and they have replied that this is the way it has always been; that the men come, like vultures, when there has been a death, to take care of the body.

I have suggested to them that men are cruel, but they have denied this, saying that men perform their God-given tasks efficiently. The men, they say, cannot be held responsible for the death of unicorns.

I mention guns. But they have no knowledge of guns, or, it turns out, of weapons of any sort. So I describe for them the deep trench that runs across the top of the ridge. I describe the parking lot behind the trench and the cars that arrive, filled with men and guns. They have no idea of the nature of cars or of their purpose — this is a red herring and I do not answer their questions about the nature of cars. I explain instead that the head of a unicorn is greatly prized by men who pay three thousand pounds for the privilege of shooting one. I explain how the men climb into the trench and wait for the unicorns to run across the moor.

When I return to the subject of guns the unicorns laugh, tossing their heads high and falling about the cave. And their leader, Moorav, smilingly warns me against blasphemy, saying that only God has the power to take life.

He tells me then how in the early days the unicorns lived for ever, being revered by both men and animals, and having no natural enemies. He says, however, that this was in pagan times, before God came into the world. God, he informs me, bestowed upon the unicorns (and I use his exact words) "the gift of death".

There is an old tale, he relates, which tells how the unicorns were brought across the water from a hot and strange land to this moor which is now their home. It was here that God gave them his promise regarding death and here, also, that He decreed that the males should live together in the caves on the North Knoll and the females in the caves on the South Knoll. These laws are still strictly observed to this day.

I ask if perhaps the God in the story had the appearance of a man. And Moorav replies that he does not think so, and that God, should he have any appearance at all, would be most likely to have the appearance of a unicorn, although he was no expert in these matters, and thought it better I ask one of the priests for confirmation of this.

I point out that it is only in the stretch between the males' cave and the females' cave — some two miles of open moorland — that the unicorns are killed, and Moorav says this is only natural, because they go nowhere else. He doesn't think it surprising that unicorns should never die in their caves — this, after all, has always been the case.

The unicorns are beginning to appear stupid to me, but this only increases my desire to protect them from the wealthy industrialists who come to hunt them.

I insist that they should guard themselves against the men who come to kill them, pointing out that God does not fire guns. They become more serious with this point, and I think perhaps I have made some progress. Moorav leaves the circle and goes to confer with others deeper in the cave.

To those remaining with me I say that if there is a God he certainly doesn't use a gun. I begin to explain the nature of the gun, its mechanism. I take as my model the Lee Enfield .303 with which I have had some little experience. I draw it in the dust of the cave floor. I explain the nature of men's wars and allude to weapons more complex and more cruel than the one I have outlined to them. I give them details of man's cruelties to man and to animals. I give, as examples, the slaughter of seals, the systematic murder of sheep and cattle, the subjection of horses, the killing of lions, the establishment of zoos and circuses.

Most of these animals, however, are unknown to them, although the lion is described in one of their legends.

I ask them what they eat. Mistaking this for a request, they bring me a meal: wild honey, brown bread, and milk. I ask them if they eat meat. They do not understand this. I explain that meat is the flesh of animals. This also is taken for a request (although I stated, explicitly, that this was not the case), and they become troubled, talking to each other in whispers.

I continue my dissertation on the crimes of men but am interrupted by Moorav, who has returned with two of his fellows. He begs me to stop my talk. I reply that I am only concerned for their safety. He introduces his two friends, one of whom is a priest, wise in the ways and laws of God. The priest is old and has a white beard, something I have not observed in the others. I explain again, for his benefit, the nature of man, his need to kill other creatures, his consumption of their flesh.

At this point I find myself pinned on two sides by young unicorns, their huge flanks almost crushing my ribcage.

The priest is saying something about blasphemy.

I say, I have only come here to save you from death. I did not come to discuss theology, only facts. I ask them if the death of a unicorn is not always accompanied by a loud bang.

The priest says that this is so, but that there are also many bangs which do not signal a death.

I revert once more to a discussion of guns, ammunition, ballistics.

The priest asks me how it is that the unicorns have never seen these instruments. I describe, once more, the deep trench that runs across the top of the ridge, and explain, again, that the men can kill from far away. I describe the way in which the unicorn's head is removed and how it is mounted on the walls of the homes of rich men. I am becoming angry. They continue to whisper among themselves, not wishing to listen. Their accents, at first pleasant, seem to have become more rustic and so more stupid.

They also, it would appear, have become disenchanted with me. My clothes are ripped from behind. They force me, somehow, to a kneeling position and make me run on all fours, coming at me from all angles with their horns. They are calling me a blasphemer. There are tears in my eyes, but not caused by pain. A large unicorn sits suddenly on me, pushing my face into the dirt. My ribs have surely broken.

There is a searing pain in my side and a dull blow to my head. That is all I can remember on that occasion.

2.

The hunters found me on the moor and, unaware of my missionary activities, treated me kindly, taking me to a nearby hospital where I was well looked after.

Upon my release, my right leg in plaster and my ribs securely taped, I returned to the moor, taking with me a rifle I had purchased. I would demonstrate to the unicorns the nature of the gun, and, with luck, arrange for them to make an exodus from the area to some more remote part of the moor where they might never be found.

I bore them no ill-will for the attack. It was the product of ignorance and I could expect no more.

3.

Moorav was surprised to see me. However, neither he nor his followers were unkind to me. They fed me well and the priest came over and ate bread beside me, asking if I had recovered. He referred to my behaviour as "your trouble" and asked me if I was better.

I said I had brought an instrument that would prove me either right or wrong. The priest smiled and said he hoped I wasn't about to start all over again. I indicated the gun and gave it its name. He looked at it and asked some questions which I answered simply enough. They related more to the materials of manufacture than to the function.

After the meal I persuaded them to come with me to the door of the cave. Moorav was nervous, but I was insistent. With the unicorns standing in a semicircle behind me I raised the gun to my shoulder and fired across the moor.

Strangely, they were not at all impressed. The bang, they said, was in no way like the bang of death, and for proof they pointed out that no one had, in fact, died. And they began, once more, to laugh at me. I, for my part, became angry and desperate that I should prove my point.

Eventually Moorav stepped forward and suggested that we should only settle the matter if I pointed the weapon at him. I said no, for it would kill him. He laughed once more and said I was frightened of failing. (I had noticed, on this second visit, that they treated me as a madman, perhaps having decided that I was ignorant but not dangerous. The charge of blasphemy was not raised again.)

Sadly, I asked Moorav if he was prepared to die for the sake of his people.

He said, it was only the unicorns in pagan times who did not die, I am not frightened of dying.

I engaged in no calculations for I knew that, should I do so, I would never prove my point. I raised the rifle and pointed it at his head. For an instant I hesitated, but then, with the unicorns behind me still laughing, I pulled the trigger. Moorav moaned and staggered. Blood rushed from the wound in his head and he sank slowly to the ground, his eyes rolling.

There was silence behind me. No one spoke.

4.

I myself buried Moorav in a shallow grave. It was a slow process as the unicorns possess no digging tools, and they still expected that a man would come to remove Moorav, a man other than myself.

5.

The cave has been quiet all day. Unicorns lie in groups but do not talk. Finally the priest approaches me and indicates that he wishes a word. He says I have done his people a grave disservice, that I had removed the gift of death from them. He says that his people will now surely move to another part of the moor, as I had wished. There will be a return to the old times and no one will die. The unicorns, without Gods or enemies, will slowly sink into deep despair and spend their hours in search of sleep, where, perhaps, they will dream of dying. They will forget, eventually, that dying was ever possible.

The priest now reveals that he has attempted to persuade the unicorns to remain where they are, but they are frightened and, should he put his authority to the test, they would not obey him. He asks me only one thing, that I should use my instrument on him. He would regard it as a great favour.

I load the rifle, sadly. Inside the cave the unicorns lie quietly, unaware that they will live for ever.

American Dreams

No one can, to this day, remember what it was we did to offend him. Dyer the butcher remembers a day when he gave him the wrong meat and another day when he served someone else first by mistake. Often when Dyer gets drunk he recalls this day and curses himself for his foolishness. But no one seriously believes that it was Dyer who offended him.

But one of us did something. We slighted him terribly in some way, this small meek man with the rimless glasses and neat suit who used to smile so nicely at us all. We thought, I suppose, he was a bit of a fool and sometimes he was so quiet and grey that we ignored him, forgetting he was there at all.

When I was a boy I often stole apples from the trees at his house up in Mason's Lane. He often saw me. No, that's not correct. Let me say I often sensed that he saw me. I sensed him peering out from behind the lace curtains of his house. And I was not the only one. Many of us came to take his apples, alone and in groups, and it is possible that he chose to exact payment for all these apples in his own peculiar way.

Yet I am sure it wasn't the apples.

What has happened is that we all, all eight hundred of us, have come to remember small transgressions against Mr Gleason, who once lived amongst us.

My father, who has never borne malice against a single living creature, still believes that Gleason meant to do us well, that he loved the town more than any of us. My father says we have treated the town badly in our minds. We have used it, this little valley, as nothing more than a stopping place. Somewhere on the way to somewhere else. Even those of us who have been here many years have never taken the town seriously. Oh yes, the place is pretty. The hills are green and the woods thick. The stream is full of fish. But it is not where we would rather be.

For years we have watched the films at the Roxy and dreamed, if not of America, then at least of our capital city. For our own town, my father says, we have nothing but contempt. We have treated it badly, like a whore. We have cut down the giant shady trees in the main street to make doors for the school house and seats for the football pavilion. We have left big holes all over the countryside from which we have taken brown coal and given back nothing.

The commercial travellers who buy fish and chips at George the Greek's care for us more than we do, because we all have dreams of the big city, of wealth, of modern houses, of big motor cars: American dreams, my father has called them.

Although my father ran a petrol station he was also an inventor. He sat in his office all day drawing strange pieces of equipment on the back of delivery dockets. Every spare piece of paper in the house was covered with these little drawings and my mother would always be very careful about throwing away any piece of paper no matter how small. She would look on both sides of any piece of paper very carefully and always preserved any that had so much as a pencil mark.

I think it was because of this that my father felt that he understood Gleason. He never said as much, but he inferred that he understood Gleason because he, too, was concerned with similar problems. My father was working on plans for a giant gravel crusher, but occasionally he would become distracted and become interested in something else.

There was, for instance, the time when Dyer the butcher bought a new bicycle with gears, and for a while my father talked of nothing else but the gears. Often I would see him across the road squatting down beside Dyer's bicycle as if he were talking to it.

We all rode bicycles because we didn't have the money for anything better. My father did have an old Chev truck, but he rarely used it and it occurs to me now that it might have had some mechanical problem that was impossible to solve, or perhaps it was just that he was saving it, not wishing to wear it out all at once. Normally, he went everywhere on his bicycle and, when I was younger, he carried me on the crossbar, both of us dismounting to trudge up the hills that led into and out of the main street. It was a common sight in our town to see people pushing bicycles. They were as much a burden as a means of transport.

Gleason also had his bicycle and every lunchtime he pushed and pedalled it home from the shire offices to his little weatherboard house out at Mason's Lane. It was a three-mile ride and people said that he went home for lunch because he was fussy and wouldn't eat either his wife's sandwiches or the hot meal available at Mrs Lessing's café.

But while Gleason pedalled and pushed his bicycle to and from the shire offices everything in our town proceeded as normal. It was only when he retired that things began to go wrong.

Because it was then that Mr Gleason started supervising the building of the wall around the two-acre plot up on Bald Hill. He paid too much for this land. He bought it from Johnny Weeks, who now, I am sure, believes the whole episode was his fault, firstly for cheating Gleason, secondly for selling him the land at all. But Gleason hired some Chinese and set to work to build his wall. It was then that we knew that we'd offended him. My father rode all the way out to Bald Hill and tried to talk Mr Gleason out of his wall. He said there was no need for us to build walls. That no one wished to spy on Mr Gleason or whatever he wished to do on Bald Hill. He said no one was in the least bit interested in Mr Gleason. Mr Gleason, neat in a new sportscoat, polished his glasses and smiled vaguely at his feet. Bicycling back, my father thought that he had gone too far. Of course we had an interest in Mr Gleason. He pedalled back and asked him to attend a dance that was to be held on the next Friday, but Mr Gleason said he didn't dance.

"Oh well," my father said, "any time, just drop over."

Mr Gleason went back to supervising his family of Chinese labourers on his wall.

Bald Hill towered high above the town and from my father's small filling station you could sit and watch the wall going up. It was an interesting sight. I watched it for two years, while I waited for customers who rarely came. After school and on Saturdays I had all the time in the world to watch the agonizing progress of Mr Gleason's wall. It was as painful as a clock. Sometimes I could see the Chinese labourers running at a jog-trot carrying bricks on long wooden planks. The hill was bare, and on this bareness Mr Gleason was, for some reason, building a wall.

In the beginning people thought it peculiar that someone would build such a big wall on Bald Hill. The only thing to recommend Bald Hill was the view of the town, and Mr Gleason was building a wall that denied that view. The top soil was thin and bare clay showed through in places. Nothing would ever grow there. Everyone assumed that Gleason had simply gone mad and after the initial interest they accepted his madness as they accepted his wall and as they accepted Bald Hill itself.

Occasionally someone would pull in for petrol at my father's filling station and ask about the wall and my father would shrug and I would see, once more, the strangeness of it.

"A house?" the stranger would ask. "Up on that hill?"

"No," my father would say, "chap named Gleason is building a wall."

And the strangers would want to know why, and my father would shrug and look up at Bald Hill once more. "Damned if I know," he'd say.

Gleason still lived in his old house at Mason's Lane. It was a plain weatherboard house, with a rose garden at the front, a vegetable garden down the side, and an orchard at the back.

At night we kids would sometimes ride out to Bald Hill on our bicycles. It was an agonizing, muscle-twitching ride, the worst part of which was a steep, unmade road up which we finally pushed our bikes, our lungs rasping in the night air. When we arrived we found nothing but walls. Once we broke down some of the brickwork and another time we threw stones at the tents where the Chinese labourers slept. Thus we expressed our frustration at this inexplicable thing.

The wall must have been finished on the day before my twelfth birthday. I remember going on a picnic birthday party up to Eleven Mile Creek and we lit a fire and cooked chops at a bend in the river from where it was possible to see the walls on Bald Hill. I remember standing with a hot chop in my hand and someone saying, "Look, they're leaving!"

We stood on the creek bed and watched the Chinese labourers walking their bicycles slowly down the hill. Someone said they were going to build a chimney up at the mine at A.1 and certainly there is a large brick chimney there now, so I suppose they built it.

When the word spread that the walls were finished most of the town went up to look. They walked around the four walls which were as interesting as any other brick walls. They stood in front of the big wooden gates and tried to peer through, but all they could see was a small blind wall that had obviously been constructed for this special purpose. The walls themselves were ten feet high and topped with broken glass and barbed wire. When it became obvious that we were not going to discover the contents of the enclosure, we all gave up and went home.

Mr Gleason had long since stopped coming into town. His wife came instead, wheeling a pram down from Mason's Lane to Main Street and filling it with groceries and meat (they never bought vegetables, they grew their own) and wheeling it back to Mason's Lane. Sometimes you would see her standing with the pram halfway up the Gell Street hill. Just standing there, catching her breath. No one asked her about the wall. They knew she wasn't responsible for the wall and they felt sorry for her, having to bear the burden of the pram and her husband's madness. Even when she began to visit Dixon's hardware and buy plaster of Paris and tins of paint and waterproofing compound, no one asked her what these things were for. She had a way of averting her eyes that indicated her terror of questions. Old Dixon carried the plaster of Paris and the tins of paint out to her pram for her and watched her push them away. "Poor woman," he said, "poor bloody woman."

From the filling station where I sat dreaming in the sun, or from the enclosed office where I gazed mournfully at the rain, I would see, occasionally, Gleason entering or leaving his walled compound, a tiny figure way up on Bald Hill. And I'd think "Gleason," but not much more.

Occasionally strangers drove up there to see what was going on, often egged on by locals who told them it was a Chinese temple or some other silly thing. Once a group of Italians had a picnic outside the walls and took photographs of each other standing in front of the closed door. God knows what they thought it was.

But for five years between my twelfth and seventeenth birthdays there was nothing to interest me in Gleason's walls. Those years seem lost to me now and I can remember very little of them. I developed a crush on Susy Markin and followed her back from the swimming pool on my bicycle. I sat behind her in the pictures and wandered past her house. Then her parents moved to another town and I sat in the sun and waited for them to come back.

We became very keen on modernization. When coloured paints became available the whole town went berserk and brightly coloured houses blossomed overnight. But the paints were not of good quality and quickly faded and peeled, so that the town looked like a garden of dead flowers. Thinking of those years, the only real thing I recall is the soft hiss of bicycle tyres on the main street. When I think of it now it seems very peaceful, but I remember then that the sound induced in me a feeling of melancholy, a feeling somehow mixed with the early afternoons when the sun went down behind Bald Hill and the town felt as sad as an empty dance hall on a Sunday afternoon.

And then, during my seventeenth year, Mr Gleason died. We found out when we saw Mrs Gleason's pram parked out in front of Phonsey Joy's Funeral Parlour. It looked very sad, that pram, standing by itself in the windswept street. We came and looked at the pram and felt sad for Mrs Gleason. She hadn't had much of a life.

Phonsey Joy carried old Mr Gleason out to the cemetery by the Parwan Railway Station and Mrs Gleason rode behind in a taxi. People watched the old hearse go by and thought, "Gleason," but not much else.

And then, less than a month after Gleason had been buried out at the lonely cemetery by the Parwan Railway Station, the Chinese labourers came back. We saw them push their bicycles up the hill. I stood with my father and Phonsey Joy and wondered what was going on.

And then I saw Mrs Gleason trudging up the hill. I nearly didn't recognize her, because she didn't have her pram. She carried a black umbrella and walked slowly up Bald Hill and it wasn't until she stopped for breath and leant forward that I recognized her.

"It's Mrs Gleason," I said, "with the Chinese."

But it wasn't until the next morning that it became obvious what was happening. People lined the main street in the way they do for a big funeral but, instead of gazing towards the Grant Street corner, they all looked up at Bald Hill.

All that day and all the next people gathered to watch the destruction of the walls. They saw the Chinese labourers darting to and fro, but it wasn't until they knocked down a large section of the wall facing the town that we realized there really was something inside. It was impossible to see what it was, but there was something there. People stood and wondered and pointed out Mrs Gleason to each other as she went to and fro supervising the work.

And finally, in ones and twos, on bicycles and on foot, the whole town moved up to Bald Hill. Mr Dyer closed up his butcher shop and my father got out the old Chev truck and we finally arrived up at Bald Hill with twenty people on board. They crowded into the back tray and hung onto the running boards and my father grimly steered his way through the crowds of bicycles and parked just where the dirt track gets really steep. We trudged up this last steep track, never for a moment suspecting what we would find at the top.

It was very quiet up there. The Chinese labourers worked diligently, removing the third and fourth walls and cleaning the bricks which they stacked neatly in big piles. Mrs Gleason said nothing either. She stood in the only remaining corner of the walls and looked defiantly at the townspeople, who stood open-mouthed where another corner had been.

And between us and Mrs Gleason was the most incredibly beautiful thing I had ever seen in my life. For one moment I didn't recognize it. I stood open-mouthed, and breathed the surprising beauty of it. And then I realized it was our town. The buildings were two feet high and they were a little rough but very correct. I saw Mr Dyer nudge my father and whisper that Gleason had got the faded U in the BUTCHER sign of his shop.

I think at that moment everyone was overcome with a feeling of simple joy. I can't remember ever having felt so uplifted and happy. It was perhaps a childish emotion but I looked up at my father and saw a smile of such warmth spread across his face that I knew he felt just as I did. Later he told me that he thought Gleason had built the model of our town just for this moment, to let us see the beauty of our town, to make us proud of ourselves and to stop the American Dreams we were so prone to. For the rest, my father said, was not Gleason's plan and he could not have foreseen the things that happened afterwards.

I have come to think that this view of my father's is a little sentimental and also, perhaps, insulting to Gleason. I personally believe that he knew everything that would happen. One day the proof of my theory may be discovered. Certainly there are in existence some personal papers, and I firmly believe that these papers will show that Gleason knew exactly what would happen.

We had been so overcome by the model of the town that we hadn't noticed what was the most remarkable thing of all. Not only had Gleason built the houses and the shops of our town, he had also peopled it. As we tiptoed into the town we suddenly found ourselves. "Look," I said to Mr Dyer, "there you are."

And there he was, standing in front of his shop in his apron. As I bent down to examine the tiny figure I was staggered by the look on its face. The modelling was crude, the paintwork was sloppy, and the face a little too white, but the expression was absolutely perfect: those pursed, quizzical lips, and the eyebrows lifted high. It was Mr Dyer and no one else on earth.

And there beside Mr Dyer was my father, squatting on the footpath and gazing lovingly at Mr Dyer's bicycle gears, his face marked with grease and hope.

And there was I, back at the filling station, leaning against a petrol pump in an American pose and talking to Brian Sparrow, who was amusing me with his clownish antics.

Phonsey Joy standing beside his hearse. Mr Dixon sitting inside his hardware store. Everyone I knew was there in that tiny town. If they were not in the streets or in their backyards they were inside their houses, and it didn't take very long to discover that you could lift off the roofs and peer inside.

We tiptoed around the streets, peeping into each other's windows, lifting off each other's roofs, admiring each other's gardens, and while we did it, Mrs Gleason slipped silently away down the hill towards Mason's Lane. She spoke to nobody and nobody spoke to her.

I confess that I was the one who took the roof from Cavanagh's house. So I was the one who found Mrs Cavanagh in bed with young Craigie Evans.

I stood there for a long time, hardly knowing what I was seeing. I stared at the pair of them for a long, long time. And when I finally knew what I was seeing I felt such an incredible mixture of jealousy and guilt and wonder that I didn't know what to do with the roof.

Eventually it was Phonsey Joy who took the roof from my hands and placed it carefully back on the house, much, I imagine, as he would have placed the lid on a coffin. By then other people had seen what I had seen and the word passed around very quickly.

And then we all stood around in little groups and regarded the model town with what could only have been fear. If Gleason knew about Mrs Cavanagh and Craigie Evans (and no one else had), what other things might he know? Those who hadn't seen themselves yet in the town began to look a little nervous and were unsure of whether to look for themselves or not. We gazed silently at the roofs and felt mistrustful and guilty.

We all walked down the hill then, very quietly, the way people walk away from a funeral, listening only to the crunch of the gravel under our feet while the women had trouble with their high-heeled shoes.

The next day a special meeting of the shire council passed a motion calling on Mrs Gleason to destroy the model town on the grounds that it contravened building regulations.

It is unfortunate that this order wasn't carried out before the city newspapers found out. Before another day had gone by the government had stepped in.

The model town and its model occupants were to be preserved. The minister for tourism came in a large black car and made a speech to us in the football pavilion. We sat on the high, tiered seats eating potato chips while he stood against the fence and talked to us. We couldn't hear him very well, but we heard enough. He called the model town a work of art and we stared at him grimly. He said it would be an invaluable tourist attraction. He said tourists would come from everywhere to see the model town. We would be famous. Our businesses would flourish. There would be work for guides and interpreters and caretakers and taxi drivers and people selling soft drinks and ice creams.

The Americans would come, he said. They would visit our town in buses and in cars and on the train. They would take photographs and bring wallets bulging with dollars. American dollars.

We looked at the minister mistrustfully, wondering if he knew about Mrs Cavanagh, and he must have seen the look because he said that certain controversial items would be removed, had already been removed. We shifted in our seats, like you do when a particularly tense part of a film has come to its climax, and then we relaxed and listened to what the minister had to say. And we all began, once more, to dream our American dreams.

We saw our big smooth cars cruising through cities with bright lights. We entered expensive nightclubs and danced till dawn. We made love to women like Kim Novak and men like Rock Hudson. We drank cocktails. We gazed lazily into refrigerators filled with food and prepared ourselves lavish midnight snacks which we ate while we watched huge television sets on which we would be able to see American movies free of charge and for ever.

The minister, like someone from our American dreams, re-entered his large black car and cruised slowly from our humble sportsground, and the newspaper men arrived and swarmed over the pavilion with their cameras and notebooks. They took photographs of us and photographs of the models up on Bald Hill. And the next day we were all over the newspapers. The photographs of the model people side by side with photographs of the real people. And our names and ages and what we did were all printed there in black and white.

They interviewed Mrs Gleason but she said nothing of interest. She said the model town had been her husband's hobby.

We all felt good now. It was very pleasant to have your photograph in the paper. And, once more, we changed our opinion of Gleason. The shire council held another meeting and named the dirt track up Bald Hill "Gleason Avenue". Then we all went home and waited for the Americans we had been promised.

It didn't take long for them to come, although at the time it seemed an eternity, and we spent six long months doing nothing more with our lives than waiting for the Americans.

Well, they did come. And let me tell you how it has all worked out for us.

The Americans arrive every day in buses and cars and sometimes the younger ones come on the train. There is now a small airstrip out near the Parwan cemetery and they also arrive there, in small aeroplanes. Phonsey Joy drives them to the cemetery where they look at Gleason's grave and then up to Bald Hill and then down to the town. He is doing very well from it all. It is good to see someone doing well from it. Phonsey is becoming a big man in town and is on the shire council.

On Bald Hill there are half a dozen telescopes through which the Americans can spy on the town and reassure themselves that it is the same down there as it is on Bald Hill. Herb Gravney sells them ice creams and soft drinks and extra film for their cameras. He is another one who is doing well. He bought the whole model from Mrs Gleason and charges five American dollars' admission. Herb is on the council now too. He's doing very well for himself. He sells them the film so they can take photographs of the houses and the model people and so they can come down to the town with their special maps and hunt out the real people.

To tell the truth most of us are pretty sick of the game. They come looking for my father and ask him to stare at the gears of Dyer's bicycle. I watch my father cross the street slowly, his head hung low. He doesn't greet the Americans any more. He doesn't ask them questions about colour television or Washington, D.C. He kneels on the footpath in front of Dyer's bike. They stand around him. Often they remember the model incorrectly and try to get my father to pose in the wrong way. Originally he argued with them, but now he argues no more. He does what they ask. They push him this way and that and worry about the expression on his face which is no longer what it was.

Then I know they will come to find me. I am next on the map. I am very popular for some reason. They come in search of me and my petrol pump as they have done for four years now. I do not await them eagerly because I know, before they reach me, that they will be disappointed.

"But this is not the boy."

"Yes," says Phonsey, "this is him all right." And he gets me to show them my certificate.

They examine the certificate suspiciously, feeling the paper as if it might be a clever forgery. "No," they declare. (Americans are so confident.) "No," they shake their heads, "this is not the real boy. The real boy is younger."

"He's older now. He used to be younger." Phonsey looks weary when he tells them. He can afford to look weary.

The Americans peer at my face closely. "It's a different boy."

But finally they get their cameras out. I stand sullenly and try to look amused as I did once. Gleason saw me looking amused but I can no longer remember how it felt. I was looking at Brian Sparrow. But Brian is also tired. He finds it difficult to do his clownish antics and to the Americans his little act isn't funny. They prefer the model. I watch him sadly, sorry that he must perform for such an unsympathetic audience.

The Americans pay one dollar for the right to take our photographs. Having paid the money they are worried about being cheated. They spend their time being disappointed and I spend my time feeling guilty, that I have somehow let them down by growing older and sadder.

The Fat Man in History

1.

His feet are sore. The emporium seems endless as he shuffles an odd-legged shuffle with the double-bed sheets under his arm. It is like a nightmare — the exit door in sight but not coming any closer, the oppressive heat, the constant swarm of bodies flowing towards him like insects drawn towards, then repelled by, a speeding vehicle.

He is sweating badly, attempting to look calm. The sheets are badly wrapped. He wrapped them himself, surprising himself with his own nerve. He took the sheets (double, because there were no singles in blue) and walked to the wrapping counter where he pulled out a length of brown paper and set to work. To an assistant looking at him queryingly he said, smiling meekly, "You don't object?" The assistant looked away.

His trousers are large, floppy, and old-fashioned. Fortunately they have very large pockets and the pockets now contain several tins of smoked oysters. The smoked oysters are easy, always in big tubs outside the entrance to the self-service section. He has often wondered why they do this, why put them outside? Is it to make them easier to steal, because they are difficult to sell? Is it their way of providing for him and his friends? Is there possibly a fat man who has retained his position in the emporium? He enjoys himself with these theories, he has a love of such constructions, building ideas like card houses, extending them until he gets dizzy and trembles at their heights.

Approaching the revolving door he hesitates, trying to judge the best way to enter the thing. The door is turning fast, spewing people into the store, last-minute shoppers. He chooses his space and moves forward, bustling to get there in time. Deirdre, as tiny and bird-like as she always was, is thrown out of the revolving door, collides with him, hisses "slob" at him, and scurries into the store, leaving him with a sense of dull amazement, surprise that such a pretty face could express such fear and hatred so quickly.

Of course it wasn't Deirdre. But Alexander Finch reflects that it could have been. As he sadly circles inside the revolving door and walks slowly along the street he thinks how strange it is that the revolution should have produced this one idea that would affect his life so drastically: to be fat is to be an oppressor, to be greedy, to be pre-revolutionary. It is impossible to say if it arose from the people or was fed to them by the propaganda of the revolution. Certainly in the years before the revolution most fat men were either Americans, stooges for the Americans, or wealthy supporters of the Americans. But in those years the people were of a more reasonable mind and could accept the idea of fat men like Alexander Finch being against the Americans and against the old Danko regime.

Alexander Finch had always thought of himself as possessing a lovable face and figure. He had not thought this from any conceit. At school they had called him "Cuddles", and on the paper everyone called him "Teddy" or "Teddy Bear". He had signed his cartoons "Teddy" and when he included himself in a cartoon he was always a bewildered, rotund man with a large bum, looking on the antics of the world with smiling, fatherly eyes.

But somehow, slowly, the way in which the world looked at Alexander Finch and, in consequence, the way Alexander Finch looked at himself altered. He was forced to become a different cartoon, one of his own "Fat Americans": grotesque, greedy, an enemy of the people.

But in the early days after the revolution the change had not taken place. Or, if it had, Finch was too busy to notice it. As secretary of the Thirty-second District he took notes, recorded minutes, wrote weekly bulletins, drafted the ten-day reports to the Central Committee of Seventy-five, and still, somehow, found time to do a cartoon for his paper every day and to remember that General Kooper was spelt with a "K" and not a "C" (Miles Cooper being one of the infamous traitors of the revolution). In addition he was responsible for inspecting and reporting on the state of properties in the Thirty-second District and investigating cases of hardship and poverty wherever he found them. And if, during these early days, he occasionally became involved in unpleasant misunderstandings he regarded them as simply that, nothing more. People were accustomed to regarding all fat officials as either American or Danko men, because only the Americans and their friends had had enough food to become fat on. Occasionally Finch attempted to explain the nature of glandular fat and to point out that he wasn't a real official but rather the cartoonist "Teddy", who had always been anti-Danko.

Finch was occasionally embarrassed by his fatness in the early days when the people were hungry. But, paradoxically, it wasn't until the situation improved, when production had reached and passed the pre-revolutionary figure and when the distribution problems had finally been more or less ironed out, that the fat question came to the fore. And then, of course, food was no problem at all. If anything there was a surfeit and there was talk of dumping grain on the world market. Instead it was dumped in the sea.

Even then the district committees and the Committee of Seventy-five never passed any motions directly relating to fat men. Rather the word "fat" entered slyly into the language as a new adjective, as a synonym for greedy, ugly, sleazy, lazy, obscene, evil, dirty, dishonest, untrustworthy. It was unfair. It was not a good time to be a fat man.

Alexander Finch, now secretary of the clandestine "Fat Men Against The Revolution," carries his stolen double-bed sheets and his cans of smoked oysters northwards through the hot city streets. His narrow slanting eyes are almost shut and he looks out at the world through a comforting curtain of eyelashes. He moves slowly, a fat man with a white cotton shirt, baggy grey trousers, and a slight limp that could be interpreted as a waddle. His shirt shows large areas of sweat, like daubs, markings deliberately applied. No one bumps him. At the traffic lights he stands to one side, away from the crowds. It seems to be a mutual arrangement.

The sheets under his arm feel heavy and soggy. He is not sure that he has gotten away with it. They may be following him still (he dares not look around), following him to the house, to discover what else he may have stolen. He smiles at the thought of all those empty cans of smoked oysters in the incinerator in the backyard, all those hundreds of cans they will find. And the beer keg Fantoni stole. And the little buddha he stole for Fantoni's birthday but somehow kept for himself, he felt so sorry for (or was it fond of?) the little fat statue. He accuses himself of self-love but reflects that a little self-love is tonic for a fat man in these times.

Two youths run past him, bumping him from either side. He assumes it was intentional but is uncertain. His whole situation is like that, a tyranny of subtlety. To be fired from his job with the only newspaper that had been continually sympathetic to Kooper and his ideas for "slovenliness" and "bad spelling". He had laughed out loud. "Bad spelling." It was almost a tradition that cartoonists were bad spellers. It was expected of them and his work was always checked carefully for literals. But now they said his spelling was a nuisance and wasteful of time, and anyway he was "generally slovenly in dress and attitude". Did "slovenly" really mean "fat"? He didn't ask them. He didn't wish to embarrass them.

2.

Milligan's taxi is parked in front of the house. The taxi is like Milligan: it is very bright and shiny and painted in stripes of iridescent blue and yellow. Milligan spray-painted it himself. It looks like a dodgem car from Luna Park, right down to the random collection of pink stars stencilled on the driver's door.

Milligan is probably asleep.

Behind Milligan's taxi the house is very still and very drab, painted in the colours of railway stations and schools: hard green and dirty cream. Rust shows through the cream paint on the cast-iron balcony and two pairs of large baggy underpants hang limply from a line on the upstairs verandah.

It is one of six such houses, all identical, surrounded by high blocks of concrete flats and areas of flat waste land where dry thistles grow. The road itself is a major one and still retains some of its pre-revolutionary grandeur: rows of large elms form an avenue leading into the city.

The small front garden is full of weeds and Glino's radishes. Finch opens the front door cautiously, hoping it will be cooler inside but knowing that it won't be. In the half-dark he gropes around on the floor, feeling for letters. There are none — Fantoni must have taken them. He can still make out the dark blotches on the door where May sat and banged his head for three hours. No one has bothered to remove the blood.

Finch stands in the dark passage and listens. The house has the feeling of a place where no one works, a sort of listlessness. May is upstairs playing his Sibelius record. It is very scratched and it makes May morose, but it is the only record he has and he plays it incessantly. The music filters through the heavy heat of the passage and

Finch hopes that Fantoni is not in the kitchen reading his "correspondence" — he doesn't wish Fantoni to see the sheets. He shuffles slowly down the passage, past the foot of the high, steep stairs, through the strange little cupboard where Glino cooks his vegetarian meals in two battered aluminium saucepans, and enters the kitchen where Fantoni, wearing a florid Hawaiian shirt and smoking a cigar, is reading his "correspondence" and tugging at the large moustache which partially obscures his small mouth. Finch has often thought it strange that such a large man should have such a small mouth. Fantoni's hands are also small but his forearms are large and muscular. His head is almost clean-shaven, having the shortest of bristles covering it, and the back of his head is divided by a number of strange creases. Fantoni is the youngest of the six fat men who live in the house. An ex-parking officer, aged about twenty-eight, he is the most accomplished thief of them all. Without Fantoni they would all come close to starving, eking out a living on their pensions. Only Milligan has any other income.

Fantoni has connections everywhere. He can arrange food. He can arrange anything but the dynamite he needs to blow up the 16 October Statue. He has spent two months looking for the dynamite. Fantoni is the leader and driving force of the "Fat Men Against The Revolution". The others are like a hired army, fighting for Fantoni's cause which is to "teach the little monkeys a lesson".

Fantoni does not look up as Finch enters. He does not look up when Finch greets him. He does nothing to acknowledge Finch's presence. Because he is occupied with "my correspondence", the nature of which he has never revealed to anyone. Finch, for once, is happy that Fantoni doesn't look up, and continues out onto the porch with the green fibreglass sunroof, past Fantoni's brand-new bicycle and Glino's herbs, along the concrete path, past the kitchen window, and comes to what is known as "the new extensions".

"The new extensions" are two bedrooms that have been added onto the back of the house. Their outside walls are made from corrugated iron, painted a dark, rusty red. Inside they are a little more pleasant. One is empty. Finch has the other. Finch's room is full of little pieces of bric-à-brac — books, papers, his buddha, a Rubens print, postcards from Italy with reproductions of Renaissance paintings. He has an early map of Iceland on the wall above the plywood bedhead, a grey goatskin rug covering the biggest holes in the maroon felt carpet, a Chinese paper lantern over the naked light globe.

He opens the door, steps back a pace, and pulls a huge comic fatman's face to register his disgust to some invisible observer.

The room has no insulation. And with each day of heat it has become hotter and hotter. At 4 a.m. it becomes a little cooler and at 7 a.m. it begins to heat up again. The heat brings out the strange smells of previous inhabitants, strange sweats and hopes come oozing out in the heat, ghosts of dreams and spilt Pine-o-Kleen.

The window does not open. There is no fly-wire screen on the door. He can choose between suffocation and mosquitoes.

Only a year ago he did a series of cartoons about housing conditions. He had shown corrugated-iron shacks, huge flies, fierce rats, and Danko himself pocketing the rent. Danko's men had called on him after the fourth one had appeared. They threatened to jail him for treason, to beat him up, to torture him. He was very frightened, but they did nothing.

And now he is living in a corrugated-iron room with huge blow-flies and the occasional rat. In a strange way it pleases him that he is no longer an observer, but it is a very small pleasure, too small to overcome the sense of despair that the smells and the suffocating heat induce in him.

He opens the roughly wrapped parcel of sheets and arranges them on the bed. The blue is cool. That is why he wanted the blue so badly, because it is cooler than white, and because it doesn't show the dirt so badly. The old sheets have turned a disgusting brown. If they were not listed in the inventory he would take them out and burn them. Instead he rolls them up and stuffs them under the bed.

If Fantoni had seen the sheets there would have been a row. He would have been accused, again, of self-indulgence, of stealing luxuries instead of food. But Fantoni can always arrange sufficient food.

He peels off the clinging, sweat-soaked clothes and throws them onto the goatskin rug. Bending over to remove his socks he catches sight of his body. He stands slowly, in amazement. He is Alexander Finch whose father was called Senti but who called himself Finch because he sold American cigarettes on the black market and thought the name Finch very American. He is Alexander Finch, thirty-five years old, very fat, very tired, and suddenly, hopelessly sad. He has four large rolls of fat descending like a flesh curtain suspended from his navel. His spare tyres. He holds the fat in his hand, clenching it, wishing to tear it away. He clenches it until it hurts, and then clenches harder. For all the Rubens prints, for all the little buddhas he is no longer proud or even happy to be fat. He is no longer Teddy. But he is not yet Fantoni or Glino — he doesn't hate the little monkeys. And, as much as he might pretend to, he is never completely convincing. They suspect him of mildness.

He is Finch whose father was called Senti, whose father was not fat, whose mother was not fat, whose grandfather may well have been called Chong or Ching — how else to explain the narrow eyes and the springy black hair?

3.

There are six fat men in the house: Finch, Fantoni, May, Milligan, Glino, and one man who has never divulged his name. The-man-who-won't-give-his-name has been here from the beginning. He is taller, heavier, and stronger than any of the others, Fantoni included. Finch has estimated his weight at twenty-two stone. The-man-who-won't-give-his-name has a big tough face with a broken nose. Hair grows from him everywhere, it issues from his nose, his ears, flourishes in big bushy white eyebrows, on his hands, his fingers and, Finch has noticed, on his large rounded back. He is the only original tenant. It was because of him that Florence Nightingale suggested the place to Fantoni, thinking he would find a friend in another fat man. Fantoni offered accommodation to Milligan. A month or so later Finch and May were strolling along 16 October Avenue (once known as Royal Parade) when they saw three men talking on the upstairs balcony outside Fantoni's room. Fantoni waved. May waved back, Milligan called to them to come up, and they did. Glino moved in a week later, having been sent with a letter of introduction from Florence Nightingale.

It was Fantoni who devised the now legendary scheme for removing the other tenants. And although the-man-who-won't-give-his-name never participated in the scheme, he never interfered or reported the matter to the authorities.

The-man-who-won't-give-his-name says little and keeps to himself. But he always says good-morning and good-night and once discussed Iceland with Finch on the day Finch brought home the map. Finch believes he was a sailor, but Fantoni claims that he is Calsen, an academic, who was kicked out of the university for seducing one of "the little scrawnies".

Finch stands in front of the mirror, his hands digging into his stomach. He wonders what Fantoni would say if he knew that Finch had been engaged to two diminutive girls, Deirdre and Anne, fragile girls with the slender arms of children who had both loved him with a total and unreasonable love, and he them, before the revolution.

4.

May turns his Sibelius record to side two and begins one more letter to his wife. He begins, Dear Iris, just a short note to say everything is all right.

5.

Finch is sitting in the kitchen leafing through the Botticelli book he has just bought. It took half the pension money. Everyone is out. He turns each page gently, loving the expensive paper as much as the reproductions.

Behind him he hears the key in the front door. He puts the book in the cupboard under the sink, among the saucepans, and begins to wash up the milk bottles; there are dozens of them, all dirty, all stinking.

There is cursing and panting in the passage. He can hear Fantoni saying, the little weed, the little fucker. Glino says something. There is an unusual sense of urgency in their voices. They both come into the kitchen at once. Their clothes are covered with dirt but Fantoni is wearing overalls.

Glino says, we went out to Deer Park.

There is an explosives factory at Deer Park. Fantoni has discussed it for months. No one could tell him what sort of explosive they made out there, but he was convinced it was dynamite.

Fantoni pushes Finch away from the sink and begins to wash the dirt off his hands and face. He says, the little weeds had guns.

Finch looks at Glino, who is leaning against the door with his eyes closed, his hands opening and closing. He is trembling. There is a small scratch on one of his round, smooth cheeks and blood is seeping through his transparent skin. He says, I thought I was going in again, I thought we'd gone for sure.

Fantoni says, shut up, Glino.

Glino says, Christ, if you've ever been inside one of those places you'll never want to see one again.

He is talking about prison. The fright seems to have overcome some of his shyness. He says, Christ I couldn't stand it.

Finch, handing Fantoni a tea towel to dry himself with, says, did you get the dynamite?

Fantoni says, well, what do *you* think! It's past your bedtime.

Finch leaves, worrying about the Botticelli book.

6.

Florence Nightingale will soon be here to collect the rents. Officially she arrives at 8 p.m., but at 7.30 she will arrive secretly, entering through the backyard, and visit Finch in "the new extensions".

Finch has showered early and shaved carefully. And he waits in his room, the door closed for privacy, checking with serious eyes to see that everything is tidy.

These visits are never mentioned to the others, there is an unspoken understanding that they never will be.

There is a small tap on the door and Florence Nightingale enters, smiling shyly. She says, wow, the heat. She is wearing a simple yellow dress and leather sandals that lace up her calves Roman-style. She closes the door with an exaggerated sort of care and tiptoes across to Finch, who is standing, his face wreathed in a large smile.

She says, hello, Cuddles, and kisses him on the cheek. Finch embraces her and pats her gently on the back. He says, the heat ...

As usual Finch sits on the bed and Florence Nightingale squats yoga-style on the goatskin rug at his feet. Finch once said, you look as if Modigliani painted you. And was pleased that she knew of Modigliani and was flattered by the comparison. She has a long straight face with a nose that is long vertically but not horizontally. Her teeth are straight and perfect, but a little on the long side. But now they are not visible and her lips are closed in a strange calm smile that suggests melancholy. They enjoy their melancholy together, Finch and Florence Nightingale. Her eyes, which are grey, are very big and very wide and she looks around the room as she does each time, looking for new additions.

She says, it got to 103 degrees ... the steering wheel was too hot to touch.

Finch says, I was shopping. I got a book on Botticelli.

Her eyes begin to circle the room more quickly. She says, where, show me?

Finch giggles. He says, it's in the kitchen cupboard. Fantoni came back while I was reading it.

She says, you shouldn't be frightened of Fantoni, he won't eat you. You've got blue sheets, *double* blue sheets. She raises her eyebrows.

He says, no significance, it was just the colour.

She says, I don't believe you. *Double* blue sheets. Florence Nightingale likes to invent a secret love life for him but he doesn't know why. But they enjoy this, this sexual/asexual flirtation. Finch is never sure what it is meant to be but he has never had any real hopes regarding Florence Nightingale, although in sleep and half-sleep he has made love to her many times. She is not quite frail enough. There is a strength that she attempts to hide with little girl's shyness. And sometimes there is a strange awkwardness in her movements as if some logical force in her mind is trying to deny the grace of her body. She sits on the floor, her head cocked characteristically on one side so her long hair falls over one eye. She says, how's the Freedom Fighter?

The Freedom Fighter was Finch's name for Fantoni. Finch says, oh nothing, we haven't done anything yet, just plans.

She says, I drove past the 16 October Statue — it's still there.

Finch says, we can't get the explosive. Maybe we'll just paint it yellow.

Florence Nightingale says, maybe you should eat it.

Finch loves that. He says, that's good, Nancy, that's really good.

Florence Nightingale says, it's your role, isn't it? The eaters? You should behave in character, the way they expect you to. You should eat everything. Eat the Committee of Seventy-five. She is rocking back and forth on the floor, holding her knees, balancing on her arse.

Finch tries not to look up her skirt. He says, a feast.

She cups her hands to make a megaphone and says, The Fat Men Against The Revolution have eaten General Kooper.

He says, and General Alvarez.

She says, the Central Emporium was devoured last night, huge droppings have been discovered in 16 October Avenue.

He says, you make me feel like the old days, good fat, not bad fat.

She says, I've got to go. I was late tonight. I brought you some cigars, some extra ones for you.

She has jumped up, kissed him, and departed before he has time to thank her. He remains on the bed, nursing some vague disappointment, staring at the goatskin rug.

Slowly he smiles to himself, thinking about eating the 16 October Statue.

7.

Florence Nightingale will soon be here to collect the rents. With the exception of Fantoni, who is in the shower, and Glino, who is cooking his vegetarian meal in his little cupboard, everyone is in the kitchen.

Finch sits on a kerosene drum by the back annexe, hoping to catch whatever breeze may come through.

Milligan, in very tight blue shorts, yellow T-shirt, and blue-tinted glasses, squats beside him, smiling to himself and rubbing his hands together. He has just finished telling a very long and involved story about a prostitute he picked up in his cab and who paid him double to let her conduct her business in the backseat. She made him turn his mirror back to front. No one cares if the story is true or not.

Milligan says, yep.

Milligan wears his clothes like corsets, always too tight. He says it is good for his blood, the tightness. But his flesh erupts in strange bulges from his thighs and stomach and arms. He looks trussed up, a grinning turkey ready for the oven.

Milligan always has a story. His life is a continual charade, a collection of prostitutes and criminals, "characters", beautiful women, eccentric old ladies, homosexuals, and two-headed freaks. Also he knows many jokes. Finch and May sit on the velvet cushions in Milligan's room and listen to the stories, but it is bad for May, who becomes depressed. The evenings invariably end with May in a fury saying, Jesus, I want a fuck, I want a fuck so badly it hurts. But Milligan just keeps laughing, somehow never realizing how badly it affects May.

May, Finch, Milligan, and the-man-who-won't-give-his-name lounge around the kitchen, drinking Glino's homemade beer. Finch has suggested that they wash the dirty milk bottles before Florence Nightingale arrives and everyone has agreed that it is a good idea. However, they have all remained seated, drinking Glino's homemade beer. No one likes the beer, but out of all the things that are hard to steal alcohol is the hardest. Even Fantoni cannot arrange it. Once he managed to get hold of a nine-gallon keg of beer but it sat in the back yard for a year before Glino got hold of a gas cylinder and the gear for pumping it out. They were drunk for one and a half days on that lot, and were nearly arrested en masse when they went out to piss on the commemorative plaque outside the offices of the Fifty-fourth District.

No one says much. They sip Glino's beer from jam jars and look around the room as if considering ways to tidy it, removing the milk bottles; doing something about the rubbish bin — a cardboard box which was full a week ago and from which eggshells, tins, and breadcrusts cascade onto the floor. Every now and then May reads something from an old newspaper, laughing very loudly. When May laughs, Finch smiles. He is happy to see May laughing because when he is not laughing he is very sad and liable to break things and do himself an injury. May's forehead is still scarred from the occasion when he battered it against the front door for three hours. There is still blood on the paintwork.

May wears an overcoat all the time, even tonight in this heat. His form is amorphous. He has a double chin and a drooping face that hangs downwards from his nose. He is balding and worries about losing hair. He sleeps for most of the day to escape his depressions and spends the nights walking around the house, drinking endless glasses of water, playing his record, and groaning quietly to himself as he tries to sleep.

May is the only one who was married before the revolution. He came to this town when he was fired from his job as a refrigerator salesman, and his wife was to join him later. Now he can't find her. She has sold their house and he is continually writing letters to her, care of anyone he can think of who might know her whereabouts.

May is also in love with Florence Nightingale, and in this respect he is no different from the other five, even Fantoni, who claims to find her skinny and undernourished.

Florence Nightingale is their friend, their confidante, their rent collector, their mascot. She works for the revolution but is against it. She will be here soon. Everybody is waiting for her. They talk about what she will wear.

Milligan, staring intently at his large Omega watch, says, peep, peep, peep, on the third stroke ...

The front door bell rings. It is Florence Nightingale.

The-man-who-won't-give-his-name springs up. He says, I'll get it, I'll get it. He looks very serious but his broken, battered face appears to be very gentle. He says, I'll get it. And sounds out of breath. He moves with fast heavy strides along the passage, his back hunched urgently like a jungle animal, a rhino, ploughing through undergrowth. It is rumoured that he is having an affair with Florence Nightingale but it doesn't seem possible.

They crowd together in the small kitchen, their large soft bodies crammed together around the door. When Florence Nightingale nears the door there is much pushing and shoving and Milligan dances around the outside of the crowd, unable to get through, crying "make way there, make way for the lady with the big blue eyes" in his high nasal voice, and everyone pushes every way at once. Finally it is Fantoni who arrives from his shower and says, "For Christ's sake, give a man some *room*."

Everybody is very silent. They don't like to hear him swear in front of Florence Nightingale. Only Fantoni would do it, no one else. Now he nods to her and indicates that she should sit down on one of the two chairs. Fantoni takes the other. For the rest there are packing cases, kerosene tins, and an empty beer keg which is said to cause piles.

Fantoni is wearing a new safari suit, but no one mentions it. He has sewn insignia on the sleeves and the epaulettes. No one has ever seen this insignia before. No one mentions it. They pretend Fantoni is wearing his white wool suit as usual.

Florence Nightingale sits simply with her hands folded in her lap. She greets them all by name and in turn; to the-man-who-won't-give-his-name she merely says "Hello". But it is not difficult to see that there is something between them. The-man-who-won't-give-his-name shuffles his large feet and suddenly smiles very broadly. He says, "Hello."

Fantoni then collects the rent which they pay from their pensions. The rent is not large, but the pensions are not large either. Only Milligan has an income, which gives him a certain independence.

Finch doesn't have enough for the rent. He had meant to borrow the difference from Milligan but forgot. Now he is too embarrassed to ask in front of Fantoni.

He says, I'm a bit short.

Florence Nightingale says, forget it, try and get it for next week. She counts the money and gives everyone a receipt. Finch tries to catch Milligan's eye.

Later, when everyone is smoking the cigars she has brought and drinking Glino's homebrew, she says, I hate this job, it's horrible to take this money from you.

Glino is sitting on the beer keg. He says, what job would you like? But he doesn't look at Florence Nightingale. Glino never looks at anyone.

Florence Nightingale says, I would come and look after you. We could all live together and I'd cook you crêpe Suzettes.

And Fantoni says, but who would bring us cigars then? And everybody laughs.

8.

Everyone is a little bit drunk.

Florence Nightingale says, Glino, play us a tune.

Glino says nothing, but seems to double up even more so that his broad shoulders become one with his large bay window. His fine white hair falls over his face.

Everybody says, come on, Glino, give us a tune. Until, finally, Glino takes his mouth organ from his back pocket and, without once looking up, begins to play. He plays something very slow. It reminds Finch of an albatross, an albatross flying over a vast, empty ocean. The albatross is going nowhere. Glino's head is so bowed that no one can see the mouth organ, it is sandwiched between his nose and his chest. Only his pink, translucent hands move slowly from side to side.

Then, as if changing its mind, the albatross becomes a gypsy, a pedlar, or a drunken troubador. Glino's head shakes, his foot taps, his hands dance.

Milligan jumps to his feet. He dances a sailor's dance, Finch thinks it might be the hornpipe, or perhaps it is his own invention, like the pink stars stencilled on his taxi door. Milligan has a happy, impish face with eyebrows that rise and fall from behind his blue-tinted glasses. If he weighed less his face might even be pretty. Milligan's face is half-serious, half-mocking, intent on the dance, and Florence Nightingale stands slowly. They both dance, Florence Nightingale whirling and turning, her hair flying, her eyes nearly closed. The music becomes faster and faster and the five fat men move back to stand against the wall, as if flung there by centrifugal force. Finch, pulling the table out of the way, feels he will lose his balance. Milligan's face is bright red and streaming with sweat. The flesh on his bare white thighs shifts and shakes and beneath his T-shirt his breasts move up and down. Suddenly he spins to one side, drawn to the edge of the room, and collapses in a heap on the floor.

Everyone claps. Florence Nightingale keeps dancing. The clapping is forced into the rhythm of the music and everyone claps in time. May is dancing with Florence Nightingale. His movements are staccato, he stands with his feet apart, his huge overcoat flapping, stamps his feet, spins, jumps, shouts, nearly falls, takes Florence Nightingale around the waist and spins her around and around, they both stumble, but neither stops. May's face is transformed, it is living. The teeth in his partly open mouth shine white. His overcoat is like some magical cloak, a swirling beautiful thing.

Florence Nightingale constantly sweeps long hair out of her eyes.

May falls. Finch takes his place but becomes puffed very quickly and gives over to the-man-who-won't-give-his-name.

The-man-who-won't-give-his-name takes Florence Nightingale in his arms and disregards the music. He begins a very slow, gliding waltz. Milligan whispers in Glino's ear. Glino looks up shyly for a moment, pauses, then begins to play a Strauss waltz.

Finch says, the "Blue Danube". To no one in particular.

The-man-who-won't-give-his-name dances beautifully and very proudly. He holds Florence Nightingale slightly away from him, his head is high and cocked to one side. Florence Nightingale whispers something in his ear. He looks down at her and raises his eyebrows. They waltz around and around the kitchen until Finch becomes almost giddy with embarrassment. He thinks, it is like a wedding.

Glino once said (of prisons): "If you've ever been inside one of those places you wouldn't ever want to be inside one again."

Tonight Finch can see him lying on his bunk in a cell, playing the "Blue Danube" and the albatross and staring at the ceiling. He wonders if it is so very different from that now: they spend their days lying on their beds, afraid to go out because they don't like the way people look at them.

The dancing finishes and the-man-who-won't-give-his-name escorts Florence Nightingale to her chair. He is so large, he treats her as if she were wrapped in crinkly cellophane, a gentleman holding flowers.

Milligan earns his own money. He asks Fantoni, why don't you dance?

Fantoni is leaning against the wall smoking another cigar. He looks at Milligan for a long time until Finch is convinced that Fantoni will punch Milligan.

Finally Fantoni says, I can't dance.

9.

They all walk up the passage with Florence Nightingale. Approaching the front door she drops an envelope. The envelope spins gently to the floor and everyone walks around it. They stand on the porch and wave goodnight to her as she drives off in her black government car.

Returning to the house Milligan stoops and picks up the envelope. He hands it to Finch and says, for you. Inside the official envelope is a form letter with the letterhead of the Department of Housing. It says, Dear Mr Finch, the department regrets that you are now in arrears with your rent. If this matter is not settled within the statutory seven days you will be required to find other accommodation. It is signed, Nancy Bowlby.

Milligan says, what is it?

Finch says, it's from Florence Nightingale, about the rent.

Milligan says, seven days?

Finch says, oh, she has a job to do, it's not her fault.

10.

May has the back room upstairs. Finch is lying in bed in "the new extensions". He can hear Milligan calling to May.

Milligan says, May?

May says, what is it?

Milligan says, come here.

Their voices, Milligan's distant, May's close, seem to exist only inside Finch's head.

May says, what do you want?

Milligan shouts, I want to tell you something.

May says, no you don't, you just want me to tuck you in.

Milligan says, no. No, I don't.

Fantoni's loud raucous laugh comes from even further away.

The-man-who-won't-give-his-name is knocking on the ceiling of his room with a broom. Finch can hear it going, bump, bump, bump. The Sibelius record jumps. May shouts, quit it.

Milligan says, I want to tell you something.

May shouts, no you don't.

Finch lies naked on top of the blue sheets and tries to hum the albatross song but he has forgotten it.

Milligan says, come *here*. May? May, I want to tell you something.

May says, tuck yourself in, you lazy bugger.

Milligan giggles. The giggle floats out into the night.

Fantoni is in helpless laughter.

Milligan says, May?

May's footsteps echo across the floorboards of his room and cross the corridor to Milligan's room. Finch hears Milligan's laughter and hears May's footsteps returning to May's room.

Fantoni shouts, what did he want?

May says, he wanted to be tucked in.

Fantoni laughs. May turns up the Sibelius record. The-man-who-won't-give-his-name knocks on the ceiling with a broom. The record jumps.

11.

It is 4 a.m. and not yet light. No one can see them. As May and Finch leave the house a black government car draws away from the kerb but, although both of them see it, neither mentions it.

At 4 a.m. it is cool and pleasant to walk through the waste lands surrounding the house. There are one or two lights on in the big blocks of flats, but everyone seems to be asleep.

They walk slowly, picking their way through the thistles.

Finally May says, you were crazy.

Finch says, I know.

They walk for a long time. Finch wonders why the thistles grow in these parts, why they are sad, why they only grow where the ground has been disturbed, and wonders where they grew originally.

He says, do they make you sad?

May says, what?

He says, the thistles.

May doesn't answer. Finally he says, you were crazy to mention it. He'll really do it. He'll *really* do it.

Finch stubs his toe on a large block of concrete. The pain seems deserved. He says, it didn't enter my mind — that he'd think of Nancy.

May says, he'll really do it. He'll bloody well eat her. Christ, you know what he's like.

Finch says, I know, but I didn't mention Nancy, just the statue.

May wraps his overcoat around himself and draws his head down into it. He says, he *looks* evil, he *likes* being fat.

Finch says, that's reasonable.

May says, I can still remember what it was like being thin. Did I tell you, I was only six, but I can remember it like it was yesterday. Jesus it was nice. Although I don't suppose I appreciated it at the time.

Finch says, shut up.

May says, he's still trying to blow up that bloody statue and he'll get caught. Probably blow himself up. Then we'll be the ones that have to pinch everything. And we'll get caught, or we'll starve more like it.

Finch says, help him get some dynamite and then dob him in to the cops. While he's in jail he couldn't eat Florence Nightingale.

May says, and we wouldn't eat anything. I wouldn't mind so much if he just wanted to screw her. I wouldn't mind screwing her myself.

Finch says, maybe he is. Already.

May pulls his overcoat tightly around himself and says, no, it's whatshisname, the big guy, that's who's screwing her. Did you see them dancing? It's him.

Finch says, I like him.

May says nothing. They have come near a main road and they wordlessly turn back, keeping away from the streetlights, returning to the thistles.

Finch says, it was Nancy's idea. She said why don't we eat the statue.

May says, you told me already. You were nuts. She was nuts too but she was only joking. You should have known that he's serious about everything. He really wants to blow up everything, not just the fucking statue.

Finch says, he's a fascist.

May says, what's a fascist?

Finch says, like Danko ... like General Kooper ... like Fantoni. He's going to dig a hole in the backyard. He calls it the barbecue.

12.

In another two hours Finch will have earned enough money for the rent. Fantoni is paying him by the hour. In another two hours he will be clear and then he'll stop. He hopes there is still two hours' work. They are digging a hole among the dock weeds in the backyard. It is a trench like a grave but only three feet deep. He asked Milligan for the money but Milligan had already lent money to Glino and May.

Fantoni is wearing a pair of May's trousers so he won't get his own dirty. He is stripped to the waist and working with a mattock. Finch clears the earth Fantoni loosens; he has a long-handled shovel. Both the shovel and the mattock are new; they have appeared miraculously, like anything that Fantoni wants.

They have chosen a spot outside Finch's window, where it is completely private, shielded from the neighbouring houses. It is a small private spot which Fantoni normally uses for sunbathing.

The top of Fantoni's bristly head is bathed in sweat and small dams of sweat have caught in the creases on the back of his head; he gives strange grunts between swings and carries out a conversation with Finch, who is too exhausted to answer.

He says, I want the whole thing ... in writing, OK? ... write it down ... all the reasons ... just like you explained it to me.

Finch is getting less and less earth on the shovel. He keeps aiming at the earth and overshooting it, collecting a few loose clods on the blade. He says, yes.

Fantoni takes the shovel from him. He says, you write that now, write all the reasons like you told me, and I'll count that as time working. How's that?

And he is not sure how it is. He cannot believe any of it. He cannot believe that he, Alexander Finch, is digging a barbecue to cook a beautiful girl called Florence Nightingale in the backyard of a house in what used to be called Royal Parade. He would not have believed it, and still cannot.

He says, thanks Fantoni.

Fantoni says, what I want, Finch, is a thing called a rationale ... that's the word isn't it ... they're called rationales.

13.

Rationale by A. Finch

The following is a suggested plan of action for the "Fat Men Against The Revolution".

It is suggested that the Fat Men of this establishment pursue a course of militant love, by bodily consuming a senior member of the revolution, an official of the revolution, or a monument of the revolution (e.g. the 16 October Statue).

Such an act would, in the eyes of the revolution, be in character. The Fat Men of this society have been implicitly accused of (among other things) loving food too much, of loving themselves too much to the exclusion of the revolution. To eat a member or monument of the revolution could be seen as a way of turning this love towards the revolution. The Fat Men would incorporate in their own bodies all that could be good and noble in the revolution and excrete that which is bad. In other words, the bodies of Fat Men will purify the revolution.

Alexander Finch shivers violently although it is very hot. He makes a fair copy of the draft. When he has finished he goes upstairs to the toilet and tries, unsuccessfully, to vomit.

Fantoni is supervising the delivery of a load of wood, coke, and kindling in the backyard. He is dressed beautifully in a white suit made from lightweight wool. He is smoking one of Florence Nightingale's cigars.

As Finch descends the stairs he hears a loud shout and then, two steps later, a loud crash. It came from May's room. And Finch knows without looking that May has thrown his bowl of goldfish against the wall. May loved his goldfish.

14.

At dinner Finch watches Fantoni eat the omelette that Glino has cooked for him. Fantoni cuts off dainty pieces. He buries the dainty pieces in the small fleshy orifice beneath his large moustache.

15.

May wakes him at 2 a.m. He says, I've just realized where she is. She'll be with her brother. That's where she'll be. I wrote her a letter.

Finch says, Florence Nightingale.

May says, my wife.

16.

Glino knows. Milligan knows. May and Finch know. Only the-man-who-won't-give-his-name is unaware of the scheme. He asked Fantoni about the hole in the backyard. Fantoni said, it is a wigwam for a goose's bridle.

17.

The deputation moves slowly on tiptoes from Finch's room. In the kitchen annexe someone trips over Fantoni's bicycle. It crashes. Milligan giggles. Finch punches him sharply in the ribs. In the dark, Milligan's face is caught between laughter and surprise. He pushes his glasses back on the bridge of his nose and peers closely at Finch.

The others have continued and are now moving quietly through the darkened kitchen. Finch pats Milligan on the shoulder. He whispers, I'm sorry. But Milligan passes on to join the others where they huddle nervously outside the-man-who-won't-give-his-name's room.

Glino looks to Finch, who moves through them and slowly opens the door. Finch sums up the situation. He feels a dull soft shock. He stops, but the others push him into the room. Only when they are all assembled inside the room, very close to the door, does everybody realize that the-man-who-won't-give-his-name is in bed with Florence Nightingale.

Florence Nightingale is lying on her side, facing the door, attempting to smile. The-man-who-won't-give-his-name seems very slow and very old. He rummages through the pile of clothes beside the bed, his breathing the only sound in the room. It is hoarse, heavy breathing that only subsides after he has found his underpants. He trips getting into them and Finch notices they are on inside out. Eventually the-man-who-won't-give-his-name says, it is generally considered good manners to knock.

He begins to dress now. No one knows what to do. They watch him hand Florence Nightingale her items of clothing so she can dress beneath the sheet. He sits in front of her then, partially obscuring her struggles. Florence Nightingale is no longer trying to smile. She looks very sad, almost frightened.

Eventually Finch says, this is more important, I'm afraid, more important than knocking on doors.

He has accepted some new knowledge and the acceptance makes him feel strong although he has no real idea of what the knowledge is. He says, Fantoni is planning to eat Florence Nightingale.

Florence Nightingale, struggling with her bra beneath the sheet, says, we know, we were discussing it.

Milligan giggles.

The-man-who-won't-give-his-name has found his dressing gown in the cupboard in the corner. He remains there, like a boxer waiting between rounds.

Florence Nightingale is staring at her yellow dress on the floor. Glino and May bump into each other as they reach for it at the same time. They both retreat and both step forward again. Finally it is Milligan who darts forward, picks up the garment, and hands it to Florence Nightingale, who disappears under the sheets once more. Finch finds it almost impossible not to stare at her. He wishes she would come out and dress quickly and get the whole thing over and done with.

Technically, Florence Nightingale has deceived no one.

Glino says, we got to stop him.

Florence Nightingale's head appears from beneath the sheets. She smiles at them all. She says, you are all wonderful ... I love you all.

It is the first time Finch has ever heard Florence Nightingale say anything so insincere or so false. He wishes she would unsay that.

Finch says, he must be stopped.

Behind him he can hear a slight shuffling. He looks around to see May, his face flushed red, struggling to keep the door closed. He makes wild signs with his eyes to indicate that someone is trying to get in. Finch leans against the door, which pushes back with the heavy weight of a dream. Florence Nightingale slides sideways out of bed and Glino pushes against Finch, who is sandwiched between two opposing forces. Finally it is the-man-who-won't-give-his-name who says, let him in.

Everybody steps back, but the door remains closed. They stand, grouped in a semicircle around it, waiting. For a moment it seems as if it was all a mistake. But, finally, the door knob turns and the door is pushed gently open. Fantoni stands in the doorway wearing white silk pyjamas.

He says, what's this, an orgy?

No one knows what to do or say.

18.

Glino is still vomiting in the drain in the backyard. He has been vomiting since dawn and it is now dark. Finch said he should be let off, because he was a vegetarian, but the-man-who-won't-give-his-name insisted. So they made Glino eat just a little bit.

The stench hangs heavily over the house.

May is playing his record.

Finch has thought many times that he might also vomit.

The blue sheet which was used to strangle Fantoni lies in a long tangled line from the kitchen through the kitchen annexe and out into the backyard, where Glino lies retching and where the barbecue pit, although filled in, still smokes slowly, the smoke rising from the dry earth.

The-man-who-won't-give-his-name had his dressing gown ruined. It was soaked with blood. He sits in the kitchen now, wearing Fantoni's white safari suit. He sits reading Fantoni's mail. He has suggested that it would be best if he were referred to as Fantoni, should the police come, and that anyway it would be best if he were referred to as Fantoni. A bottle of Scotch sits on the table beside him. It is open to anyone, but so far only May has taken any.

Finch is unable to sleep. He has tried to sleep but can see only Fantoni's face. He steps over Glino and enters the kitchen.

He says, may I have a drink please, Fantoni?

It is a relief to be able to call him a name.

19.

The-man-who-won't-give-his-name has taken up residence in

Fantoni's room. Everybody has become used to him now. He is known as Fantoni.

A new man has also arrived, being sent by Florence Nightingale with a letter of introduction. So far his name is unknown.

20.

"Revolution in a Closed Society — A Study of Leadership among the Fat"
by Nancy Bowlby

Leaders were selected for their ability to provide materially for the welfare of the group as a whole. Obviously the same qualities should reside in the heir-apparent, although these qualities were not always obvious during the waiting period; for this reason I judged it necessary to show favouritism to the heir-apparent and thus to raise his prestige in the eyes of the group. This favouritism would sometimes take the form of small gifts and, in those rare cases where it was needed, shows of physical affection as well.

A situation of "crisis" was occasionally triggered, *deus ex machina*, by suggestion, but usually arose spontaneously and had only to be encouraged. From this point on, as I shall discuss later in this paper, the "revolution" took a similar course and "Fantoni" was always disposed of effectively and the new "Fantoni" took control of the group.

The following results were gathered from a study of twenty-three successive "Fantonis". Apart from the "Fantoni" and the "Fantoni-apparent", the composition of the group remained unaltered. Whilst it can be admitted that studies so far are at an early stage, the results surely justify the continuation of the experiments with larger groups.

The Uses of Williamson Wood

1.

The mornings in the Lost and Found were better than the afternoons. In the mornings she didn't think about the afternoons, yet the knowledge of their coming hung behind her eyes like great grey cloud banks that would soon blot out the sky.

Few people came to the Lost and Found at any time. Sometimes in the mornings they would have a businessman looking for an umbrella or a schoolgirl looking for a lost coat. But few came to collect the great library of treasure that was stacked in its high dusty canyons. Sometimes in the mornings she would simply wander through the great grey alleyways between the metal shelves and then she would visit her favourite objects: the cases of butterflies that were stacked in the high shelves above the railway goods yards, the old gardening books on the top of the ancient gramophone, the strange and beautiful building materials that lay in a tangled heap just near the loading dock. She would sit here sometimes, perched on a bag of concrete looking at the big lumps of four by two and imagining what she might do with them if she had a chance. The wood was grey and heavy, each piece marked with the name "Williamson" and she often wondered who Williamson had been and how anyone could be so careless as to misplace such a wonderful treasure. She longed to steal that four by two, to grow even taller than her five feet ten inches and somehow put it under an overcoat and walk out with it in the same way that Jacobs walked out each day with watches and transistors and small items of value. Mr Jacobs used the Lost and Found as a private business, as if the whole sawtooth-roofed warehouse had been built by the government for the express purpose of making Mr Jacobs rich.

Mr Jacobs didn't give a damn for butterflies or books or four by two. He cared solely for money, and he cared for it with a fierce energy that she found alien and disturbing.

In the mornings when he spoke to her he often talked about

money, its value, its uses, the freedom he would purchase with it. In two years, he predicted, he would no longer use his battered brown briefcase to smuggle goods from the Lost and Found, but instead use it to collect rents in the afternoons. In the mornings he planned to stay in bed.

Mr Jacobs was a small neat man who combed his hair flat with Californian Poppy hair oil. In his grey dustcoat he could look almost frail. In fewer clothes he revealed the alarming strength of his muscular forearms, disproportionate arms that belonged to a far bigger body than his. Sometimes she saw the arms in nightmares. Yet when he arrived in the morning wearing a suit and carrying a briefcase he looked to her like a respectable businessman. She was always shocked, in the mornings, to see how respectable he looked, and how his eyes, peering behind his rimless glasses, had a soft, almost mouse-like quality. He looked like a character from one of those cartoons which feature henpecked husbands. If you hadn't known Mr Jacobs you could have imagined him saying "Yes dear, no dear", but then you wouldn't have known about the forearms, nor the afternoons, nor his angry bachelorhood. A wife, Mr Jacobs said, was a waste of money.

She had never known anyone like Mr Jacobs, but she had little experience of people. When she was a child they had lived in a poor mining area where her mother's lovers had tried to gouge some unknown wealth from a bleak clay-white landscape. Around their tin shack were the high white clay piles of other men's attempts. The ground was dotted with deep shafts and for her first four years she had only been able to play in a special leather harness which was strapped to a length of fencing wire. She had run up and down the wire like a dog on a chain, safe from the dangers of mine shafts. It must have been there, in that white hot place, that she had learned how to go somewhere else, to dream of green places and cool clear rain, to ignore what her eyes saw or her body felt.

People do not love those whose eyes show that they are somewhere else. Her mother had not liked it. Her mother's lovers, in varying degrees, had been enraged or irritated by her withdrawals. She had learned not to hear their words or feel their blows. Now, at nineteen, her long thin legs still bore the ghost of their rages, the stripe of a heavy piece of wire, the spot of a cigarette. Yet they had not touched her.

Now it was morning in the Lost and Found and Mr Jacobs was talking about money again. He was sitting at his desk behind the great grimy counter and she was leaning against the wall, hugging herself with her thin arms, her head on one side, her waving fair hair falling over one eye as she watched Mr Jacobs with curiosity. She asked her ritual question with the untiring curiosity of a child who wants to be told the same frightening story once again.

"Mr Jacobs, would you really do anything for money, really?"

"You bet." He lit a long thin cigar and put his feet on the desk. Each time he put the cigar to his mouth the terrible forearms emerged from his grey dustcoat. She thought of octopuses lurking beneath rocks in shallow pools.

"Would you walk naked in the street for a thousand dollars?"

"I'd do it for five hundred, doll."

"You'd go to jail."

"No, I'd be fined. I could pay the fine and still make a profit."

"Would you drink, you know ..." she faded off, suddenly embarrassed by what she had said.

"No, I don't know." He smirked. She hated his smirk. He knew what she meant because he had said he would do it before. He had said he would drink piss if there were money in it. She wanted to hear him say it again.

"You know, drink 'it'."

"Piss, would I drink piss for money?"

"Yes." Her pale face burned. "That."

"How much piss?"

"A teaspoonful."

"Forty dollars." It was strange the way he said that, the same tone of voice that he used when he was quoting a price for unredeemed property. It meant he was cheating. It meant, she thought, that he would probably do it for ten dollars.

"I'd do a pint for eighty."

"What about the other?"

"What 'other'?"

"You know."

"Shit?"

She nodded.

"That'd be more expensive. I'd want a hundred and fifty for that."

"What about dog's stuff?"

"Two hundred."

She shook her head, appalled at the thought of it.

"You don't believe me?"

"I believe you." She pulled a face. She couldn't help it. The thought of it. The strange respectable little face, the neat clipped moustache smeared with stinking muck.

"Don't pull faces at me, young lady." She heard the tone in the voice and began to drift away. It was the nasty voice.

"I wasn't," she said, and then, seeing the rage growing on his face, corrected herself. "I was, but I'm sorry. I can't help it."

The confession pacified him. "Look, sweetheart, you don't live in the real world. In two years' time I'll be free, just collecting rent."

"Who'll come here then?" Maybe, she thought, there will be someone nice. The thought cheered her. It had never occurred to her before.

"I'm fucked if I know. Somebody. You'll be stuck here and I'll be free just going around collecting rent."

"Oh," she said, "I won't be here either."

He laughed then. "You'll be here, my little biddy, until you're a shrunken-up old woman. How will you get out?"

She smiled then, so secretly that he started to get angry again.

"What are you smiling about?" He took his feet down off the desk.

"It's nothing," she said, but she was already edging her way along the wall, trying to escape. She couldn't tell him.

"Tell me." He was standing now and moving towards her. There was really no point in running. She would have to tell him something. Tell him anything.

"Tell me." He was beside her now. His hand took her wrist. What would he do? She began to retreat. She started collecting coloured stones under water. She liked doing that. Swimming through the pale green water with the bucket, a beautiful turquoise bucket. The stones lay on the bright sandy bottom.

He was twisting her wrist. It was called "A Chinese Burner". He had told her that before. He put two hands around her wrist and twisted different ways.

"I'll get married," she lied, picking up a glowing ruby-coloured stone, "and go away and have children."

That satisfied him. He believed in confessions under pain. He believed in pain as he believed in money. He released her wrist and went back to sit behind his desk. Soon he would make a few false entries in the book, then he would go out to lunch, and then it would be afternoon.

During lunch she retreated into the depths of the Lost and Found. She crouched on the floor, reading in the dusty light: "Harvesting is not easy in a large mango tree, for the fruit must be picked carefully and placed gently into the picking boxes."

There were no photographs of mangoes and she had never seen one.

She waited for the afternoon, placing glowing blue fruit into a pinewood box. She dropped pink tissues into the box and bedded the blue mangoes into it. She loved the feel of them, as soft and gentle as a baby's cheek.

2.

It was afternoon and he stank of drink. He did not want it straight away. He made some phone calls and she waited, desperately flying through dusty corridors looking for beautiful things.

There was so much ugliness.

She saw shelves of dog turds lined up like buns in a bakery. She saw lengths of electrical flex hanging like whips. She looked for coloured stones but when she picked them up they were warm and squelchy in her hands and smelt of unmistakable filth. She searched on while he talked, looking for the forest, finding at last cool green paths below dripping trees. In the distance the bright blue mangoes shone like magic things and now she walked towards them, her bare feet caressed by a soft sandy path.

He was taking her hand now and leading her into the warehouse.

He wanted her to talk. He tugged at her clothes. The smell of liquor assailed her. She saw the bottled snake in her mind, soaked in formaldehyde. She hated the smell of the drink.

"Tell me you want to fuck me."

"I want to fuck you."

She said it. She shed her clothes and stood shivering. She didn't see him. She tried to walk down the sandy path and reach the mangoes.

She felt the blow. He liked to hit her. They all liked to hit her. Why did they like it? Why did they always want to hit her? They didn't like her walking down sandy paths. They were jealous and could not see the mangoes.

"I want to fuck you." She tried to say it better. She tried to look at his hard brown eyes which glinted at her behind the horrible spectacles. She felt the moustache on her lips, trying to eat her alive, and she thought of it covered with muck.

He grunted above her now but she was able to feel nothing. She said the words he wanted her to say.

When it was over she remained lying on the old pile of carpet, looking up through the canyons of shelves towards the distant skylights.

He stood above her, pulling his trousers on.

"You've got no tits," he said, "it's like fucking a beanpole." He threw her clothes to her. "Get dressed, for Chrissakes, I can't stand looking at you."

The clothes fell on her and she smiled at him. "Could I take home some of that wood?"

"Which bloody wood?" He was embarrassed now. He always was. If she smiled it made it worse.

"The four by two."

"How will you get it out?"

"I'll just cut a piece off."

"All right," he said, "I'll cut it for you."

She'd rather have cut it herself, but she let him do it.

"What do you want it for?"

"I just want it," she said.

"Well, get dressed."

As she got dressed she listened to him sawing the wood. He would saw it crooked but it didn't matter, she only wanted it for practice.

3.

It was late at night.

She lay in her narrow bed in her YWCA room, her wide pale eyes following the footsteps in the corridor above. On the floor beside the bed were several very short sawn pieces of the four by two. She had cut the pieces as thin as possible, eking out her length of "Williamson" wood.

She gazed down at the cut pieces, reached down a long arm and picked one up. The cut was straight, but not straight enough. She got out of bed and picked up a piece of Williamson wood again, putting it over the edge of the dressing table. This one would be perfect. She drew the pencil lines using the set square she had bought at the newsagent's. Then, very quietly, she began to saw. Sometimes the wood slipped but when she had finished she looked at the cut she had made. The faintest trace of grey pencil line was visible around it. It was a beautiful cut. She smiled at it with satisfaction.

The rest of the Williamson could be used for nailing.

She took the pillow from the bed and placed it on the dresser. Then she placed the wood on the pillow and began to drive in a three-inch nail. The pillow deadened the noise a little, but didn't make the hammering any easier.

They were knocking on the wall but she finished six nails before she got into bed, taking the hammer and saw and cut pieces of wood with her.

Soon the floor superintendent would be there to complain. She would be sound asleep then, and their voices would not be able to reach her.

4.

He had taken to hitting her more lately, as if he had tapped a new and extraordinary vein of pleasure. While he grunted above her he called her horrible names, names so vile that they broke through the soft pink walls of her jungle dreams and hurt her even there. The passionate blows lay on jungle paths like brightly coloured snakes and their fangs sawed and ripped at her running legs. They would not leave her alone. She built houses on high stilts and climbed into the leafy heart of the mango tree but they were everywhere and pain oozed through the air, covering everything with its black ink.

Her sanctuary was violated. The blue sky was torn to ribbons.

Afterwards she retired deep into the recesses of the Lost and Found, like a hurt animal in search of a place to recuperate. He left her alone then and went to smoke cigars in the front office. She climbed the high steel ladders and lay stretched out on shelves twenty feet from the concrete floor. It was on one of these shelves that she found the old pillow. She placed it under her aching head and stared at the grey metal of the shelf above, dimly recognizing that she had come to a crisis from which she could not escape.

If only there could be another job, but there were no other jobs to be had. Even as he assaulted her, he liked to remind her of this. Even as he bent her arms behind her back, he increased his pleasure by taunting with this hard steel fact, as cruel as a serrated knife.

If he threatened the peace of her private places she would have to fight him. She had never fought. She did not know how. She had been a tree, or a rock, and hate and anger were strangers to her. Storms had assailed her, rivers washed over her, but they had not hurt her. Now she lay on the uncomfortable pillow and felt the hate come, like a visit to the toilet too long postponed because of other business. She was surprised at the pleasure it gave her. It came from her in a long slow flood and she felt suffused by a lovely warmth which she kindled with puzzlement and wonder.

Her revenges were far-fetched and extravagant but they began to radiate the blue light of her beloved mangoes.

5.

She hid from pain. Twice she avoided him for a whole afternoon, lying on the high shelf just below the ceiling. She lay in dread, barely moving while he bellowed with rage in the canyons below. He screamed her name and threatened her with horrible pains. He shouted tortures through the air and chanted the chilling litanies of dismissal.

Yet in the mornings he was a quiet respectable man with a brief-case. He pretended nothing had happened. She sensed a strange embarrassment about him, as if he knew that he had behaved badly. But that did nothing to stop the tangled schemes she continually constructed for his punishment.

It was on a third afternoon, lying in her hiding place, that her nervous fingers began to explore the peculiarly uncomfortable stuff-ing in the pillow. As Mr Jacobs began to climb other ladders and look into high shelves three rows away, her closely bitten fingernails plucked at the threads of the pillow. She explored the soft kapok interior more through agitation than curiosity and when her hands touched the bank notes she played with them for a while before she thought to pull them out and see what they were.

There were five hundred and six of them, all single dollar notes. While Mr Jacobs threatened death, she calmly counted them. When she had finished, she counted again.

6.

She lay the notes across her bed so they were like a patchwork quilt.

She put them in one single pile and wrapped them in tissue paper.

She spent three of them on a chisel.

She bought a three-foot section of four by two.

She stood outside the bank for half an hour before she got the courage to go in and then she told them what she wanted.

When she emerged fifteen minutes later she had deposited two hundred dollars in a savings account and she had a withdrawal form with her.

7.

It was morning. Mr Jacobs sat at his desk smoking his thin black cigar. She leant, as usual, against the wall. But this was not usual. Nothing was usual. She trembled with excitement at the impossible thing she was going to do. She watched him closely, her heart beating wildly, her fear dominating all other emotions.

Today she would teach him to leave her alone. Today she had money.

"What's the matter with you, stupid?"

"Nothing," she said. She was going to have to say something else soon. Say it now, she thought, say it now.

"What is it?" The voice was already becoming blotched with anger. She was not prepared for a Chinese Burner. She was the one who would give Chinese Burners today.

It was time to say.

"Mr Jacobs, would you really eat dog's poo for two hundred dollars?" She said it as she always said it, with innocent curiosity.

"I told you I would."

"I bet you wouldn't." There. She had started. She had never doubted him before.

"Listen, doll, I said I would, I meant I would. What's the matter with you? What the fuck are you smiling about?"

She had it behind her back, wrapped in a little piece of clear thin plastic film. Now she held it out.

"There it is," she smiled.

He looked at her in disbelief. He took the cigar out of his mouth and put it on the ashtray. He wasn't looking properly and the cigar rolled off the ashtray and lay on the desk, quietly blistering the varnish.

"What's that?"

"Dog's poo."

"Pull the other leg, honey." But his eyes were riveted on the strange little parcel.

She walked over to his desk and unwrapped it gently. It wasn't a very big piece, about three inches long and three-quarters of an inch in diameter.

"You dirty little bitch." He was staring at her with astonishment.

"Will you eat it?" She was surprised how controlled her voice was, how quiet and firm and reasonable.

"Two hundred dollars," he said, but the voice trailed off at the end and lacked conviction. He was staring at the turd which lay on the desk in front of him. The neglected cigar was making a strange smell but he didn't seem to notice.

She took the bank book and withdrawal form and placed it beside the turd. She saw then just how little he wanted to eat it.

"It's all right," she goaded him softly, "I knew you wouldn't."

"Sign the form," Jacobs said thickly.

"I'll sign it when you've eaten it."

"Sign it now."

"No. Afterwards."

There was silence then. She picked up the cigar and put it in the ashtray. Jacobs stared at the turd and poked at it with a pencil.

"I didn't think you would," she said.

He didn't say anything for a moment and when he looked up his eyes looked strange and dead. "Get me a glass of water."

She got him the glass of water and placed it beside the turd.

Now when she realized that he was going to do what she hoped, she no longer wanted him to. She saw the flaws in her revenge. She saw that it would solve nothing. It would make it worse. She felt that she had a tiger pinned to the ground and her triumph was fractured by the knowledge that sooner or later she would have to let it go.

"Don't," she pleaded, "please don't, Mr Jacobs."

"Piss off." His little eyes glinted behind his spectacles and he passed his tongue nervously over his lower lip. He bit his neatly trimmed moustache. He daintily pulled back the sleeves of his grey dustcoat. He looked like a high-jumper about to make his run.

"No," she said, "please. I didn't mean it. It was a joke."

His eyes were alight with triumph. "I'll do it, damn you. I'll take your fucking money." But still he didn't touch it. She stared in horror.

It was not what she wanted. It was not what she thought. There would be no pleasure here.

He took the turd like an old lady picking up a lamington, and bit it.

She retched first.

When Jacobs retched nothing came up. He drank the water and smeared the glass. Then he bit again, and swallowed. She could not stand it. It was not what she wanted. She only wanted peace. She only wanted to be somewhere else, to walk soft sandy paths, to build a little house in a warm tropical place. She had wasted her money. She had thrown it away.

Mr Jacob's face was contorted in a horrible grimace. He stood and knocked over his chair and then rushed from the room. She could hear him vomitting.

When he came back he was wiping his face with the back of his hand.

"Now," he said, "sign the form."

She signed it, full of dread. His voice had been like a surgical instrument.

"Now," he said, "give me a kiss."

She ran then, darting around him and fleeing into the doorway that led to her great shelved refuge. He was behind her. There was no hiding. She came to a ladder. It was not her ladder. It led to no refuge, merely to piles of cement bags. She was high up the ladder when he reached the bottom. She didn't look down. She could hear his breathing.

She tried to be somewhere else. She had to be somewhere else. When she dropped the cement bag down the ladder she was already walking down the sandy path to the mango tree. Somewhere far away, she heard a grunt. As she dropped the second bag she knew that the grunt had come from a tangled mess of the bright painful snakes.

"No snakes here," she said.

She descended the ladder beside the path and found the snakes snapping around her ankles.

"Go away," she said, "or I will have to kill you. No snakes here."

But the snakes would not go away and writhed and twisted about each other making their nasty sounds.

It took her a while to mix the cement with sand and carry enough water, but soon she had it mixed and she buried the groaning snakes in concrete where they would do no harm.

When she looked at the concrete, trowelled neatly and squared off, she realized that it was as good a place as any to build.

She walked off down the path towards the mango tree. There she found some pieces of wood with "Williamson" written on them.

She started sawing then, and by the time dusk came she had built the beginning of her new home.

That night she slept on a high platform above the path, but two nights later she was asleep within her new house.

The moon shone through the sawtoothed sky and she dreamed that she was trapped in a white arid landscape, strapped in a harness and running helplessly up and down on a wire, but that was only a dream.

Exotic Pleasures

1.

Lilly Danko had a funny face, but the actual point where one said "this is a funny face" rather than "this is a pretty face" was difficult to establish. Certainly there were little creases around the eyes and small smile lines beside the mouth, yet they had not always been there and she had always had a funny face. It was a long face with a long chin and perhaps it was the slight protuberance of her lower lip that was the key to it, yet it was not pronounced and could be easily overlooked and to make a fuss about it would be to ignore the sparkle in her pale-blue eyes. Yet all of this is missing the point about faces which are not static things, a blue this, a long that, a collection of little items like clues in a crossword puzzle. For Lillian Danko had a rubber face which squinted its eyes, pursed its lips, wrinkled its nose and expressed, with rare freedom, the humours of its owner.

At the age of eight she had written in a school composition that she wished, when fully grown, to take the profession of clown. And although she had long since forgotten this incident and the cold winter's afternoon on which she had written it, she would not now, at the age of thirty, sitting in a boiling old Chevrolet at the Kennecott Interstellar Space Terminal, have found anything to disown.

Here she was, knitting baby clothes in a beaten-up car, while Mort, dressed up in a suit like a travelling salesman, walked the unseen corridors inside the terminal in search of a job as a miner on one of the company's planets, asteroids or moons. She was not likely to share any jokes on the subject with Mort, who was stretched as tight as a guitar string about to break. And she wished, as she had found herself wishing more and more lately, that her father had been alive to share the idiocies of the world with.

She would have astonished him with the news, made him laugh and made him furious all at once. Here, she would have said, we have the romance of space and pointed to the burnt ugly hulk of an interstellar cargo ship lowering itself onto the earth like a dirty old hen going down on its nest. Space had yielded no monsters, no Martians, no exotic threats or blessings. The ship roaring bad-temperedly on the platform would contain nothing more beautiful than iron ingots, ball-bearings, and a few embittered workers who were lucky enough to have finished their stint in the untidy back-yards of space.

It wasn't funny unless you made it funny and Lilly, four months pregnant, with twenty dollars in her purse, a car that needed two hundred dollars and a husband who was fighting against three million unemployed to get a job, had no real choice but to make it funny.

"C'est la bloody guerre," she said, holding up her knitting and reflecting that two hundred miles of dusty roads had not done a lot for the whiteness of the garment.

Fuck it, she thought, it'll have to do.

When the face appeared in the open window by her shoulder she got such a fright she couldn't remember whether she'd said "fuck" out loud or just thought it.

"I beg your pardon," she said to the bombed-out face that grinned crookedly through the window.

"Pardon for what?" He was young and there was something crazy about him. His black eyes looked as sleepy as his voice sounded. He was neglected and overgrown with wild curling black hair falling over his eyes and a bristling beard that was just catching up to an earlier moustache.

"I thought I may have said something."

"If you said something," he said, "I didn't hear it. I am definitely at least half deaf in one ear."

"I probably didn't say it then," she said carefully, wondering if he was going to rob her or if he was just crazy. "Are you looking for a lift?"

"Not me." He stood back from the windows so she could see his white overalls with their big Kennecott insignia. He was tall and thin like a renegade basketball player. "This," he gestured laconically to include the whole area of car park, administration building, docking platforms and dry parched earth, "this is my home. So," he paused for a moment as if what he had said had made him inexplicably sad, "so I don't need a lift, thank you."

"Any jobs in there?"

"Let's say there are an awful lot of people in there waiting to be told no."

Lilly nodded. "Yeah, well ..."

"You want to see something?"

"Well, that depends what it is."

He walked smoothly back to a little white cleaner's trolley he had left marooned a few yards from the car and trundled it back, whistling like one who carries rare gifts.

"If anyone comes," he whispered, "you're asking me directions, OK?"

"OK."

"This," he reached a large hand into the white cart, "is really something special."

He was not exaggerating. For what he now pushed through the window and onto her lap was the most beautiful bird that Lilly Danko had ever dreamed might be possible, more exquisite and delightful than a bird of paradise, a flamingo, or any of the rare and beautiful species she had ever gazed at in picture books. It was not a large bird, about the size of a very big pigeon, but with a long supple neck and a sleek handsome head from which emerged a strong beak that looked just like mother of pearl. Yet such was the splendour of the bird that she hardly noticed the opaline beauty of the beak, or the remarkable eyes which seemed to have all the colours of the rainbow tucked into a matrix of soft brown. It was the bird's colouring that elicited from her an involuntary cry. For the feathers that ran from its smooth head to its graceful tail were of every blue possibly imaginable. Proud Prussian blue at the head then, beneath a necklace of emerald green, ultramarine and sapphire which gave way to dramatic tail feathers of peacock blue. Its powerful chest revealed viridian hidden like precious jewels in an aquamarine sea.

When she felt the first pulse of pure pleasure she imagined that it came from the colours themselves and later when she tried to explain this first feeling to Mort she would use the word "swoon", savouring the round smooth strangeness of the word.

"Don't it feel nice when you touch it?"

"Oh yes."

And even as she answered she realized that it was not the colours that gave such pleasure, but that the feeling was associated with stroking the bird itself. "It's like having your back rubbed."

"Better."

"Yes," she said, "better. It gets you right at the base of the neck."

"It gets you just about everywhere." And something about the way he said it made her realize that he wasn't showing her this bird out of idle interest, but that he was going to offer it for sale. It was an exotic, of course, and had probably been smuggled in by some poor miner looking for an extra buck. If the crew-cut Protestants who had begun the push into space with such obsessive caution had seen the laxness of the space companies with quarantine matters they would have shrieked with horror. But NASA had wilted away and no terrible catastrophe had hit the earth. There were exotic shrubs which needed to be fed extraterrestrial trace elements to keep them alive, a few dozen strange new weeds of no particular distinction, and a poor small lizardish creature raised for its hallucinogenic skin.

But there had been nothing as strange and beautiful as this and she calculated its value in thousands of dollars. When she was invited to make an offer she reluctantly handed it back, or tried to, because as she held it up to the man he simply backed away.

"You've got to make an offer. You can't not make an offer."

She put the bird, so placid she thought it must be drugged, back on her lap and stroked sadly. "OK, I'll be the bunny. How much do you want?"

He held up two hands.

"Ten dollars?"

"Is that cheap or is it cheap?"

"It's cheap, but I can't."

"You should have made an offer."

"I can't," she said hopelessly, thinking of Mort and what he would say. God knows the world pressed in on him heavily enough. Yet the thrilling thought that she could own such a marvel, that she need never hand it back, crept into her mind and lodged there, snug and comfortable as a child sleeping beneath a soft blanket.

"I can only offer five," she said, thinking that she couldn't offer five at all.

"Done."

"Oh, shit."

"You don't want it?"

"Oh yes, I want it," she said drily, "you know I want it." She put the bird down on the seat, where it sat waiting for nothing more than to be picked up again, and took five of their precious dollars from her handbag. "Well," she said, handing over the money, "I guess we can always eat it." Then, seeing the shocked look on the wild young face: "Just joking."

"If you don't want it ..."

"I want it, I want it. What does it eat? Breakfast cereal and warm milk?"

"I've got feed for it, so don't sweat."

"And the feed is extra, right?"

"My dear Dolores," he said, "where this bird comes from, the stuff it eats grows on trees. If you'd be nice enough to open the boot I'll give you a bag of it and our transaction, as they say, will be finito."

She opened the boot and he wheeled round his cleaner's trolley and hoisted a polythene sack into the car.

"What do I do when it's eaten all this?"

But he was already gliding across the car park towards the administration building. "Well, *then*," he giggled over his shoulder, "you're going to have to *eat* it."

The giggling carried across the hot tarmac and got lost in the heat haze.

Lilly went back to the car and was still stroking the bird when Mort came back.

Through pale veils of pleasure she saw him walking back across the blistering car park and she knew, before he arrived at the car, exactly what his eyes would look like. She had seen those eyes more and more recently, like doors to comfortable and familiar rooms that suddenly open to reveal lift wells full of broken cables. She should have taken him in her arms then and held him, stroked his neck until the lights came back on in those poor defeated eyes, eyes which had once looked at the world with innocent certainty, which had sought nothing more than the contentment of being a good gardener, calm eyes without fear and ambition. She should have taken him in her arms, but she had the bird and she sat there, stroking it stupidly, like someone who won't leave a hot shower until the water goes cold.

He came and sat behind the wheel, not looking at her.

"Take off your coat, honey," she said gently, putting a hand on his. "Come on, take it off."

It was then that he saw the bird.

"What's that?"

Her left hand was still stroking it. She ran a finger down its opaline bill, across its exquisitely smooth head and down its glowing blue back. "It's a bird. Stroke it." She tugged his hand, a hand which each day had become smoother and softer, towards the bird, and the bird, as if understanding, craned its supple neck towards him. "It'll make you feel better."

But Mort put both hands on the steering wheel and she saw his knuckles whiten. She was frightened then. He was a dark well she had only thought of as calm and still, but that was in the easy confidence of employment, in times without threat. Now, when she said what she had to say, something would happen.

"Mort, I'm sorry. I paid five dollars for it. I'm sorry, Mort."

He opened the door and walked slowly around the car. She watched him. He didn't look at her. He walked around the car a second time and she saw his face colouring. Then he started kicking it. He moved slowly, methodically, kicking it every couple of feet as if he wished to leave no part of its dull chalky body unpunished. When he had finished he came and sat down again, resting his head against the wheel.

Lilly got out of the car and walked to the driver's side.

"Come on, bugalugs," she said, "move over. I'm driving."

She slid behind the wheel, thinking that in another month she wouldn't be able to fit behind it, and when he moved over she passed him the bird. By the time they had left the terminal he was stroking it. His face had relaxed and resumed its normal quiet innocence and she remembered the days they had worked together as gardeners on the Firestone Estate as if this were some lost paradise from which they had been inexplicably expelled by a stern fascist god.

"Let's stay in a motel," she said. "Let's have a hot shower and a good meal and get drunk and have a nice fuck in a big bed."

"And be broke in the morning," he said, but smiled.

"One morning we'll be broke. We might as well have fun doing it."

Mort stroked the bird slowly, dreamily.

"Do you like our bird?" she asked.

He smiled. "You're a crazy person, Lilly."

"Do you still love me?"

"Yes," he said, "and I like the bird. Let's have champagne and piss off without paying."

"Champagne it is."

As it turned out, the motel they chose didn't have champagne, but it had an architecture well suited to their plans. Its yellow painted doors faced the highway and when they backed the car into the space in front of the room there was nothing in their way to prevent a fast getaway.

2.

Lilly lay on the bed stroking the bird which sat comfortably between her breasts and her swollen belly. The bottle of wine which stood amongst the debris of a meal on the table beside her was very nearly empty.

Mort, his hair wet, sat naked in a chair staring at the television. She envied him his looseness, his easy sexual satisfaction.

"Why don't you put it down?" he said.

"In a minute."

"Come and rub my back."

"You're a greedy bugger, Morto."

"You want to be careful with that bird. It probably should have injections or something. You shouldn't fuck around with exotics when you're pregnant."

"You're the only exotic I fuck around with." She looked at him and thought for the millionth time how pretty he was with his smooth skin and his hard muscles and that beautiful guileless face. "Let's get another bottle." The drunk Mort was more like the old Mort.

Without waiting for an answer she reached over and picked up the phone. She ordered the wine, put the bird in the bathroom with a saucer of seed, threw Mort a pair of trousers and picked up her own dress from where she had dropped it.

It was the manager himself who brought the wine. He wasn't content to hand it through the door. "I'll just pick up the trays," he said, and Lilly noted that he already had his foot in the door, like an obnoxious encyclopedia salesman.

He was a short, slim man, handsome in an overripe way, with a mole near his eye and waving dark hair. Lilly didn't like him. She didn't like his highly shined shoes or his neatly pressed flannel trousers. She didn't like the way he looked at the wet towel lying on the floor and the rumpled disordered bed freshly stained from lovemaking.

She sat on the bed while he busied himself with the trays. When she saw he was actually counting the knives and forks she started mimicking him behind his back.

When he announced that a saucer was missing she nearly burst out laughing, as if anyone would pinch one of his stupid tasteless saucers.

"It's in the bathroom," she said, and was wondering if she should add "where it belongs" when the man took the opportunity to inspect the bathroom.

When he came back he was holding the bird in one hand and the saucer in the other. Lilly took the bird from him and watched him drop the seeds into the rubbish bin.

"There is a house rule against pets. It's quite clearly displayed."

"It's not a pet," she said.

"I can't have people bringing pets here."

She saw Mort put his head in his hands as he anticipated one more setback, one more razor-nick defeat.

She took the saucer from the manager's manicured hand. "Just stroke it," she said, "it has special properties," and smiled inwardly to hear herself use a word like "properties", a leftover from her wasted education.

The manager looked at her with supercilious eyes and was about to give her back the bird when she firmly took hold of his free hand (which she was astonished to find damp with anxiety) and rubbed it down the bird's back. When she took her hand away he continued to stroke it mechanically, the threatened light of authority still shining in his eyes.

"Go on," she encouraged, "it feels nice."

In spite of a private conviction that he was being made a fool of, the manager stroked the bird, at first tentatively and then more surely. The bird, as if understanding the importance of the occasion, brushed its cheek against the manager's and then for a minute or two very little moved in the room but the manager's hand.

Lights from the highway flowed across the wall.

On the television a mute reporter held a microphone towards a weeping man.

Twice Lilly saw the manager trying to give the bird back and twice she saw him fail.

"Feels nice, doesn't it?"

The manager nodded his head and looked embarrassed. She could see that pleasure had made his eyes gooey as marshmallow.

"Now," she said briskly, holding out her hands for the bird, "I'll put it in the car so we won't be breaking the rules."

"No." He was like a two-year-old with a teddy bear.

"You'll exhaust it," Lilly said, "and we need it for tomorrow. It's our business. That's what I mean about it not being a pet."

"Your business?" the manager asked, and in truth every person in the room was trying to think how this beautiful bird might be anyone's "business".

"It's a Pleasure Bird," Lilly said, lighting a cigarette although she had given them up three months ago. It gave her time to think. "We charge a dollar a minute for people to stroke it."

"You people in show business?"

"Sure am." Lilly exhaled luxuriously and sat down on the bed.

"Dollar a minute, eh. Good work if you can get it." He was being nice now and she allowed herself the luxury of not despising him for it.

"You think that's too expensive?" She held out her arms for the bird. "We've charged more and no one's ever complained."

The manager stepped back from the extended arms, cooing over the bird like a mother keeping its baby from harm.

Lilly started talking. Ideas came to her so fast that she hardly knew how the sentence would end when she started it. "You can have it for half an hour." She watched the manager glow. "In return for the price for this room and the food."

"Done."

"And wine, of course."

"Done."

"For an extra five dollars in cash you can take it to the office so we won't disturb you. We'll get it when time's up."

"Done."

"What's the time, Mort?"

Mort picked up his wristwatch from the top of the mute television. "Nine twenty-three."

"OK, it is now nine twenty-three." She opened the door and

ushered the manager out into the night. "I'll pick it up from you at exactly nine fifty-three."

When she shut the door she was grinning so broadly her face hurt. She hugged Mort and said, "I'm a genius. Tell me I'm a genius."

"You're a genius," he said, "but you were crazy to let him take it away."

"Why, for Chrissakes?"

"He mightn't give it back."

"Oh fuck, Mort. Stop it."

"I'm sorry, it was just a thought."

"Be positive."

"I am positive."

"Well, pour me a glass of wine and tell me I'm beautiful."

The manager had taken the corkscrew and they had to shove the cork in with a pencil.

As it turned out they made an extra twenty dollars' cash that night. It was ten-thirteen before they persuaded the manager to relinquish the bird. They stood in his office holding the wristwatch while the man bought minute after minute of extra time from his petty cash. The phone rang and wasn't answered.

As they left his office, the bird ruffled its feathers and shat on the concrete.

3.

Mort didn't want to look at the empty wine bottle or the plan he had agreed to so easily the night before. When Lillian got up he curled himself into a ball and pretended he was still asleep. Lilly knew he wasn't asleep and knew why he was pretending.

"Come on, Mort, don't be chicken shit."

Mort moaned.

"Come on, Mort honey, or we won't get a stall." She rattled a coffee cup near his ear. "Do you want to get rich or do you want to stay poor? Here's your coffee, baby. It's getting cold."

When Mort finally emerged, tousle-headed and soft as a child's toy, he was in no way prepared for what he saw. Lilly was wearing white overalls and clown's make-up. There were stars round her eyes and padding in her bum.

"Oh Christ, Lilly, please."

"Please what? Drink your coffee."

"Oh shit, please don't. We don't have to do that."

"You heard what I told the man. We're in show business."

"Take it off, please. I don't mind the business with the bird, but we don't have to do all this."

"Drink your coffee and I'll take Charley-boy out for a shit."

When he drove to the markets it was in strained silence. The clown held the bird. The straight man was at the wheel. When the car finally lost its muffler neither of them said anything.

4.

The markets had sprung up to meet the needs of the new poor and were supplied and operated by an increasingly sophisticated collection of small-time crooks. The police, by mutual agreement, rarely entered their enclosures and business was thus conducted with some decorum, whether it was the purchase of stolen clothing or illicit drugs (the notorious Lizard Dust was sold here and it was only the poor who tolerated the violent illnesses that preceded its more pleasant effects). Here you could buy spare parts for rubber thongs, fruit, vegetables, motor cars of questionable origin, poisonous hot dogs and bilious-coloured drinks.

The market they drove to was a vast concrete-paved car park which, at nine o'clock in the morning, was already unpleasantly hot. A blustery wind carried clouds of dust through the stalls, rattled the canvas roofs, and lodged a fine speck of dust in Mort's eye. So it was Lilly who joined the queue for temporary stalls while Mort adjourned, more in embarrassment than pain, to minister to his eye in the men's toilets.

The stall number was 128. It was nothing more than a wooden trestle table with a number painted on the top. Canvas awnings were a luxury they could not yet afford.

Mort stood behind the stall in his suit and tie, red-eyed and sulky. The bird stood stoically on the table. Lilly, resplendent in overalls and clown's face, waddled to and fro in front, a balloon of swollen belly and padded bum.

"It won't work."

"Of course it'll work," she said. But her stomach was a mass of nerves and the baby, probably nervous of the life she had in store for it, kicked irritably inside her. "Don't look like that," she hissed. "I can't do it when you're looking at me like that."

"Do what?"

And she started to do it. She felt a fool. She did badly what she had dreamed would be easy. Her voice sounded high and when she tried to lower it, it came out worse. What she said was hardly impressive and rarely funny. But she began to lumber amongst the crowds clapping her hands and making a fuss.

"See the Pleasure Bird at stall 128," she yelled. "First three customers get a minute of pleasure for free. Oh yes, oh yes, oh yes. One dollar, one minute. They say it's better than sex. One dollar, one minute and the first three customers get it free."

A crowd of ragged children followed her. She did a cake walk. She danced a waltz with a black man in a pink suit. She fell over a guy-rope and made it look intentional. She attracted a small crowd by the simple device of placing a matchbox on the ground and making a big show of jumping over it, bowing and smiling when the jump was done. The matchbox jump was the most successful stunt of all and she gave the laughing crowd the news about stall 128 and the Pleasure Bird.

By the time she'd got lost in an alley of used car parts and been threatened by a woman who was trying to sell bruised apples she was exhausted. She had blisters on her feet from Mort's sandshoes which were four sizes too big and a cut on her hand from the fall over the guy-rope. She limped back to the stall to find an enormous crowd huddled around an old woman who was dreamily stroking the bird. Mort stood beside her with his watch in his hand. The crowd was strangely silent and the woman crooning to the bird seemed vulnerable and rather sad.

"Ten minutes," said Mort.

The woman reluctantly handed the bird back and, from a pocket of her voluminous black dress, produced a half-unravelled blue sock from which she counted out, in notes and coins, ten dollars.

As Mort handed the bird to the next person in the queue, the quiet solemnity of the recipient's face reminded Lilly of a face in her childhood taking communion in a small country church. He was an Italian, a labourer with a blue singlet and dusty boots and he had only had the bird for thirty seconds when he cradled it in one arm and dragged a bundle of notes from his pockets which he placed on the table in a crumpled heap.

"Tell me when time's up," he said, and sat on the trestle table, hunched over the bird, lost in his own private world, impervious to the mutterings of the impatient crowd.

After that they limited the time to three minutes.

They could have worked the market all day but Mort, rather than sharing Lilly's ever increasing sense of triumph, became more and more upset with her costume.

"Take it off. You don't need it now."

"No."

"Please."

"Don't be silly, Mort. It's part of the act."

"You look a fool. I can't stand people laughing at you."

They hissed at each other until one o'clock when Mort, his face red and sullen, suddenly dumped the bird in Lilly's lap and walked away.

At two o'clock she closed the stall and limped painfully back to the car. The bird shat once or twice on the way back, but apart from that seemed none the worse for its handling. Mort didn't seem to have fared so well. He was sitting woodenly inside the boiling car and when she asked him how much he'd taken he simply handed her the money.

She counted two hundred and thirty dollars in notes and didn't bother with the silver.

5.

The balcony of their room looked across the wide graceful river which was now silvery and cool in the late light. A rowing eight moved with svelte precision through a canopy of willows and two black swans descended from the sky above the distant city and Lilly, watching them, imagined the pleasant coolness of the water on their hot bodies.

Her make-up was gone now and she wore a loose white cheese-cloth dress. The ice clinked in her gin and tonic and even the small chink of the glass as it touched the metal filigree table sounded cool and luxurious to her ears. She put her blistered feet up on the railing and stroked the bird gently, letting the pleasure saturate her body.

"Mort."

"Yes."

"You feel OK now?"

He leant across and put his arm on her shoulder. His face was sunburnt and there was a strange red V mark on his chest. He nodded. "Put the bird inside."

"In a minute."

He took his hand back and filled his glass.

Lillian was feeling triumphant. She had a fair idea of the worms that were eating at Mort and she was surprised and a little guilty to discover that she didn't care excessively. She felt cool and rich and amazingly free. After a few minutes she picked up the bird and put it in front of the bathroom mirror where, she discovered, for all its unearthly qualities, it behaved just like a budgerigar.

She went back to the balcony and stood behind Mort, rubbing his broad back and loosening the tense muscles in his neck.

"Tell me I was terrific," she said. "Please say I was great."

Mort hesitated and she felt the muscles under her fingers knot again. "Let's not talk about it now."

She smiled just the same, remembering checking into this hotel, Mort dressed in his salesman's suit, she in her clown's make-up, the bird quietly hidden in a plastic shopping bag.

"Lillian," she said, "you were terrific."

The river was almost black now and, when two birds cut across it towards a certain tree, it was too dark to see the stunning colours by which she might have identified them.

6.

Their days were lined with freeways and paved with concrete. They limped south with a boiling radiator and an unmuffled engine. They worked markets, factory gates and even, on one occasion, a forgotten country school where the children let down their tyres to stop them leaving.

Mort no longer complained about the clown, yet his resentment and embarrassment grew like a cancer inside him and he seldom thought of anything else. He had long since stopped touching the Pleasure Bird and the full force of his animosity was beamed towards its small colourful eyes which seemed to contain a universe of malignant intentions.

"God, Jesus, it likes freeways." Lilly held the bird in the air, displaying its ruffled feathers, a signal that it was going to shit.

Mort didn't appear to hear.

"Well, stop the car. You're the one who's always worried about where it shits."

Slowly, irritatingly slowly, Mort pulled the car into the white emergency lane and the bird hopped out, shat quickly and effectively, and hopped back in.

"This bird seems intent on spreading shit from one end of Highway 31 to the other."

Mort pulled back onto the road.

"It's really crazy for doing it on nice clean roads. Do you notice that, Morty?"

"Why don't you put it down for a while. You're getting like a bloody junkie."

Lilly said nothing. Her clown's face showed no emotions but those she had painted on it, and in truth she did not allow herself to think anything of Mort's jealousies. She stroked her index finger slowly down the bird's sensuous back and the slow waves of pleasure blotted out anything else that might have worried her. Even the police siren, when it sounded outside the window, did not startle her. It reached her distantly, having no more importance than a telephone ringing in someone else's dream.

She watched the police car park in front of them and watched the policeman walk back towards their car, pink book in his hand. She heard him talk to Mort about the muffler and saw them both walk around the car looking at the tyres. Even when the policeman stood beside her window and spoke to her she did not think that the words were really addressed to her.

"What sort of bird is that?"

It was only when the question was repeated that she managed to drag her mind to the surface and stare blinking into the strangely young face.

"It's a Pleasure Bird," she smiled, "here." And she passed the passive bird into the big white hands.

"Sure does give a lot of pleasure."

"Sure does."

The bird was passed back and the pink notebook opened.

"Now," he said, "how about we start by you telling me where you got this."

"Why?"

"Because it's an exotic."

"No. It's from New Guinea."

"Look, madam, you've chosen the wrong fellow to lay that on. This bird comes from Kennecott 21. I was there two years."

"Fancy that," said Lilly, "we were told it was from New Guinea." The notebook closed. "I'll have to take it."

Lilly was struck by the early rumbles of panic. "You can't take it. It's how we earn our living."

But the policeman was already leaning over into the car, his hands ready to engulf the plump jewel-like body.

Then he was suddenly lurching back from the car window with his hands to one eye. Blood streamed down across his knuckles. The bird was pecking at the fingers which covered the other eye. The noise was terrible. She saw Mort running around the car and he was beside her starting the engine, and the bird, as if nothing had happened, was back sitting on her lap.

"Don't go," she said. "Mort. Don't."

But Mort was white with panic and as he accelerated onto the highway Lilly turned helplessly to watch as the policeman staggered blindly onto the road, where a giant container truck ran over the top of him.

Even as she watched she stroked the bird in her lap so she had the strange experience of seeing a man killed, of feeling guilt, horror and immeasurable pleasure all at once. The floodgates lifted. Seven colours poured into her brain and mixed into a warm sickly brown mud of emotion.

They turned east down a dusty road which led through the rusting gates of neglected farms. Grass grew through the centre of the road and swished silkily beneath the floor. Lilly began to remove her make-up. Mort, pale and shaken, hissed inaudible curses at the dusty windscreen.

7.

Yet their life did not stop, but limped tiredly on through a series of markets and motel rooms and if their dreams were now marred by guilt and echoes, neither mentioned it to the other.

They bought a small radio and listened to the news, but nothing was ever said about the policeman and Lilly was shocked to find herself hoping that his head had been crushed, obliterating the evidence of the attack.

Mort drew away from her more and more, as if the crime had been hers and hers alone. When he spoke, his sentences were as cold and utilitarian as three-inch nails.

He took to calling the bird "the little murderer". There was something chilling in the way that dreamy childlike face moved its soft lips and said such things as: "Have you fed the little murderer?"

He was filled with anger and resentment and fear which had so many sources he himself didn't know where the rivers of his pain began, from which wells they drew, from which fissures they seeped.

He watched Lillian perform at the markets, saw the bird shit on every hard surface that came its way, and he watched it narrowly, warily, and on more than one occasion thought he saw the bird watching him. Once, removing the bird from bedroom to bathroom for the night against Lilly's will, he thought that the bird had burned him.

At the markets he did less and less and now it was Lilly who not only attracted the crowds but also took the money and kept time. He felt useless and hopeless, angry at himself that he was too stiff and unbending to do the things that he should to earn a living, resentful that his wife could do it all without appearing to try, angry that she should accept his withdrawal so readily, angry that she showed no guilt or remorse about a man's death, angry when she met his silences with her own, angry that he who hated the bird should continue to want the money it brought him.

They spent three hundred dollars on the car. Its radiator no longer boiled. A shiny new muffler was bolted securely into place. Yet the sight of that clean metal exhaust pipe sticking out from beneath the rear bumper made him close his eyes and suck in his breath.

He drank champagne without pleasure and made love with silent rage while Lilly's eyes followed invisible road maps on the ceiling.

With sticky tissues still between her legs she brought the bird to bed and stroked it till she drifted into sleep. Even the ease of her sleep enraged him, giving him further proof of her cold self-sufficiency.

And it was on one such night, with his wife asleep on the twin bed beside him, with a cheap air-conditioner rattling above his head, that he saw the current affairs bulletin on the latest quarantine breakdown. He watched it without alarm or even any particular interest. There had been many such breakdowns before and there would be many again in the future. As usual there were experts who were already crying catastrophe, and these were, of course, balanced by optimists who saw no serious threat to the terrestrial environment.

The breakdown in this case involved a tree, named by journalists as the Kennecott Rock-drill. The seeds of this tree took to their new home with a particular enthusiasm. Adapted for a harsh, rocky environment the seeds had a very specialized survival mechanism. Whereas a terrestrial seed secreted mucus, the Kennecott Rock-drill secreted a strong acid much as a lichen did. When dropped on the rocky surfaces of its home planet the secreted acid produced a small hole. In this self-made bed the root tips expanded, using osmosis, and little by little cracked the rock, pushing a strong and complicated root system down a quarter of a mile if need be. In a terrestrial environment the whole process was speeded up, moisture and a less formidable ground surface accelerating the growth rate to such an extent that a single seed could emerge as a small tree on a busy freeway in less than seven days.

Mort watched the programme with the same detachment with which earlier generations had greeted oil spills or explosions in chemical plants.

Service stations in the north were overcome by green vegetation. Men in masks sprayed poisons which proved ineffective. People lay in hospital beds seriously ill from drinking water contaminated by this same herbicide. Fire, it seemed, rather than slowing the spread of the Rock-drill merely accelerated the germination of the seeds. Mort watched an overgrown house sacrificed to fire and then the result, a week later, when giant Rock-drills grew in the burnt-out ruins. He would have turned complacently to the late movie on another channel had they not shown film of the Rock-drill's home environment.

There he watched the strange rocky outcrops of a Kennecott planet, saw the miners working beneath a merciless sun and silently thanked God he had not succeeded in getting a job there. He admired the beauty of the giant trees silhouetted against a purple sunset and then, sitting up with a cry of recognition, saw the flocks of birds that crowded the gnarled branches.

The birds were identical to the one which sat silently on the end of Lilly's bed.

He sat shaking his head, as puzzled and secretly pleased as any lost citizen who finds his hated neighbour on public television.

8.

The argument started the next morning at breakfast and flickered and flared for the next two days as they pursued an ever more erratic course, dictated more by Mort's perversity than the location of markets. His eyes blazed, bright, righteous and triumphant. A strange pallor lay like a sheet across his tucked-in face.

To Lilly he became a mosquito buzzing on the edges of an otherwise contented sleep. She slapped at the mosquito and wished it would go away. The bird, now officially outlawed for its role in spreading the Rock-drill seed, sat contentedly in her lap as she stroked it. The stroking rarely stopped now. It was as if she wanted nothing more from life than to stroke its blue jewelled back for ever and it seemed, for the bird, the arrangement was perfect.

"Are you listening to me?"

"Yes." She hadn't been.

"We'll have to hand it in."

"No we won't." There was no anger in her voice.

Mort sucked in breath through clenched teeth.

She heard the intake of air but it caused her no concern. No matter how he shouted or hissed, no matter what he said about the bird, there was only one danger to Mort and it had nothing to do with quarantine breakdowns. From the depths of the blue well she now lived in, Lilly acknowledged the threat posed by the Kennecott Rock-drill and in her mind she had fulfilled her obligation to the world by collecting the bird's shit in a cardboard box. It was as simple as that. As for the potential violence of the bird, she saw no problem in that either. It was only violent when it was threatened. It was wiser not to threaten it.

These simple answers to the problem did not satisfy Mort and she concluded, correctly, that there must be other things which threatened him more directly.

"Do you know why you want me to get rid of this bird?" she said.

"Of course I bloody know."

"I don't think you do."

"All right," he said slowly, "you tell me."

"First, you don't like the bird because you hate to see me being able to earn a living. Then you hate yourself because you can't. You're so fucked up you can't see I'm doing it for both of us."

"Bullshit."

"No, Morty. Not bullshit, fact. But most of all," she paused, wondering if it was wise to say all this while he was driving.

"Yes, most of all ..."

"Most of all it is because you're frightened of pleasure. You can't have pleasure yourself. You don't know how. You can't stand the sight of me having pleasure. You can't give me pleasure, so you're damned if anything else is going to."

The car swung off the road and onto the verge. It skidded in gravel. For a moment, as the wheels locked and the car slid sideways, she thought that it would roll. It turned 180 degrees and faced back the way it had come, its engine silent, red lights burning brightly on the dash.

"You're saying I'm a lousy fuck."

"I'm saying you give me no pleasure."

"You used to make enough noise."

"I loved you. I wanted to make you happy."

Mort didn't say anything for a moment. The silence was a tight pink membrane stretched through pale air.

She looked at the warning lights, thinking the ignition should be turned off.

She was expecting something, but when the blow came she did not know what happened. It felt like an ugly granite lump of hate, not a fist. Her head was hit sideways against the window.

Everything that happened then was slow and fast all at once. She felt wetness on her face and found tears rather than the blood she had expected. At the same time she saw the bird rise from her lap and fly at Mort. She saw Mort cower beneath the steering wheel and saw the bird peck at his head. She saw, like a slow-motion replay, the policeman walk onto the road howling with pain. She quietly picked up the bird in both hands as she had done it a hundred times every day, and quietly wrung its neck.

She held the body on her lap, stroking it.

She watched Mort, whom she did not love, weep across the steering wheel.

9.

They drove in grey silence for there was nothing else to do. It was as if they travelled along the bottom of the ocean floor. If there was sun they didn't see it. If there were clouds they took no note of their shapes or colours.

If they had come to a motel first it is possible that the ending might have been different but, turning down a road marked A34, they came to their first forest of Kennecott Rock-drill. It grew across the road like a wall. It spread through a shopping complex and across a service station. Water gushed from broken pipes.

When they left the car the smell of gasoline enveloped them and in the service station they saw a huge underground tank pushed up through a tangle of roots and broken concrete, its ruptured skin veiled by an inflammable haze.

Lilly heard a sharp noise, a drumming, and looked to see Mort hammering on the car's bonnet with clenched fists, drumming like a child in a tantrum. He began screaming. There were no words at first. And then she saw what he had seen. Above their heads the branches of the trees were crowded with the birds, each one as blue and jewel-like as the dead body that lay in the front seat of the car. Through mists of gasoline Lilly saw, or imagined she saw, a curious arrogance in their movements, for all the world like troops who have just accomplished a complicated and elegant victory.

A Schoolboy Prank

It is Monday morning and the prank will not be played until seven o'clock tonight. The backyards are quiet: paling fences, trim grass and gum leaves floating in suburban swimming pools. In the middle of this a man stands crying, gulping in the blue early summer air in huge desperate breaths.

The noise is frightening, like curtains rending in temples, ancient statues falling, the woes of generations in pyres of lace curtains and tinder-dry wood.

A neighbour stands peering from his back steps, standing with the shocked uncertainty of those who witness motor accidents.

Turk Kershaw is weeping.

Turk Kershaw is a large man, hard, gnarled, knurled, lumped like a vine that has been cut and pruned and retained and restrained so that he has grown strong and old against the restrictions placed on him. He has grown around them like a tree grows around fencing wire. He has grown under them and his roots have slid into rock crevices, coarse-armed, fine-haired, searching for soft soil and cool water.

He is red-necked, close-barbered, with a gnome-like forehead, a thick neck and a strong pugnacious chin. The noise he now makes is strange and frightening to him and does not seem to be his. It has erupted from him out of nowhere.

Turk Kershaw is sixty-six years old and his dog, old and worn as a hallway carpet, lies beside his foot, dead.

When Turk wept for the dog he wept for many things. He wept for a man who had died five years before and left his bed cold and empty. He wept for parents who had died twenty years before that. He wept for lost classrooms full of young faces, prayers after meals, the smell of floor polish, blue flowers in a pickle-jar vase. He wept because he was totally alone.

At seven o'clock in the morning Turk Kershaw began digging. The ground was dry and hard, too hard for a spade. He walked slowly back to the house to get a mattock.

2.

It was five o'clock in the afternoon. He waited at the Golden Nugget Bar to see what time had done to his pupils. They had idolized him and wished to please him with their success. He had had meetings like this before and he had always enjoyed the display of their triumphs, achievements as smooth and predictable as hens' eggs.

But today, in the gaudy darkness of the Golden Nugget amidst the cufflinks and the high-heeled shoes, all he could think was that his dog had died. He took a large gulp of the expensive whisky, gritted his teeth and swallowed hard. He was terrified that he might cry again. It was ridiculous. It would be seen to be ridiculous for him to cry because his dog died. It would not be acceptable to these bright young men who would shortly arrive. Yet he could think of nothing but the emptiness of the house without the dog. There were too many empty things in the house anyway: a bed that was now too large, a pottery kiln that was no longer used, a dining room that had been vacated in favour of the chromium table in the kitchen. And now there was a metal food bowl which the dog had nightly nuzzled into a corner as he had eaten his food. There was an old chipped porcelain bowl still filled with water and, on the kitchen bench, a half-empty packet of dry dog food. He should have thrown them out.

It was ridiculous, it would be seen to be ridiculous. He had loved his dog. A man can love a dog. There was no one to explain this to.

Turk Kershaw was a legend and a character and tears did not form part of his myth.

The waitress who brought him his second Scotch, a Scotch he couldn't afford, did not treat him as a myth or a legend. She saw only a seedy old man in a tweed sportscoat who might once have been good-looking. He was a large man and his leather-patched sports-coat was a little too small for him. He counted the money for the drink from a small leather purse and as she waited for him to add up the coins she wondered if he was an old queen. Whatever he was, he didn't belong here and she managed to let him know it, tapping her foot impatiently while he provided her with exactly the right money. No tip. Fuck you, she thought, you're going to wait a long

time for your next drink. She left him disdainfully, an old man with
dandruff on his shoulders who ate Lifesavers with his Scotch.

Turk Kershaw barely remembered the students who would meet
him today, yet he missed them dreadfully. Somewhere in the midst
of the smells of tobacco and perfume he smelt the very distinctive
odour of floor polish and he ached for the comforts of boarding
school where floor polish was the dominant perfume of innocent
romances, crushes and night assignations. He had, of course, not
participated in any of this but had enjoyed being amongst them,
feeling like an old bull in the midst of nuzzling calves.

It had made him soft, he reflected, reliant on the company of
others, left him ill-equipped to handle life on his own, made him
place all his weight on a dog so the death of a dog was like the death
of a lover or a parent. He could see the craziness of it. He had seen
it this morning whilst he dug the grave and placed the body of the
little fox terrier in it. But seeing the craziness did not stop the pain.

He needed a drink. He caught the waitress's eye but she turned
the other way. He didn't feel up to this meeting. He didn't feel he
could be the Turk Kershaw they wanted him to be.

Turk Kershaw had been a rough old bastard and had been loved
for it. He had taken thousands of boys through the junior school and
changed them from pampered little rich boys into something a little
better. He had been obsessed with teaching them the skills of survival. He had taught them how to exist in the bush for a week without
fire or prepared foods. He had shown them how to build shelter from
the shed bark of giant trees. He had forced the weak to become strong
and the strong to become disciplined.

And today, he knew, his success with these boys would frighten
him as it had sometimes frightened him on other such meetings.
They would appear to him as iron men who control companies and
countries. The sons of the rich, the rulers, whom he had equipped so
skilfully to defend what they had. He had misunderstood the reali-
ties of power and had taught them as he would have taught himself.
It would have been better to soften them, to teach them to touch each
other gently, to show compassion to the weak, to weep shamelessly
over losses. Sometimes it occurred to him that he had been a
Frankenstein, obsessively creating the very beings who had the
power to crush him totally. For he had not been honest with them.

He had tried to remake them so that they wouldn't suffer what he had suffered when there was no likelihood they ever would.

They would not shed tears over the death of dogs. He had taught them how to despise anyone who did.

3.

Sangster found the drink that Turk couldn't. He attracted the waitress with one careless wave of his arm, ordered a Scotch for Turk and a bourbon for himself and, after a few polite inquiries about Turk's retirement, proceeded to chronicle his success as a husband, father, and newspaper proprietor.

The newspaper had, of course, been his father's and had become his with his father's death. Turk hardly listened. He had read it all in the papers. The boardroom battles. The takeover bids. The fierce sackings throughout the company after the younger Sangster took the chair.

He was busy trying to defeat waves of sadness and loss with his third Scotch. He tried to remember Sangster before dark whiskers and expensive lunches had forced their attention on his slender, olive-skinned face. Turk recalled the early battles they had had, when Sangster, who was fast and skilful in using his mind and his body, had refused to try. Sangster had wanted to be liked and had feared excellence. Turk had taught him, painfully, to ignore that fear. He had pushed him and bullied him until fear of Turk was a more serious motivating force than fear of his friends' envy.

Looking at the new Sangster, he missed the old one, who was languid and lazy and imbued with an easy grace.

4.

Davis and McGregor arrived together. They shook hands eagerly and laughed too much. Turk sensed their disappointment in him. He was different from how they'd remembered him. He was not what they wanted to meet. He remembered the dandruff and brushed his shoulder. McGregor saw him do it. Their eyes met for a second and McGregor got him another Scotch.

McGregor, stocky, red-haired, no longer blushed as he had when his name was mentioned in class. He still had his bullish awkwardness but it was now combined with a drawling aggressiveness that Turk found almost unpleasant.

McGregor, now the marketing director of a large company, had no idea what to say to Turk Kershaw. He was shocked by the seediness of the man, his sloppiness, his age, the strange puffy eyes. There was also something funny, almost effeminate, about the way he held his cigarette. And those bloody Lifesavers. He turned to Sangster and began to question him about a case that was being heard by the Trade Practices Commission. It had some relevance to the way advertising space would be bought in newspapers.

Turk Kershaw had no interest in the subject. He felt vaguely contemptuous of McGregor and wished the meeting to be over soon.

Davis, short and meticulous, seemed the one who was most as he had been. His good looks had not become overripe as had Sangster's. Neither had success made him as disdainful of Turk as it had McGregor. Whilst Sangster and McGregor continued their conversation with earnest exclusiveness, Davis talked quietly and modestly to Turk about his hospital work. And it was Davis, pointedly ignoring the other conversation, who asked Turk about his dog, a different dog who had been less important to him.

The question almost brought Turk undone.

He had another swallow of Scotch before he answered.

"It died," he said.

Davis nodded, sensing the pain, but not understanding it. "How long ago?"

"Ten years," Turk said. "You would have been at university by then." He remembered a story that Davis had written in first form. It came to him then. The ten-year-old boy standing beside his desk reading aloud a work that verged on the erotic. He had read it to a tittering class without embarrassment. Turk had said nothing about the story. He had given it an average mark, yet it had touched him, it had been a strange eruption from a sea of mediocrity. Why had he given it an average mark? Had he been embarrassed too? Why had he wished to discourage him?

McGregor was talking about some ideas he had to stop the problem of dole cheats. Sangster was obviously bored with the conversation. He was staring intently at a Malaysian air hostess who was drinking alone at the next table.

"Did you get another one?" Davis asked.

"Another what ... I'm sorry." Turk had been watching the air hostess smile at Sangster and had been pleased to note McGregor's annoyance when he saw the same thing.

"Another dog."

The word cut into him. He thought, I must not think of the metal dish. And then immediately he thought of it, and the chipped water bowl and the small grave, and the shed hair on the bedclothes, and the weight of the dog when it came to lie on his bed after the fire had gone cold at night.

He swallowed and sucked in his breath. "It died too, I'm afraid." He looked at Davis. He wondered if Davis understood anything. He had a sensitive face. It was a face his patients would have trusted. Davis listened to Turk, and his dark-brown eyes never left his face. "This morning ... I ... had to bury him." Turk tried to smile, but he was too distressed and didn't trust himself to say more. He could handle it. He would handle it. He had drunk too much, but he would handle it because there was no way not to handle it. Turk Kershaw did not weep.

He blew his nose and caught Sangster looking at him warily. The air hostess had left. McGregor was talking to the waitress.

Then Davis did something which he had not expected. He put his hand on Turk's shoulder and said, "I'm sorry."

It was because of the concern, the kindness, the surgeon's understanding of the total emptiness that he now felt that his defences crumbled. It was because of this that he now cried, very quietly, holding his snot-wet handkerchief to his eyes.

It did not last long. But when he had put his handkerchief back in his pocket the table had new drinks on it, there was a clean ashtray, and everyone seemed uncomfortable.

The awkwardness of the situation summoned up reserves in Turk that he had thought long gone. With red eyes and a blocked nose he fought his way out of his sentimentality, his loneliness, his empty house, and began to ease the conversation back to normality by helping them talk about what they wanted to talk about: the school, its characters, the people they had all once known.

He was impatient and in a hurry to settle things, and it was this haste which made his first choice such a bad one. For he turned to McGregor and said, "Tell me, Mac, do you ever see Masterton?"

It was only when he saw McGregor redden till his face was the bright crimson he had shown so readily at the age of twelve that he realized what he had said and how unacceptable the memory must be to McGregor. Masterton had been several years younger than McGregor, a blond boy with fine exquisite features, long lashes, and a prettiness of a type that is more commonly admired in females. McGregor had loved him hotly, chastely, with puzzled intensity. Their friendship had been one of those small, delightful scandals but one which had lasted longer than most. Turk had known all this but had never thought anything of it, had enjoyed it all, had watched the young lovers with the protective happiness of a parent. In his haste it had not occurred to him that McGregor might wish to forget it.

Nor had it occurred to him that talk of Masterton and McGregor might make Sangster and Davis more than a little uncomfortable. For they too had had their affairs of the heart and simpler more obvious releases of adolescent lust.

So they found themselves, all three, confronted with things they had no wish to remember. They did not wish to know that they had sucked the cocks of boys who had grown up to be married men or that they had loved other boys in the peculiarly intense way that the marketing director had loved Masterton.

Davis's foot accidently touched Sangster's leg and he withdrew it quickly as if stung.

Sangster, the newspaper proprietor, had no wish to remember that he had coated his cock with Vaseline hair tonic and slipped it gently into Davis, the surgeon's, arse. Nor did Davis wish to remember the hot painful wonder of it, the shameful perplexing door of a world he had not known existed.

None of the young men who sat at this table with Turk Kershaw wanted to recall the euphemistic way they had come to proposition one another by saying "Let's inspect the plumbing", which was delightfully ambiguous for them and meant, on the simplest level, crawling beneath the locker rooms, the dark damp space beneath the floor where they made love from curiosity and Sunday boredom and hot adolescent need.

It had been another world, another time, with other rules.

Now in the Golden Nugget they experienced the fear of dreams where you walk naked into crowded churches.

They looked at Turk Kershaw and saw that he was, in spite of his obvious discomfort, smiling. There was a twinkle in his red eyes. And they knew that a hundred pieces of gossip and scandal were contained in that great domed head. He was ridiculous in his dirty old sportscoat. His sleeves were too short. His shirt was not properly ironed. He moved his hands in ways which were not conventionally masculine. If he had not been Turk Kershaw they would never have spoken to him. But there he was, sitting across the table, a glimmer of a smile betraying the dirty secrets he still carried with him. They looked at Turk Kershaw and could not forgive him for being their past.

5.

It was McGregor who was most angry with Turk. He had been made to look a fool and he could not forgive that. He had become the master of both the cudgel and the stiletto, using both of them with equal skill. He had learned the art of the lethal memo and knew how to maximize its effects: who to send copies to and how to list their names in orders both ingratiating and insulting. He had become an expert in detecting weaknesses and never hesitated to hit the weak spots when the moment was right. He had had his predecessor fired and he would be managing director within two years. He no longer remembered that it was Turk himself who had first shown him the benefits of intelligent analysis of your enemies' weaknesses. It was Turk who had coached McGregor's bullish bowling, and had made him look at each batsman as a separate problem. "Pick the weakness," Turk had said, "everybody has a weak point. When you've found it, pound away at it."

So now McGregor waited while the others played "remember when". And when he was ready he took advantage of a natural pause in the conversation. He smiled at Turk and said, "Remember how you used to get the kids doing exercises in the morning, in front of your bedroom window?"

He drew blood. He watched with satisfaction as the colour came into Turk's face. He reacted to the colour like a shark tasting blood in the water. He attacked politely, never once abandoning his perfect manners.

"Why did you get them to do it in front of your bedroom window? Frankly," he smiled, "I find that curious."

Turk watched him warily. He saw, out of the corner of his eye, Sangster grinning broadly. "I saw no reason to get out of bed simply because you lot couldn't behave yourselves. The punishment was for you, not me."

He looked at Davis. Davis looked away. He looked to Sangster. Was Sangster for him or against him? McGregor folded his arms and smiled complacently.

"Come on, Turk," said Sangster, "you've got to admit, it's a bit strange when you look at it. Lying in bed watching twelve-year-old boys doing their exercises. In their underwear."

Even as they spoke they began to wonder if it wasn't true. Was it possible that Turk Kershaw was an old queen? They watched for other clues now, although the thought itself shocked them. For now they remembered how Turk had wrestled with them at night when he had come round to put the lights out, how they had attempted, four or five at a time, to overpower him. They thought of themselves as boys wrestling with an old queen. They felt foolish and disgusted with themselves and it was finally Davis (you too, Davis, thought Turk) who said: "You used to like wrestling."

Turk reddened again. He watched their smiling faces and detested them. He thought of their wives, whom he had seen in the social pages of *Vogue*, which he bought for just this reason. He saw the wives, one as beautiful as the next and almost identical in their style, each reduced to a charming doll in the small black and white photographs. While the men came to show the marks of character and experience on their faces, the women paid fortunes so that their experience and pain didn't show, so they looked, each one, like people who had discovered nothing. And when, finally, their lives burst out through the treatments and the creams and showed on their faces they would feel it was the beginning of the end. He felt pity for the wives with their swimming-pool parties and charity balls and anger at their husbands, who displayed their deeds and emotions so proudly on their faces yet refused to allow their wives the same privilege.

"No," he said slowly with a quietness they all remembered with not some little fear. "No, it was you who enjoyed the wrestling." He watched them, one by one, saw their anger and apprehension, hesitated, and finally decided it wiser not to say the words that were already formed in his mind: your little dicks were stiff with excitement.

They paused then, aware of a new strength in him. They watched him carefully and found no weakness. The wound had closed.

Sangster had none of McGregor's political sense. It had never been necessary for him to have any. So now he continued where the other held back. "Tell us," he said, toying with his drink, "where you buried your dog."

Turk looked at him with narrowed eyes. He felt Davis shift uneasily in his chair. "I buried the dog," he said, "beneath the fig tree in the backyard of my house." His head was perfectly clear now and he would not weep. He was vulnerable to pity or love but not to a crude bullying attack like that.

There was silence at the table then. At other tables the habitués of the Golden Nugget conducted their business, boasted, made assignations and confessions and went to the telephone to tell lies with complicated plots.

The attack on Turk had lost its momentum and the three students were temporarily marooned in the midst of battle, nervous, embarrassed by what they had done.

But McGregor wouldn't give up. While Turk was looking for his matches McGregor looked across at Sangster and made a limp-wristed caricature of a homosexual.

Turk saw it.

McGregor smiled back insultingly.

Turk stood, slowly, feeling the weight of the whisky for the first time.

McGregor waited.

"McGregor," Turk smiled, "surely, if you're honest, you'll admit that you miss Masterton. He did have such a firm little arse."

He walked from the bar before McGregor could recover, full of rage yet not for a second denying the pleasure he felt in saying the unsayable.

In the bar three successful men in their early thirties stayed to plan their revenge.

It was not a revenge at all, the way they discussed it.

It was a prank.

6.

Sangster's Mercedes arrived at the house before Turk's bus could hope to. Davis, unsure and worried, lost courage at the last moment and sat in the car. He was beginning to feel sick and had no appetite for what was planned. He remembered a childhood afternoon when he had fired air-rifle pellets into a large, slow-moving lizard, only realizing the atrocity he was committing after he had fired twenty slugs into the slow body and saw the blood spots and the open eyes of the terribly silent being which stubbornly refused to die.

He waited in the dark street, fearful of both Turk's arrival and his friends' activity. He considered leaving but he lacked the courage, just as he had lacked the courage to speak against the prank.

In the gloom he saw Sangster and McGregor carrying something. Their laughter was sharp and clear.

They were on the porch now. He heard the giggling, and then the hammering as they nailed the muddy body of Turk's fox terrier to his front door.

They made him come then, to admire the work.

The surgeon in the dark suit walked up the steps of the house where he joined a marketing director and a newspaper proprietor in looking at the body of a dead dog nailed to a door.

At that moment they were not to know that they had made an enduring nightmare for themselves, that the staring eyes of the dead dog would peer into the dirty corners of their puzzled dreams for many years to come.

For the people they continued to make love to in their dreams did not always have vaginas and the dog looked on, its tongue lewdly lolling out, observing it all.

The Journey of a Lifetime

1.

How I have waited for the train, dreamed about it, studied its every detail. It has been my ambition, my obsession, a hope too far-fetched for one of my standing. My poor, dimly lit room is lined with newspaper cuttings, postcards, calendars (both cheaply and expensively printed) celebrating its glories, the brutal power of its locomotive, the velvety luxury of its interiors.

On stifling summer nights I have lain on my bed and lingered over the pages of my beautiful scrapbooks, particularly the one titled "Tickets, Reservations, etc.". Possibly it is the best collection of its type. I do not know. But I have been fortunate indeed to have superiors who have not only known of my interest but have been thoughtful enough to hand on what bits and pieces have come their way.

I imagine them at dinner parties: the clink of fine crystal, the witty conversation, the French wines and white-shouldered women.

"Ah," one would say, "so you have been north on the train?"

"Yes," said nonchalantly, as if the train were nothing, a bicycle, a bowl of soup.

"I wonder perhaps if I may have your tickets. I have a clerk who has an interest ..."

Even now, imagining this conversation, I hold my breath. I wait on tenterhooks. Have the tickets been thrown away? Have they been kept? If so will my superior remember to ask about dining-room reservation cards, a menu, baggage tickets?

"Well, yes, I believe I have them still."

Will he get them now? Or will he merely intend to fetch them but stay talking for a moment and then, finally, forget the matter entirely.

No. No. He stands. A tall man, very white-skinned, a rather cruel aristocratic nose. A kindly smile flickers around his thin lips. "Best to get it now," he says, "lest one forget."

It is a large house of course and he is away some time. He walks lightly up the great curving staircase where he passes maids in black dresses and white aprons. He greets them kindly, knowing each one by name. I follow him down wide corridors and into a study, book-lined, a large green lamp hanging over a cedar table on which sits a stamp collection in eight leather-bound volumes. One album lies open revealing blue stamps, almost identical, but with slight differences in printing.

He fossicks in the drawer of a mahogany desk. I cannot make out what he has. Ah, an envelope. Now, down the corridors. Oh, the agony of waiting. On the staircase he stops to talk with a servant, inquiring about the man's father. The conversation drags on. It seems as if we will be here all night. But no, no, it is over. The servant proceeds upstairs, his master downstairs.

Finally at the dinner table the envelope is presented to my superior. He opens it. Thank God. I thought for a moment he was going to put it in his pocket without even looking.

And, oh, what treasures we have.

First, two small blue first-class tickets. The blue denotes a journey in excess of one thousand miles. Rare enough, but across the blue is a faint green stripe which denotes the Family Saloon. I imagine the saloon, recalling the colour gravure calendar which displays its glories. The oak door leading to the observation platform. The high arched roof with the clerestory windows. The two quilted chairs upholstered in rich rust-coloured velvet. There is also a couch with two loose cushions, one with tassels, one bearing an insignia the nature of which remains mysterious to me. There is a writing table with a lamp of graceful design. The windows of the carriage are large, affording a panorama of the most spectacular scenery by day, curtained by ingenious blinds at night.

In addition the envelope contains reservations for the dining car, a lavishly printed menu and two unusual luggage labels denoting the high rank of the traveller.

They will go into my scrapbook, of course, and be held there not by anything as coarse as glue, but by the small transparent hinges used by stamp collectors. The scrapbook will lie under my bed as always. On a hot night I will lean down and take it out, and slowly, having all the time in the world, I will peruse its contents.

If the fat bitch in the next room roars and moans in her stinking lust I will not become distressed. I will not even hear her. While her organ grips and slides over her latest lover's aching penis, I will be far away. Nothing will touch me. I will not hammer on the wall in rage. Nor will I be so base as to press my ear closer to catch the obscenities she mutters or the details of the perversions she commands him to perform.

I will travel first through the old tickets, pale gold with ornate copperplate, then over the commemorative journeys with their ornamental insignia, their laurels, crests and specially commissioned engravings. The list, although not endless, is certainly long. There are five hundred and thirty-three separate tickets.

If the following day is a Sunday I will wake early and travel by blue bus to the Central Station. It is not permitted to visit the platform itself but one can look through the wire grille and watch the activity. The passengers, beautifully dressed, occasionally accompanied by servants, stroll to and fro on the platform. One may also catch a glimpse of a courtesan, white-skinned and dark-eyed, her position in life denoted by the small white umbrella she holds in one small gloved hand. Porters bustle. Waiters in red uniform, their faces as empty of expression as the glass window they stand behind, examine the status of those whom they will shortly serve. At one time a string quartet was established in a long white carriage and when the train at last departed it was possible to hear the sweet music of a cello above the muscular sound of the locomotive.

Doubtless you think me a poor fellow, forever watching, never travelling, my red hands gripped around the wire mesh, doomed to be left behind, to watch from cuttings, to peer from bridges, to stand amongst thistles in driving rain whilst the train passes me by and leaves me to walk two miles through muddy paddocks and wait for a bus to take me back to my room. If you think me pitiful, you are not alone. My co-workers have belittled me, taken every opportunity to play some cruel trick on me and in general have acted as if they are in some way superior, and all the while they have complained about their own lot, the monotony of their lives, the injustice of the state, the cruelty of their superiors. Little did they know how I pitied them, how I laughed at their presumption that they might one day control their own destiny.

But I, I have not complained. I have worked day in, day out, forever filing away the mountains of paper which record the business of the state: births, deaths, marriages, all tucked away in the right place so they can easily be found when needed. I have filed acts of parliament, executions, stays of execution, punishments of greater and lesser degree, exhumations, cremations, promotions and so on. When my clothes have become worn I have spent my precious savings in order that I might do honour to my lowly position and not disgrace my superiors.

My colleagues' frayed cuffs and stained suits have appalled me. Their scuffed shoes, their dirty hair, their missing buttons have affronted me day in and day out for nearly thirty years.

They have thought me vain, foolish, lonely, pathetic but they, like you, do not know everything, and when they hear of my reward, my gift, my privilege, we will see who is laughing at who.

For I, Louis Morrow Baxter Moon, am to travel on the train on official business.

Ha.

Today I have been to the bank and withdrawn my savings, every penny. I have purchased a new suit, a pair of shoes, one pair of dark socks, and I still have some not insubstantial amount left to cover such items as tips and wine. The state, of course, will pay normal expenses but I do not intend to travel as a lackey.

In addition I intend to drink gin and tonic.

2.

The ticket is palest pink, denoting a journey of two thousand miles. A black diagonal line across the corner entitles me to a private salon of the second rank which, humble as it may sound to the uninitiated, is more sumptuous than anything my co-workers will experience if they live to be three hundred years old.

The ticket is held between two gloved fingers. I hand it to the man on the gate. He looks at me quizzically. Does he remember me? Has he seen me here on Sunday mornings and is he now indignant that I shall at last pass through his gate? I stare him down. He waves me through and I enter the platform with my heavy suitcase.

I had expected a porter to rush to my service, but this is not the case. All around porters carry cases belonging to other passengers. Perhaps my dress is not of the style normally worn by travellers. I carry my case without complaint. In any case it will save me the difficulty of tipping. I would rather save the money for other things.

I experience a strange sense of unreality, perhaps explained by my sleepless night, the curious nature of the mission that has been given me, the experience of walking, after so many years, on the platform itself. How often have I dreamed of just this moment: seeing myself reflected in the large windows of the carriages, a ticket in my hand, ready to board the train.

Through the windows of the dining car I see maids laying tables with fine silver. Three wine glasses are with each setting and do not think that when the time comes I will not use at least two of them.

I present myself at car 23 and hand my ticket to the steward.

"Who is this for?" he asks. He is red-haired and freckled-faced. His elegant uniform does not disguise his common upbringing. I do not like his tone.

"It is for me. Mr Moon. A booking made on the account of the State, on whose business I am travelling."

"Ah yes, I see." He seems almost disappointed to have found my name in his register. His manner is not what I would have expected.

He allocates me the salon next to his office.

"Here we are."

"Is this over the wheels?" I ask this as planned. It is well known that a salon directly over the wheels is less comfortable than one between the wheels even though the rails are now laid in quarter-mile sections, thus eliminating the clickety-clack commonly associated with trains.

"It don't float on air," he says and somehow thinks that he has made a great joke. He leaves, laughing loudly, and in my confusion I forget to open the envelope I had marked "Tips".

Any feeling (and I will admit to the presence of certain feelings) that he has somehow given me an inferior salon soon disappears as I investigate.

3.

The salon, in fact, was roughly the same size as my room. But there the similarity ended. The floor, to begin at the bottom, was covered with a plush burgundy carpet so soft and luxurious that I removed my shoes and socks immediately. There were two couches, not velvet, as I had expected, but upholstered with soft old leather and studded along the fronts with brass brads, each one gleaming and newly polished. The bed stood along one wall, a majestic double bed with high iron ends in which I discovered porcelain plaques depicting rural scenes. The bed, of course, could be curtained off from the rest of the salon and one reached the toilet and shower through a small door disguised as panelling. The wallpaper was a rich wine red, embossed with fleurs-de-lys.

I placed my case high on the rack above the bed, put my shoes and socks back on, and retired to the leather couch. From this privileged position I could watch the other passengers pass by my window without appearing in the least inquisitive. Then, remembering the matter of the tip, I removed two notes from the envelope in my breast pocket, folded them, and slipped them lightly into my side pocket. Then I rang the bell.

He took long enough to come.

"Yes?" He just stood at the door, staring in. I would have no more of this.

"Please enter."

He entered reluctantly, tapping a pencil against his leg with obvious impatience.

First, the tip. I'm afraid the manoeuvre was not gracefully executed. Perhaps he thought I wished to hold his hand, how can I tell? But he stepped away. I clutched after him, missed, and finally stood up. Abandoning all pretence at subtlety I displayed the notes. His manner changed.

"Now," I said, retiring to the couch, "there are services I shall require."

"Yes, sir."

It would be an exaggeration to say that there was respect in his voice, but at least he used the correct form of address.

"For a start I will be drinking gin and tonic."

"Gin and tonic, sir."

"And I wish there to be plenty of ice. On occasions I believe the ice can run out very early, is this so?"

"You don't need to worry, sir."

"Then I shall require a reservation in the dining car and after dinner I wish a ..." and here, I blush to remember, I hesitated. I had been so intent on not hesitating that I did.

"You wish, after dinner?"

"A courtesan."

"A what, sir?"

"A courtesan."

"You mean a woman, sir?" I swear he smirked. He had me there. Perhaps the term courtesan was not in common use amongst the lower classes from which he came.

"A woman, a courtesan," I insisted.

"And ice."

"And ice."

"Will that be all, sir?"

"That will be all."

He left me. Was he smiling? I couldn't be sure.

My pleasure in the train's departure was marred by my embarrassment over this incident, but as the train passed through the slums I called for my first gin and tonic. The ice was clear and cold and the drink quickly restored my good spirits.

I sat back deep in the couch and prepared to enjoy the journey of a lifetime.

4.

How to describe the afternoon? A long slow dream in which everything was as it should be. I perused my "Tickets" album and resisted the temptation to place my current ticket in it although I had brought hinges for just this purpose. I drank gin and tonic as planned and had a light lunch brought to my salon. The train left the city very quickly, edged slowly around Mount Speculation, and by three o'clock we were already entering that poor dry country which marks the edges of the Great Eastern Desert. Here and there I saw bands of prisoners working on some task, guarded by soldiers, and I was reminded, against my will, of the mission that awaited me two thousand miles hence. I will confess that I drank a little more than might be considered correct and by four o'clock I was sound asleep.

I woke at five thirty, feeling a little the worse for wear, showered, dressed, and, with nothing else planned, decided on an early visit to the dining car.

This was not the right thing to do. My impatience got the better of me. For had I not imagined this moment for so many years, the moment I would take my place beside my superiors at dinner. To remain sitting in my salon was thus beyond my power.

Yet, as I said, this was a mistake. The dining car was practically empty and I thought at first that I had mistaken the hour. However,

I soon noticed, at the far end of the carriage, an old gentleman already eating. I thought to join him, to engage in travellers' conversation, but the waiter, resplendent in red coat and black trousers, escorted me to an obscure corner behind the dessert trolley where, as he pointed out, I could enjoy some privacy.

Here is not perhaps the place to record the meal for it is all entered in the menu which I quietly slipped into my jacket. But I would wish to record that I drank a bottle of Château Smith Haut-Laffite which many consider one of the finest wines in the world, although it did have the unfortunate effect of drying my mouth and making my tongue a trifle furry.

I retired without enjoying a cigar and, feeling a little below par, decided to cancel the courtesan.

The wine cannot be held responsible for the violent sickness which beset me during the night. Doubtless it was due to overexcitement on my part. But here again, even in the midst of such upheaval, I appreciated the little luxuries the train provided, for the toilet was but a short step from my bed.

5.

The morning revealed the truth which our most experienced travellers have so often related: that there is a certain monotony in a long journey through the desert. I was pleased to find that my view coincided with that of my superiors.

We were well and truly in the desert now and even a cluster of poor rocks was welcomed as something new, eagerly awaited, studied on arrival, and reluctantly farewelled.

I strolled the corridors a little and, not feeling up to much conversation, merely nodded to those ladies and gentlemen I met. Their smiles were in no way condescending.

In the afternoon I composed my instructions to the courtesan which I took great care over, drafting them several times and, to be honest, feeling not a little aroused by the activities I described. She was to visit me before dinner. I had the money in an envelope marked "Courtesan". I placed it under the pillow where I considered it would be easily reached when the time came.

6.

"And this is what you want?" she said. She was so beautiful I could barely look at her.

"Yes."

"You have written it all by hand."

"Yes." I wore my dressing gown, explaining that I had just had a shower. And in fact I had wet my hair a little just to go along with the story. All this was as planned.

She wore a long blue dress, very low-cut at the front. Her skin was white, so very, very white, and she smelt like a garden of flowers. A little smile played around her full lips.

"You have very beautiful handwriting," she said.

"Thank you."

"Shall we start then?"

"Very well."

"You want to start with," she consulted the instructions, paused, smiled, "number one."

"Yes."

"Oh, master," she began. And fell upon my ear, licking it furiously.

"Not ears," I shouted, "not ears."

She consulted the list again and soon realized her mistake. After that she seemed to become more familiar with my handwriting.

7.

At dinner I was strangely pleased to hear that the dining car had run out of ice. Yet I had enjoyed ice aplenty in the gin and tonic I had ordered in my salon just fifteen minutes before. The practice of tipping had brought me rewards and I felt immensely pleased with myself in every respect.

After dinner I took a constitutional, walking the complete length of the train several times, feeling very much at peace with the world. True, the nature of my mission sometimes clouded this perfect happiness but there were so many things to observe, so many small memorabilia to collect, that the clouds soon passed.

It was near car 33 that I passed a large storage compartment and, looking in, saw the steward, my steward from car 23. He was bent over a cabinet, or so I thought it, scooping ice into a silver bucket.

"Ah," I thought, "the devil has his own supply." And seeking to congratulate him on his initiative I stepped inside.

"Good evening," I said, and smiled to see him jump with fright, for he had not noticed my presence.

My smile, alas, was short-lived. For as he turned I looked into the cabinet and found it to be not a cabinet at all, but rather a coffin of sorts. To my horror I saw a man's naked corpse inside and, packed around his pale corpulence, great quantities of ice floating in water. So this was the ice the rascal had been giving me.

I said not a word, but turned on my heel.

As I hurried along the corridor I heard him coming after me. I went into my salon and locked the door. I did not answer when he knocked, and in fact was unable to, for I was in the toilet, my stomach rent with uncontrollable spasms.

8.

How can it be that our dreams are so vulnerable, so tender, so frail that the spasms of the body can serve to rip them apart in so short a time. For that is what occurred in the long night that followed. It was as if every cell in my body rebelled against the train, its motion, its food, its passengers, its wine, and most particularly my mission which floated before me, pale, bloated and surrounded by ice.

My stomach was emptied but my body produced a green poison in order that there should be something to expel. Near as the cabinet was it was not always possible to arrive in time. And what dreams, what visions came to assail me: wide staring eyes, matted hair, pale hands floating in cold water. The taste of gin, foul and perfumed, surrounded me. I prayed to God that the spasms would stop and wished for nothing more than to be home in my poor bed.

But my prayers were shunned and all night the blackness was sliced into sickening strips by the hiss of a guillotine.

9.

The train moved like a merciless juggernaut, dragging my dead weight from grey dawn to pale day. I did not welcome it. For now I could see only the price which I, in my madness, had agreed to pay for this journey.

I wanted the courtesan, dreamed of her for so many years, wanted her breasts in my mouth, her legs wrapped around me, but when it was done, it was done and I couldn't wait to get her out of my salon. So too it was with the train: I had had it and wanted it no more. But now the price I had agreed to in passion and lust must be paid on this cold grey morning when my lust seemed ugly and the blindfold of desire had been ripped away.

The assignment I had accepted was to be the executioner (I! Executioner!) of Frederick Myrdal, a man whom even the professional executioner shrank from killing.

Even now they will be waiting for me on the platform in their grey suits and long coats.

I will step onto the platform.

"Please, sir," they will say, "come this way."

The Chance

It was three summers since the Fastalogians had arrived to set up the Genetic Lottery, but it had got so no one gave a damn about what season it was. It was hot. It was steamy. I spent my days in furies and tempers, half-drunk. A six-pack of beer got me to sleep. I didn't have the money for more fanciful drugs and I should have been saving for a Chance. But to save the dollars for a Chance meant six months without grog or any other solace.

There were nights, bitter and lonely, when I felt beyond the Fastalogian alternative, and ready for the other one, to join the Leapers in their suicidal drops from the roofs of buildings and the girders of bridges. I had witnessed a dozen or more. They fell like overripe fruit from the rotten trees of a forgotten orchard.

I was overwhelmed by a feeling of great loss. I yearned for lost time, lost childhoods, seasons, for Chrissake, the time when peaches are ripe, the time when the river drops after the snow has all melted and it's just low enough to wade and the water freezes your balls and you can walk for miles with little pale crayfish scuttling backwards away from your black-booted feet. Also you can use a dragonfly larva as live bait, casting it out gently and letting it drift downstream to where big old brown trout, their lower jaws grown long and hooked upwards, lie waiting.

The days get hot and clear then and the land is like a tinderbox. Old men lighting cigarettes are careful to put the burnt matches back into the matchbox, a habit one sometimes sees carried on into the city by younger people who don't know why they're doing it, messengers carrying notes written in a foreign language.

But all this was once common knowledge, in the days when things were always the same and newness was something as delightful and strange as the little boiled sweets we would be given on Sunday morning.

Those were the days before the Americans came, and before the

Fastalogians who succeeded them, descending in their spaceships from God knows what unimaginable worlds. And at first we thought them preferable to the Americans. But what the Americans did to us with their yearly car models and two-weekly cigarette lighters was nothing compared to the Fastalogians, who introduced concepts so dazzling that we fell prey to them wholesale like South Sea Islanders exposed to the common cold.

The Fastalogians were the universe's bush-mechanics, charlatans, gypsies: raggle-taggle collections of equipment always going wrong. Their Lottery Rooms were always a mess of wires, the floors always littered with dead printed circuits like cigarette ends.

It was difficult to have complete faith in them, yet they could be persuasive enough. Their attitude was eager, frenetic almost, as they attempted to please in the most childish way imaginable. (In confrontation they became much less pleasant, turning curiously evasive while their voices assumed a high-pitched, nasal, wheedling characteristic.)

In appearance they were so much less threatening than the Americans. Their clothes were worn badly, ill-fitting, often with childish mistakes, like buttoning the third button through the fourth buttonhole. They seemed to us to be lonely and puzzled and even while they controlled us we managed to feel a smiling superiority to them. Their music was not the music of an inhuman oppressor. It had surprising fervour, like Hungarian rhapsodies. One was reminded of Bartók, and wondered about the feelings of beings so many light years from home.

Their business was the Genetic Lottery or The Chance, whatever you cared to call it. It was, of course, a trick, but we had nothing to question them with. We had only accusations, suspicions, fears that things were not as they were described. If they told us that we could buy a second or third Chance in the Lottery most of us took it, even if we didn't know how it worked, or if it worked the way they said it did.

We were used to not understanding. It had become a habit with the Americans, who had left us with a technology we could neither control nor understand. So our failure to grasp the technicalities or even the principles of the Genetic Lottery in no way prevented us from embracing it enthusiastically. After all, we had never grasped the technicalities of the television sets the Americans sold us. Our curiosity about how things worked had atrophied to such an extent that few of us bothered with understanding such things as how the tides worked and why some trees lost their leaves in autumn. It was enough that someone somewhere understood these things. Thus we had no interest in the table of elements that make up all matter, nor in the names of the atomic subparticles our very bodies were built from. Such was the way we were prepared, like South Sea Islanders, like yearning gnostics waiting to be pointed in the direction of the first tin shed called "God".

So now for two thousand intergalactic dollars (IG$2,000) we could go in the Lottery and come out with a different age, a different body, a different voice and still carry our memories (allowing for a little leakage) more or less intact.

It proved the last straw. The total embrace of a cancerous philosophy of change. The populace became like mercury in each other's minds and arms. Institutions that had proved the very basis of our society (the family, the neighbourhood, marriage) cracked and split apart in the face of a new shrill current of desperate selfishness. The city itself stood like an external endorsement to this internal collapse and recalled the most exotic places (Calcutta, for instance) where the rich had once journeyed to experience the thrilling stink of poverty, the smell of danger, and the just-contained threat of violence born of envy.

Here also were the signs of fragmentation, of religious confusion, of sects decadent and strict. Wild-haired holy-men in loincloths, palm-readers, seers, revolutionaries without followings (the Hups, the Namers, the L.A.K.). Gurus in helicopters flew through the air, whilst bandits roamed the countryside in search of travellers who were no longer intent on adventure and the beauty of nature, but were forced to travel by necessity and who moved in nervous groups, well armed and thankful to be alive when they returned.

It was an edgy and distrustful group of people that made up our society, motivated by nothing but their self-preservation and their blind belief in their next Chance. To the Fastalogians they were nothing but cattle. Their sole function was to provide a highly favourable intergalactic balance of payments.

It was through these streets that I strode, muttering, continually on the verge of either anger or tears. I was cut adrift, unconnected. My face in the mirror that morning was not the face that my mind had started living with. It was a battered, red, broken-nosed face, marked by great quizzical eyebrows, intense black eyes, and tangled wiry hair. I had been through the lottery and lost. I had got myself the body of an ageing street-fighter. It was a body built to contain furies. It suited me. The arrogant Gurus and the ugly Hups stepped aside when I stormed down their streets on my daily course between the boarding house where I lived and the Department of Parks and Gardens where I was employed as a gardener. I didn't work much. I played cards with the others. The botanical gardens were slowly being choked by "Burning Glory", a prickly crimson flowering bush the Fastalogians had imported either by accident or design. It was our job to remove it. Instead, we used it as cover for our cheating card games. Behind its red blazing hedges we lied and fought and, on occasion, fornicated. We were not a pretty sight.

It was from here that I walked back to the boarding house with my beer under my arm, and it was on a Tuesday afternoon that I saw her, just beyond the gardens and a block down from the Chance Centre in Grove Street. She was sitting on the footpath with a body beside her, an old man, his hair white and wispy, his face brown and wrinkled like a walnut. He was dressed very formally in a three-piece grey suit and had an old-fashioned watch chain across the waistcoat. I assumed that the corpse was her grandfather. Since the puppet government had dropped its funeral assistance plan this was how poor people raised money for funerals. It was a common sight to see dead bodies in rented suits being displayed on the footpaths. So it was not the old man who attracted my attention but the young woman who sat beside him.

"Money," she said, "money for an old man to lie in peace."

I stopped willingly. She had her dark hair cut quite short and rather badly. Her eyebrows were full, but perfectly arched, her features were saved from being too regular by a mouth that was wider than average. She wore a khaki shirt, a navy blue jacket, filthy trousers and a small gold earring in her right ear.

"I've only got beer," I said. "I've spent all my money on beer."

She grinned a broad and beautiful grin which illuminated her face and made me echo it.

"I'd settle for a beer." And I was surprised to hear shyness.

I sat down on the footpath and we opened the six-pack. Am I being sentimental when I say I shared my beer without calculation? That

I sought nothing? It seems unlikely for I had some grasping habits as you'll see soon enough. But I remember nothing of the sort, only that I liked the way she opened the beer bottle. Her hands were large, a bit messed up. She hooked a broken-nailed finger into the ring-pull and had it off without even looking at what she was doing.

She took a big swallow, wiped her mouth with the back of her hand and said: "Shit, I needed that."

I muttered something about her grandfather, trying to make polite conversation. I was out of the habit.

She shrugged and put the cold bottle on her cheek. "I got him from the morgue."

I didn't understand.

"I bought him for 3 IGs." She grinned, tapping her head with her middle finger. "Best investment I've ever made."

It was this, more than anything, that got me. I admired cunning in those days, smart moves, cards off the bottom of the deck, anything that tricked the bastards — and "the bastards" were everyone who wasn't me.

So I laughed. A loud deep joyful laugh that made passers-by stare at me. I gave them the fingers-up and they looked away.

She sat on her hands, rocking back and forth on them as she spoke. She had a pleasantly nasal, idiosyncratic voice, slangy and relaxed. "They really go for white hair and tanned faces." She nodded towards a paint tin full of coins and notes. "It's pathetic, isn't it? I wouldn't have gotten half this much for my real grandfather. He's too dark. Also, they don't like women much. Men do much better than women."

She had the slightly exaggerated toughness of the very young. I wondered if she'd taken a Chance. It didn't look like it.

We sat and drank the beer. It started to get dark. She lit a mosquito coil and we stayed there in the gloom till we drank the whole lot.

When the last bottle was gone, the small talk that had sustained us went away and left us in an uneasy area of silence. Now suspicion hit me with its fire-hot pinpricks. I had been conned for my beer. I would go home and lie awake without its benefits. It would be a hot sleepless night and I would curse myself for my gullibility. I, who was shrewd and untrickable, had been tricked.

But she stood and stretched and said, "Come on, now I've drunk your beer, I'll buy you a meal."

We walked away and left the body for whoever wanted it. I never saw the old man again.

The next day he was gone.

2.

I cannot explain what it was like to sit in a restaurant with a woman. I felt embarrassed, awkward, and so pleased that I couldn't put one foot straight in front of the other.

I fancy I was graciously old-fashioned.

I pulled out her chair for her, I remember, and saw the look she shot me, both pleased and alarmed. It was a shocked, fast flick of the eyes. Possibly she sensed the powerful fantasies that lonely men create, steel columns of passion appended with leather straps and tiny mirrors.

It was nearly a year since I'd talked to a woman, and that one stole my money and even managed to lift two blankets from my sleeping body. Twelve dull stupid drugged and drunken months had passed, dissolving from the dregs of one day into the sink of the next.

The restaurant was one of those Fasta Cafeterias that had sprung up, noisy, messy, with harsh lighting and long rows of bright white tables that were never ever filled. The service was bad and in the end we went to the kitchen where we helped ourselves from the long trays of food, Fastalogian salads with their dried intoxicating mushrooms, and that strange milky pap they are so fond of. She piled her plate high with everything and I envied the calm that allowed her such an appetite. On any other night I would have done the same, guzzling and gorging myself on my free meal.

Finally, tripping over each other, we returned to our table. She bought two more beers and I thanked her for that silently.

Here I was. With a woman. Like real people.

I smiled broadly at the thought. She caught me and was, I think, pleased to have something to hang on to. So we got hold of that smile and wrung it for all it was worth.

Being desperate, impatient, I told her the truth about the smile. The directness was pleasing to her. I watched how she leant into my words without fear or reservation, displaying none of the shiftiness that danced through most social intercourse in those days. But I was as calculating and cunning as only the very lonely learn how to be. Estimating her interest, I selected the things which would be most pleasing for her. I steered the course of what I told, telling her things about me which fascinated her most. She was pleased by my confessions. I gave her many. She was strong and young and confident. She couldn't see my deviousness and, no matter what I told her of loneliness, she couldn't taste the stale self-hating afternoons or suspect the callousness they engendered.

And I bathed in her beauty, delighting in the confidence it brought her, the certainty of small mannerisms, the chop of that beautiful rough-fingered hand when making a point. But also, this: the tentative question marks she hooked on to the ends of her most definite assertions. So I was impressed by her strength and charmed by her vulnerability all at once.

One could not have asked for more.

And this also I confessed to her, for it pleased her to be talked about and it gave me an intoxicating pleasure to be on such intimate terms.

And I confessed why I had confessed.

My conversation was mirrors within mirrors, onion skin behind onion skin. I revealed motives behind motives. I was amazing. I felt myself to be both saint and pirate, as beautiful and gnarled as an ancient olive. I talked with intensity. I devoured her, not like some poor beggar (which I was) but like a prince, a stylish master of the most elegant dissertations.

She ate ravenously, but in no way neglected to listen. She talked impulsively with her mouth full. With mushrooms dropping from her mouth, she made a point. It made her beautiful, not ugly.

I have always enjoyed women who, whilst being conventionally feminine enough in their appearance, have exhibited certain behavioural traits more commonly associated with men. A bare-breasted woman working on a tractor is the fastest, crudest approximation I can provide. An image, incidentally, guaranteed to give me an aching erection, which it has, on many lonely nights.

But to come back to my new friend, who rolled a cigarette with hands which might have been the hands of an apprentice bricklayer, hands which were connected to breasts which were connected to other parts doubtless female in gender, who had such grace and beauty in her form and manner and yet had had her hair shorn in such a manner as to deny her beauty.

She was tall, my height. Across the table I noted that her hands

were as large as mine. They matched. The excitement was exquisite.
I anticipated nothing, vibrating in the crystal of the moment.

We talked, finally, as everyone must, about the Lottery, for the
Lottery was life in those days and all of us, most of us, were saving
for another Chance.

"I'm taking a Chance next week," she said.

"Good luck," I said. It was automatic. That's how life had got.

"You look like you haven't."

"Thank you," I said. It was a compliment, like saying that my shirt
suited me. "But.I've had four."

"You move nicely," she smiled. "I was watching you in the
kitchen. You're not awkward at all."

"You move nicely too," I grinned. "I was watching you too. You're
crazy to take a Chance, what do you want?"

"A people's body." She said it fast, briskly, and stared at me
challengingly.

"A what?"

"A people's body." She picked up a knife, examined it and put it
down.

It dawned on me. "Oh, you're a Hup."

Thinking back, I'm surprised I knew anything about Hups. They
were one of a hundred or more revolutionary crackpots. I didn't give
a damn about politics and I thought every little group was more
insane than the next.

And here, goddamn it, I was having dinner with a Hup, a rich
crazy who thought the way to fight the revolution was to have a body
as grotesque and ill-formed as my friends at the Parks and Gardens.

"My parents took the Chance last week."

"How did it go?"

"I didn't see them. They've gone to ..." she hesitated "... to another place where they're needed." She had become quiet now, and
serious, explaining that her parents had upper-class bodies like hers,
that their ideas were not at home with their physiognomy (a word I
had to ask her to explain), that they would form the revolutionary
vanguard to lead the misshapen Lumpen Proletariat (another term
I'd never heard before) to overthrow the Fastas and their puppets.

I had a desperate desire to change the subject, to plug my ears, to
shut my eyes. I wouldn't have been any different if I'd discovered
she was a mystic or a follower of Hiwi Kaj.

"Anyway," I said, "you've got a beautiful body."

"Why did you say that?"

I could have said that I'd spent enough of my life with her beloved Lumpen Proletariat to hold them in no great esteem, that the very reason I was enjoying her company so much was because she was so unlike them. But I didn't want to pursue it. I shrugged, grinned stupidly, and filled her glass with beer.

Her eyes flashed at my shrug. I don't know why people say "flashed", but I swear there was red in her eyes. She looked hurt, stung, and ready to attack.

She withdrew from me, leaning back in her chair and folding her arms. "What do you think is beautiful?"

Before I could answer she was leaning back into the table, but this time her voice was louder.

"What is more beautiful, a parrot or a crow?"

"A parrot, if you mean a rosella. But I don't know much about parrots."

"What's wrong with a crow?"

"A crow is black and awkward-looking. It's heavy. Its cry is unattractive."

"What makes its cry unattractive?"

I was sick of the game, and exhausted with such sudden mental exercise.

"It sounds forlorn," I offered.

"Do you think that it is the crow's intention, to sound forlorn? Perhaps you are merely ignorant and don't know how to listen to a crow."

"Certainly, I'm ignorant." It was true, of course, but the observation stung a little. I was very aware of my ignorance in those days. I felt it keenly.

"If you could kill a parrot or a crow which would you kill?"

"Why would I want to kill either of them?"

"But if you had to, for whatever reason."

"The crow, I suppose. Or possibly the parrot. Whichever was the smallest."

Her eyes were alight and fierce. She rolled a cigarette without looking at it. Her face suddenly looked extraordinarily beautiful, her eyes glistening with emotion, the colour high in her cheeks, a peculiar half-smile on her wide mouth.

"Which breasts are best?"

I laughed. "I don't know."

"Which legs?"

"I don't know. I like long legs."

"Like the film stars."

Like yours, I thought. "Yes."

"Is that really your idea of beautiful?"

She was angry with me now, had decided to call me enemy. I did not feel enemy and didn't want to be. My mind felt fat and flabby, unused, numb. I forgot my irritation with her ideas. I set all that aside. In the world of ideas I had no principles. An idea was of no worth to me, not worth fighting for. I would fight for a beer, a meal, a woman, but never an idea.

"I like grevilleas," I said greasily.

She looked blank. I thought as much! "Which are they?" I had her at a loss.

"They're small bushes. They grow in clay, in the harshest situations. Around rocks, on dry hillsides. If you come fishing with me, I'll show you. The leaves are more like spikes. They look dull and harsh. No one would think to look at them twice. But in November," I smiled, "they have flowers like glorious red spiders. I think they're beautiful."

"But in October?"

"In October I know what they'll be like in November."

She smiled. She must have wanted to like me. I was disgusted with my argument. It had been cloying and saccharine even to me. I hadn't been quite sure what to say, but it seems I hit the nail on the head.

"Does it hurt?" she asked suddenly.

"What?"

"The Chance. Is it painful, or is it like they say?"

"It makes you vomit a lot, and feel ill, but it doesn't hurt. It's more a difficult time for your head."

She drained her beer and began to grin at me. "I was just thinking," she said.

"Thinking what?"

"I was thinking that if you have anything more to do with me it'll be a hard time for your head too."

I looked at her grinning face, disbelievingly.

I found out later that she hadn't been joking.

3.

To cut a long and predictable story short, we got on well together, if you'll allow for the odd lie on my part and what must have been more than a considerable suppression of common sense on hers.

I left my outcast acquaintances behind to fight and steal, and occasionally murder each other in the boarding house. I returned there only to pick up my fishing rod. I took it round to her place at Pier Street, swaggering like a sailor on leave. I was in a flamboyant, extravagant mood and left behind my other ratty possessions. They didn't fit my new situation.

Thus, to the joys of living with an eccentric and beautiful woman I added the even more novel experience of a home. Either one of these changes would have brought me some measure of contentment, but the combination of the two of them was almost too good to be true.

I was in no way prepared for them. I had been too long a grabber, a survivor.

So when I say that I became obsessed with hanging on to these things, using every shred of guile I had learned in my old life, do not judge me harshly. The world was not the way it is now. It was a bitter jungle of a place, worse, because even in the jungle there is co-operation, altruism, community.

Regarding the events that followed I feel neither pride nor shame. Regret, certainly, but regret is a useless emotion. I was ignorant, short-sighted, bigoted, but in my situation it is inconceivable that I could have been anything else.

But now let me describe for you Carla's home as I came to know it, not as I saw it at first, for then I only felt the warmth of old timbers and delighted in the dozens of small signs of domesticity everywhere about me: a toothbrush in a glass, dirty clothes overflowing from a blue cane laundry basket, a made bed, dishes draining in a sink, books, papers, letters from friends, all the trappings of a life I had long abandoned, many Chances ago.

The house had once been a warehouse, long before the time of the Americans. It was clad with unpainted boards that had turned a gentle silver, ageing with a grace that one rarely saw in those days.

One ascended the stairs from the Pier Street wharf itself. A wooden door. A large key. Inside: a floor of grooved boards, dark with age.

The walls showed their bones: timber joists and beams, roughly nailed in the old style, but solid as a rock.

High in the ceiling was a sleeping platform, below it a simple kitchen filled with minor miracles: a hot-water tap, a stove, a refrigerator, saucepans, spices, even a recipe book or two.

The rest of the area was a sitting room, the pride of place being given to three beautiful antique armchairs in the Danish style, their carved arms showing that patina which only age can give.

Add a rusty-coloured old rug, pile books high from the floor, pin Hup posters here and there, and you have it.

Or almost have it, because should you open the old high sliding door (pushing hard, because its rollers are stiff and rusty from the salty air) the room is full of the sea, the once-great harbour, its waters rarely perturbed by craft, its shoreline dotted with rusting hulks of forgotten ships, great tankers from the oil age, tugs, and ferries which, even a year before, had maintained their services in the face of neglect and disinterest on all sides.

Two other doors led off the main room: one to a rickety toilet which hung out precariously over the water, the other to a bedroom, its walls stacked with files, books, loose papers, its great bed draped in mosquito netting, for there was no wiring for the customary sonic mosquito repellents and the mosquitoes carried Fasta Fever with the same dedicated enthusiasm that others of their family had once carried malaria.

The place revealed its secrets fast enough, but Carla, of course, did not divulge hers quite so readily. Frankly, it suited me. I was happy to see what I was shown and never worried about what was hidden away.

I mentioned nothing of Hups or revolution and she, for her part, seemed to have forgotten the matter. My assumption (arrogantly made) was that she would put off her Chance indefinitely. People rarely plunged into the rigours of the Lottery when they were happy with their life. I was delighted with mine, and I assumed she was with hers.

I had never known anyone like her. She sang beautifully and played the cello with what seemed to me to be real accomplishment. She came to the Park and Gardens and beat us all at poker. To see her walk across to our bed, moving with the easy gait of an Islander, filled me with astonishment and wonder.

I couldn't believe my luck.

She had been born rich but chose to live poor, an idea that was beyond my experience or comprehension. She had read more books in the last year than I had in my life. And when my efforts to hide my ignorance finally gave way in tatters she took to my education with the same enthusiasm she brought to our bed.

Her methods were erratic, to say the last. For each new book she gave me revealed a hundred gaps in my knowledge that would have to be plugged with other books.

I was deluged with the whole artillery of Hup literature: long and difficult works like Gibson's *Class and Genetics*, Schumacher's *Comparative Physiognomy*, Hale's *Wolf Children*.

I didn't care what they were about. If they had been treatises on the history of Rome or the Fasta economic system I would have read them with as much enthusiasm and probably learned just as little.

Sitting on the wharf I sang her "Rosie Allan's Outlaw Friend", the story of an ill-lettered cattle thief and his love for a young school mistress. My body was like an old guitar, fine and mellow with beautiful resonance.

The first star appeared.

"The first star," I said.

"It's a planet," she said.

"What's the difference?" I asked.

She produced a school book on the known solar system at breakfast the next morning.

"How in the hell do you know so little?" she said, eating the omelette I'd cooked her.

I stared at the extraordinary rings of Saturn, knowing I'd known some of these things long ago. They brought to mind classrooms on summer days, dust, the smell of oranges, lecture theatres full of formally dressed students with eager faces.

"I guess I just forgot," I said. "Maybe half my memory is walking around in other bodies. And how in the fuck is it that you don't know how to make a decent omelette?"

"I guess," she grinned, "that I just forgot."

She wandered off towards the kitchen with her empty plate but got distracted by an old newspaper she found on the way. She put the plate on the floor and went on to the kitchen where she read the paper, leaning back against the sink.

"You have rich habits," I accused her.

She looked up, arching her eyebrows questioningly.

"You put things down for other people to pick up."

She flushed and spent five minutes picking up things and putting them in unexpected places.

She never mastered the business of tidying up and finally I was the one who became housekeeper.

When the landlord arrived one morning to collect the rent she introduced me as "my house-proud lover". I gave the bastard my street-fighter's sneer and he swallowed the smirk he was starting to grow on his weak little face.

I was the one who opened the doors to the harbour. I swept the floor, I tidied the books and washed the plates. I threw out the old newspapers and took down the posters for Hup meetings and demonstrations which had long since passed.

She came in from work after my first big clean-up and started pulling books out and throwing them on the floor.

"What in the fuck are you doing?"

"Where did you put them?"

"Put what?"

She pulled down a pile of old pamphlets and threw them on the floor as she looked between each one.

"What?"

"My posters, you bastard. How dare you."

I was nonplussed. My view of posters was purely practical. It had never occurred to me that they might have any function other than to adverise what they appeared to advertise. When the event was past the poster had no function.

Confused and angry at her behaviour, I retrieved the posters from the bin in the kitchen.

"You creased them."

"I'm sorry."

She started putting them up again.

"Why did you take them down? It's your house now, is it? Would you like to paint the walls, eh? Do you want to change the furniture too? Is there anything else that isn't to your liking?"

"Carla," I said, "I'm very sorry. I took them down because they were out of date."

"Out of date," she snorted. "You mean you think they're ugly."

I looked at the poster she was holding, a glorification of crooked forms and ugly faces.

"Well, if you want to put it like that, yes, I think they're fucking ugly."

She glowered at me, self-righteous and prim. "You can only say that because you're so conditioned that you can only admire looks like mine. How pathetic. That's why you like me, isn't it?"

Her face was red, the skin taut with rage.

"Isn't it?"

I'd thought this damn Hup thing had gone away, but here it was. The stupidity of it. It drove me insane. Her books became weapons in my hands. I threw them at her, hard, in a frenzy.

"Idiot. Dolt. You don't believe what you say. You're too young to know anything. You don't know what these damn people are like," I poked at the posters, "you're too young to know anything. You're a fool. You're playing with life." I hurled another book. "Playing with it."

She was young and nimble with a boxer's reflexes. She dodged the books easily enough and retaliated viciously, slamming a thick sociology text into the side of my head.

Staggering back to the window I was confronted with the vision of an old man's face, looking in.

I pulled up the window and transferred my abuse in that direction.

"Who in the fuck are you?"

A very nervous old man stood on a long ladder, teetering nervously above the street.

"I'm a painter."

"Well, piss off."

He looked down into the street below as I grabbed the top rung of the ladder and gave it a little bit of a shake.

"Who is it?" Carla called.

"It's a painter."

"What's he doing?"

I looked outside. "He's painting the bloody place orange."

The painter, seeing me occupied with other matters, started to retreat down the ladder.

"Hey." I shook the ladder to make him stop.

"It's only a primer," he pleaded.

"It doesn't need any primer," I yelled. "Those bloody boards will last a hundred years."

"You're yelling at the wrong person, fellah." The painter was at the bottom of the ladder now, and all the bolder because of it.

"If you touch that ladder again I'll have the civil police here." He backed into the street and shook his finger at me. "They'll do you, my friend, so just watch it."

I slammed the window shut and locked it for good measure. "You've got to talk to the landlord," I said, "before they ruin the place."

"Got to?"

"Please."

Her face became quiet and secretive. She started picking up books and pamphlets and stacking them against the wall with exaggerated care.

"Please, Carla."

"You tell them," she shrugged. "I won't be here." She fetched the heavy sociology text from beneath the window and frowned over the bookshelves, looking for a place to put it.

"What in the hell does that mean?"

"It means I'm a Hup. I told you that before. I told you the first time I met you. I'm taking a Chance and you won't like what comes out. I told you before," she repeated, "you've known all along."

"Be buggered you're taking a Chance."

She shrugged. She refused to look at me. She started picking up books and carrying them to the kitchen, her movements uncharacteristically brisk.

"People only take a Chance when they're pissed off. Are you?"

She stood by the stove, the books cradled in her arms, tears streaming down her face.

Even as I held her, even as I stroked her hair, I began to plot to keep her in the body she was born in. It became my obsession.

4.

I came home the next night to find the outside of the house bright orange and the inside filled with a collection of people as romantically ugly as any I had ever seen. They betrayed their upper-class origins by dressing their crooked forms in such romantic styles that they were in danger of creating a new foppishness. Faults and infirmities were displayed with a pride that would have been alien to any but a Hup.

A dwarf reclined in a Danish-style armchair, an attentuated hand waving a cigarette. His overalls, obviously tailored, were very soft, an expensive material splattered with "original" paint. If he hadn't been smoking so languorously he might have passed for real.

Next to him, propped against the wall, was the one I later knew as Daniel. The grotesque pockmarks on his face proudly accentuated by the subtle use of make-up and, I swear to God, colour co-ordinated with a flamboyant pink scarf.

Then, a tall thin woman with the most pronounced curvature of the spine and a gaunt face dominated by a most extraordinary hooked nose. Her form was clad in the tightest garments and from it emanated the not unsubtle aroma of power and privilege.

If I had seen them anywhere else I would have found them laughable, not worthy of serious attention. Masters amusing themselves by dressing as servants. Returned tourists clad in beggars' rags. Educated fops doing a bad charade of my tough, grisly companions in the boarding house.

But I was not anywhere else. This was our home and they had turned it into some spider's-web or nightmare where dog turds smell like French wine and roses stink of the charnel-house.

And there squatting in their midst, my most beautiful Carla, her eyes shining with enthusiasm and admiration whilst the hook-nosed lady waved her bony fingers.

I stayed by the door and Carla, smiling too eagerly, came to greet me and introduce me to her friends. I watched her dark eyes flick nervously from one face to the next, fearful of everybody's reaction to me, and mine to them.

I stood awkwardly behind the dwarf as he passed around his snapshots, photographs taken of him before his Chance.

"Not bad, eh?" he said, showing me a shot of a handsome man on the beach at Cannes. "I was a handsome fellow, eh?"

It was a joke, but I was confused about its meaning. I nodded, embarrassed. The photograph was creased with lines like the palm of an old man's hand.

I looked at the woman's curved back and the gaunt face, trying to find beauty there, imagining holding her in my arms.

She caught my eyes and smiled. "Well, young man, what will you do while we have our little meeting?"

God knows what expression crossed my face, but it would have been a mere ripple on the surface of the feelings that boiled within me.

Carla was at my side in an instant, whispering in my ear that it was an important meeting and wouldn't take long. The hook-nosed woman, she said, had an unfortunate manner, was always upsetting everyone, but had, just the same, a heart of gold.

I took my time in leaving, fussing around the room looking for my beautiful light fishing rod with its perfectly preserved old Mitchell reel. I enjoyed the silence while I fossicked around behind books, under chairs, finally discovering it where I knew it was all the time.

In the kitchen, I slapped some bait together, mixing mince meat, flour and garlic, taking my time with this too, forcing them to indulge in awkward small talk about the price of printing and the guru in the electric cape, one of the city's recent contributions to a more picturesque life.

Outside the painters were washing their brushes, having covered half of the bright orange with a pale blue.

The sun was sinking below the broken columns of the Hinden Bridge as I cast into the harbour. I used no sinker, just a teardrop of mince meat, flour and garlic, an enticing meal for a bream.

The water shimmered, pearlescent. The bream attacked, sending sharp signals up the delicate light line. They fought like the fury and showed themselves in flashes of frantic silver. Luderick also swam below my feet, feeding on long ribbons of green weed. A small pink cloud drifted absent-mindedly through a series of metamorphoses. An old work boat passed, sitting low in the water like a dumpy brown duck, full of respectability and regular intent.

Yet I was anaesthetized and felt none of what I saw.

For above my head in a garish building slashed with orange and blue I imagined the Hups concluding plans to take Carla away from me.

The water became black with a dark-blue wave. The waving reflection of a yellow-lighted window floated at my feet and I heard the high-pitched wheedling laugh of a Fasta in the house above. It was the laugh of a Fasta doing business.

That night I caught ten bream. I killed only two. The others I returned to the melancholy window floating at my feet.

5.

The tissues lay beneath the bed. Dead white butterflies, wet with tears and sperm.

The mosquito net, like a giant parody of a wedding veil, hung over us, its fibres luminescent, shimmering with light from the open door.

Carla's head rested on my shoulder, her hair wet from both our tears.

"You could put it off," I whispered. "Another week."

"I can't. You know I can't. If I don't do it when it's booked I'll have to wait six months."

"Then wait ..."

"I can't."

"We're good together."

"I know."

"It'll get better."

"I know."

"It won't last, if you do it."

"It might, if we try."

I damned the Hups in silence. I cursed them for their warped ideals. If only they could see how ridiculous they looked.

I stroked her brown arm, soothing her in advance of what I said. "It's not right. Your friends haven't become working class. They have a manner. They look disgusting."

She withdrew from me, sitting up to light a cigarette with an angry flourish.

"Ah, you see," she pointed the cigarette at me. "Disgusting. They look disgusting."

"They look like rich fops amusing themselves. They're not real. They look evil."

She slipped out from under the net and began searching through the tangled clothes on the floor, separating hers from mine. "I can't stand this," she said, "I can't stay here."

"You think it's so fucking great to look like the dwarf?" I screamed. "Would you fuck him? Would you wrap your legs around him? Would you?"

She stood outside the net, very still and very angry. "That's my business."

I was chilled. I hadn't meant it. I hadn't thought it possible. I was trying to make a point. I hadn't believed.

"Did you?" I hated the shrill tone that crept into my voice. I was a child, jealous, hurt.

I jumped out of the bed and started looking for my own clothes. She had my trousers in her hand. I tore them from her.

"I wish you'd just shut up," I hissed, although she had said nothing. "And don't patronize me with your stupid smart talk." I was shaking with rage.

She looked me straight in the eye before she punched me.

I laid one straight back.

"That's why I love you, damn you."

"Why?" she screamed, holding her hand over her face. "For God's sake, why?"

"Because we'll both have black eyes."

She started laughing just as I began to cry.

6.

I started to write a diary and then stopped. The only page in it says this:

"Saturday. This morning I know that I am in love. I spend the day thinking about her. When I see her in the street she is like a painting that is even better than you remembered. Today we wrestled. She told me she could wrestle me. Who would believe it? What a miracle she is. Ten days to go. I've got to work out something."

7.

Wednesday. Meeting day for the freaks.

On the way home I bought a small bag of mushrooms to calm me down a little bit. I walked to Pier Street the slow way, nibbling as I went.

I came through the door ready to face the whole menagerie but they weren't there, only the hook-nosed lady, arranged in tight brown rags and draped across a chair, her bowed legs dangling, one shoe swinging from her toe.

She smiled at me, revealing an uneven line of stained and broken teeth.

"Ah, the famous Lumpy."

"My name is Paul."

She swung her shoe a little too much. It fell to the floor, revealing her mutant toes in all their glory.

"Forgive me. Lumpy is a pet name?" She wiggled her toes. "Something private?"

I ignored her and went to the kitchen to make bait in readiness for my exile on the pier. The damn mince was frozen solid. Carla had tidied it up and put it in the freezer. I dropped it in hot water to thaw it.

"Your mince is frozen."

"Obviously."

She patted the chair next to her with a bony hand.

"Come and sit. We can talk."

"About what?" I disconnected the little Mitchell reel from the rod and started oiling it, first taking off the spool and rinsing the sand from it.

"About life." She waved her hand airily, taking in the room as if it were the entire solar system. "About ... love. What ... ever." Her speech had that curious unsure quality common in those who had taken too many Chances, the words spluttered and trickled from her mouth like water from a kinked and tangled garden hose. "You can't go until your mince ... mince has thawed." She giggled. "You're stuck with me."

I smiled in spite of myself.

"I could always use weed and go after the luderick."

"But the tide is high and the weed will be ... impossible to get. Sit down." She patted the chair again.

I brought the reel with me and sat next to her, slowly dismantling it and laying the parts on the low table. The mushrooms were beginning to work, coating a smooth creamy layer over the gritty irritations in my mind.

"You're upset," she said. I was surprised to hear concern in her voice. I suppressed a desire to look up and see if her features had changed. Her form upset me as much as the soft rotting faces of the beggars who had been stupid enough to make love with the Fastas. So I screwed the little ratchet back in and wiped it twice with oil.

"You shouldn't be upset."

I said nothing, feeling warm and absent-minded, experiencing that slight ringing in the ears you get from eating mushrooms on an empty stomach. I put the spool back on and tightened the tension knob. I was running out of things to do that might give me an excuse not to look at her.

She was close to me. Had she been that close to me when I sat down? In the corner of my eye I could see her gaunt bowed leg, an inch or two from mine. My thick muscled forearm seemed to belong to a different planet, to have been bred for different purposes, to serve sane and sensible ends, to hold children on my knee, to build houses, to fetch and carry the ordinary things of life.

"You shouldn't be upset. You don't have to lose Carla. She loves you. You may find that it is not so bad ... making love ... with a Hup." She paused. "You've been eating mushrooms, haven't you?"

The hand patted my knee. "Maybe that's not such a bad thing."

What did she mean? I meant to ask, but forgot I was feeling the hand. I thought of rainbow trout in the clear waters at Dobson's Creek, their brains humming with creamy music while my magnified white hands rubbed their underbellies, tickling them gently before grabbing them, like stolen jewels, and lifting them triumphant in the sunlight. I smelt the heady smell of wild blackberries and the damp fecund odours of rotting wood and bracken.

"We don't forget how to make love when we change."

The late afternoon sun streamed through a high window. The room was golden. On Dobson's Creek there is a shallow run from a deep pool, difficult to work because of overhanging willows; caddis flies hover above the water in the evening light.

The hand on my knee was soft and caressing. Once, many Chances ago, I had my hair cut by a strange old man. He combed so slowly, cut so delicately, my head and my neck were suffused with pleasure. It was in a classroom. Outside someone hit a tennis ball against a brick wall. There were cicadas, I remember, and a water sprinkler threw beads of light onto glistening grass, freshly mown. He cut my hair shorter and shorter till my fingers tingled.

It has been said that the penis has no sense of right or wrong, that it acts with the brainless instinct of a venus fly-trap, but that is not true. It's too easy a reason for the stiffening cock that rose, stretching blindly towards the bony fingers.

"I could show," said the voice, "that it is something quite extraordinary ... not worse ... better ... better ... better by far, you have nothing to fear."

I knew, I knew exactly in the depth of my clouded mind, what was happening. I didn't resist it. I didn't want to resist it. My purpose was as hers. My reasons probably identical.

Softly, sonorously she recited:

"Which trees are beautiful?"

All trees that grow.

Which bird is fairest?"

A zipper undone, my balls held gently, a finger stroked the length of my cock. My eyes shut, questions and queries banished to dusty places.

"The bird that flies.

Which face is fairest?

The faces of the friends of the people of the earth."

A hand, flat-palmed on my rough face, the muscles in my shoulders gently massaged, a finger circling the lips of my anal sphincter.

"Which forms are foul?

The forms of the owners.

The forms of the exploiters.

The forms of the friends of the Fastas."

Legs across my lap, she straddled me. "I will give you a taste ... just a taste ... you won't stop Carla ... you can't stop her."

She moved too fast, her legs gripped mine too hard, the hand on my cock was tugging towards her cunt too hard.

My open eyes stared into her face. The face so foul, so misshapen, broken, the skin marked with ruptured capillaries, the green eyes wide, askance, alight with premature triumph.

Drunk on wine I have fucked monstrously ugly whores. Deranged on drugs, blind, insensible, I have grunted like a dog above those whom I would as soon have slaughtered.

But this, no. No, no, no. For whatever reason, no. Even as I stood, shaking and trembling, she clung to me, smiling, not understanding. "Carla will be beautiful. You will do things you never did."

Her grip was strong. I fought through mosquito nets of mushroom haze, layer upon layer that ripped like dusty lace curtains, my arms flailing, my panic mounting. I had woken under water, drowning.

I wrenched her hand from my shoulder and she shrieked with

pain. I pulled her leg from my waist and she fell back onto the floor, grunting as the wind was knocked from her.

I stood above her, shaking, my heart beating wildly, the head of my cock protruding foolishly from my unzipped trousers, looking as pale and silly as a toadstool.

She struggled to her feet, rearranging her elegant rags and cursing. "You are an ignorant fool. You are a stupid, ignorant, reactionary fool. You have breathed the Fastas' lies for so long that your rotten body is soaked with them. You stink of lies … Do you … know who I am?"

I stared at her, panting.

"I am Jane Larange."

For a second I couldn't remember who Jane Larange was, then it came to me. "The actress?" The once beautiful and famous.

I shook my head. "You silly bugger. What in God's name have you done to yourself?"

She went to her handbag, looking for a cigarette. "We will kill the Fastas," she said, smiling at me, "and we will kill their puppets and their leeches."

She stalked to the kitchen and lifted the mince meat from the sink. "Your mince is thawed."

The mince was pale and wet. It took more flour than usual to get it to the right consistency. She watched me, leaning against the sink, smoking her perfumed cigarette.

"Look at you, puddling around with stinking meat like a child playing with shit. You would rather play with shit than act like a responsible adult. When the adults come you will slink off and kill fish." She gave a grunt. "Poor Carla."

"Poor Carla." She made me laugh. "You try and fuck me and then you say 'poor Carla'!"

"You are not only ugly," she said, "you are also stupid. I did that for Carla. Do you imagine I like your stupid body or your silly mind? It was to make her feel better. It was arranged. It was her idea, my friend, not mine. Possibly a silly idea, but she is desperate and unhappy and what else is there to do? But," she smiled thinly, "I will report a great success, a great rapture. I'm sure you won't be silly enough to contradict me. The lie will make her happy for a little while at least."

I had known it. I had suspected it. Or if I hadn't known it, was trying a similar grotesque test myself. Oh, the lunacy of the times!

"Now take your nasty bait and go and kill fish. The others will be here soon and I don't want them to see your miserable face."

I picked up the rod and a plastic bucket.

She called to me from the kitchen. "And put your worm back in your pants. It is singularly unattractive bait."

I said nothing and walked out the door with my cock sticking out of my fly. I found the dwarf standing on the landing. It gave him a laugh, at least.

8.

I told her the truth about my encounter with the famous Jane Larange. I was a fool. I had made a worm to gnaw at her with fear and doubt. It burrowed into the space behind her eyes and secreted a filmy curtain of uncertainty and pain.

She became subject to moods which I found impossible to predict.

"Let me take your photograph," she said.

"All right."

"Stand over there. No, come down to the pier."

We went down to the pier.

"All right."

"Now, take one of me."

"Where's the button?"

"On the top."

I found the button and took her photograph.

"Do you love me? Now?"

"Yes, damn you, of course I do."

She stared at me hard, tears in her eyes, then she wrenched the camera from my hand and hurled it into the water.

I watched it sink, thinking how beautifully clear the water was that day.

Carla ran up the steps to the house. I wasn't stupid enough to ask her what the matter was.

9.

She had woken in one more mood, her eyes pale and staring, and there was nothing I could do to reach her. There were only five days to go and these moods were thieving our precious time, arriving with greater frequency and lasting for longer periods.

I made the breakfast, frying bread in the bacon fat in a childish attempt to cheer her up. I detested these malignant withdrawals. They made her as blind and selfish as a baby.

She sat at the table, staring out the window at the water. I washed the dishes. Then I swept the floor. I was angry. I polished the floor and still she didn't move. I made the bed and cleaned down the walls in the bedroom. I took out all the books and put them in alphabetical order according to author.

By lunchtime I was beside myself with rage.

She sat at the table.

I played a number of videotapes I knew she liked. She sat before the viewer like a blind deaf-mute. I took out a recipe book and began to prepare beef bourguignon with murder in my heart.

Then, some time about half past two in the afternoon, she turned and said "Hello."

The cloud had passed. She stood and stretched and came and held me from behind as I cooked the beef.

"I love you," she said.

"I love you," I said.

She kissed me on the ear.

"What's the matter?" My rage had evaporated, but I still had to ask the stupid question.

"You know." She turned away from me and went to open the doors above the harbour. "Let's not talk about it."

"Well," I said, "maybe we should."

"Why?" she said. "I'm going to do it so there's nothing to be said."

I sat across from her at the table. "You're not going to go away," I said quietly, "and you are not going to take a Chance."

She looked up sharply, staring directly into my eyes, and I think she finally knew that I was serious. We sat staring at each other, entering an unreal country as frightening as any I have ever travelled in.

Later she said quietly, "You have gone mad."

There was a time, before this one, when I never wept. But now as I nodded tears came, coursing down my cheeks. We held each other miserably, whispering things that mad people say to one another.

10.

Orgasm curved above us and through us, carrying us into dark places where we spoke in tongues.

Carla, most beautiful of women, crying in my ear, "Tell me I'm beautiful."

Locked doors with broken hinges. Bank vaults blown asunder. Blasphemous papers floating on warm winds, lying in the summer streets, flapping like wounded seagulls.

11.

In the morning the light caught her. She looked more beautiful than the Bonnards in Hale's *Critique of Bourgeois Art*, the orange sheet lying where she had kicked it, the fine hairs along her arm soft and golden in the early light.

Bonnard painted his wife for more than twenty years. Whilst her arse and tits sagged he painted her better and better. It made my eyes wet with sentimental tears to think of the old Mme Bonnard posing for the ageing M. Bonnard, standing in the bathroom or sitting on the toilet seat of their tiny flat.

I was affected by visions of constancy. In the busy lanes behind the central market I watched an old couple helping each other along the broken-down pavement. He, short and stocky with a country man's arms, now infirm and reduced to a walking stick. She, of similar height, overweight, carrying her shopping in an old-fashioned bag.

She walked beside him protectively, spying out broken cobble-stones, steps, and the feet of beggars.

"You walk next to the wall," I heard her say, "I'll walk on the outside so no one kicks your stick again."

They swapped positions and set off once more, the old man jutting his chin, the old lady moving slowly on swollen legs, strangers to the mysteries of the Genetic Lottery and the glittering possibilities of a Chance.

When the sun, in time, caught Carla's beautiful face, she opened her eyes and smiled at me.

I felt so damned I wished to slap her face.

It was unbelievable that this should be taken from us. And even as I held her and kissed her sleep-soft lips, I was beginning, at last, to evolve a plan that would really keep her.

As I stroked her body, running one feathery finger down her shoulder, along her back, between her legs, across her thighs, I was designing the most intricate door, a door I could fit on the afternoon before her Chance-day, a door to keep her prisoner for a day at least. A door I could blame the landlord for, a door painted orange, a colour I could blame the painters for, a door to make her miss her appointment, a door that would snap shut with a normal click but would finally only yield to the strongest axe.

The idea, so clearly expressed, has all the tell-tale signs of total madness. Do not imagine I don't see that, or even that I didn't know it then. Emperors have built such monuments on grander scales and entered history with the grand expressions of their selfishness and arrogance.

So allow me to say this about my door: I am, even now, startled at the far-flung originality of the design and the obsessive craftsmanship I finally applied to its construction. Further, to this day I can think of no simpler method by which I might have kept her.

12.

I approached the door with infinite cunning. I took time off from work, telling Carla I had been temporarily suspended for insolence, something she found easy enough to believe.

On the first day I built a new doorframe, thicker and heavier than the existing one, and fixed it to the wall struts with fifty long brass screws. When I had finished I painted it with orange primer and rehung the old door.

"What's all this?" she asked.

"Those bloody painters are crazy," I said.

"But that's a new frame. Did the painters do that?"

"There was a carpenter too," I said. "I wish you'd tell the landlord to stop it."

"I bought some beer," she said, "let's get drunk."

Neither of us wanted to talk about the door, but while we drank I watched it with satisfaction. The orange was a beautiful colour. It cheered me up no end.

13.

The dwarf crept up on me and found me working on the plans for the door, sneaking up on his obscene little feet.

"Ah-huh."

I tried to hide it, this most complicated idea which was to lock you in, which on that very afternoon I would begin making in a makeshift workshop I had set up under the house. This gorgeous door of iron-hard old timber with its four concealed locks, their keyholes and knobs buried deep in the door itself.

"Ah," said the dwarf, who had been a handsome fellow, resting his ugly little hand affectionately on my elbow. "Ah, this is some door."

"It's for a friend," I said, silently cursing my carelessness. I should have worked under the house.

"More like an enemy," he observed. "With a door like that you could lock someone up in fine style, eh?"

I didn't answer. The dwarf was no fool but neither was he as crazy as I was. My secret was protected by my madness.

"Did it occur to you," the dwarf said, "that there might be a problem getting someone to walk through a doorway guarded by a door like this? A good trap should be enticing, or at least neutral, if you get my meaning.

"It is not for a jail," I said, "or a trap, either."

"You really should see someone," he said, sitting sadly on the low table.

"What do you mean, 'someone'?"

"Someone," he said, "who you could see. To talk to about your problems. A counsellor, a shrink, someone …" He looked at me and smiled, lighting a stinking Fasta cigarette. "It's a beautiful door, just the same."

"Go and fuck yourself," I said, folding the plans. My fishing rod was in the corner.

"After the revolution," the dwarf said calmly, "there will be no locks. Children will grow up not understanding what a lock is. To see a lock it will be necessary to go to a museum."

"Would you mind passing me my fishing rod. It's behind you."

He obliged, making a small bow as he handed it over. "You should consider joining us," he said, "then you would not have this problem you have with Carla. There are bigger problems you could address your anger to. Your situation now is that you are wasting energy being angry at the wrong things."

"Go and fuck yourself," I smiled.

He shook his head. "Ah, so this is the level of debate we have come to. Go and fuck yourself, go and fuck yourself." He repeated my insult again and again, turning it over curiously in his mind.

I left him with it and went down to talk to the bream on the pier. When I saw him leave I went down below the house and spent the rest of the day cutting the timber for the door. Later I made dovetail joints in the old method before reinforcing them with steel plates for good measure.

14.

The door lay beneath us, a monument to my duplicity and fear.

In a room above, clad by books, stroked slowly by Haydn, I presented this angry argument to her while she watched my face with wide wet eyes. "Don't imagine that you will forget all this. Don't imagine it will all go away. For whatever comfort you find with your friends, whatever conscience you pacify, whatever guilt you assuage, you will always look back on this with regret and know that it was unnecessary to destroy it. You will curse the schoolgirl morality that sent you to a Chance Centre and in your dreams you will find your way back to me and lie by my side and come fishing with me on the pier and everyone you meet you will compare and find lacking in some minor aspect."

I knew exactly how to frighten her. But the fear could not change her mind.

To my argument she replied angrily: "You understand nothing."

To which I replied: "You don't yet understand what you will understand in the end."

After she had finished crying we fucked slowly and I thought of Mme Bonnard sitting on the edge of the bath, all aglow like a jewel.

15.

She denied me a last night. She cheated me of it. She lied about the date of her Chance and left a day before she had said. I awoke to find only a note, carefully printed in a handwriting that seemed too young for the words it formed. Shivering, naked, I read it.

Dear Lumpy,
 You would have gone crazy. I know you. We couldn't part like that. I've seen the hate in your eyes but what I will remember is love in them after a beautiful fuck.

I've got to be with Mum and Dad. When I see beggars in the street I think it's them. Can't you imagine how that feels? They have turned me into a Hup well and proper.

You don't always give me credit for my ideas. You call me illogical, idealist, fool. I think you think they all mean the same thing. They don't. I have no illusions (and I don't just mean the business about being sick that you mentioned). Now when I walk down the street people smile at me easily. If I want help it comes easily. It is possible for me to do things like borrow money from strangers. I feel loved and protected. This is the privilege of my body which I must renounce. There is no choice. But it would be a mistake for you to imagine that I haven't thought properly about what I am doing. I am terrified and cannot change my mind.

There is no one I have known who I have ever loved a thousandth as much as you. You would make a perfect Hup. You do not judge, you are objective, compassionate. For a while I thought we could convert you, but c'est la vie. You are a tender lover and I am crying now, thinking how I will miss you. I am not brave enough to risk seeing you in whatever body the comrades can extract from the Fastas. I know your feelings on these things. It would be too much to risk. I couldn't bear the rejection.

I love you, I understand you,

Carla

I crumpled it up. I smoothed it out. I kept saying "Fuck", repeating the word meaninglessly, stupidly, with anger one moment, pain the next. I dressed and ran out to the street. The bus was just pulling away. I ran through the early morning streets to the Chance Centre, hoping she hadn't gone to another district to confuse me. The cold autumn air rasped my lungs, and my heart pounded wildly. I grinned to myself thinking it would be funny for me to die of a heart attack. Now I can't think why it seemed funny.

16.

Even though it was early the Chance Centre was busy. The main concourse was crowded with people waiting for relatives, staring at the video display terminals for news of their friends' emergence. The smell of trauma was in the air, reminiscent of stale orange peel and piss. Poor people in carpet slippers with their trousers too short sat hopefully in front of murals depicting Leonardo's classic proportions. Fasta technicians in grubby white coats wheeled patients in and out of the concourse in a sequence as aimless and purposeless

as the shuffling of a deck of cards. I could find Carla's name on none
of the terminals.

I waited the morning. Nothing happened. The cards were shuf-
fled. The coffee machine broke down. In the afternoon I went out
and bought a six-pack of beer and a bottle of Milocaine capsules.

17.

In the dark, in the night, something woke me. My tongue furry, my
eyes like gravel, my head still dulled from the dope and drink,
half-conscious I half saw the woman sitting in the chair by the bed.

A fat woman, weeping.

I watched her like television. A blue glow from the neon lights in
the street showed the coarse, folded surface of her face, her poor lank
greying hair, deep creases in her arms and fingers like the folds in
babies' skin, and the great drapery of chin and neck was reminiscent
of drought-resistant cattle from India.

It was not a fair time, not a fair test. I am better than that. It was
the wrong time. Undrugged, ungrogged, I would have done better.
It is unreasonable that such a test should come in such a way. But in
the deep grey selfish folds of my mean little brain I decided that I
had not woken up, that I would not wake up. I groaned, feigning
sleep and turned over.

Carla stayed by my bed till morning, weeping softly while I lay
with my eyes closed, sometimes sleeping, sometimes listening.

In the full light of morning she was gone and had, with bitter
reproach, left behind merely one thing: a pair of her large grey
knickers, wet with the juices of her unacceptable desire. I placed
them in the rubbish bin and went out to buy some more beer.

18.

I was sitting by the number five pier finishing off the last of the beer.
I didn't feel bad. I'd felt a damn sight worse. The sun was out and
the light dancing on the water produced a light dizzy feeling in my
beer-sodden head. Two bream lay in the bucket, enough for my
dinner, and I was sitting there pondering the question of Carla's flat:
whether I should get out or whether I was meant to get out or
whether I could afford to stay on. They were not difficult questions
but I was managing to turn them into major events. Any moment I'd

be off to snort a couple more caps of Milocaine and lie down in the sun.

I was not handling this well.

"Two fish, eh?"

I looked up. It was the fucking dwarf. There was nothing to say to him.

He sat down beside me, his grotesque little legs hanging over the side of the pier. His silence suggested a sympathy I did not wish to accept from him.

"What do you want, ugly?"

"It's nice to hear that you've finally relaxed, mm? Good to see that you're not pretending any more." He smiled. He seemed not in the least malicious. "I have brought the gift."

"A silly custom. I'm surprised you follow it." It was customary for people who took the Chance to give their friends pieces of clothing from their old bodies, clothing that they expected wouldn't fit the new. It had established itself as a pressure-cooked folk custom, like brides throwing corsages and children putting first teeth under their pillows.

The dwarf held out a small brown-paper parcel.

I unwrapped the parcel while he watched. It contained a pair of small white lady's knickers. They felt as cold and vibrant as echoes across vast canyons: quavering questions, cries, and thin misunderstandings.

I shook the dwarf by his tiny hand.

The fish jumped forlornly in the bucket.

19.

So long ago. So much past. Furies, rages, beer and sleeping pills. They say that the dwarf was horribly tortured during the revolution, that his hands were literally sawn from his arms by the Fastas. The hunchback lady now adorns the 50 IG postage stamps, in celebration of her now famous role at the crucial battle of Haytown.

And Carla, I don't know. They say there was a fat lady who was one of the fiercest fighters, who attacked and killed without mercy, who slaughtered with a rage that was exceptional even in such a bloody time.

But I, I'm a crazy old man, alone with his books and his beer and his dog. I have been a clerk and a pedlar and a seller of cars. I have been ignorant, and a scholar of note. Pockmarked and ugly I have wandered the streets and slept in the parks. I have been bankrupt and handsome and a splendid conman. I have been a river of poisonous silver mercury, without form or substance, yet I carry with me this one pain, this one yearning, that I love you, my lady, with all my heart. And on evenings when the water is calm and the birds dive amongst the whitebait, my eyes swell with tears as I think of you sitting on a chair beside me, weeping in a darkened room.

Fragrance of Roses

I have looked for the village in an atlas and cannot find it. It is a poor town, made from the same grey granite as the mountain it clings to. The cobbled streets are of the same grey stone, often wet with rain, occasionally covered with a heavy blanket of snow.

There are twenty-five houses in the village and the old man lived at the very last one on the high side, above the school. The house was as bleak and unremarkable as any other house in the village. But behind it was the most intricately wrought glasshouse, as delicate and weblike as the glasshouse in Kew Gardens in London.

In this house the old man grew roses. It is probable that the glasshouse was warmer than his own mean bedroom and his bleak kitchen. If the ashes in his stove were often white and cold, the furnace for the glasshouse never died through the winter. And in the very worst months he would move his mattress into the glasshouse and spend his nights there.

He spoke Spanish very badly and often irritated the storekeeper with his requests. The people in the village had never had a foreigner in their midst before and after twenty-five years he was seen as more of a pest than a novelty.

His mail was often needlessly delayed by the post office clerk, an idle and malicious game which gave less pleasure than teasing the old peasant woman who waited for letters from her son. The clerk tormented the old man quietly and determinedly, placing his parcels in full view on the shelf and insisting they were not for him.

The old man accepted this quietly, and called at the post office persistently, day after day, waiting patiently at the counter, rubbing his small dry hands together and breathing into them to make them warm. He never complained. He never explained that the books were about the production of hybrid roses, and it would have made no difference if he had.

When his books were finally made available he walked painfully back to his house, a small grey figure who looked fragile and pitiable in this village where everything seemed so cold and massive and unsympathetic.

Earlier he had donated a large clock for the small village school. The gift had been received with embarrassment. A year later the clock stopped. The opinion in the village was that the clock had been of inferior quality.

So its hands were still showing eighteen minutes past seven when two more foreigners arrived in the village fifteen years afterwards.

They asked questions at the post office and the clerk gladly told them everything he knew about the old man with the glasshouse. He even gave them two parcels he had been keeping for over a month.

That night the old man left the village with the other two foreigners, who were members of the Israeli security service.

Later the town was to learn that the small, quiet foreigner had been none other than the former commandant of Auschwitz.

The locals will now tell you that when they visited the old man's glasshouse they discovered the most beautiful rose that anyone could ever dream of. It was twice the size of a man's fist and was almost black in colour, with just the faintest hint of red in its velvety petals.

When I visited the town in the spring of 1974, the rose, or one of its descendants, was still there, carefully nurtured by the townspeople and shown with pride to visitors.

The locals insist that you can smell the mass graves of Auschwitz in the glasshouse, and that the heavy, sweet odour of death emanates from this one black rose.

They have named it "The Auschwitz Rose" and have printed a cheap colour postcard to celebrate their peculiar good fortune.

He Found Her in Late Summer

1.

He found her in the later summer when the river ran two inches
deep across glistening gravel beds and lay resting in black pools
in which big old trout lay quietly in the cool water away from the
heat of the sun. Occasionally a young rainbow might break the
surface in the middle of the day, but the old fish did no such thing,
either being too well fed and sleepy or, as the fisherman would
believe, too old and wise to venture out at such a time.

Silky oaks grew along the banks and blackberries, dense and
tangled, their fruit long gone into Dermott's pies, claimed by birds,
or simply rotted into the soil, vigorously reclaimed the well-trodden
path which wound beside fallen logs, large rocks, and through
fecund gullies where tree ferns sent out tender new fronds as soft
and vulnerable as the underbellies of exotic moths.

In one such gully a fallen tree had revealed a cave inside a rocky
bank. It was by no means an ideal cave. A spring ran continually
along its floor. Great fistfuls of red clay fell frequently and in the heat
of the day mosquitoes sheltered there in their swarming thousands.

Three stalks of bracken outside its dirty mouth had been broken
and the sign of this intrusion made him lower his hessian bag of
hissing crayfish and quietly peer inside.

It was there he found her, wild and mud-caked, her hair tangled,
her fair skin scratched and festered and spotted with infected insect
bites. She was no more than twenty years old.

For a long time they regarded each other quietly. He squatted on
his heels and slapped at the mosquitoes that settled on his long, wiry
brown legs. She, her eyes swollen, fed them without complaint.

He rolled down the sleeves of his plaid shirt and adjusted his
worn grey hat. He pulled up his odd grey socks and shifted his
weight.

She tugged at her dress.

At last he held out his hand in the way that one holds out a hand to a shy child, a gentle invitation that may be accepted or rejected.

Only when the hand was lowered did she hold hers out. It was small and white, a city hand with the last vestiges of red nail polish still in evidence. He took the hand and pulled her gently to her feet, but before a moment had passed she had collapsed limply onto the muddy floor.

Dermott adjusted his hat.

"I'm going to have to pick you up," he said. It was, in a way, a question, and he waited for a moment before doing as he'd said. Then, in one grunting movement, he put her on his shoulders. He picked up the bag of crayfish and set off down the river, wading carefully, choosing this way home to save his passenger from the blackberry thorns which guarded the path along the banks.

Neither spoke to the other, but occasionally the girl clenched his shoulder tightly when they came to a rapid or when a snake, sleeping lightly on a hot rock, slipped silkily into the water as they approached.

Dermott carried his burden with pleasure yet he did not dwell on the reason for her presence in the cave or attempt to invent theories for her being so many hundred miles from a town. For all of these things would be dealt with later and to speculate on them would have seemed to him a waste of time.

As he waded the river and skirted the shallow edges of the pools he enjoyed his familiarity with it, and remembered the time twenty years ago when it was as strange to him as it must be to his silent guest. Then, with the old inspector, he had done his apprenticeship as his mother had wished him to, read books, learned to identify two hundred different dragonflies, studied the life cycle of the trout, and most particularly the habits of the old black crayfish which were to be his alone to collect. It was an intensive education for such a simple job, and he often reflected in later years that it may not have been, in an official sense, compulsory, but rather a private whim of the old inspector who had loved this river with a fierce protectiveness.

The examination had been a casual affair, a day trek in late spring from where the old Chinese diggings lay in soft mossy neglect to the big falls five miles upriver, yet at the end of it he had successfully identified some two hundred trees, thirty insects, three snakes, and described to the old inspector's satisfaction the ancient history of the rocks in the high cliffs that towered above them.

It was only much later, after a child had died, a wife had left and floods had carried away most of his past, that he realized exactly what the old man had given him: riches more precious than he could ever have dreamed of. He had been taught to know the river with the quiet confident joy of a lover who knows every inch of his beloved's skin, every hair, every look, whether it denoted the extremes of rage and passion or the quieter more subtle moods that lie between.

Which is not to suggest that he was never lonely or that the isolation did not oppress him at times, but there were few days in which he did not extract some joy from life, whether the joys be as light as the clear web of a dragonfly or as turbulent as the sun on the fast water below Three Day Falls.

The winters were the hardest times, for the river was brown and swollen then and crayfish were not to be had. Then he occupied himself with a little tin mining and with building in stone. His house, as the years progressed, developed a unique and eccentric character, its grey walls jutting out from the hillside, dropping down, spiralling up. And if few walls were quite vertical, few steps exactly level, it caused him no concern. Winter after winter he added more rooms, not from any need for extra space, but simply because he enjoyed doing it. Had ten visitors descended on him there would have been a room for each one, but there were few visitors and the rooms gave shelter to spiders and the occasional snake which feasted on mice before departing.

Once a gypsy had stayed during a period of illness and repaid his host with a moth-eaten rug of Asiatic origin. Other items of furniture were also gifts. An armchair with its stuffing hanging out had been left by a dour fisheries inspector who had carried it eighty miles on top of his Land Rover, knowing no other way to express his affection for this man on the river with his long silences and simple ways.

Books also were in evidence, and there was an odd assortment. Amongst them was a book on the nature of vampires, the complete works of Dickens, a manual for a motor car that now lay rusting in a ravine, and a science fiction novel entitled *Venus in a Half-Shell*. He had not, as yet, read any of them although he occasionally picked one up and looked at it, thinking that one day he would feast on the knowledge contained within. It would never have occurred to him that the contents of these books might reflect different levels of truth or reality.

"Nearly home," he said. They had left the river and passed through the high bracken of Stockman's Flat. He trudged in squelching boots along the rutted jeep track that led to the house. He was hot now, and tired. "Soon be there," he said, and in a moment he had carried her through the thick walls of his house and gently lowered her down into the old armchair.

She huddled into the armchair while he filled a big saucepan with water and opened the draught on the stained yellow wood stove.

"Now," he said, "we'll fix you up."

From the armchair the girl heard the words and was not frightened.

2.

There was about him a sense of pain long past, a slight limp of the emotions. His grey eyes had the bittersweet quality of a man who has grasped sorrow and carries it with him, neither indignant at its weight nor ignorant of its value. So if his long body was hard and sinewy, if his hair was cut brutally short, there was also a ministering gentleness that the girl saw easily and understood.

He brought warm water in a big bowl to her chair and with it two towels that might once, long ago, have been white.

"Now," he said, "one of us is going to wash you."

He had large drooping eyelids and a shy smile. He shifted awkwardly from one waterlogged boot to the other. When she didn't move he put the towels on the arm of the chair and the bowl of water on the flagstone floor. "Don't worry about getting water on the floor," he said.

She heard him squelch out of the room and, in a moment, imagined she heard a floor being swept elsewhere in the house. Outside the odd collection of windows she could see the tops of trees and below, somewhere, she heard the sound of the river.

She picked up a grey towel and went to sleep.

3.

The tin roof was supported by the trunks of felled trees. The stone walls were painted white, veiled here and there by the webs of spiders and dotted with the bodies of dead flies. In one corner was a bed made from rough logs, its lumpy mattress supported by three thicknesses of hessian. A tree brushed its flowers against the window and left its red petals, as fine and delicate as spider legs, caught in the webs that adorned the glass.

She lay naked on the bed and let him wash her.

Only when he came in embarrassed indecision to the vulva did she gently push his hand away.

When the washing was over he took a pair of tweezers, strangely precise and surgical, and removed what thorns and splinters he found in her fair skin. He bathed her cuts in very hot water, clearing away the yellow centres of red infections, and dressed each one with a black ointment from a small white jar which bore the legend, "For Man or Beast".

He denied himself any pleasure he might have felt in touching her naked body, for that would have seemed wrong to him. When the wounds were all dressed he gave her an old-fashioned collarless shirt to wear for a nightdress and tucked her into bed. Only then did he allow himself the indulgence of thinking her pretty, seeing behind the cuts and swellings, the puffed eyelids, the tangled fair hair, a woman he might well have wished to invent.

She went to sleep almost immediately, her forehead marked with a frown.

He tiptoed noisily from the room and busied himself tidying up the kitchen in a haphazard fashion. But even while he worried over such problems as where to put a blackened saucepan his face broke continually into a grin. "Well," he said, "wonders will never cease."

When dinner came he presented her with two rainbow trout and a bowl of potatoes.

4.

It would be two days before she decided to walk and he passed these much as he would normally have, collecting the crayfish both morning and afternoon, gardening before lunch, fishing before dinner. Yet now he carried with him a new treasure, a warm white egg which he stored in some quiet dry part of his mind, and as he worked his way down the rows of tomato plants, removing the small green grubs with his fingers, he smiled more often than he would have done otherwise.

When a shadow passed over the tangled garden and he looked up to admire the soft drift of a small white cloud, he did not look less long than he would have normally but there was another thing which danced around his joy, an aura of a brighter, different colour.

Yet he was, through force of habit, frugal with his emotions, and he did not dwell on the arrival of the girl. In fact the new entry into his life often slipped his mind completely or was squeezed out by his concentration on the job at hand. But then, without warning, it would pop up again and then he would smile. "Fancy that," he'd say. Or: "Well, I never."

The girl seemed to prefer staying in the house, sometimes reading, often sleeping with one of Dermott's neglected books clutched to her chest. The swellings were subsiding, revealing a rather dreamy face with a wide, sad mouth and slightly sleepy blue eyes. A haze of melancholy surrounded her. When she walked it was with the quiet distraction of a sleepwalker. When she sat, her slow eyes followed Dermott's progress as he moved to and fro across the room, carrying hot water from the fire to the grimy porcelain sink, washing a couple of dishes, or one knife or two forks, stewing peaches from the tree in the garden, brewing a herb tea with a slightly bitter flavour, sweeping the big flagstone floor while he spread dirt from his hobnailed boots behind him, cleaning four bright-eyed trout, feeding the tame magpie that wandered in and out through the sunlit patch in the back door.

He whistled a lot. They were old-fashioned optimistic songs, written before she was born.

When, finally, she spoke, it was to talk about the sweeping.

"You're bringing more dirt in than you're sweeping out."

He did not look surprised that she had spoken but he noted the softness of her voice and hoarded it away with delight. He considered the floor, scratching his bristly head and rubbing his hand over his newly shaven chin. "You're quite correct," he said. He sat on the long wooden bench beneath the windows and began to take off his boots, intending to continue the job in stockinged feet.

"Here," she said, "give it to me."

He gave her the broom. A woman's touch, he smiled, never having heard of women's liberation.

5.

That night at dinner she told him her story, leaning intently over the table and talking very softly.

It was beyond his experience, involving drugs, men who had abused her, manipulated her, and finally wished to kill her. He was too overwhelmed by it to really absorb it. He sat at the table absently cleaning a dirty fork with the tablecloth. "Fancy that," he would say. Or: "You're better off now." And again: "You're better off without them, that's all."

From the frequency of these comments she judged that he wished her to be quiet, but really they were produced by his feeling of inadequacy in the face of such a strange story. He was like a peasant faced with a foreigner who speaks with a strange accent, too overcome to recognize the language as his own.

What he did absorb was that Anna had been treated badly by the world and was, in some way, wounded because of it.

"You'll get better here," he said. "You've come to the right place."

He smiled at her, a little shyly, she thought. For a brief instant she felt as safe and comfortable as she had ever been in her life and then fear and suspicion, her old friends, claimed her once more. Her skin prickled and the wind in the trees outside sounded forlorn and lonely.

She sat beside the kerosene lamp surrounded by shadows. That the light shone through her curling fair hair, that Dermott was almost unbearably happy, she was completely unaware.

6.

Weeks passed and the first chill of autumn lay along the river. Dermott slowly realized that Anna's recovery would not be as fast as he had imagined, for her lips remained sad and the sleepy eyes remained lustreless and defeated.

He brought things for her to marvel at — a stone, a dried-out frog, a beetle with a jewel-like shell — but she did not welcome the interruptions and did not try to hide her lack of interest, so he stood there with the jewel in his hand feeling rather stupid.

He tried to interest her in the river, to give to her the pleasure the old inspector had given him, but she stood timidly on the bank wearing a dress she had made from an old sheet, staring anxiously at the ground around her small flat feet.

He stood in the water wearing only baggy khaki shorts and a battered pair of tennis shoes. She thought he looked like an old war photo.

"Nothing's going to bite you," he said. "You can stand in the water."

"No." She shook her head.

"I'll teach you how to catch crays."

"No."

"That's a silky oak."

She didn't even look where he pointed. "You go. I'll stay here."

He looked up at the sky with his hands on his hips. "If I go now I'll be away for two hours."

"You go," she insisted. The sheet dress made her look as sad as a little girl at bedtime.

"You'll be lonely. I'll be thinking that you're lonely," he explained, "so it won't be no fun. Won't you be lonely?"

She didn't say no. She said, "You go."

And he went, finally, taking that unsaid no with him, aware that his absence was causing her pain. He was distracted and cast badly. When a swarm of caddis flies hatched over a still dark pool he did not stay to cast there but pushed on home with the catch he had: two small rainbows. He had killed them without speaking to them.

He found her trying to split firewood, frowning and breathing hard.

"You're holding the axe wrong," he said, not unkindly.

"Well, how should I hold it then?"

She stood back with her hands on her hips. He showed her how to do it, trying to ignore the anger that buzzed around her.

"That's what I was doing," she said.

He retired to tend the garden and she thought he was angry with her for intruding into his territory. She did not know that his mother had been what they called "a woman stockman" who was famous for her toughness and self-reliance. When she saw him watching her she thought it was with disapproval. He was keeping an anxious eye on her, worried that she was about to chop a toe off.

7.

"Come with me."

"No, you go."

That is how it went, how it continued to go. A little litany.

"Come, I'll teach you."

"I'm happy here."

"When I get back you'll be unhappy."

Over and over, a pebble being washed to and fro in a rocky hole.

"I can't enjoy myself when you're unhappy."

"I'm fine."

And so on, until when he waded off downstream he carried her unhappiness with him and a foggy film lay between him and the river.

The pattern of his days altered and he in no way regretted the change. Like water taking the easiest course down a hillside, he moved towards those things which seemed most likely to minimize her pain. He helped her on projects which she deemed to be important, the most pressing of which seemed to be the long grass which grew around the back of the house. They denuded the wild vegetable garden of its dominant weed. He had never cared before and had let it grow beside the tomatoes, between the broad leaves of the pumpkin, and left it where it would shade the late lettuce.

As he worked beside her it did not occur to him that he was, in fact, less happy than he had been, that his worry about her happiness had become the dominant factor of his life, clouding his days and nagging at him in the night like a sore tooth. Yet even if it had occurred to him, the way she extended her hand to him one evening and brought him silently to her bed with a soft smile on her lips would have seemed to him a joy more complex and delightful than any of those he had so easily abandoned.

He worked now solely to bring her happiness. And if he spent many days in shared melancholy with her there were also rewards of no small magnitude: a smile, like a silver spirit breaking the water, the warmth of her warm white body beside him each morning.

He gave himself totally to her restoration and in so doing became enslaved by her. Had he been less of an optimist he would have abandoned the project as hopeless.

And the treatment was difficult, for she was naked and vulnerable, not only to him, to the world, but to all manner of diseases which arrived, each in their turn, to lay her low. In moments of new-found bitterness he reflected that these diseases were invited in and made welcome, evidence of the world's cruelty to her, but these thoughts, alien to his nature and shocking for even being thought, were banished and put away where he could not see them.

She lay in his bed pale with fever. He picked lad's love, thyme, garlic and comfrey and ministered to her with anxious concern.

"There," he said, "that should make you better."

"Do you love me, Dermott?" she asked, holding his dry dusty hand in her damp one. They made a little mud between them.

He was surprised to hear the word. It had not been in his mind, and he had to think for a while about love and the different things he understood by it.

"Yes," he said at last, "I do."

He felt then that he could carry her wounded soul from one end of the earth to the other. He was bursting with love.

8.

As he spent more and more time dwelling with her unhappiness he came to convince himself that he was the source of much of her pain. It was by far the most optimistic explanation, for he could do nothing to alter her past even if he had been able to understand it. So he came to develop a self-critical cast of mind, finding fault with himself for being stubborn, silent, set in his ways, preferring to do a thing the way he always had rather than the way she wished.

Eager to provide her with companionship he spent less and less time on the river, collecting the crays just once, early in the morning while she slept. In this way he lost many but this no longer seemed so important.

When she picked up a book to read in the afternoons he did likewise, hoping to learn things that he might share with her. He felt himself unlettered and ignorant. When he read he followed the lines of words with his broken-nailed finger and sometimes he caught her watching his lips moving and he felt ashamed. He discovered things to wonder at in every line and he often put his book down to consider the things he had found out. He would have liked to ask Anna many things about what he read but he imagined that she found his questions naive and irritating and did not like to be interrupted. So he passed over words he did not understand and marvelled in confused isolation at the mysteries he found within each page.

The True Nature of Vampires had been written long ago by a certain A.A. Dickson, a man having no great distinction in the world of the occult, whose only real claim to public attention had been involved with extracting twenty thousand pounds from lonely old women. Needless to say, none of this was mentioned in the book.

Dermott, sitting uncomfortably on a hard wooden bench, looked like a farmer at a stock sale. He learned that vampirism does not necessarily involve the sucking of blood from the victim (although this often is the case) but rather the withdrawal of vital energy, leaving the victim listless, without drive, prey to grey periods of intense boredom.

– On page ten he read, "The case of Thomas Deason, a farmer in New Hampshire, provides a classic example. In the spring of 1882 he befriended a young woman who claimed to have been beaten and abandoned by her husband. Deason, known to be of an amiable disposition, took the woman into his home as a housekeeper. Soon the groom and farm workers noticed a change in Deason: he became listless and they remarked on the 'grey pallor of his skin'. The groom, who was a student of such matters, immediately suspected vampirism and, using rituals similar to those described in the Dion Fortune episode, drove the woman from the house. It was, however, too late to save Deason, who had already become a Vampire himself. He was apprehended in a tavern in 1883 and brought to trial. After his conviction and execution there was still trouble in the area and it was only after a stake was driven through the heart of his exhumed corpse in 1884 that things returned to normal in the area."

One night, when making love, Anna bit him passionately on the neck. He leapt from her with a cry and stood shivering beside the bed in the darkness.

Suspicion and fear entered him like worms, and a slow anger began to spread through him like a poison, nurtured and encouraged each day by further doses of A.A. Dickson's musty book. His mind was filled with stories involving marble slabs, bodies that did not decompose, pistol wounds and dark figures fleeing across moonlit lawns.

His eyes took on a haunted quality and he was forever starting and jumping when she entered the room. As he moved deeper and deeper into the book his acknowledgment of his own unhappiness became unreserved. He felt that he had been tricked. He saw that Anna had taken from him his joy in the river, turned the tasks he had enjoyed into chores to be endured.

He began to withdraw from her, spending more and more time by himself on the river, his mind turning in circles, unable to think what to do. He moved into another bed and no longer slept with her. She did not ask him why. This was certain proof to him that she already knew.

Yet his listlessness, his boredom, his terrible lethargy did not decrease, but rather intensified.

When the jeep arrived to pick up the crayfish its driver was staggered to see the haunted look in Dermott's eyes and when he went back to town he told his superiors that there was some funny business with a woman down at Enoch's Point. The superiors, not having seen the look in Dermott's eyes, smiled and clucked their tongues and said to each other: "That Dermott, the sly old bugger."

9.

He had nightmares and cried in his sleep. He dreamed he had made a silver stake and driven it through her heart. He dreamed that she cried and begged him not to, that he wept too, but that he did it anyway, driven by steel wings of fear. He shrieked aloud in his sleep and caused the subject of his dreams to lie in silent terror in her bed, staring into the blackness with wide open eyes.

He thought of running away, of leaving the river and finding a new life somewhere else, and this is almost certainly what he would have done had he not, returning from a brooding afternoon beside the river, discovered the following note: "Dear Dermott, I am leaving because you do not like me any more and I know that I am making you unhappy. I love you. Thank you for looking after me when I was sick. I hate to see you unhappy and I know it is me that is doing it." It was signed: "With all the love in my heart, Anna."

The words cut through him like a knife, slicing away the grey webs he had spun around himself. In that moment he recognized only the truth of what she wrote and he knew he had been duped, not by her, but by a book.

It was evening when he found her, sitting on the bank of a small creek some three miles up the jeep track. He said nothing, but held out his hand. They walked back to the river in darkness.

He did not doubt that she was a vampire, but he had seen something that A.A. Dickson with his marble tombs and wooden stakes had never seen: that a vampire feels pain, loneliness and love.

If vampires fed on other people, he reflected, that was the nature of life: that one creature drew nourishment and strength from another.

When he took her to his bed and embraced her soft white body he was without fear, a strong animal with a heavy udder.

War Crimes

1.

In the end I shall be judged.

They will write about me in books and take care to explain me so badly that it is better that I do it myself. They will write with the stupid smugness of middle-class intellectuals, people of moral rectitude who have never seriously placed themselves at risk. They have supported wars they have not fought in, and damned companies they have not had the courage to destroy. Their skins are fair and pampered and their bellies are corseted by expensively made jeans.

They will write about me as a tyrant, a psychopath, an aberrant accountant, and many other things, but it would never once occur to them that I might know exactly what I am doing. Neither would they imagine that I might have feelings other than those of a mad dog.

But they do not have a monopoly on finer feelings, as you shall soon see.

I cannot begin to tell you how I loathe them, how I have, in weaker moments, envied them, how I longed to be accepted by them and how at the first hint of serious threat from them I would not have the faintest qualms about incarcerating them all.

The vermin, may they feast on this and cover it with their idiot footnotes.

2.

The most elegant Barto was driving the car, a Cadillac Eldorado with leaking air-conditioning. In a purple T-shirt and waist-length fur coat, he looked the very embodiment of sexual decadence; his shoulder-length raven hair, his large nose and chin made him as severely handsome as an Indian on a postage stamp.

Beside him, I felt graceless and boring. My trousers were shapeless and baggy. My hair was tangled and knotted, my glasses filthy, and my unshaven face looked pasty, patchy and particularly unhealthy. It was a face made to appear in the dock, a poor man's face, squinting nervously into the future.

I had filled the trunk of the Eldorado with an armoury of modern weapons but I carried a small .22 under my arm. The .22 is a punk's weapon. It was my secret and I shared it with no one.

Barto kept a Colt .45 in the glove box. It was big and heavy and perfectly melodramatic. "If it doesn't scare the cunts to death we can always shoot them."

It was a hard time and only the most unconventional methods were succeeding in business. Certainly we didn't look like the popular image of businessmen. We were special. Once you appreciated the power we held, you could only be astonished at our cleverness. For me, my grubbiness had become a habit so long ingrained that it is difficult to think back to how it started or why it continued. But it was, finally, a perverse identification with the poor people I was raised amongst. Excepting the years when I was a young accountant, I have continued to wear the marks of my caste for they are stamped, not only on my face, but also on my poorly fed bones. No matter what rich clothes I wore, I would deceive no one. So I wear them proudly. They stink. The most casual observer will know that I am someone of great note: to dress like a beggar and be given the accord due to a prince. It was a costume fit for an age which had begun by proudly proclaiming its lack of regimentation and ended railing at its own disarray.

Unemployment had become a way of life and the vagabonds had formed into bands with leaders, organizations and even, in some cases, apocalyptic religions whose leaders preached the coming of the millennium. These last were as rare as threatened species, cosseted, protected and filmed by bored journalists eager for symbols of the times. The rest of the bands roamed the country, godless, hungry and unpublicized.

We saw only one group on the six-hundred-mile journey north. They were camped by a bridge at the Thirty-two Mile Creek. As we approached they attempted to drag a dead tree across the road.

I felt Bart hesitate. The cowboy boot came back off the accelerator, making a stoned decision at eighty miles an hour.

"Plant it," I said. I said it fast and hard.

He planted it. The Cadillac responded perfectly. I heard the crunch of breaking wood. Tearing noises. Looking back I saw two bundles of rags lying on the road.

"Shit." The word was very quiet. I looked at Bart. He looked a little pale.

"How did it feel?"

He considered my question. "I don't know," he drawled out the words, beginning to luxuriate in the puzzle they contained, "just sort of *soft*. Sort of ..." he furrowed his brow, "sort of did-it-happen, didn't-it-happen type of thing."

I leant into the back seat and pulled up a bag of dope and rolled an exceedingly large trumpet-shaped joint. The Cadillac devoured the miles while the faulty air-conditioner dripped cold water onto Bart's cowboy boots, and I thought once again how genuinely strange our lives had become. I often stepped back and looked at myself from the outside. I was unthinkable to myself. Now I found it amazing to consider that only a week ago I had been making a most unconventional presentation to a highly conservative board of directors. The success of the presentation was the reason we were now heading north in this elegant motor car.

The board, of course, knew a great deal about us before we made the presentation. They were prepared for, and wanted, the unconventional. They expected to be frightened. They also expected to be given hope. Given their desire to believe in us, it would have been exceedingly difficult to do the presentation badly.

I dressed as badly as they would have expected me to, and spoke as arrogantly as they had been led to expect I would. There was nothing terribly original in the way we analysed the ills of the frozen meals subsidiary. It was simply professional, a quality that was lacking in the subsidiary's present management. We presented a market analysis, and pointed out that their company was in a unique position to take advantage of the present economic conditions. We presented a profit projection for the next twelve months and claimed a fee of half this figure, or whatever profit was finally delivered. If there was no profit we would ask for no fee. This money was to be delivered to us, in whatever way their lawyers could discover, tax-free.

We demanded complete autonomy during those twelve months and asked the board's guarantee that they would not interfere.

It was not difficult to imagine that they would buy it. They were making heavy losses and we were obviously confident of making considerable profits. In addition I had two successes behind me: a pharmaceutical company and a supermarket chain, both of which had been rescued from the hands of the receivers and turned into profitable businesses.

It would never have occurred to them that now, on this road heading towards their factory, I would be so tense and nervous that my stomach would hurt. I had gained a perverse pleasure from their respect. Now I would live in terror of losing it.

Outside the car, the scrub was immersed in a hot haze. The world seemed full of poisonous spiders, venomous snakes, raw red clay, and the bitter desperate faces of disenfranchised men.

3.

The factory belched smoke into the sky and looked beyond saving. We parked by the bridge and watched white-coated men in an aluminium boat inspect the dead fish which were floating there.

The dead fish and the foul smoke from the plant assumed the nature of a feverish dream. Flies descended on our shirt backs and our faces. We waved at them distractedly. Through the heat haze I observed the guard at the factory gate. His scuttling behaviour seemed as alien and inexplicable as that of a tropical crab. It took some time to realize that we were the object of his uncertain attentions: he kept walking out towards us and shouting. When we didn't respond, he quickly lost all courage and nervously scuttled back to his post.

The Cadillac was confusing him.

Around the plant the country was scrubby, dense, prickly and unattractive. Certain grasses betrayed the presence of swamp and the air itself was excessively humid and almost clinging. The prospect of spending twelve months here was not a pleasant one.

Behind the anxious guard the factory stood quietly rusting under a heavy grey sky. It looked like nothing more than a collection of eccentric tin huts. One might expect them to contain something dusty and rotten, the leftovers from a foreign war in disordered heaps, broken instruments with numbered dials and stiff canvas webbing left to slowly rust and decay.

Yet the plant was the largest frozen food processing and storage facility in the country. The storerooms, at this moment, contained one and a half million dollars' worth of undistributed merchandise, household favourites that had lost their popularity in the market-place. It was hard to reconcile the appearance of the plant with the neat spiral-bound report titled "Production and Storage Facilities".

I knew at that moment I didn't want to go anywhere near that plant. I wanted to be in a nice bar with soft music playing, the air-conditioning humming, a little bowl of macadamia nuts and a very long gin and tonic in front of me. I got back into the Cadillac and took some Mylanta for my stomach.

At the gate the guard seemed reluctant to let us in and Bart pulled out the Colt. It was an unnecessary move but he enjoyed it. His gangster fantasies had never been allowed for in corporate life.

He looked like a prince of darkness, standing at the gate in a purple T-shirt, a fur coat, the fingernails of his gun-hand painted in green and blue. I smiled watching him, thinking that capitalism had surely entered its most picturesque phase.

4.

The hate in the staff canteen was as palpable as the humidity outside. It buzzed and stung, finding weak spots in my carefully prepared defences. We had played the videotape with the chairman's speech to the employees but it did nothing to dilute the feelings of the office staff, who behaved like a subject race.

The girls giggled rudely. The men glowered, pretending to mis-understand the nature of the orders we gave them. I felt that their threat might, at any instant, become physical and an attack be made. Barto, more agitated than usual, produced the .45. He was laughed at. He stood there aghast, no longer feeling as cool as he would have liked.

It was a particularly bad start. I requested the sales, marketing and production managers to escort me to my new office where we could discuss their futures.

When I left the canteen I was burning with a quiet rage. My hands were wet. My stomach hurt. I was more than a little fright-ened. I began to understand why men raze villages and annihilate whole populations. The .22 under my arm nagged at me, produc-ing feelings that were intense, unnameable, and not totally un-pleasurable.

5.

I fed on my fear and used it to effect. It was my strength. It hardened me and kept my mind sharp and clear. It gave me the confidence of cornered men. It made sleep almost impossible.

We worked from the old general manager's office, the brown smudge of his suicide an unpleasant reminder of the possibility of failure. We found the floor more convenient than the desk and spread papers across it as we attempted to piece the mess together.

It became obvious very early that the marketing manager was a fool. His understanding of conditions in the market-place was minimal. His foolishly optimistic report had been a major contributing factor in the present state of affairs.

He had taken too many store buyers to too many lunches. It must have been a little awkward for the buyers to tell him they weren't taking any more of his products.

It was also difficult for me to tell him that he could not continue as marketing manager. He was large and weak and watery. He had the softness of those who lie long hours in hot baths before dressing carefully in tailor-made suits. He could not adjust to me. He could not think of me as a threat, merely as someone who needed a wash. When I dismissed him he did not understand. He returned to his office the next day and continued as usual.

When you kill flathead you put a knife in their foreheads. Their eyes roll and sometimes pop out. The marketing manager reacted in a similar manner when it occurred to him that he was being fired. His mouth opened wide with shock and I was reminded of a flathead when I looked at his eyes.

As with the fish, I found it necessary not to think too much about what I was doing. I consoled myself with the knowledge that there would have been no job for him if we had not arrived. He had been thorough enough to have destroyed any hope of his own survival. He had covered it from every angle.

With the marketing manager's departure I discovered a whole filing cabinet full of documents that he had withheld from me. As I examined them I felt like a surgeon who comes to remove a small growth and finds a body riddled with secondary cancers. I had promised the board of directors things which, given all the available information, had seemed reasonable at the time. But here the gap between the diseased body and my promises of glowing health seemed an inseparable gulf.

I began to feel that I might be less remarkable than the glorious picture the board had of me. When I had presented my credentials and broad methods to them I had felt myself to be quite glamorous, a superior being who could succeed where they and their underlings had failed. It was a good picture. I preened myself before it as if it were a mirror.

I claimed to despise the board but I didn't want that mirror taken away from me. It was very important that they hold me in high esteem.

Incensed by the appalling news we found in marketing, we re-called the sales force and threatened them with violence and torture if they did not succeed. I am thin and not particularly strong but I had a gun and I had the genuine craziness of a man who will do anything to get what he wants. Anger filled me like electricity. My fingertips were full of it. They felt so tight and tense I couldn't keep them still. Bart stood smoking a joint and waving the Colt around the office with the most carefree abandon, sighting down the barrel at first one head and then another. We spoke to them quietly and politely about the sales targets we expected them to meet in the coming year.

Whether through accident or design Bart let off a shot into the ceiling and the sales manager involuntarily wet his pants. His staff laughed out loud at his misfortune. I thought how ugly they looked with their big cufflinks and silly grins.

It was not the ideal way to do business, but the times were hard, other job opportunities non-existent, and the competition in the trade intense. Our products had been de-listed by five major chains and were in danger of being kicked out of another three. Only our cheapest lines survived, and these — frozen dinners of exceptionally low quality and price — would have to spearhead our return to the market. They were cheap and filling and there were a lot of people who needed cheap filling meals.

I gave Bart control of the marketing function and watched him nervously like a driver who takes his hands from the wheel but is ready to take it back at any serious deviation. Apart from twelve months as a trainee product manager with Procter and Gamble, Bart's previous experience had been totally in advertising agencies.

There was really nothing but my intuitive judgment to say that he'd be a success in this new role.

I needn't have worried. He had a business brain the like of which is rarely seen, as cool and clean as stainless steel and totally without compassion. It was Bart who dumped two warehouses full of frozen food straight into the river, thus clearing a serious bottleneck in the system and creating space for products that could actually be sold. He budgeted for the eight-hundred-dollar fine and spent another eight hundred dollars on the finest cocaine to celebrate with. I approved these expenses without question. The goods had been sitting in the warehouse for two years and had been written down in value by a thoughtful accountant who seemed the only person to have anticipated the company's present plight.

Bart doubled the advertising budget, a move which terrified me but which I approved. He planned to stop advertising altogether in the second half and plough an equivalent amount into promotions. It was pressure-cooked marketing. It was unorthodox and expensive but it was the sort of brutal tactic that could be necessary for our success.

Bart pursued the practice of business with the logic of an abstract artist. Things were, for him, problems of form, colour and design. He pursued cool acts with relentless enthusiasm.

From my office I watched him walk across the wide bitumen apron to fire the production manager. His hair was now dyed a henna red, and his cowboy boots made his out-turned toes look curiously elegant. He walked as casually as a man who has run out of cigarette papers taking a stroll to a corner shop.

6.

The typists had stopped staring at us and were actually managing to get some work done. However, I still continued to have trouble with my secretary. She was nearly forty-five, matronly in style, and as the secretary to the most senior executive, she was the leader of the others. She was pursuing some guerrilla war of her own, expressing her distaste for me in a hundred little ways which were almost impossible to confront directly.

On this occasion she found me alone in my office. I was sitting on the floor going through the computer print-outs from the Nielsen survey when she crept up behind me and hissed in my ear.

"May I have a word."

The bitch. She made me jump. I turned in time to catch the last sign of a smirk disappearing from her face.

I stood up. The idea of looking up her dress was beyond contemplation. I thought, as I stumbled to my feet, that I should fire her or at least exchange her with someone who could handle her. As she continued to disapprove of me she was making me more and more irritable. Yet she seemed able to bully me. I felt awkward and embarrassed every time I talked to her.

"I think," she declared, "there is something you should know."

"Yes." I put the Nielsen survey carefully on the desk. Her face was pinched and her lips had become tightly pursed. If there had been a smirk it had well and truly been superseded by this angry, self-righteous expression.

"I have come to tell you that I can't work for you."

I felt enormously relieved. "I'm sorry to hear that," I said.

"I don't suppose you'd be interested in why."

"Yes, of course I would."

This would be her moment and I would pay attention. I did as she wished.

"I cannot respect you." Her sanctimonious little face gave me the shits.

"Oh," I said, "and why not?"

"Because you are not worthy of respect." She stood stiffly upright, tapping her lolly-pink suit with a ballpoint pen which was putting little blue flecks all over it.

"You don't respect yourself." She cast a derisive glance over me as if I were someone at the back door begging for sandwiches. So she didn't like the way I dressed. "You don't respect yourself, how can I respect you."

"Oh," I laughed, "I respect myself, please don't concern yourself on that one."

"You've obviously had a good education. Why don't you use it?"

She was beginning to push it a bit far. Her complete ridiculousness didn't stop her from upsetting me. I should have been beyond all this. "I'm your general manager," I said, "surely that's using my education."

She tossed her head. "Ah, but you're not the *real* general manager."

She shouldn't have upset me at all. Her values were nothing like mine. She was trapped and helpless and had to work for me. She had no education, no chance of change. All she had was the conviction that I was worthless. It shouldn't have upset me, but it is exactly the sort of thing that upsets me. The thing she wouldn't give me was the only thing I wanted from her. I felt my temper welling up.

"Do you realize the power I have over you?" I asked her.

"You have no power over me, young man."

She didn't understand me. She thought I was just a scruffy punk who had come to make a mess in her old boss's office. She couldn't know that I have a terrible character weakness, a temper that comes from nowhere and stuns even me with its ferocity and total unreasonableness.

She shouldn't have spoken to me like that, but she wouldn't stop. She wouldn't leave when I asked her to. I stood in my office and I asked the old bitch to leave. I asked her coolly and nicely and politely, but she continued to berate me.

I watched her mouth move. It became unreal. I had the .22 under my arm, and my feelings were not like the real world, they were hot and pleasurable and electrically intense.

It was rage.

She had just repeated herself. She had just said something about respect when I drew the pistol and shot her in the foot.

She stopped talking. I watched the red mark on her stockinged foot and thought how amazingly accurate I had been.

She sat on the floor with surprise and a slight grunt.

Barto came running through the door and I stood there with the gun in my hand feeling stupid.

Later the incident made me think about myself and what I wanted from life.

7.

The provincial city nearest the plant was a most unappealing place, catering to the tastes of farmers and factory hands. We devised, therefore, quarters of our own at the plant itself and managed to create a very pleasant island within the administration block.

Here a quite unique little society began to evolve, hidden from a hostile environment by dull red-brick walls. Here we devoted ourselves to the pursuit of good talk, fanciful ideas and the appreciation of good music.

We introduced fine old Belouch rugs, rich in colour, others from Shiraz, Luristan, old Khelims, mellow and pleasant, glowing like jewels. Here we had huge couches and leather armchairs, soft and old and vibrating with the dying snores of retired soldiers, the suppleness of ancient leathers a delight to the senses. We had low, slow, yellow lights, as gentle as moonlight, and stereo equipment, its fidelity best evoked by considering the sound of Tibetan temple bells. The food, at first, was largely indifferent but the drugs and wine were always plentiful, of extraordinary variety and excellent quality.

In these conditions we marvelled at ourselves, that we, the sons of process workers and hotelkeepers, should live like this. We were still young enough to be so entranced by our success and Barto, whose father sold stolen goods in a series of hotels, was eager that a photograph be taken.

Barto seemed the most innocent of men. He approached life languidly, rarely rising before ten and never retiring before three. Ideas came from him in vast numbers and hardly ever appeared to be anything but wisps of smoke.

Lying on the great Belouch saddlebag, graceful as a cat in repose, he would begin by saying, "What if ..." It was normally Bart who said "What if ..." and normally me who said "yes" or "no". His mind was relentless in its logic, yet fanciful in style, so the most circuitous and fanciful plans would always, on examination, be found to have cold hard bones within their diaphanous folds.

We were all-powerful. We only had to dream and the dream could be made real. We planned the most unlikely strategies and carried them out, whole plots as involved and chancy as movie scenarios. It was our most remarkable talent. For instance, we evolved a plan for keeping a defecting product manager faithful by getting him a three-bag smack habit and then supplying it.

Our character judgment was perfect. We were delighted by our astuteness.

The product manager stayed but unfortunately killed himself a few months later, so not everything worked out as perfectly as we would have hoped.

We saw ourselves anew, mirrored in the eyes of each new arrival, and we preened ourselves before their gaze.

Thelma was the first to arrive. She came to be with Bart and was astounded, firstly by the ugliness of the plant, secondly by the beauty of our private world, and thirdly by the change she claimed had occurred in Bart. She found him obsessed with the business enterprise and unbearably arrogant about his part in it. This she blamed me for. She sat in a corner whispering with Bart and I fretted lest she persuade him to go away with her. She was slender and elegant and dark as a gypsy. She had little needle tracks on her arms, so later on I was able to do a deal with her whereby she agreed to go away for a while.

Ian arrived to take over the sales force and we delighted in his company. He thought our methods of enthusing the salesmen historically necessary but not the most productive in the long term. He took them fifteen miles into town and got drunk with them for two days. He had two fist fights and, somewhere along the line, lost the representative for southern country districts, a point he continued to remain vague about.

He was the perfect chameleon and won them over by becoming vulgar and loud-mouthed. He affected big cufflinks and changed his shirt twice a day. He had his hair cut perfectly and he looked handsome and macho with his smiling dark eyes.

The sales force loved him, having the mistaken idea that he was normal. Naturally he didn't discuss his enthusiastic appetite for a substance called A.C.P., a veterinary tranquillizer normally administered to nervous horses which he took, rather ostentatiously, from a teaspoon marked "Souvenir of Anglesea".

It was Ian who persuaded me to fly in Sergei from Hong Kong. With his arrival, a huge weight was lifted from my shoulders and I had more time to relax and enjoy the music and talk. Sergei was unknown to me and I found him, in some respects, alarming. It was as if he found nothing remarkable in our situation. He made no comment on the decor of our private quarters, our penchant for drugs, or the brilliance of our strategies. It was as if we stood before a mirror which reflected everything but ourselves. He made me nervous. I didn't know how I stood with him.

Yet he was the most ordinary of men: short, slim, and dark, moving with a preciseness which I found comforting in such a skilled accountant. He was eccentric in his dress, choosing neatly pressed grey flannel trousers, very expensive knitted shirts, and slip-on shoes of the softest leather. Only the small silver earring on his left earlobe gave an indication that he was not totally straight.

Sergei talked little but went quietly about the business of wrestling with our cash flow. In the first week he completely reprogrammed our computer to give us a simpler and faster idea of our situation. Each week's figures would be available on the Monday of the next week, which made life easier for all of us.

After three weeks I gave over the financial function almost completely to his care and tried to spend some time evolving a sensible long-term strategy suited to the economic climate.

Whilst the unemployed continued to receive government assistance there would be a multi-million-dollar business in satisfying their needs. Companies which should have had the sense to see this continued to ignore it. Obviously they viewed the present circumstances as some temporary aberration and were planning their long-term strategies in the belief that we would shortly be returning to normal market conditions.

My view was that we were experiencing "normal" market conditions.

I instructed our new product development team to investigate the possibility of producing a range of very simple frozen meals which would be extremely filling, could be eaten cold when cooking facilities were not available, and would be lower in cost than anything comparable. I had a series of pie-like dishes in mind but I left the brief open. It seemed like a golden opportunity.

Whilst I was engaged in this, word came from Ian that they had had a highly successful sell-in of our existing lines of frozen meals. He had given the trade substantial discounts and we were operating on very low profit margins, hoping to achieve a very high volume turnover and, more importantly, get our relationship with the trade back to a healthier state.

The telex from Ian was very short: "They love us till their balls ache. Sell-in is 180 per cent of forecast."

I looked out my window as Barto and Sergei walked towards the storeroom which hid the plant itself from my view. Bart's Colt now sat snugly in a hand-tooled leather holster he had spent the last few nights making.

Beside Bart's pointy-toed languid walk, Sergei looked as strict as a wound-up toy.

I watched them thoughtfully, thinking that they had the comic appearance of truly lethal things.

8.

My father lost his hand in a factory. He carried the stump with him as a badge of his oppression by factories. When I was very small I saw that my father had no hand and concluded that my hand would also be cut off when the time came. I carried this belief quietly in the dark part of the mind reserved for dreadful truths. Thus it was with a most peculiar and personal interest that I watched the beheading of chickens, the amputation of fox-terriers' tails, and even the tarring of young lambs. My fear was so intense that all communication on the subject was unthinkable. It would be done just as they had mutilated my cock by cutting off the skin on its head.

I envied my two sisters, who, I was sure, would be allowed to have two hands like my mother.

The factories my father worked in were many and various. I remember only their dark cavernous doors, their dull, hot metal exteriors, the various stinks they left in my father's hair, and the tired sour smell of sweaty clothes that could never be washed often enough.

In the sleep-out behind the house I pinned pictures of motor cars to the walls and masturbated. The yellow walls were decorated with dull brown ageing sellotape and the breasts of impossible girls even less attainable than the motor cars. It was here that I waited to be sent to the factory. Here on hot, stinking afternoons I planned the most fantastic escapes and the most bloodcurdling retaliations. It was here, at night, that I was struck dumb by nightmares. The nightmares that assailed me were full of factories which, never really seen and only imagined, were more horrifying than anything my father could have encountered. They cut and slashed at me with gleaming blades and their abysses and chasms gaped before my fearful feet. Their innards were vast and measureless, and they contained nothing but the machinery of mutilation.

The dreams pursued me throughout life and now, at thirty, I still have the same horrible nameless nightmare I first learned when I was five years old. I play it as if it were the music of hell, neatly notated, perfectly repeatable, and as horribly frightening as it was the first time. I am a rabbit caught in the headlights of my dream.

The time had now come to go and confront the factory which was mine. I had done everything in my power to stay away. It was easy enough to make decisions based on engineers' reports and the advice of the production manager. But finally the day came when the excuses began to look ridiculous.

When we left the central admin block the heat came out of the scrubland and hung on us. I had not been outside for three weeks and the heat which I had seen as air-conditioned sunshine now became a very raw reality. A northerly wind lifted stinging dust out of the scrub and flies tried to crawl up my nose and into my ears, as if they wished to lay eggs inside my brain.

The plant and storerooms blinded me with their metallic glare which was not diminished by the streaks of rust decorating their surfaces, hints of some internal disorder.

Barto, walking beside me on the soft, sticky bitumen, said: "How's your nightmare?"

His hair seemed surreal, haloed, blue sky above it and shining silver behind. Already I could hear the rumbling of the plant. A rivulet of dirty water came running from the No. 2 to meet us. Barto hopped across it nimbly, his cowboy boots still immaculately clean.

"Not good," I said. I regretted my confession most bitterly. A confession is nothing but a fart. I have despised those who make confessions of their fears and weaknesses. It is a game the middle class play but they are only manufacturing razorblades which will be used to slash their own stupid white throats.

The door of the No. 2 yawned cavernous in front of me. The floor was an inch deep in filthy water.

Bart stopped. "Fuck, I can't go in there."

"Why not?" The bastard had to go with me. I wasn't going by myself. We stopped at the door. A foul smell of something cooking came out and engulfed us. I thought I was going to be sick. "Why not?" I asked. "What's the matter?" I tried to make my voice sound normal.

"I'll get my fucking boots fucked." Bart stood at the door, legs apart, a hand on his hip, a knee crooked, looking down at his cowboy boots. "Fuck," he said, "I'm sorry."

"I'll buy you a new pair." I shouldn't have said that.

"No, there's none left to buy. Shit, I'm sorry." I could see that he was. I could see that there was no way I could talk him into coming with me. I was going to have to do the factory tour alone.

"Fuck your fucking boots."

"I'm sorry. It's just that you can't buy them any more."

I walked gingerly into the lake and kept going, leaving Bart to feel whatever guilt he was capable of.

In waking life it was not only the machinery I was frightened of, although it was terrifying enough. The vats were huge and their sheer bulk was so unrelated to anything human that I felt my throat block off at the consideration of the weight of food they would contain. The production line itself was also particularly old, clanking, wheezing, full of machinery that oozed grease and farted air, and which lifted and pulled and lifted without any regard for life and limb.

It was the people I didn't want to see.

The heat was impossible, far worse than outside. It mixed with the noise to produce an almost palpable substance which should have suffocated all life. The belt stretched on through this giant corrugated-iron oven, and men and women in grubby white stood beside the line, doing operations that had been perfectly described on the production report.

Line No. 3: four female packers, one male supervisor.

The information on the report was enough. It didn't help me to know that one of the female packers was tall and thin with a baleful glare she directed accusingly at management, that her companion was just as tall but heavier, that next to her was a girl of sixteen with wire spectacles and a heat rash that extended from her forehead to her hands, that one other, an olive-skinned girl with a smooth Mediterranean Madonna face, would have the foolishness to smile at me. And so on.

I have seen enough factories, God knows, but they continue to be a problem to me. They should not be. My fear is irrational and should be overcome by habituation. But nothing dulls me to the assault of factories and I carry with me, still, the conviction that I will end up at the bottom of the shit pile, powerless against the machines in factories. So I look at the people a little too hard, too searchingly, wondering about them in a way that could make my job impossible. The fish in my hand cannot be thought of as anything more than an operation to be performed. The minute one considers the feelings of the fish the act becomes more difficult. So, in factories, I have a weakness, a hysterical tendency to become the people I see there, to enter their bodies and feel their feelings, and see the never-ending loud, metallic, boring days. And I become bitterly angry for them. And their anger, of course, is directed at me, who isn't them. It is a weakness. A folly. An idiot's hobby.

I got my arse out of the factory as fast as I could.

Bart met me at the door of the No. 2. "How's your nightmare?"

I was still in its grip. I was shaking and angry. "It's really shitty in there. It is *really* shitty."

Bart polished his cowboy boot, rubbing the right toe on the back of his left leg. "What are you going to do about it?" he asked, innocently enough.

A confession is a fart. You should never make a confession, no matter what dope you're on. "I'm not going to do anything, pig face. There's not a fucking thing to do, if I wanted to. That's what factories are like." My suede boots were soaked in muck. I flicked a pea off and watched it bounce across the bitumen.

"Listen," the word drawled out of Bart as slow and lazy as the kicking pointy-toed walk he was walking. The word was inquisitive, tentative, curious and also politely helpful. "Listen, do you think they hate you?"

"Yes." I said it before I had time to think.

"Well," the word came out as lazily as the "listen", "I'll tell you what I'll do in the next two months."

I grinned at him. "What'll you do, smart-arse?"

"I'll fucking make them love you, smart-arse, if that's what you want."

He was grinning delightedly, his hands in his back pockets, his great Indian face turned up towards the screaming sun as if he was drinking power from it.

"And how will you do that?"

"Delegate, delegate," he drawled, "you've got to learn to delegate. Just leave it to me and I'll fix it for you." He finished the conversation in my office. "Easy," he said, "easy-peasy."

9.

Almost without noticing it, we became quite famous. This gave me a lot of pleasure, but also disappointed me. You imagine it will amount to more, that it will feel more substantial than it is. This, after all, is the bit you've dreamed of in all the grubby corners of your life. It is almost the reason you've done what you've done. This is where the world is forced to accept you no matter what you wear, no matter what you look like, no matter what your accent is. You redefine what is acceptable. This is when they ask you for your comments on the economy and war and peace, and beautiful girls want to fuck you because you are emanating power which has been the secret of all those strong physiques which you lack, which you needlessly envied. This is what you dreamed about, jerking off in your stinking hot bungalow, treasuring your two hands. It is what you told the red-mouthed naked girl in the *Playboy* pin-up when you came all over the glossy page, and what you wished while you wiped the come off the printed image, so as to keep it in good condition for next time.

The middle-class intellectuals were the first to discover us and we were happy enough to have them around. They came up from the south pretending they weren't middle class. They drank our wine and smoked our dope and drove around in our Cadillac and did tours of the factory. They were most surprised to find that we dressed just like they did. We were flattered that they found us so fascinating and delighted when they were scandalized. In truth we despised them. They were comfortable and had fat-arsed ideas. They went to bed early to read books about people they would try to copy. They didn't know whether to love us or hate us.

We bought a French chef and we had long dinners with bottles of Château Latour, Corton, Chambertin, and old luscious vintages of Château d'Yquem. They couldn't get over the wine.

We discussed Dada, ecology, Virginia Woolf, Jean-Paul Sartre, and the whole principle of making stacks of money and going to live in Penang or the south of France.

Occasionally we had rows on important issues and we normally resolved these by the use of violence.

The simplicity of this ploy struck me as obvious and delightful, yet they were too stupid to learn the lessons we could have taught them. They couldn't get past the style. They'd seen too many movies

and hung around with too many wardrobe mistresses. They couldn't
see or understand that we were no different from Henry Ford or any
of the other punks.

We were true artists. We showed them the bones of business and
power. We instructed them in the uses of violence. Metaphorically,
we shat with the door open.

They learned nothing, but were attracted to the power with the
dumb misunderstanding of lost moths. They criticized us and asked
us for jobs.

Finally, of course, the media arrived and allowed themselves to
be publicly scandalized by the contradiction in our lives.

The *Late Night* man couldn't understand why we kept playing
"Burning and a-Looting" by Bob Marley and the Wailers. I can still
see his stupid good-looking face peering at me while he said: "But
how can you listen to that type of material? They're singing about
you. They want to burn and loot *you*."

The television audience was then treated to the sight of Ian, stoned
out of his head on horse tranquillizer, smiling blissfully without even
the politeness to act uncomfortable.

"We are," he said, "the Andy Warhols of business."

In the first six months we had achieved almost 100 per cent
distribution, increased sales by 228 per cent, introduced a new line
of low-price dinners, and, as the seventh month finished, we began
to look as if we might meet the profit forecast we had made.

We entertained the board of directors at a special luncheon. They
were delighted with us.

10.

The camp fires of the unemployed flicker around the perimeter.
Tonight, once more, their numbers have increased. They grew from
three to six, to twenty. Now I choose not to count them. The unemployed have assumed the nature of a distinct and real threat. Yet they
have done nothing. During grey days they have been nothing but
poorly defined figures in a drab landscape, sitting, standing, concerned with matters I cannot imagine. They have done nothing to
hamper trucks full of raw materials. Neither have they tried to
intercept the freezer vans. Their inactivity sits most uneasily with
their cancerous multiplication.

I can hear some of them singing. They sound like men on a bus coming home from a picnic.

The night buzzes with insects and great grey clouds roll across the sky, whipped across by a high, warm wind. Occasionally lightning flickers around the edge of the sky. Out in the scrub the mosquitoes must be fierce and relentless. It must be a poor feast for them.

Although the gate is guarded and the perimeter patrolled I have chosen to set up my own guard in this darkened window. It was not a popular decision. An open window makes the air-conditioning behave badly. Sergei thinks that I am being an alarmist but I have always been an alarmist.

I have spent my life in a state of constant fear that could be understood by very few. I have anticipated disaster at every turn, physical attack at every instant. To be born small and thin and poor, one learns, very quickly, of one's vulnerability. My fear kept me in constant readiness and it also gave me fuel for my most incredible defence. My strength has been my preparedness to do anything, to be totally crazy, to go past the limits that only the strongest will dare to contemplate. The extent of my terrible quaking fear was in exact correspondence with the degree of my craziness. For I performed unthinkable acts of cruelty to others, total bluffs that would prevent all thought of retaliation.

I learned this early, as a child, when I got my nose busted up by a boy four years older and much, much bigger. I can still remember the bastard. He had wire-framed glasses and must have been blind in one eye because he had white tape obscuring one lens. I can remember the day after he bashed me. I can remember as if it were yesterday. I waited for him just around the side of the Catholic church. There was a lane there which he always walked down and beside the lane was a big pile of house bricks, neatly stacked. I was eight years old. I waited for the bastard as he came down the lane kicking a small stone. He looked arrogant and self-confident and I knew I couldn't afford to fail. As he passed me I stood up and threw the first brick. It sounded soft and quiet as it hit his shoulder, but I'd thrown it so hard it knocked him over. He looked round with astonishment but I already had the second brick in the air. It gashed his arm. He started crying. His glasses had gone. They were on the ground. I stood on them. Then I kicked him for good measure.

The effectiveness of this action was greatly enhanced by the fact that I had been seen by others. It helped me get a reputation. I built on this with other bricks and great lumps of wood. I cut and burned and slashed. I pursued unthinkable actions with the fearful skill and sensitivity of someone who can't afford to have his bluff called. I developed the art of rages and found a way to let my eyes go slightly mad and, on occasions, to dribble a little. It was peculiar that these theatrical effects often became real. I forgot I was acting.

But there was no real defence against the fires of the unemployed. They were nothing more than threatening phantoms licking at the darkness. My mind drifted in and out of fantasies about them and ended, inevitably, with the trap corridors of a maze, at the place where they killed or tortured me.

Below me Bart was sitting on the steps. I could hear him fiddling with his weapon. All week he has been working on a new, better, hand-tooled leather holster. Now it is finished he wears it everywhere. He looks good enough for the cover of *Rolling Stone*.

The unemployed are singing "Blowing in the Wind". Bart starts to hum the tune along with them, then decides not to. I can hear him shifting around uncomfortably, but there is nothing I can say to him that would make his mind any more at ease.

The unemployed will have the benefit of their own holy rage.

It is difficult to see across the plant. The spotlights we rigged up seem to create more darkness than light. I stare into the darkness, imagining movements, and thinking about my day's work. Today I went through the last three months' cost reports and discovered that our raw material costs are up over 10 per cent on eight of our lines. This is making me edgy. Something nags at me about it. I feel irritable that no one has told me. But there is nothing that can be done until tomorrow.

The movement across the face of the No. 1 store is vague and uncertain. I rub my eyes and squint. Below me I can hear Bart shift. He has taken off his boots and now he moves out towards the No. 1, sleek as a night cat, his gun hand out from his side like a man in a movie. I hold my breath. He fades into almost-dark. The figure near the No. 1 stops and becomes invisible to me. At that moment there is a shot. The figure flows out of the dark, dropping quietly like a shadow to the ground.

I am running down the stairs and am halfway across the apron before Bart has reached the No. 1. I pray to God he hasn't shot a guard.

"Not bad, eh? That's about fifty yards."

I don't say anything. He is fussing over his gun, replacing the dead shell with a live bullet. I let him walk ahead. I'm not going to get any fun out of this. He walks forward, as nonchalant as if he were going to change a record or go and get another drink.

I see his flashlight turn on and then a pause as he kneels to look at the body. And then the light goes out and he is running around and around in circles. He is yelping and running like a dog whose foot has been run over. As he circles he says, "Shit, Shit, Shit, oh fucking Christ." He looks comical and terrible dancing in his bare feet. He can't stay still. He runs around saying shit.

Then I am looking at the body. In the yellow light of my flashlight I see the face of a sixteen-year-old boy. I notice strange things, small details: golden down on the cheeks, bad pimples, and something else. At first, in dumb shock, I think it's his guts coming up. And a pea rolls out. In his mouth is a chunk of TV dinner, slowly thawing.

11.

When I was six years old I threw a cat into an incinerator. It wasn't until the cat came running out the grate at the bottom, burning, screaming, that I had any comprehension of what I had done.

The burning cat still runs through my dreams, searing me with its dreadful knowledge.

When I saw the dead boy I knew it was Bart's burning cat.

He is like the girls in *Vogue*, wearing combat clothes and carrying guns and smoking pink cigarettes. He is like the intellectuals: he lives on the wrong side of the chasm between ideas and action. The gap is exactly equal to the portion of time that separates the live cat from the burning cat.

That is the difference between us.

It should be said to him: "If you wear guns on your hip you will need to see young boys lying dead at your feet and confront what 'dead' is. That is what it takes to live that fantasy. If you cannot do this, you should take off your uniform. Others will perform the unpleasant acts for you. It is the nature of business that as a result of your decisions some people will starve and others be killed. It is simply a matter of confronting the effects of your actions. If you can grasp this nettle you will be strong. If you cannot you are a fool and are deluding yourself."

12.

Our burning cats are loose.

Bart's is sedated, slowed down, held tightly on a fearful leash by Mandies or some other downer. Perhaps he has been shooting up with morphine. His eyes are dull and his movements clumsy but his cat stirs threateningly within him, intimidating him with its most obvious horror.

My cat is loose and raging and my eyes are wide. Black smoke curls like friendly poison through my veins and bubbles of rage course through my brain. My cat is clawing and killing, victim and killer. I am in an ecstasy. I can't say. My eyes stretch wide and nostrils, also, are flaring.

Oh, the electricity. The batteries of torches firing little hits of electricity behind the eyes. To stretch my fingers and feel the tautness behind the knuckles like full sails under heavy wind.

For I have found out.

I have discovered a most simple thing. The little bastard Sergei has been cheating me in such a foolish and simple way that I cannot contain my rage at the insult to my intelligence. He has been siphoning funds like a punk. A dull stupid punk without inventiveness. He is someone trying to club a knife-fighter to death. He is so stupid I cannot believe it.

Ah, the rage. The rage, the fucking rage. He has no sense. He hasn't even the sense to be afraid. He stands before me, Bart by his side. Bart does not live here. He is away on soft beds of morphine which cannot ease his pain. Sergei is threatening. He is being smart. He thinks I'm a fool. He casts collusive glances towards Bart, who is like a man lobotomized. Smiling vaguely, insulated by blankets of morphine from my rage, like man in an asbestos suit in the middle of a terrible fire.

Oh, and fire it is.

For the cost of raw materials has not risen by 10 per cent. The cost of raw materials has not risen at all. Sergei, the fool, has been paying a fictitious company on his cheque butts and using the actual cheques to both pay the real suppliers and himself.

I only do this for the profit, for the safety, for the armour and strength that money gives. That I may be insulated from disaster and danger and threats and little bastards who are trying to subvert my friends and take my money.

And now there will be an example.

For he is trying to place me in a factory. He is trying to take my power. He shall be fucking well cut, and slashed, and shall not breathe to spread his hurt.

He is smart and self-contained. He speaks with the voice of the well educated and powerful. His eyebrows meet across his forehead.

It took me three hours to trace his schoolboy fiddle. And it only took that long because the bastards who were doing the company's search took so long to confirm that the company he's been writing on his cheque butts doesn't exist. It took me five minutes to check that his prices were inflated. Five minutes to guess what he was up to.

The body of Bart's victim has been tied to the top of the perimeter fence. Let that warn the bastards. Even the wind will not keep down the flies. The unemployed shall buzz with powerless rage.

And now Sergei. An example will be made. I have called for his suit and his white business shirt and black shoes. The suit is being pressed. The shoes are being polished. It will be a most inventive execution, far more interesting than his dull childish cheating.

Under my surveillance his hair is being cut. Very neat. He is shaved cleanly. He is shaved twice. The poor idiot does not know what is happening. Bart watches with dumb incomprehension, helping the girl who is cutting the hair. He holds the bowl of hot water. He brings a towel. He points out a little bit of sideburn that needs trimming better. He is stumbling and dazed. Only I know. I have Bart's gun, just in case.

The suit is pressed. Bart helps with the tie. He fusses, tying and retying. Sergei's eyes have started to show fear. He tries to talk casually to me, to Bart. He is asking what is happening but Bart is so far away that his mind is totally filled with the simple problem of tying the tie, its loops and folds provide intricate problems of engineering and aesthetics.

I never liked Sergei. He never treated me with respect. He showed disdain.

I will donate him a briefcase. I have a beautiful one left me by the old general manager. It is slim and black with smart snappy little chrome clips on it. In it I place Sergei's excellent references and about five hundred dollars' worth of cash. It is a shame about the money, but no one must ever think him poor or helpless.

I order him to hold the briefcase. He looks so dapper. Who could not believe he was a senior executive? Who indeed!

It is time now for the little procession to the gate. The knowledge of what is happening hits Sergei on this, his walk to the scaffold. He handles it well enough, saying nothing I remember.

High on the wire the dead boy stands like a casualty of an awkward levitation trick.

I have the main gate opened and Sergei walks out of it. The guards stand dumbly like horses in a paddock swishing flies away. I am watching Bart's eyes but they are clouded from me. He has become a foreign world veiled in mists. I know now that we will not discuss Kandinsky again or get stoned together. But he will do what I want because he knows I am crazy and cannot be deceived.

He seems to see nothing as the great wire mesh gate is rolled back into place and locked with chains. Sergei walks slowly down the gravel road away from us.

A grey figure slides out from the scrub a mile or so away. They will welcome him soon, this representative of management with his references in his briefcase.

The fact of Sergei's execution could not possibly be nearly as elegant as my plan. I return to my office, leaving the grisly reality of it to the watchers at the gate.

13.

In the night they put Sergei's head on the wire. It stares towards my office in fear and horror, a reminder of my foolishness.

For now it appears that I misunderstood the situation. It appears that he was acting on Bart's instructions, that the siphoned funds were being used to rebuild the inside of the factory.

To please me, dear God.

How could I have guarded against Bart's "What if ..." or protected us all from his laconic "easy-peasy"? If one lives with dreamers and encourages their aberrations something is bound to go wrong. Now I understand what it is to be the parent of brilliant children, children reared with no discipline, their every fantasy pandered to. Thus one creates one's own assassins.

The factory tour is over now and Bart sits in my office eyeing me with the cunning of a dog, pretending servility, but with confused plans and strategies showing in his dog-wet eyes.

He understood nothing of factories or my fear of them. His model factory is a nightmare far more obscene than anything my simple mind could have created.

For they have made a factory that is quiet. They have worried about aesthetics.

Areas of peaceful blue and whole fields of the most lyrical green. In these ideal conditions people perform insulting functions, successfully imitating the functions of mid-twentieth-century machinery.

This is Bart and Sergei's masterpiece, their gift to me. They have the mentality of art students who think they can change the world by spraying their hair silver.

They make me think of other obscenities. For instance, a Georg Jensen guillotine made from the finest silver and shaped with due concern for function and aesthetic appeal. Alternatively, condemned cells decorated with pretty blue bunny patterns from children's nurseries.

In order to achieve these effects they have reduced profit by 6.5 per cent.

In here it is very quiet. No noise comes from the staff outside. I have seen them, huddled together in little groups at the windows staring at Sergei. They seem anaesthetized. They have the glazed eyes of people too frightened to see anything that might get them into trouble. Thus they avoided Bart's eyes. He pranced through like a spider, his hand on his gun, the fury in his veins bursting to fill the room like black ink in water.

Now in the silence of my office I see the extent to which he is afflicted by hurt and misunderstanding. Trying to talk to him, I put my hand on his arm. He flinches from me. In that terrible instant I am alone on the pack ice, the string inside me taut and all that lonely ice going in front of me no matter which way I turn. And he, Bart, looking at me guilty and afraid and angry and does he want to kill me?

Yes, he does.

He will learn to use his burning cat. He hates me because I killed his friend. It was a misunderstanding. It was his fault, not mine. If they hadn't cheated I would never have made the mistake. His friend Sergei, the little turd, he thought he was clever but he was a fool. Sergei, his stupid mouth dribbling black blood on the top of the wire fence. If only his siphoning of funds had been more subtle. There were two other ways to do it, but he did it like a petty-cash clerk. It was this which upset me the most. It was this which put me over the line and left me here, alone, threatened by the one person I thought my friend.

He may wish to kill me.

But I, alone on the ice, have eyes like the headlights of a truck. I have power. I will do anything. And I have made enough bad dreams that one more dying face will make not the slightest scrap of difference. Anyone who wants to cling on to their life won't fuck around with me too willingly, though their hand might easily encircle my wrist, though they have the strength to crush me with their bare arms, for I am fearful and my fear makes me mighty.

And I am not mad, but rather I have opened the door you all keep locked with frightened bolts and little prayers. I am more like you than you know. You have not inspected the halls and attics. You haven't got yourself grubby in the cellars. Instead you sit in the front room in worn blue jeans, reading about atrocities in the Sunday papers.

Now Bart will do as I wish for he wishes to live and is weak because of it. I am a freight train, black smoke curling back, thundering down the steel lines of terrible logic.

So now I speak to him so quietly that I am forcing him to strain towards me. Trucks have been destroyed attempting to enter the plant. It is time, I tell him, that the scrub be cleared of unemployed.

It will give him something to do. It will give him a use for his rage. He can think about his friend, whom I didn't kill. He was killed by the people in the scrub, whoever they are. They are the ones holding up trucks and stopping business, and business must go on. BUSINESS MUST GO ON. That is what the hell we are here for. There is no other reason for this. This is the time that is sold to the devil. It is time lost, never to be relived, time stolen so it can be OK later and I can live in white sheets and ironed shirts and drink gin and tonic in long glasses, well away from all this.

Then I can have the luxury of nightmares, and pay the price

gladly, for it will only be my sleep which will be taken and not my waking hours as well.

14.

All around the plant seemed very, very still. The sun had gone down, leaving behind a sky of the clearest blue I had ever seen. But even as I watched, this moment passed and darkness claimed it.

I watched Bart lead his contingent of workers through the dusk in the direction of the front gate. Each man had a flamethrower strapped to his back and I smiled to think that these men had been producing food to feed those whom they would now destroy.

I watched the operation from the roof of the canteen, using binoculars Sergei had left behind.

As I watched men run through the heat, burning other men alive, I knew that thousands of men had stood on hills or roofs and watched such scenes of terrible destruction, the result of nothing more than their fear and their intelligence.

In the scrub the bodies of those who hated me were charred and smouldering.

I touched my arm, marvelling at the fineness of hairs and skin, the pretty pinkness glowing through the fingernails, the web-like mystery of the palm, the whiteness underneath the forearm and the curious sensitivity where the arm bends.

I wished I had been born a great painter. I would have worn fine clothes and celebrated the glories of man. I would have stood aloft, a judge, rather than wearily kept vigil on this hill, hunchbacked, crippled, one more guilty fool with blood on his hands.

A Letter to Our Son

Before I have finished writing this, the story of how you were born, I will be forty-four years old and the events and feelings which make up the story will be at least eight months old. You are lying in the next room in a cotton jump-suit. You have five teeth. You cannot walk. You do not seem interested in crawling. You are sound asleep.

I have put off writing this so long that, now the time is here, I do not want to write it. I cannot think. Laziness. Wooden shutters over the memory. Nothing comes, no pictures, no feelings, but the architecture of the hospital at Camperdown.

You were born in the King George V Hospital in Missenden Road, Camperdown, a building that won an award for its architecture. It was opened during the Second World War, but its post-Bauhaus modern style has its roots in that time before the First World War, with an optimism about the technological future that we may never have again.

I liked this building. I liked its smooth, rounded, shiny corners. I liked its wide stairs. I liked the huge sash-windows, even the big blue-and-white-checked tiles: when I remember this building there is sunshine splashed across those tiles, but there were times when it seemed that other memories might triumph and it would be remembered for the harshness of its neon lights and emptiness of the corridors.

A week before you were born, I sat with your mother in a four-bed ward on the eleventh floor of this building. In this ward she received blood transfusions from plum-red plastic bags suspended on rickety stainless-steel stands. The blood did not always flow smoothly. The bags had to be fiddled with, the stand had to be raised, lowered, have its drip-rate increased, decreased, inspected by the sister who had been a political prisoner in Chile, by the sister from the Solomon Islands, by others I don't remember. The blood entered your mother through a needle in her forearm. When the vein collapsed, a new one had to be found. This was caused by a kind of bruising called "tissuing". We soon knew all about tissuing. It made her arm hurt like hell.

She was bright-eyed and animated as always, but her lips had a slight blue tinge and her skin had a tight, translucent quality.

She was in this room on the west because her blood appeared to be dying. Some thought the blood was killing itself. This is what we all feared, none more than me, for when I heard her blood-count was so low, the first thing I thought (stop that thought, cut it off, bury it) was cancer.

This did not necessarily have a lot to do with Alison, but with me, and how I had grown up, with a mother who was preoccupied with cancer and who, going into surgery for suspected breast cancer, begged the doctor to "cut them both off". When my mother's friend Enid Tanner boasted of her hard stomach muscles, my mother envisaged a growth. When her father complained of a sore elbow, my mother threatened the old man: "All right, we'll take you up to Doctor Campbell and she'll cut it off." When I was ten, my mother's brother got cancer and they cut his leg off right up near the hip and took photographs of him, naked, one-legged, to show other doctors the success of the operation.

When I heard your mother's blood-count was low, I was my mother's son. I thought: cancer.

I remembered what Alison had told me of that great tragedy of her grandparents' life, how their son (her uncle) had leukaemia, how her grandfather then bought him the car (a Ford Prefect? a Morris Minor?) he had hitherto refused him, how the dying boy had driven for miles and miles, hours and hours while his cells attacked each other.

I tried to stop this thought, to cut it off. It grew again, like a thistle whose root has not been removed and must grow again, every time, stronger and stronger.

The best haematological unit in Australia was on hand to deal with the problem. They worked in the hospital across the road, the Royal Prince Alfred. They were friendly and efficient. They were not at all like I had imagined big hospital specialists to be. They took blood samples, but the blood did not tell them enough. They returned to take marrow from your mother's bones. They brought a big needle with them that would give you the horrors if you could see the size of it.

The doctor's speciality was leukaemia, but he said to us: "We

don't think it's anything really nasty." Thus "nasty" became a code
for cancer.

They diagnosed megaloblastic anaemia which, although we did
not realize it, is the condition of the blood and not the disease itself.

Walking through the streets in Shimbashi in Tokyo, your mother
once told me that a fortune-teller had told her she would die young.
At the time she told me this, we had not known each other very long.
It was July. We had fallen in love in May. We were still stumbling over
each other's feelings in the dark. I took this secret of your mother's
lightly, not thinking about the weight it must carry, what it might
mean to talk about it. I hurt her; we fought, in the street by the
Shimbashi railway station, in a street with shop windows advertising cosmetic surgery, in the Dai-Ichi Hotel in the Ginza district of
Tokyo, Japan.

When they took the bone marrow from your mother's spine, I
held her hand. The needle had a cruel diameter, was less a needle
than an instrument for removing a plug. She was very brave. Her
wrists seemed too thin, her skin too white and shiny, her eyes too big
and bright. She held my hand because of pain. I held hers because I
loved her, because I could not think of living if I did not have her. I
thought of what she had told me in Tokyo. I wished there was a God
I could pray to.

I flew to Canberra on 7 May 1984. It was my forty-first birthday.
I had injured my back and should have been lying flat on a board.
I had come from a life with a woman which had reached, for both of
us, a state of chronic unhappiness. I will tell you the truth: I was on
that aeroplane to Canberra because I hoped I might fall in love. This
made me a dangerous person.

There was a playwrights' conference in Canberra. I hoped there
would be a woman there who would love me as I would love her.
This was a fantasy I had had before, getting on aeroplanes to foreign
cities, riding in taxis towards hotels in Melbourne, in Adelaide, in
Brisbane. I do not mean that I was thinking about sex, or an affair,
but that I was looking for someone to spend my life with. Also —
and I swear I have not invented this after the fact — I had a vision
of your mother's neck.

I hardly knew her. I met her once at a dinner when I hardly noticed
her. I met her a second time when I saw, in a meeting room, the back

of her neck. We spoke that time, but I was argumentative and I did not think of her in what I can only call "that way".

And yet as the aeroplane came down to land in Canberra, I saw your mother's neck, and thought: maybe Alison Summers will be there. She was the dramaturge at the Nimrod Theatre. It was a playwrights' conference. She should be there.

And she was. And we fell in love. And we stayed up till four in the morning every morning talking. And there were other men, everywhere, in love with her. I didn't know about the other men. I knew only that I was in love as I had not been since I was eighteen years old. I wanted to marry Alison Summers, and at the end of the first night we had been out together when I walked her to the door of her room, and we had, for the first time, ever so lightly, kissed on the lips — and also, I must tell you, for it was delectable and wonderful, I kissed your mother on her long, beautiful neck — and when we had kissed and patted the air between us and said "all right" a number of times, and I had walked back to my room where I had, because of my back injury, a thin mattress lying flat on the floor, and when I was in this bed, I said, aloud, to the empty room: "I am going to live with Alison."

And I went to sleep so happy I must have been smiling.

She did not know what I told the room. And it was three or four days before I could see her again, three or four days before we could go out together, spend time alone, and I could tell her what I thought.

I had come to Canberra wanting to fall in love. Now I was in love. Who was I in love with? I hardly knew, and yet I knew exactly. I did not even realize how beautiful she was. I found that out later. At the beginning I recognized something more potent than beauty: it was a force, a life, an energy. She had such life in her face, in her eyes — those eyes which you inherited — most of all. It was this I loved, this which I recognized so that I could say — having kissed her so lightly — I will live with Alison. And know that I was right.

It was a conference. We were behaving like men and women do at conferences, having affairs. We would not be so sleazy. After four nights staying up talking till 4 a.m. we had still not made love. I would creep back to my room, to my mattress on the floor. We talked about everything. Your mother liked me, but I cannot tell you how long it took her to fall in love with me. But I know we were discussing marriages and babies when we had not even been to bed together. That came early one morning when I returned to her room after three hours' sleep. There we were, lying on the bed, kissing, and then we were making love, and you were not conceived then, of course, and yet from that time we never ceased thinking of you and when, later in Sydney, we had to learn to adjust to each other's needs, and when we argued, which we did often then, it was you more than anything that kept us together. We wanted you so badly. We loved you before we saw you. We loved you as we made you, in bed in another room, at Lovett Bay.

When your mother came to the eleventh floor of the King George V Hospital, you were almost ready to be born. Every day the sisters came and smeared jelly on your mother's tight, bulging stomach and then stuck a flat little octopus-type sucker to it and listened to the noises you made.

You sounded like soldiers marching on a bridge.

You sounded like short-wave radio.

You sounded like the inside of the sea.

We did not know if you were a boy or a girl, but we called you Sam anyway. When you kicked or turned we said, "Sam's doing his exercises." We said silly things.

When we heard how low Alison's blood-count was, I phoned the obstetrician to see if you were OK. She said there was no need to worry. She said you had your own blood-supply. She said that as long as the mother's count was above 6 there was no need to worry.

Your mother's count was 6.2. This was very close. I kept worrying that you had been hurt in some way. I could not share this worry for to share it would only be to make it worse. Also I recognize that I have made a whole career out of making my anxieties get up and walk around, not only in my own mind, but in the minds of readers. I went to see a naturopath once. We talked about negative emotions — fear and anger. I said to him, "But I *use* my anger and my fear." I talked about these emotions as if they were chisels and hammers.

This alarmed him considerably.

Your mother is not like this. When the haematologists saw how she looked, they said: "Our feeling is that you don't have anything nasty." They topped her up with blood until her count was 12 and, although they had not located the source of her anaemia, they sent her home.

A few days later her count was down to just over 6.

It seemed as if there was a silent civil war inside her veins and arteries. The number of casualties was appalling.

I think we both got frightened then. I remember coming home to Louisa Road. I remember worrying that I would cry. I remember embracing your mother — and you too, for you were a great bulge between us. I must not cry. I must support her.

I made a meal. It was salade niçoise. The electric lights, in memory, were all ten watts, sapped by misery. I could barely eat. I think we may have watched a funny film on videotape. We repacked the bag that had been unpacked so short a time before. It now seemed likely that your birth was to be induced. If your mother was sick she could not be looked after properly with you inside her. She would be given one more blood transfusion, and then the induction would begin. And that is how your birthday would be on 13 September.

Two nights before your birthday I sat with Alison in the four-bed ward, the one facing west, towards Missenden Road. The curtains were drawn around us. I sat on the bed and held her hand. The blood continued its slow viscous drip from the plum-red bag along the clear plastic tube and into her arm. The obstetrician was with us. She stood at the head of the bed, a kind, intelligent woman in her early thirties. We talked about Alison's blood. We asked her what she thought this mystery could be. Really what we wanted was to be told that everything was OK. There was a look on Alison's face when she asked. I cannot describe it, but it was not a face seeking medical "facts".

The obstetrician went through all the things that were not wrong with your mother's blood. She did not have a vitamin B deficiency. She did not have a folic acid deficiency. There was no iron deficiency. She did not have any of the common (and easily fixable) anaemias of pregnancy. So what could it be? we asked, really only wishing to be assured it was nothing "nasty".

"Well," said the obstetrician, "at this stage you cannot rule out cancer."

I watched your mother's face. Nothing in her expression showed what she must feel. There was a slight colouring of her cheeks. She nodded. She asked a question or two. She held my hand, but there was no tight squeezing.

The obstetrician asked Alison if she was going to be "all right". Alison said she would be "all right". But when the obstetrician left she left the curtains drawn.

The obstetrician's statement was not of course categorical and not everyone who has cancer dies, but Alison was, at that instant, confronting the thing that we fear most. When the doctor said those words, it was like a dream or a nightmare. I heard them said. And yet they were not said. They could not be said. And when we hugged each other — when the doctor had gone — we pressed our bodies together as we always had before, and if there were tears on our cheeks, there had been tears on our cheeks before. I kissed your mother's eyes. Her hair was wet with her tears. I smoothed her hair on her forehead. My own eyes were swimming. She said: "All right, how are we going to get through all this?"

Now you know her, you know how much like her that is. She is not going to be a victim of anything.

"We'll decide it's going to be OK," she said, "that's all."

And we dried our eyes.

But that night, when she was alone in her bed, waiting for the sleeping pill to work, she thought: If I die, I'll at least have made this little baby.

When I left your mother I appeared dry-eyed and positive, but my disguise was a frail shell of a thing and it cracked on the stairs and my grief and rage came spilling out in gulps. The halls of the hospital gleamed with polish and vinyl and fluorescent light. The flower-seller on the ground floor had locked up his shop. The foyer was empty. The whisker-shadowed man in admissions was watching television. In Missenden Road two boys in jeans and sand-shoes conducted separate conversations in separate phone booths. Death was not touching them. They turned their backs to each other. One of them — a redhead with a tattoo on his forearm — laughed.

In Missenden Road there were taxis NOT FOR HIRE speeding towards other destinations.

In Missenden Road the bright white lights above the zebra crossings became a luminous sea inside my eyes. Car lights turned into necklaces and ribbons. I was crying, thinking it is not for me to cry: crying is a poison, a negative force; everything will be all right; but I was weeping as if huge balloons of air had to be released from inside my guts. I walked normally. My grief was invisible. A man rushed past me, carrying roses wrapped in cellophane. I got into my car. The floor was littered with car-park tickets from all the previous days of blood transfusions, tests, test results, admission etc. I drove out of the car park. I talked aloud.

I told the night I loved Alison Summers. I love you, I love you, you will not die. There were red lights at the Parramatta Road. I sat there, howling, unroadworthy. I love you.

The day after tomorrow there will be a baby. Will the baby have a mother? What would we do if we knew Alison was dying? What would we do so Sam would know his mother? Would we make a videotape? Would we hire a camera? Would we set it up and act for you? Would we talk to you with smiling faces, showing you how we were together, how we loved each other? How could we? How could we think of these things?

I was a prisoner in a nightmare driving down Ross Street in Glebe. I passed the Afrikan restaurant where your mother and I ate after first coming to live in Balmain.

All my life I have waited for this woman. This cannot happen.

I thought: Why would it *not* happen? Every day people are tortured, killed, bombed. Every day babies starve. Every day there is pain and grief, enough to make you howl to the moon for ever. Why should we be exempt, I thought, from the pain of life?

What would I do with a baby? How would I look after it? Day after day, minute after minute, by myself. I would be a sad man, for ever, marked by the loss of this woman. I would love the baby. I would care for it. I would see, in its features, every day, the face of the woman I had loved more than any other.

When I think of this time, it seems as if it's two in the morning, but it was not. It was ten o'clock at night. I drove home through a landscape of grotesque imaginings.

The house was empty and echoing.

In the nursery everything was waiting for you, all the things we had got for "the baby". We had read so many books about babies, been to classes where we learned about how babies are born, but we still did not understand the purpose of all the little clothes we had folded in the drawers. We did not know which was a swaddle and which was a sheet. We could not have selected the clothes to dress you in.

I drank coffee. I drank wine. I set out to telephone Kathy Lette, Alison's best friend, so she would have this "news" before she spoke to your mother the next day. I say "set out" because each time I began to dial, I thought: I am not going to do this properly. I hung up. I did deep breathing. I calmed myself. I telephoned. Kim Williams, Kathy's husband, answered and said Kathy was not home yet. I thought: She must know. I told Kim, and as I told him the weeping came with it. I could hear myself. I could imagine Kim listening to me. I would sound frightening, grotesque, and less in control than I was. When I had finished frightening him, I went to bed and slept.

I do not remember the next day, only that we were bright and determined. Kathy hugged Alison and wept. I hugged Kathy and wept. There were isolated incidents. We were "handling it". And, besides, you were coming on the next day. You were life, getting stronger and stronger.

I had practical things to worry about. For instance: the bag. The bag was to hold all the things we had been told would be essential in the labour ward. There was a list for the contents of the bag and these contents were all purchased and ready, but still I must bring them to the hospital early the next morning. I checked the bag. I placed things where I would not forget them. You wouldn't believe the things we had. We had a cassette-player and a tape with soothing music. We had rosemary and lavender oil so I could massage your mother and relax her between contractions. I had a Thermos to fill with blocks of frozen orange juice. There were special cold packs to relieve the pain of a backache labour. There were paper pants — your arrival, after all, was not to happen without a great deal of mess. There were socks, because your mother's feet would almost certainly get very cold. I packed all these things, and there was something in the process of this packing which helped overcome my fears and made me concentrate on you, our little baby, already so loved although we did not know your face, had seen no more of you than the ghostly blue image thrown up by the ultrasound in the midst of whose shifting perspectives we had seen your little hand move. ("He waved to us.")

* * *

On the morning of the day of your birth I woke early. It was only just light. I had notes stuck on the fridge and laid out on the table. I made coffee and poured it into a Thermos. I made the bagel sandwiches your mother and I had planned months before — my lunch. I filled the bagels with a fiery Polish sausage and cheese and gherkins. For your mother, I filled a spray-bottle with Evian water.

It was a Saturday morning and bright and sunny and I knew you would be born but I did not know what it would be like. I drove along Ross Street in Glebe ignorant of the important things I would know that night. I wore grey stretchy trousers and a black shirt which would later be marked by the white juices of your birth. I was excited, but less than you might imagine. I parked at the hospital as I had parked on all those other occasions. I carried the bags up to the eleventh floor. They were heavy.

Alison was in her bed. She looked calm and beautiful. When we kissed, her lips were soft and tender. She said: "This time tomorrow we'll have a little baby."

In our conversation, we used the diminutive a lot. You were always spoken of as "little", as indeed you must really have been, but we would say "little" hand, "little" feet, "little" baby, and thus evoked all our powerful feelings about you.

This term ("little") is so loaded that writers are wary of using it. It is cute, sentimental, "easy". All of sentient life seems programmed to respond to "little". If you watch grown dogs with a pup, a pup they have never seen, they are immediately patient and gentle, even solicitous, with it. If you had watched your mother and father holding up a tiny terry-towelling jump-suit in a department store, you would have seen their faces change as they celebrated your "littleness" while, at the same time, making fun of their own responses — they were aware of acting in a way they would have previously thought of as saccharine.

And yet we were not aware of the torrents of emotion your "littleness" would unleash in us, and by the end of 13 September we would think it was nothing other than the meaning of life itself.

When I arrived at the hospital with the heavy bags of cassette-players and rosemary oil, I saw a dark-bearded, neat man in a suit sitting out by the landing. This was the hypnotherapist who had arrived to help you come into the world. He was serious, impatient, eager to start. He wanted to start in the pathology ward, but in the end he helped carry the cassette-player, Thermoses, sandwiches, massage oil, sponges, paper pants, apple juice, frozen orange blocks, rolling pin, cold packs, and even water down to the labour ward where — on a stainless-steel stand eight feet high — the sisters were already hanging the bag of oxytocin which would ensure this day was your birthday.

It was a pretty room, by the taste of the time. As I write it is still that time, and I still think it pretty. All the surfaces were hospital surfaces — easy to clean — laminexes, vinyls, materials with a hard shininess, but with colours that were soft pinks and blues and an effect that was unexpectedly pleasant, even sophisticated.

The bed was one of those complicated stainless-steel machines which seem so cold and impersonal until you realize all the clever things it can do. In the wall there were sockets with labels like "Oxygen". The cupboards were filled with paper-wrapped sterile "objects". There was, in short, a seriousness about the room, and when we plugged in the cassette-player we took care to make sure we were not using a socket that might be required for something more important.

The hypnotherapist left me to handle the unpacking of the bags. He explained his business to the obstetrician. She told him that eight hours would be a good, fast labour. The hypnotherapist said he and Alison were aiming for three. I don't know what the doctor thought, but I thought there was not a hope in hell.

When the oxytocin drip had been put into my darling's arm, when the water-clear hormone was entering her veins, one drip every ten seconds (you could hear the machine click when a drip was released), when these pure chemical messages were being delivered to her body, the hypnotherapist attempted to send other messages of a less easily assayable quality.

I tell you the truth: I did not care for this hypnotherapist, this pushy, over-eager fellow taking up all this room in the labour ward. He sat on the right-hand side of the bed. I sat on the left. He made me feel useless. He said: "You are going to have a good labour, a fast labour, a fast labour like the one you have already visualized." Your mother's eyes were closed. She had such large, soft lids, such tender and vulnerable coverings of skin. Inside the pink light of the womb, your eyelids were the same. Did you hear the messages your mother was sending to her body and to you? The hypnotherapist said: "After just three hours you are going to deliver a baby, a good, strong, healthy baby. It will be an easy birth, an effortless birth. It will last three hours and you will not tear." On the door the sisters had tacked a sign reading: QUIETPLEASEHYPNOTHERAPYINPROGRESS. "You are going to be so relaxed, and in a moment you are going to be even more relaxed, more relaxed than you have ever been before. You are feeling yourself going deeper and deeper and when you come to, you will be in a state of waking hypnosis and you will respond to the trigger-words Peter will give you during your labour, words which will make you, once again, so relaxed."

My trigger-words were to be "Breathe" and "Relax".

The hypnotherapist gave me his phone number and asked me to call when you were born. But for the moment you had not felt the effects of the oxytocin on your world and you could not yet have suspected the adventures the day would have in store for you.

You still sounded like the ocean, like soldiers marching across a bridge, like short-wave radio.

On Tuesday nights through the previous winter we had gone to classes in a building where the lifts were always sticking. We had walked up the stairs to a room where pregnant women and their partners had rehearsed birth with dolls, had watched hours of videotapes of exhausted women in labour. We had practised all the different sorts of breathing. We had learned of the different positions for giving birth: the squat, the supported squat, the squat supported by a seated partner. We knew the positions for first and second stage, for a backache labour, and so on, and so on. We learned birth was a complicated, exhausting and difficult process. We worried we would forget the methodology of breathing. And yet now the time was here we both felt confident, even though nothing would be like it had been in the birth classes. Your mother was connected to the oxytocin drip which meant she could not get up and walk around. It meant it was difficult for her to "belly dance" or do most of the things we had spent so many evenings learning about.

In the classes they tell you that the contractions will start far apart, that you should go to hospital only when they are ten minutes apart: short bursts of pain, but long rests in between. During this period your mother could expect to walk around, to listen to music, to enjoy a massage. However, your birth was not to be like this. This was not because of you. It was because of the oxytocin. It had a fast, intense effect, like a double Scotch when you're expecting a beer. There were not to be any ten-minute rests, and from the time the labour started it was, almost immediately, fast and furious, with a one-minute contraction followed by no more than two minutes of rest.

If there had been time to be frightened, I think I would have been frightened. Your mother was in the grip of pains she could not escape from. She squatted on a bean bag. It was as if her insides were all . tangled, and tugged in a battle to the death. Blood ran from her. Fluid like egg-white. I did not know what anything was. I was a man who had wandered onto a battlefield. The blood was bright with oxygen. I wiped your mother's brow. She panted. *Huh-huh-huh-huh*. I ministered to her with sponge and water. I could not take her pain for her. I could do nothing but measure the duration of the pain. I had a little red stop-watch you will one day find abandoned in a dusty drawer. (Later your mother asked me what I had felt during labour. I thought only: I must count the seconds of the contraction; I must help Alison breathe, now, now, now; I must get that sponge — there is time to make the water in the sponge cool — now I can remove that bowl and cover it. Perhaps I can reach the bottle of Evian water. God, I'm so *thirsty*. What did I think during the labour? I thought: When this contraction is over I will get to that Evian bottle.)

Somewhere in the middle of this, in these three hours in this room whose only view was a blank screen of frosted glass, I helped your mother climb onto the bed. She was on all fours. In this position she could reach the gas mask. It was nitrous oxide, laughing gas. It did not stop the pain, but it made it less important. For the gas to work your mother had to anticipate the contraction, breathing in gas before it arrived. The sister came and showed me how I could feel the contraction coming with my hand. But I couldn't. We used the stop-watch, but the contractions were not regularly spaced, and sometimes we anticipated them and sometimes not. When we did not get it right, your mother took the full brunt of the pain. She had her face close to the mattress. I sat on the chair beside. My face was close to hers. I held the watch where she could see it. I held her wrist.

I can still see the red of her face, the wideness of her eyes as they bulged at the enormous *size* of the pains that racked her.

Sisters came and went. They had to see how wide the cervix was. At first it was only two centimetres, not nearly enough room for you to come out. An hour later they announced it was four centimetres. It had to get to nine centimetres before we could even think of you being born. There had to be room for your head (which we had been told was big — well, we were told wrong, weren't we?) and your shoulders to slip through. It felt to your mother that this labour would go on for eight or twelve or twenty hours. That she should endure this intensity of pain for this time was unthinkable. It was like running a hundred-metre race which was stretching to ten miles. She wanted an epidural — a pain blocker.

But when the sister heard this she said: "Oh do try to hang on. You're doing *so* well."

I went to the sister, like a shop steward.

I said: "My wife wants an epidural, so can you please arrange it?"

The sister agreed to fetch the anaesthetist, but there was between us — I admit it now — a silent conspiracy: for although I had pressed the point and she had agreed it was your mother's right, we both believed (I, for my part, on her advice) that if your mother could endure a little longer she could have the birth she wanted — without an epidural.

The anaesthetist came and went. The pain was at its worst. A midwife came and inspected your mother. She said: "Ten centimetres."

She said: "Your baby is about to be born."

We kissed, your mother and I. We kissed with soft, passionate lips as we did the day we lay on a bed at Lovett Bay and conceived you. That day the grass outside the window was a brilliant green beneath the vibrant petals of fallen jacaranda.

Outside the penumbra of our consciousness trolleys were wheeled. Sterile bags were cut open. The contractions did not stop, of course.

The obstetrician had not arrived. She was in a car, driving fast towards the hospital.

I heard a midwife say: "Who can deliver in this position?" (It was still unusual, as I learned at that instant, for women to deliver their babies on all fours.)

Someone left the room. Someone entered. Your mother was pressing the gas mask so hard against her face it was making deep indentations on her skin. Her eyes bulged huge.

Someone said: "Well get her, otherwise I'll have to deliver it myself."

The door opened. Bushfire came in.

Bushfire was Aboriginal. She was about fifty years old. She was compact and taciturn like a farmer. She had a face that folded in on itself and let out its feelings slowly, selectively. It was a face to trust, and trust especially at this moment when I looked up to see Bushfire coming through the door in a green gown. She came in a rush, her hands out to have gloves put on.

There was another contraction. I heard the latex snap around Bushfire's wrists. She said: "There it is. I can see your baby's head." It was you. The tip of you, the top of you. You were a new country, a planet, a star seen for the first time. I was not looking at Bushfire. I was looking at your mother. She was all alight with love and pain.

"Push," said Bushfire.

Your mother pushed. It was you she was pushing, you that put that look of luminous love on her face, you that made the veins on her forehead bulge and her skin go red.

Then — it seems such a short time later — Bushfire said: "Your baby's head is born."

And then, so quickly in retrospect, but one can no more recall it accurately than one can recall exactly how one made love on a bed when the jacaranda petals were lying like jewels on the grass outside. Soon. Soon we heard you. Soon you slipped out of your mother. Soon, exactly three hours after the labour had begun, you came slithering out not having hurt her, not even having grazed her. You slipped out, as slippery as a little fish, and we heard you cry. Your cry was so much lighter and thinner than I might have expected. I do not mean that it was weak or frail, but that your first cry had a timbre unlike anything I had expected. The joy we felt. Your mother and I kissed again, at that moment.

"My little baby," she said. We were crying with happiness. "My little baby."

I turned to look. I saw you. Skin. Blue-white, shiny-wet.

I said; "It's a boy."

"Look at me," your mother said. I turned to her. I kissed her. I was crying, just crying with happiness that you were there.

* * *

The room you were born in was quiet, not full of noise and clattering. This is how we wanted it for you. So you could come into the world gently and that you should — as you were now — be put onto your mother's stomach. They wrapped you up. I said: "Couldn't he feel his mother's skin?" They unwrapped you so you could have your skin against hers.

And there you were. It was you. You had a face, the face we had never known. You were so calm. You did not cry or fret. You had big eyes like your mother's. And yet when I looked at you first I saw not your mother and me, but your two grandfathers, your mother's father, my father; and, as my father, whom I loved a great deal, had died the year before, I was moved to see that here, in you, he was alive.

Look at the photographs in the album that we took at this time. Look at your mother and how alive she is, how clear her eyes are, how all the red pain has just slipped off her face and left the unmistakable visage of a young woman in love.

We bathed you (I don't know whether this was before or after) in warm water and you accepted this gravely, swimming instinctively.

I held you (I think this must be before), and you were warm and slippery. You had not been bathed when I held you. The obstetrician gave you to me so she could examine your mother. She said: "Here."

I held you against me. I knew then that your mother would not die. I thought: "It's fine, it's all right." I held you against my breast. You smelled of lovemaking.